Shifter BONDS

MIAMI SCORCHER SERIES COLLECTION

SAVANNAH STUART

Shifter Bonds
Copyright © Katie Reus & Savannah Stuart 2009-2015

All rights reserved. Except as permitted under the U.S. Copyright Act of 1976, no part of this publication may be reproduced, distributed, or transmitted in any form or by any means, or stored in a database or retrieval system, without the prior written permission of the author. Thank you for buying an authorized version of this book and complying with copyright laws. You're supporting writers and encouraging creativity.

Cover art: Jaycee of Sweet 'N Spicy Designs
Formatting: Author EMS
Author Website: www.katiereus.com

Publisher's Note: This is a work of fiction. Names, characters, places, and incidents are either the products of the author's imagination or used fictitiously, and any resemblance to actual persons, living or dead, or business establishments, organizations or locales is completely coincidental.

Shifter Bonds/Savannah Stuart – 1st ed.

ISBN-10: 1-942447-86-8
ISBN-13: 978-1-942447-86-3

CONTENTS

UNLEASHED TEMPTATION   1

WORTH THE RISK   105

POWER UNLEASHED   201

DANGEROUS CRAVING   293

DESIRE UNLEASHED   379

UNLEASHED TEMPTATION

The sexiest man she's ever met turns out to be her new boss...

After finding out her boyfriend has been cheating on her with her boss, Carly decides her life needs a makeover. She trades in her winter coat for a bikini and heads south to Miami, Florida. Almost as soon as she arrives, she falls in lust with the sexiest man she's ever laid eyes on. Too bad he's her new boss.

He also just happens to be a shifter...

Alpha werewolf Nick gave up hope of finding his mate a century ago. When sexy redhead Carly comes to work for him, she disrupts his entire world. Although he desperately wants to come clean about what he is, he keeps running into problems. Like the fact that an ancient enemy has set his sights on Carly. Nick discovers he'll go to any lengths to keep her safe. Even if it means losing her in the process.

CHAPTER ONE

"I'm going to need a bigger moving trailer." Carly Kendall entered her bedroom carrying another empty moving box.

Stacie, Carly's best friend of fifteen years and roommate of four, shook her head as she grabbed the box from her. "What you need is a sexy man in your bed."

Carly rolled her eyes and picked up a handful of thick, winter scarves from the floor. That was Stacie's answer to everything. "No, what I *need* is a change of scenery. I'm tired of Chicago and I'm tired of this weather. Miami is the perfect place for a new start. Sunny weather year round."

"What about hurricanes?"

Carly shrugged and dumped her handful on the bed. "Better than snowstorms and blackouts."

Stacie sat on the edge of Carly's bed and held up the scarves. "What do you want me to do with these?"

"Keep half of them and put the rest in the box marked winter clothes. I won't need them where I'm going." She grinned at her friend as she turned back toward her closet.

"And this has nothing to do with that snake Dan?" Stacie asked.

Carly turned to find her friend digging through her jewelry. "Hey, I said you could take some scarves, not half my room... And no, this has nothing to do with him."

"Hmm." Stacie avoided her gaze as she opened a drawer and dumped it into one of the boxes.

Carly cringed at her friend's lack of organization. She'd be digging through boxes for days trying to figure out what went where. "Okay, maybe it has a little to do with him, but a lot to do with the fact that I need to mix it up. I don't have any family here—"

"Hey!" The hurt look on Stacie's face made Carly cringe.

"I didn't mean it like that. You know you're like family to me. It's just...I don't know, I need something different right now. I can't explain it." Sighing, she flopped down on her bed. Finding out her boyfriend—now ex-boyfriend—had been cheating on her hadn't bothered her much. That was a sign in itself that she should have broken up with Dan months ago. Hell, with their conflicting schedules they hadn't had sex in over four months. And they hadn't had *good* sex in she couldn't remember how long.

The only thing that pissed her off was that he'd been screwing *her* boss. Certainly explained all that overtime she'd been roped into doing. At least she had a nice savings account. She wasn't worried about finding work, and now she'd have time to relax and learn her way around the city before job hunting. Not to mention she planned to hit the beach as soon as she got there.

"Fine, I guess I understand. But I reserve the right to come visit you anytime."

"As if that was ever an issue. You better come visit me."

"I can't believe you're living with your grandmother." Stacie snickered as she dumped the contents of another drawer into the same box.

Carly jumped off the bed and scooted her friend out of the way with her hip. "How about you stick with boxing my clothes and I'll take over this dresser… And, I'm not living with her. I'm living in the apartment behind her house."

"Same thing," Stacie mumbled.

It wasn't, but Carly didn't correct her. She knew her friend was bummed she was leaving and the truth was, Stacie was the only reason she'd even contemplated staying in Chicago in the first place. Carly's grandmother had moved to Florida two years ago and she'd almost left then, but back then she'd loved her job and friends. She still loved her friends, but it was time to take control of her life. She had no desire to get stagnant or settled.

As she unhooked a string of beads she and Stacie had gotten at the last St. Patrick's Day parade, an unexpected wave of emotions threatened to overwhelm her. She really was going to miss Stacie. "You want to put off packing and head to Cullen's Bar for happy hour?"

Stacie swiveled from the closet. She dropped the bundle of shirts in her hand and grinned. "Hell yeah."

Carly pulled the ponytail holder from her hair and gave herself a quick glance in the mirror. One night of partying with her friend wouldn't make a difference in how soon she got to Miami.

Two Weeks Later

Scrubbing a hand over his face, Nick Lazos sank into his comfortable chair with a sigh. He turned on his computer and sat back, waiting for it to start. After the last disastrous interview, he seriously hoped he had some new responses to his want ad. He couldn't keep doing all this admin stuff on top of everything else.

When there was a soft knock at his office door he glanced at the wall clock. Inwardly he groaned. Even though he needed a new accountant, he'd been hoping the last interviewee wouldn't show up today. His mother had talked him into interviewing one of her friend's granddaughters. If she was anything like the last woman his mom had recommended — he fought off a shudder.

"Come in," he barked. Better get this over with.

The door creaked open and for a moment, he forgot to breathe. This could *not* be the woman here to interview.

A pretty redhead took a couple tentative steps inside. Her ivory cheeks were flushed a delectable shade of pink. "Hi, I'm Carly Kendall. I hope I'm not late."

Somehow he found his voice. "You're right on time." Instinctively he stood and motioned for her to sit across the desk. Now he wished he'd taken a few minutes to straighten up.

She wore a respectable dark blue pencil skirt and button-down blouse, but the effect on her was 'naughty librarian'. Which was the last thing he should be thinking about. The shape of her perfectly rounded breasts pressed against her top and all he could think about doing was unbuttoning it and peeling it open slowly, inch by inch, as her delectable body was revealed to him.

What the *fuck* was wrong with him? He mentally shook himself, needing to get his shit together.

He wasn't some horny fucking adolescent, but something about her scent was making him crazy. It was unusual, like a spring rain and a hint of raspberries — Crap, she was saying something.

"I appreciate you taking the time to interview me. I wasn't sure if you had it so here's my résumé." She slid it across the desk as she spoke.

"Why don't you tell me a little about yourself and why you want to work here?" There, he got out a coherent sentence. He deserved a freaking medal for being able to talk when she was staring at him with those big blue eyes, begging him to do all sorts of bad things. Damn, he could practically feel his canines extending. As a werewolf, he'd learned to control his urges as a pup. For some reason, his primal instinct was overruling all those ingrained rules. When she nervously moistened her lips he realized he was staring a little too hard.

Nick quickly glanced at her résumé. "Finance?" Good for him. Another word. He looked up again.

A real smile touched her shiny pink, oh-so-kissable lips. "Yes. After college I started working at…"

Oh shit. Shit, shit, shit! He'd always had a thing for redheads. Funny that he'd never dated one, but especially not a human one. And now his living, breathing fantasy wanted to work for him. She wasn't glamorous or exotic — *or a shifter* — but she was *exactly* his type. Something he hadn't realized he even had until she'd walked through the door of his office. Adorable freckles splattered her nose and cheeks, giving her an innocent quality he usually detested.

He wanted a woman with experience. Too bad his dick had other plans. It had taken one look at sexy Ms. Kendall and gone on red alert. What *the fuck* was wrong with him? He'd been in her presence sixty seconds and he felt like one of his barbaric ancestors, ready to take her back to his cave and claim her. Hell, maybe his ancestors had been on to something because that sounded like a damn good idea.

"And with five years of experience I think I can be a great asset to your company." She sat there staring at him expectantly.

What had she been saying? Was she expecting a response? He cleared his throat and glanced down at her résumé, mainly so he wouldn't freak her out by staring. She certainly had the right work history. More than enough to do this job. Dealing with his roughneck employees is what had caused the last assistant to leave though. Of course, she'd had a permanent stick up her ass so he'd been happy to see that one go even if she had left him high and dry.

"Mr. Lazos?" Carly — Ms. Kendall — crossed her toned legs and bit her bottom lip.

She stared at him with those intoxicating eyes and he knew he needed to say something. Anything. Before the words were out, he was completely aware he was going to regret this, but what choice did he have. He didn't have time to go through a dozen more interviews and she had more than enough qualifications. Not to mention, viable candidates weren't banging down the door to work here. So what if he ended up walking around with a permanent hard-on. He'd get used to it.

He cleared his throat. "This all looks very impressive. If you started here, you'd be in charge of payroll and handle all the accounting for this shop and the other two I own. I have about forty-five employees, but I plan to expand soon. Do you think that's something you could handle?"

Smiling, she nodded. "At my last job I handled the payroll for close to two hundred people and I'm a certified CPA so I could take care of all your taxes at the end of the year too."

Turning her down simply because she made him hot would be a mistake. Carly Kendall was a dream employee. She had all the qualifications and then some. And…he didn't want to let her walk out that door without knowing he'd see her again. "I pay bi-weekly and if it works out, after thirty days you get medical and dental, two weeks paid vacation, and ten paid sick days." He rattled off the salary and when she blinked, he knew she'd take the job if he offered it.

"Can you start this week?" he managed to choke out.

Her gorgeous blue eyes widened as if that had been the last thing she'd expected. Her mouth dropped open for a fraction of a second before she contained herself. "Yes, of course. Tomorrow, if you want. Uh, don't you want to check my references?"

Good God, where was his head? "I plan to make the necessary calls today. If there's a problem, I'll contact you. If not, I'll see you tomorrow."

"Wonderful." She smiled, revealing a perfect row of white teeth. The pleasure rolling off her was sweet and palpable.

His heart rate kicked up about a thousand degrees. "Be here at nine." He gritted his teeth and tried to discreetly shift in his seat. His cock pressed painfully against the zipper of his pants.

"What exactly is the dress code here?"

"Dress code?" He stared dumbly at her.

"Well, I know the mechanics wear…uh, coveralls, or whatever those things are called, but what do I wear?"

"The last assistant I had wore skirts and dresses. Nothing fancy though." He bit back the momentary twinge of guilt as she nodded enthusiastically. His last assistant had worn jeans and polo T-shirts. It was an auto shop for God's sake. The customers didn't give a shit what they wore so long as they fixed their cars and didn't rip them off. Nick, however, wanted to see those long legs again so he flat-out lied.

"Great. Well if that's all, I guess I'll see you tomorrow morning. Thank you for this opportunity, Mr. Lazos." She stood and held out a slim, elegant hand.

He stared at it for a moment before grasping it in his much bigger one. He started to stand then stopped himself. If he did, she'd no doubt see his reaction to her and run for the hills. Then he'd have to start the interview process all over again. "See you tomorrow. And call me Nick," he said before blindly picking up a stack of papers and purposely ignoring her.

As soon as the door shut behind her he let out a long breath and let his head fall against the desk. "You are an idiot," he muttered to himself.

Seconds later the door swung open, interrupting his internal curses.

"Who was the cute redhead?" Jimmy, one of his mechanics asked.

"She's the new office manager."

Jimmy's lusty grin grew wider and Nick could smell the man's arousal as it rolled over the room. Hell, even without his extrasensory abilities, he knew exactly what the man was thinking—because he was thinking it too. "She's the most qualified applicant we've had and she's off limits. To you, to everyone. Spread it around because she starts tomorrow."

Jimmy held up his hands in mock defense and the lust Nick had smelled dissipated almost immediately. "Calm down, boss. All I said was she was cute. I'll let everyone know."

"Good. And watch your fucking language around her too!" Carly had class written all over her and he didn't want his guys running her off.

Not bothering to hide his laughter, Jimmy shut the door behind him on his way out.

Nick looked around his office and cringed. Stacks of paper were everywhere, and a dirty carburetor sat on one of the shelves. The room hadn't been cleaned in—hell, he couldn't remember how long. Muttering to himself, he started straightening up. Technically it was his office, but she'd be using it the majority of the day and he wanted it to be comfortable for her.

As he moved around the small room, his body tensed. Her raspberry scent lingered in the air, assaulting all his senses and making his wolf agitated, hungry. His entire body tensed as his canines extended. Unless he was being threatened, he normally had complete control over his body. Taking a few calming breaths, he sat and clutched the armrest of his chair until the threat of change subsided.

CHAPTER TWO

Nick jerked upright in bed, his breathing erratic. A light sheen of sweat covered his neck and chest. He scrubbed a hand over his face and shook his head, trying to clear the cobwebs of sleep. Yesterday had been long as hell and it felt like he'd *just* dozed off.

For a second he was disoriented until he spotted the digital clock on his nightstand. Time to get ready for work. As he swung his legs off the bed, he groaned when his sheet rubbed against his rock-hard cock.

He shoved the thin cover off himself and headed for the bathroom, acutely aware of the aching between his legs. The tile cooled his feet but it did little to cool the memories of the particularly erotic dream he'd been having about Carly.

She'd been on his mind since yesterday. He'd thought about her on the drive home, *at* home, and when his head had hit the pillow last night.

As he drew the shower curtain back and turned on the water, his other hand automatically fisted around his cock. It was as if his hand had a mind of its own. Maybe he should be embarrassed to fantasize about Carly while getting off, but damn, he couldn't get the vixen out of his head.

He'd spoken to her for all of twenty minutes and he was waking up with a hard-on for her. He couldn't remember the last time he'd actually dreamt about a woman not featured in a magazine. Now he was waking up panting like some randy pup. Sure, it had been a while since he'd had sex, but not so long that he should be acting like this.

As he stepped under the powerful jet stream, he started working his fist in long, fluid motions. Images of working Carly into a sexual frenzy entered his mind unbidden and all his senses heightened.

He could practically smell her sweet raspberry scent surrounding him as if she were standing right in front of him. Hell, if she was here right now, he'd kiss and taste every inch of her body until she was wet and begging for him. The overwhelming need to dominate her shouldn't surprise him, but it did.

What he wanted from her was different than anything he'd experienced and he barely knew the woman. As his free hand pressed against the tile to support himself, her face swam before him, taunting him, teasing him.

What he wouldn't give to feel her nails dig into his back or to taste between her legs. He could just imagine stroking his tongue along her slick folds.

At the sound of the metal hooks scraping against the shower rod, Nick's eyes flew open. His shoulders tensed but before he could react, the curtain was drawn back and in stepped Carly.

Completely naked.

For a moment, he forgot to breathe. Pale pink nipples were barely visible underneath the long hair cascading over her chest and a soft tuft of fine, red hair covered her mound.

He automatically reached out to touch her. Where, it didn't matter. He simply needed his hands on her.

In the recesses of his mind, reality screamed at him and his hand froze. What the hell was going on? This was definitely a dream. He shook his head, uncaring. If it was, he didn't want to wake up.

"What are you doing here?" he rasped out.

"Shh." She pressed a long finger to his lips before drawing the curtain back into place.

She turned to face him and her eyes darkened as they roved over his body. His cock jerked under her scrutiny. It felt like a heavy club between his legs and she was the only woman who could relieve him.

With a trembling hand, he pushed aside any thoughts that this might be a dream and reached out to touch her smooth skin. Her waist was slim but her hips flared out into perfect curves. Just enough for him to grasp onto as he pounded into her.

Or as she rode him. Either way, it didn't matter as long as his cock was inside her.

Wordlessly, she stepped toward him, pressing her luscious body against the full length of his. He was aware of water rushing over them, but the main thing he felt was her hard nipples brushing against his chest.

As she moved against him, the pebbles teased his skin. Nick shuddered as their bodies connected. Unable to stand it anymore and not caring if this was a fantasy he'd concocted, he threaded his fingers through her thick hair and slanted his mouth over hers.

Damn, the woman even tasted like raspberries. Sweet and succulent.

He groaned into her mouth as he imagined licking her pussy. His tongue stroked inside her as he cupped her head tightly. If he were a betting man, he'd guess she tasted just as sweet between her legs.

At that thought, his other hand strayed lower. If he couldn't taste her, he'd settle for second best. Normally he liked to explore all of a woman's body before making a break straight for her pussy, but he couldn't wait. The need to touch her most intimate area was overwhelming.

Cupping her soft mound, he slid his middle finger over her clit and between her folds. At that, her body jolted against his. It was slight, but he could feel the ripple straight to where their mouths were connected.

Just as he suspected, she was tight. Her inner walls clamped around his finger as he slowly inserted it. Dragging his finger back out, he ran it over her clit, covering the sensitive area with her own slickness.

"Ahh." She let out a tiny moan against him.

"Do you like that?" he murmured against her mouth in between kisses.

Her answer wasn't audible, but she nodded her approval.

Taking a chance, he eased another finger inside her and was rewarded by a surprised gasp. For a split second he paused, wondering if he'd hurt her, but when her hips surged forward, he pushed deeper.

She clutched at his shoulders and he increased his movement between her legs. Not too fast, but a steady rhythm. In and out, nice and slow. If the way her body trembled under his touch was any indication, she was close to climaxing.

Hell, he was close to coming and she was barely touching him.

With each stroke, he pressed his fingers against her inner walls, loving the way her tight body clenched around him.

Unable to stand just feeling her aroused nipples against his chest anymore, he released his grip from her head and reached between their bodies to cup her breast. His hands were callused from work but she didn't seem to notice.

When he rubbed the pad of his thumb across her distended nipple, her hips gave an erratic jerk against his other hand.

"I take it you like that too," he whispered as he feathered a few more kisses along her jaw.

"Don't stop." Her voice was ragged and unsteady.

Though he didn't want to pull away from kissing her, he knelt down and gently flicked her clit with his tongue.

She was taller than average for a woman, but everything about her was delicate. Long arms, long legs, and he didn't want to do anything to hurt the soft folds between those legs.

Her knees trembled so she leaned back against the tiled wall, using it as support. The position was perfect for what he wanted.

He could feel how close she was. With each stroke, her tight sheath clenched around his fingers. She just needed the right stimulation. When he sucked on her clit; that was all it took for her to lose control. Her hands gripped his head as her inner walls spasmed around him.

As she rode through the last surge of her climax, the jerky movements of her hips subsided until she was simply trembling against the wall. Her hands fell away from him and when he looked up at her, her lips were parted slightly in bliss.

He stood, ready to gather her into his arms. As he reached out to touch her she swatted his hands away and knelt in front of him.

Wordlessly, she grasped his cock at the base and licked the underside of his shaft. She started at the bottom and worked her way to the head.

Then she repeated the movement over and over, licking him everywhere. His brain was barely functioning as she ran her tongue and lips over every inch of his cock.

With one hand he reached for the wall and used it for support. Oh yeah, this was definitely a dream. This couldn't be happening. It sure felt real enough though.

The running water of the shower pounded against his back but he was big enough that she was barely sprayed.

Not that she seemed to notice, she was so intent on what she was doing. Finally, she stopped teasing him and took his head fully in her mouth. He tried to bite it back, but a loud groan escaped as she lowered her lips over him.

As she worked his length, he closed his eyes and focused on the pleasure. What felt like tiny zings of electricity zapped down his spine and through his legs, all the way to his toes. He was so close to release, it bordered on painful.

She continued working him with her mouth and pumping him with her hand. The dual movements proved to be the perfect rhythm. When she lightly tugged on his sac, the unexpected sensation pushed him over the edge.

His balls pulled up tight and his hips jerked erratically. Before he could even think to warn her, he exploded. Long, hot streams of come hit the back of her throat but she didn't stop sucking him until she'd taken all he had to give.

Breathing heavily, he waited a moment before opening his eyes because he feared what he'd see. When he did, he let out a long sigh.

He wasn't in his shower, but in his big bed.

Alone.

Even though he'd been fairly sure it had all been a dream, his gut tightened. As if on cue, the buzzing of his alarm went off. Perfect freaking timing. How the hell was he going to work with Carly and keep his hands to himself after this?

Normally he ran in the evenings, but because of how he felt, he'd need another run this morning. Throwing off the covers, he opened the sliding glass door that led from his bedroom to the lanai.

He didn't bother covering himself as he stepped outside. His pack owned miles and miles of private beach in the Key Biscayne area. He wasn't worried about anyone but the seagulls seeing him naked. Many werewolves and shifters preferred the mountains, but after years of living in mountainous terrain all over the globe, his father—his Alpha—had decided to settle in Miami.

As long as they had a place to run free, the pack could live in peace. Changing was a part of who they were. If they weren't free to change on a regular basis, they'd have no control over themselves and would eventually go crazy or get sick and die.

The sun was just peeking over the horizon so shadows danced off palm trees and other foliage. As he glanced along the beach, his gaze narrowed when he saw a familiar dark wolf standing by one of the sand dunes.

Without pausing, Nick changed. The pain was inevitable. It would hit like lightning, then fade just as quickly, blending into something much more pleasurable. As his bones shifted and broke and realigned, he focused on the rush of rapture that surged over him once he was in animal form.

Bounding over to his brother, he knocked Stephan down in a playful gesture. *What are you doing out this early?* he projected with his mind.

Stephan jumped up and swatted at the sand with his paw, kicking up the grains. *I just got off a late shift and need to blow off some steam.*

Nick loved his brother but the last thing he wanted to do now was talk. *Think you can beat me to Aunt Caro's house?*

In response, Stephan leapt away from him and darted toward the harder, wet earth lining the beach.

Nick chose to run along the softer sand as he raced down the shore. It was harder on his muscles, but it kept him in shape. In wolf form, everything was intensified. The salty smell of the ocean, the crisp breeze, the sand underneath his paws. As his muscles strained, a much-needed calmness rolled over him. An extra run was exactly what he needed.

CHAPTER THREE

Carly glanced at herself in the rearview mirror of her car one more time before getting out. A wave of heat immediately greeted her. First day jitters hummed through her body as she walked toward the glass door. She couldn't believe she'd gotten a job so quickly. Interviewing at Nick's Auto Shop had been part of her plan to get used to interviews again. As a way to ease back into the job-hunting game.

For some reason she couldn't get rid of the queasy sensation in her gut. She'd never been nervous about a job before. If only her new boss didn't have that tall, dark, and sexy thing going on. Dark hair, pale gray eyes, bronzed skin, and incredible muscles. The sleeves of his mechanic coveralls had been rolled up yesterday, revealing corded arms and a couple interesting-looking tattoos. She usually dated lawyers, CPAs or other white-collar guys and while most of the men she'd been with were in decent shape, no one had ever compared to the hulking Nick Lazos.

Not that she should even be thinking about her boss in that capacity. She'd been so nervous in the interview yesterday she hadn't been able to stop herself from rambling. At least he hadn't seemed to notice. Hell, he hadn't seemed interested in one word she'd said. That was why she couldn't believe he'd even hired her.

Nervously she smoothed a hand down her wrap dress then inwardly gave herself a pep talk. She was really good at what she did. Working in an auto shop was something she'd never done before but numbers were numbers. Didn't matter where she worked. So even if he intimidated her, she knew what she was doing.

The little bell jingled above the door as she entered. To her surprise, Mr. Lazos—Nick—stood behind the main counter. She'd assumed since he was the owner he'd come in later.

Immediately butterflies took flight in her stomach as they made eye contact but she managed a smile. "Morning."

"Morning." He watched her with that pale gaze, as if he knew she was attracted to him.

Well thank God he couldn't actually read her mind. If he could, she'd be in serious trouble. As her thoughts strayed to what lay beneath his coveralls, she cursed having the complexion of a redhead. She could actually feel her cheeks heat up.

"Hot out there," he grunted.

"Yeah. Still getting used to this weather." She unhooked her purse from her shoulder as she walked around the counter.

"All your references had great things to say about you. Why'd you move to Miami anyway?"

"Needed a change of scenery and my grandmother lives here." She avoided his gaze as she brushed past him toward the small office. No way was she telling him all the details of why she'd left Chicago. "Should I just put my purse in here?"

He followed her in so that she had no choice but to lean against the desk.

"Yeah. Listen, my last assistant left without any notice. I've already turned on the computer for you and that stack over there is everyone's time cards. Payroll needs to be finished by Friday."

"That shouldn't be a problem. What program do you use?"

When he rattled off the name of an accounting program she was familiar with, she breathed an inward sigh of relief. She'd been expecting someone to train her, but it looked like she was going to be doing everything herself.

He continued. "From what I can tell everything looks in order, but if you have any questions, don't hesitate to grab me from the pit. In a few weeks I'll have you help out with the phones but for now, I've forwarded everything to the pit. I just want you focusing on payroll. My people need to get paid on time."

"Okay."

"Oh, you get an hour for lunch. Take it whenever you want, just let me or one of the guys know."

She nodded and he left before she could think if she had any questions. Okay then, looked like she really was on her own. She was thankful he wasn't a micromanager, but she was still a little nervous that he was trusting her with so much. Tucking a strand of hair behind her ear, she looped around the desk and sat.

At least the office wasn't as messy as yesterday. Once she'd gotten used to her job, she was definitely cleaning this place up. And maybe she'd hang up a couple of pictures. It wasn't that the room was dirty, just unorganized and bland.

As she pulled up the program and got to work, relief coursed through her as she started cross-checking the time cards and employees. It would be time-consuming to get caught up with everything, but for the most part, everything was preset.

Three hours later, she was massaging the back of her neck when a female voice caused her to glance up.

"You must be the new girl." A pretty brunette wearing one of the blue jumpsuits stepped into the office.

"Uh, yeah."

"I'm Alexandra but you can call me Alex."

Carly stood. "I'm Carly. I didn't know there were any female…" She stopped, realizing how sexist she sounded.

The other woman grinned. "I get that all the time but I grew up working on cars. I'm about to head to lunch. You want to come with me?"

"Sure." She grabbed her purse from under the desk and followed Alex out. Nick had said she could go to lunch when she wanted and she needed a mental break.

The petite woman opened the glass door that led to the pit and shouted that they were leaving to eat.

Once they were outside, Carly automatically walked toward her car but Alex stopped her and motioned across the street to a one-story Cuban restaurant. "Want to go to Molina's?"

"Sure." Even though she'd been in Miami a couple weeks, Carly hadn't had as much time to get used to the area as she'd hoped.

"So why'd you move to Miami?" Alex asked as they waited at the crosswalk.

"I wanted to be closer to my grandmother but I also needed a change of scenery."

"Because of a man?" Alex's teasing voice instantly put her at ease.

She shrugged and decided to be honest. "That was part of the reason."

"There are plenty of men here. Just don't date anyone at the shop. They're all pigs. Well, except Nick. He's my cousin though so I kind of have to say that." Alex stepped onto the road as the light changed.

"Trust me, I don't plan on dating anyone for a while." Getting settled into a new place and a new job was enough to take up her time without worrying about jumping back into the dating game.

"No, *trust me*, you'll change your mind once you see all the hot men on South Beach."

She couldn't disagree with her there. "I actually got to check out the beach last week."

"And?"

Carly bit back a grin. "Okay, you're right. There were a lot of good-looking men but I don't want to date a man who works out more than me."

Alex chuckled under her breath. "Stick with me and I'll introduce you to all the eligible men worth meeting. My brother's birthday is this Friday and we're having a big party at my parents' house if you want to come," she said as she opened the door to the restaurant.

Carly avoided answering as the hostess greeted them. Alex was really sweet but she also looked like she was barely twenty-one. Something told Carly she was still into partying and clubbing. Carly had definitely done her share of partying in college, but staying out until three in the morning didn't interest her anymore. Still, she couldn't help but wonder if Nick would be there.

Nick glanced up as Alex strolled back into the garage. He was bent over the open hood of a '65 Impala, but he pushed up. The other guys were still at lunch so he nodded her over. "Alex, got a sec?"

"What's going on?"

"How was your lunch?"

Her brow furrowed, probably because he'd never asked her before. "Fine."

Okay, so she wasn't going to make this easy and he couldn't make his attraction to Carly obvious. "Do you think Carly's going to work out?"

His cousin nodded. "I hope so. She's a little quiet but I really like her. Oh, I invited her to Phillip's party Friday."

Phillip's party? He frowned, trying to remember what the party was for. In their family, there was always a birthday or anniversary to go to. Considering most of the pack was at least a century old, it was a lot of events to remember.

"Don't tell me you forgot! It's his birthday."

"I didn't forget," he muttered.

"Yeah, right." She cleared her throat and glanced over her shoulder toward the office. "Boss, I know everyone else can't smell you but good Lord, tone it down. If you don't, even Carly's going to know you want to jump her bones."

Damn it. Alex was from a much younger generation and she was still learning to control the impressions she put off. The fact that she felt the need to remind *him*, told him he might have a problem. He thought he'd done a pretty good job of masking his lust, but apparently not. Hell, after the vivid, practically multicolored dream from last night, who the hell could blame him.

"Noted. Now get back to work, slacker." He grinned as she rolled her eyes.

Even though she was young and sometimes unpredictable, Alex was one of the best employees he had. Besides, she was his cousin. He wasn't sure how he felt about her hanging around with Carly though. Alex was too wild. Grabbing a rag, he wiped off his hands and headed inside.

He found Carly shutting one of the drawers of the desk. She didn't notice him at first and when she saw him, she gave a slight jump, the scent rolling off her a mix of surprise and...not exactly guilt, but close to it. Maybe embarrassment. It was too difficult to tell. "Hey," she said, her voice slightly trembling.

"Everything okay?"

"Yeah," she said a little too quickly. It was subtle and she probably wasn't aware of it but her gaze darted back to the drawer she'd just closed.

He wasn't even going to pretend he wasn't interested. He doubted she was stealing from him since there wasn't much for her to take in here, but he didn't like that scent. "What's in the drawer?"

Her cheeks flushed pink and to his annoyance, he found he liked that way too much. "I... Okay, I don't want you to think I was doing this during work hours, especially not on my first day. Or at all, even. I'd planned to use my lunch break, but then Alex asked me so...and now I'm rambling." She slid the door open to reveal a tote bag next to her purse.

She hadn't brought the bag in this morning so she must have grabbed it after lunch or sometime earlier.

"I pulled this out of my car because I didn't want it sitting out in the heat."

"What is it?" He could see rolled yarn and a long needle sticking out.

"Ah, it's my knitting bag. And yes, I know I have the hobby of an eighty year old lady and I don't care." Her cheeks were crimson now, her scent almost defensive.

He snickered, unable to stop himself. Well, hell, she wasn't stealing, she just knitted. He found that beyond adorable. "You were hiding your knitting?"

"I didn't want you to think I was slacking off."

"What do you knit?"

She blinked in surprise. "Oh, ah, well mainly just scarves, though I won't need them down here very often. Around the holidays I make these miniature little sweaters and use them as gift ornaments. They're insanely cute. And I've made throws, but only if I can find really fantastic wool...and I'm rambling again. You were just being polite." The blush was back.

The sight of her flustered did strange things to him. He'd never liked that whole innocent quality to a woman before, but damn it, he liked it on Carly. Way too much "No, I'm really interested. Maybe you can make me something." He wanted to take the words back as soon as he'd said them, but then she smiled and relaxed.

"Maybe I will." She glanced back at the computer, sending a lock of that silky red hair cascading over her shoulder. He wondered what it would feel like sliding between his fingers. "I've done a lot of reviewing so far today and the last accountant left everything in pretty good order."

"Good. Listen, when all the guys get back I'll introduce you to everyone." He couldn't believe he hadn't done it earlier, but he hadn't been thinking straight around her. Actually, he hadn't been thinking at all. At least not with his brain.

"Sounds good." Her words came out a little breathless, sending an alert straight to his cock.

Nope, he wasn't doing this, wasn't going to be attracted to her. He would simply fight his urges. He nearly snorted at the stupidity of his own thought. "I hear you're coming to my cousin's party Friday."

"Yeah. That was really sweet of Alex to invite me." Carly turned in her chair to face him.

"I'll probably see you there." What the hell was the matter with him? He shouldn't be hanging around her office making small talk. Every second that ticked by, his cock got harder.

At his words, a light shade of pink played across her cheeks. "Okay."

It wasn't overt, but a whiff of something akin to desire tickled his nose. He wished he knew what was going on in that pretty head of hers, but his brain froze, making any further conversation impossible. He grunted something and left her in peace. He'd never had a problem around women. Talking to women came as naturally as breathing. Of course he'd never been around a woman who made his tongue swell and his cock hard without any sort of stimulation. Just talking to her and he felt like a randy pup again with his first crush.

"Can you take a look at this, boss?" Jimmy asked as he walked across the garage.

Nick stopped by the Mercedes Jimmy was working on. "Yeah. What's up?"

"I can't figure out..."

Nick made the mistake of glancing toward the store. The garage and store were connected by glass doors and glass windows so he could see practically everything going on inside. His office was the only room he couldn't see, but Carly wasn't in there. He knew that because she was talking to one of his guys. Jimmy's words faded away as he watched Rodrigo, his newest hire, leaning against one of the counters talking to Carly.

Whatever he was saying must be fucking hilarious. Carly's red hair swished seductively around her shoulders as she clutched her stomach laughing. All he could think about was the fictional memory of watching her hair cascade around his cock while she sucked him. It made him want to walk inside and slam his fist across Rodrigo's face for simply talking to her.

Despite being raised in a shifter family where the alpha and beta lines were clearly drawn, he'd always considered himself fairly enlightened when it came to the opposite sex—shifter or human. He'd never before experienced such barbaric inclinations about any woman.

Rodrigo was lucky he was still breathing. Gritting his teeth, he tore his gaze away and inwardly groaned. What the hell had he been thinking by hiring her?

CHAPTER FOUR

Carly shut the computer down with a satisfied sigh. Her first day had flown by surprisingly fast. Alex had told her that most of the guys were pigs, but everyone she'd talked to had been so nice.

A lot nicer than where she'd worked in Chicago. Maybe it had something to do with the sunny weather, but practically everyone she'd come in contact with in Miami was friendly.

"You getting out of here?" Nick's deep voice cut through her thoughts.

God, how did he do that? The man was like a ghost. "Yeah. Unless you need me to stay…"

"No, we're shutting down too. Unless there's an emergency, I don't keep my guys past five."

She grabbed her purse from the drawer in her desk and fished her keys out. Nick was still standing by the door and she wondered if she was supposed to say something else. She'd noticed him looking at her a few times today and of course it had been when she was talking to one of the employees. Maybe he thought she wasn't taking her job seriously. She frowned at the thought.

"So how was your first day?" His lips pulled up at the corners but she couldn't figure out if that was supposed to be his version of a smile. He was incredibly hard to read, but he didn't seem annoyed with her so that was good.

"It was great. I hope it's okay, but I made a couple changes with the way some of your billing is set up." She snapped her mouth shut because she could feel herself starting to ramble. *Again.* Since she'd already embarrassed herself with that little knitting revelation, she didn't need to add to it.

"I'd like to review any changes you make." His deep voice sent shivers to all her nerve endings.

She nodded and swallowed the lump in her throat. "I figured. I kept notes of everything I changed — which wasn't much," she added hastily.

"If you're ready, I'll walk you to your car." There was something positively sensual about the way he looked at her.

She was sure it wasn't intentional, but when he stared at her with those pale eyes, she wanted to do bad, bad things to him. And that wasn't like her at all. Carly normally dated a man for weeks, usually months before even contemplating sleeping with him. Nick Lazos only needed to look at her and she was ready to strip her clothes off and let him have his way with her. Ugh. He was her *boss*, she reminded herself for the hundredth time that day.

Somehow she ordered her legs to move. She needed to get out of there before she did or said something incredibly stupid. No need to embarrass herself in front of the sexy man.

The sweltering Florida heat wasn't as bad as it had been in the early afternoon, but her face and body warmed the instant they stepped outside. She'd parked directly out front so she wasn't exactly sure why he wanted to walk with her. Jangling her keys in her hand she smiled at him. "Well, thanks. I'll see you tomorrow."

He nodded, but to her dismay he waited while she got into her car. For the past week she'd been having trouble with her little two-door car. Her normally trusty car had gotten her through college and then some, but the drive to Florida had been pretty rough. She turned the ignition and held her breath when she turned the key. "Come on, baby, don't let me down now." Not in front of Nick.

This morning it had sputtered and sputtered until it finally started. This evening, it didn't even do that much for her. "Do not do this to me. Come on," she ordered through gritted teeth. She tried turning the key again but it simply made a clicking sound.

She had no choice but to turn when Nick knocked on her window. Taking a deep breath, she took the key out and opened the door. "My car's been giving me some trouble, but it's no big deal. My grandmother will pick me up so — "

"I'll give you a ride." He held out a big, callused hand.

Briefly she wondered what it would be like to feel that hand stroking over her bare skin. Just as quickly she felt her cheeks heat up. Oh yeah, she definitely didn't need to be in an enclosed space with her sexy as sin boss if that was the direction of her thoughts. "Oh, no — "

"If you give me your car key, I'll come back tonight and see if I can figure out what's wrong with it."

Carly clutched the keys in her hand. "That's okay. I couldn't ask you to do that."

"Carly. You work at an auto shop. Take advantage of the free labor." His words were low and somehow sensual, but they almost sounded like an order. Maybe that should rub her the wrong way, but she wouldn't mind him ordering her around. At least in the bedroom.

Something told her people rarely said no to him. Especially women. Averting her gaze, she slid the key off the ring and placed it in his outstretched palm. When her fingers brushed his, an electric current sent an unexpected shock straight to her core.

Her gaze flew to his and she almost stumbled at what she saw. Pure, raw lust flared in his eyes. It was only there for a split second but she knew what she'd seen.

Well, that was unexpected—and not exactly unwelcome. Clearing her throat, she found her voice. "If you're sure you don't mind taking me home, I'm ready."

"I definitely don't mind," he murmured, his tone sensual.

Oh hell. Her boss was interested in her. It was probably just a simple little attraction that would never amount to anything, but knowing a man that hot thought she was attractive did something crazy to her libido.

Carly knew what she looked like. She was cute in a girl-next-door kind of way, but men like Nick rarely looked twice at her. Maybe the men in Miami were different. Another score for the sunny city.

"Wait here, I'll pull my car around." He turned and had disappeared back inside the garage before she could blink.

Placing a hand on her abdomen, she took a few deep breaths. *Get it together*, she ordered herself. She was being ridiculous.

A few seconds later she heard Nick before she saw him. His two-door muscle car rumbled quietly as he drove around from the back of the building. She didn't know exactly what kind of car it was, but it was definitely hot. And it totally fit him.

He stopped a few feet from her and before she could move, he jumped out and opened the door for her.

Oh, this was bad. Very, very bad. He was sexy and chivalrous. "I live off La Salle Street," she said a few seconds later when he slid into the driver's seat.

"I know where that is." He didn't glance at her as he spoke.

She asked another question just to hear his voice. "How long have you lived in Miami?"

"I grew up here."

Okay, so maybe he didn't feel like making conversation. That normally wouldn't bother her. It was actually a pet peeve of hers when people felt the need to fill all silences. She clutched her purse in her lap as he turned down a side street.

The muscles in her arms and legs were incredibly tense. It was nice that he'd offered her a ride home, but it was also making her very aware that maybe her little crush was growing out of control. Which seemed insane on too many levels. She'd just met the man. "Do you mind if I turn on the radio?"

"Go ahead." There he went with that smooth voice again.

With the exception of the radio, the rest of the ride to her place was in silence, which was a little unnerving. When he started to pull into the driveway of the main house, she pointed to the extended drive along the side of the house.

"I live in the apartment back there." To her annoyance her voice had dropped a couple notches, taking on an almost sensual quality. Good Lord, she needed to get away from this man and fast.

"Do you need a ride in the morning?" he asked as he put his car in park.

"No, I'll be okay. I really appreciate you taking me home though. See you tomorrow." Holding her purse, she hurried out.

To her dismay, he opened his door and followed her up the short stone walk.

Nick raked a hand through his dark hair and cleared his throat. "Listen, Carly, I'm sorry if I've made you feel uncomfortable or anything."

She blinked. "Uncomfortable?"

"Shit. I can't think straight around you," he muttered.

"Wait, *what*?" Did he mean what she thought he did?

Those pale gray eyes of his locked with hers and her heart stuttered in her chest. He was only a few inches from her now. Their surroundings seemed to funnel out as they watched each other.

Before she realized what he intended, he cupped her cheek with his big hand. The feel of his callused palm against her skin sent a foreign flutter to her stomach. She could feel the vein in her neck pump as anticipation hummed through her.

What was he doing? Okay, she knew what he planned to do, could see it clearly in his eyes. Was she insane for letting him? Maybe so but it was hard to care. Nervously she licked her lips. The small motion tore his gaze away from hers as he zeroed in on her mouth.

Yep, she was right. He was going to kiss her. This had disaster written all over it, but that didn't stop her from wanting a taste of him.

Lips that had looked hard and unforgiving were surprisingly gentle as they covered hers. As soon as they made contact, her body molded against his. There were a dozen different reasons she knew this was the dumbest thing she'd ever done, but all she could focus on was the way he tasted.

Sweet and minty. Another surprise.

His tongue moved over hers in erotic little strokes. As if they had a will of their own, her hands wound their way around his neck.

The hand that had been cupping her cheek now clutched the back of her head in a tight, possessive grip. Moaning, she pressed her body against the full length of him, savoring the feel of her breasts against his muscular chest. Unfortunately there was a whole mess of clothes in their way. She wanted to feel his skin against hers. That thought should have brought her up short, but as she kissed him, she craved so much more.

A slow-moving heat slid down her belly and between her legs like hot lava. She'd never been so affected by anyone before. And she'd never been bowled over by one kiss either.

Heat and cream dampened her panties as he slowly trailed a hand down her back toward her backside. When he cupped her ass and squeezed, she moaned into his mouth.

This was crazy. They needed to get inside now before she let him take her up against her front door for anyone to see. Pulling her head back she kept her fingers linked around the back of his neck. Before she could say a word, however, he stepped away from her.

"Shit," he muttered and raked a hand through his hair. "I'm sorry...I'm..." His words trailed off as he turned on his heel and jogged toward his vehicle.

A tight knot formed in her stomach as he tore out of the driveway. What the hell had just happened? She'd been ready to throw herself at her boss. Her boss!

Groaning aloud, she opened her front door and locked the door tightly behind her. Part of her wanted to hide her head in the sand and not go into work tomorrow. Or ever. But she knew she couldn't do that. Finding a job so quickly had been a miracle. Not to mention the pay and the benefits were fantastic. Besides, he was the one who'd kissed her. If he had a problem, then too bad. He could just deal with it.

CHAPTER FIVE

Three Days Later

Nick steered his 1968 Dodge Charger into his Aunt Melina's long driveway. Unlike most of the pack, his aunt preferred living closer to the city limits of Miami instead of in Key Biscayne. There were almost a dozen cars already lining the street and three currently in the driveway. He didn't see Carly's car, but Alex had told him she was picking up the redheaded vixen he couldn't get out of his head so he knew she was already here.

For the past three days he'd been able to avoid her. There had been a few awkward moments, but he'd mastered his Houdini act. Kissing her had been the dumbest move he could have made. He wanted to talk to her about it and apologize, but he was afraid if he tried to talk to her, he'd kiss her again. Not to mention, he wasn't sorry and he doubted he could fake it.

A bang on his window made him turn to find his younger brother, Stephan, standing there. He inwardly cursed his lack of awareness. For the past week all his senses had been off kilter. He should have smelled Stephan. Instead all his energy and thoughts were focused on Carly.

Immediately he opened the door. "Hey, surprised to see you here. Tell me I'm not the last one."

"Just about." Stephan slapped him on the back and pulled him into a tight hug.

"Are you working a case right now?" Nick locked his car before shutting the door.

"Nah. Just came off one. Thought I'd see the family before I got reassigned." His brother raked a hand through his dark hair.

"You need a haircut." He shook his head as they walked up the steps.

UNLEASHED TEMPTATION | 25

Stephan had been working for the Drug Enforcement Administration for the past four years.

"Tell me about it... Hey, who's the hot redhead human Alex brought? She smells like sex and —"

"She's off limits. To you, to anyone. She's *mine*," Nick growled. The second the words were out of his mouth, he knew it was true. It was the only thing that made sense. Carly *was* his. He'd stopped looking for a mate a long time ago. And he'd never thought his mate would be a human. But it was the only thing that explained his intense attraction to her.

"Oh, shit. Never thought I'd see the day. You actually think she's your mate? A human?" Stephan asked as they reached the front door of his aunt's two-story Mediterranean-style house.

"Just stay away from her," he bit out. It was a struggle to simply keep his wolf in check right now.

"Hmm, if you haven't claimed her, she's fair game." Stephan's voice was taunting as he opened the front door.

The only thing keeping Nick from actually punching his brother was that he knew Stephan was just fucking with him. "I'd hate to kick your ass if —"

The second they stepped onto the tiled foyer, his Aunt Melina grabbed both their arms. For such a small female, she had a wicked grip. "Stephanos, where did you sneak off to? Nicolas, you're *late*! And where's Thomas?"

"I think he's working, but Stephan wanted to ask you about that salon you go to. He needs a haircut." Nick dropped a quick kiss on her cheek and headed down the long hallway toward the kitchen. He threw a glance over his shoulder and gave his scowling brother the finger.

If he allowed her, his aunt would hold his ear captive for half an hour. And he had more important things to worry about. Like finding Carly.

In the kitchen he found three of his younger female cousins whispering around the table. When they saw him they all giggled.

"What's so funny?" He looked back and forth between them.

Athena, one of his favorites, answered. "Nothing much. Alex just told us a story about you when you were our age."

He frowned. Athena wasn't more than fifteen or sixteen. She was barely a pup. When she turned twenty, her aging process would slow down immensely, allowing her to live hundreds of years. Hell, maybe longer. It wasn't as if it was an exact science.

He remembered quite well what he'd been like back then. It had been over a century ago and he'd been living in Greece.

Sighing, he thought of his hometown of Leontio. Being a shifter had been a lot easier back then. Greeks in general had a lot of respect for wolves and mythology and the thought of the paranormal wasn't scoffed at as it was in so many other places around the globe. "Where exactly is Alex?" he asked through gritted teeth.

With a big, knowing grin plastered on her face, Athena nodded toward the back of the house. "Back porch. Hey, where's Thomas? I haven't seen him in like, a month, and he promised to help me with a school project on the history of Greece."

"He's working," he answered absently as he opened the back door.

Wherever Alex was, Carly was sure to be also. As he stepped onto the back porch, he swept his gaze around the throng of people. There were about twenty-five of his relatives and friends of friends, shifters and humans alike, eating and drinking. A few sat in lounge chairs around the Olympic-sized pool, some stood in clusters, and one of his uncles and two male cousins stood around the grill arguing about a football game. His Uncle Cosmo had remarried a few decades ago and now his pack had a new generation of werewolves who were more in touch with their human side. They'd all grown up in the city and while they understood their heritage and their order in the pack, they didn't seem to take things as seriously as his generation.

Nick mentally shook himself as he zeroed in on Carly. Even if he hadn't been able to smell her sweet scent, she was the easiest to spot. In a sea of dark-haired men and women, her red hair and fair skin was like a beacon.

Unwanted jealousy jolted through him, sharp and deadly, when he spotted her talking to a man he didn't recognize. She held a glass of white wine in one of her slim hands and was smiling politely while that randy bastard practically undressed her with his eyes.

Fuck that.

If she was his mate, he needed to clear the air with Carly if he was ever going to get a decent night's sleep again. Not to mention he owed her a big apology.

In a few long strides he stood in front of Carly and the man.

"Carly." Her name rolled off his tongue with ease. For the past couple nights he'd fantasized about saying her name as that long hair fanned against his chest while she rode him.

Her pretty blue eyes widened as she shifted to face him. "Oh hi, Nick." When she bit her bottom lip in that adorable way he was coming to love, he bit back a groan. He wanted to be the one biting that lip.

"I'm Dennis." The other man nodded at him politely, but he couldn't mask the wave of annoyance that rolled off him.

Nick stared at the man for a moment. His green eyes had a strange quality, but Nick couldn't place him. The guy smelled human, but there was something else there too. Something earthy and slightly familiar? Nick inwardly cursed himself. He was sizing this guy up just because he was talking to his woman. He didn't give a shit what the guy smelled like. "Nice to meet you," he said through clenched teeth. "Hope you don't mind if I steal Carly for a second. Shop talk."

Nick didn't wait for a response as he hooked his hand under Carly's elbow and steered her toward two lone chairs by the pool.

"What are you doing?" she muttered.

"Do you want to sit?" He motioned to the lounge chair.

"Fine." She sat and when she crossed those long legs, his cock jumped to attention.

Following suit, he sat next to her. She wore white shorts that showcased her sinfully long legs and a turquoise halter top that showed off her graceful neck. The thought of raking his teeth over that delicate skin caused another unwanted reaction.

"How's your car running?" It had taken him about an hour Tuesday night to figure out what was wrong, but it had been an easy fix. He'd even changed her oil.

"Better than before, actually, thank you. Do you really want to talk about my car?" she asked quietly.

He cleared his throat and forced himself to maintain eye contact. "We haven't had a chance to talk since…ah…" He cleared his throat again. Damn, it shouldn't be this hard to talk to her.

"Since you kissed me." Her words were tight and restrained.

"Right."

"And whose fault is that? You've been ignoring me all week," she snapped. The unexpected fire in her eyes and the heat in her voice made him change tactics.

He hadn't realized just how feisty Carly was. "You're right. I should have talked to you sooner. I've never behaved like that with an employee and I owe you an apology. Hell, I owe you more than that. If you want to file a sexual harassment charge against me, you have more than enough right to. I won't fight you." Werewolf or not, he was a man first and he'd had no right to treat Carly the way he had. Even if Carly had returned the kiss, he was her boss and he'd put her in an awkward position.

She watched him carefully, her expression far too neutral. "Did you enjoy the kiss?"

Did she even have to ask? "It's all I've thought about the past three days."

A smiled teased her very kissable mouth. "Me too… I don't want to file a harassment charge against you, Nick. Trust me."

"Then what do you want?"

"You." Her lips parted a fraction, as if she'd surprised herself with the admission. "Damn, I shouldn't have had that second glass," she murmured as she placed her near-empty wineglass next to her chair.

Shit, the woman was sending all his good intentions out the window. The twinge of lust he'd smelled a few days ago was now full blown. The spicy scent rolled over him with an unexpected intensity. He'd been walking around with a permanent hard-on the past few days and feeling doubly guilty for practically mauling his new employee on her first day. And she still wanted him? "Do you want to get out of here?" he rasped out.

Her eyes widened for a split second, but she simply nodded.

"Good. I'll tell Alex you're not feeling well and that I'm taking you home." He glanced over his shoulder. No one was paying attention to them. "Head through the house and I'll meet you out front in a few minutes."

Her cheeks had turned pink, but she nodded and stood on shaky legs.

He waited in his seat for a minute longer to compose himself. Once he'd managed to get his thoughts and body under control, he found his cousin, gave her a quick excuse, then managed to avoid talking to anyone as he escaped out the front door. He knew Alex hadn't believed him and considering the lusty vibe he knew he was putting off, Nick guessed every shifter in the house knew *exactly* why he was leaving.

He didn't give a shit.

Nick found Carly leaning against his car and his breath caught in his throat. All he could envision was her stretched out on his hood wearing nothing but a pair of heels.

"Do you want to grab a bite to eat or hit up some of the clubs? My older brother owns one on South Beach." Somehow he managed to string multiple coherent sentences together. She might have said she wanted to leave, but she didn't say she wanted to head back to his place and fuck for hours. That was what *he* wanted to do.

She glanced down at herself then back up at him. "If we go downtown I'll need to change first."

He bit back his disappointment. "No problem." He hated the Miami nightlife and if it wasn't for the fact that his brother owned a club, he'd never go in the first place. He might have offered to take her out, but all he really wanted to do was get her back to his place and flat on her back.

Or against a wall. Or bent over the side of his bed. Or hell, right on his car. He'd take her wherever and whenever she let him.

After opening the door for her he rounded the car and slid into the driver's seat.

"Was one of your brothers here earlier?"

He glanced in the rearview mirror before backing out. "Yeah, why?"

"I did a double take when I saw him. I thought it was you until he turned around."

He understood what she meant. They all had similar builds but both Nick's brothers had dark eyes. "That was Stephan. He's two years younger than me. Thomas is my older brother. He's the one who owns the club downtown."

"So it's just the three of you?" Out of the corner of his eye, he watched her shift in her seat and cross her legs toward him.

He forced himself to keep his gaze on the road and *not* her legs. Hard to do when all he could seem to think about was what it would be like to have those legs tossed over his shoulders as he tasted her. "Yep." Making any sort of conversation was damn near impossible. Nick racked his brain, trying to think of anything nonsexual to talk about. "Do you like Miami so far?"

Her face lit up instantly. "I love it here. The summers in Chicago are hot too so I'm looking forward to spending a fall here with no snow."

There, that wasn't so bad. He could talk like a normal human being. "What about the shop? I know we didn't get a chance to talk much this week, but are you figuring everything out okay?"

"Yeah. Most of the accounting stuff is time consuming since everyone has such different hours, but the programs you've got are great. And everyone has been really nice too, especially Alex."

He grunted at his cousin's name.

"What?"

"Nothing. She's just a pain in the ass sometimes. Needs a man to take care of her."

Carly's nose crinkled as she laughed aloud. The sweet sound enveloped him. "I can't believe you just said that. That's so chauvinistic."

He shrugged and glanced over his shoulder before switching lanes. Chauvinistic or not, it was true. For the next fifteen minutes he managed to talk to her like a normal person. That was a feat in itself.

Once they reached her place she invited him in while she got changed. Her apartment was small but from what he could see, it fit her. Large black-and-white prints of various American cities hung on two of the sage-colored walls. Bright afghan blankets were thrown across the back of the loveseat and couch and a vase of fresh sunflowers stood proudly on the coffee table. He wondered if she'd knitted the throws. If so, she was talented.

Carly's scent and movements caused him to look up from the magazine he'd grabbed off the coffee table. She was standing in the entryway of the hallway. He hadn't been actually reading, just staring at the pages and thinking of her. Everything inside him stilled at the sight of her. She wore a slim fitted two-toned purple and white dress with strappy heels. The cut was high, boat-neck, he thought maybe it was called, with some sort of lace overlay over the entire thing. "What do you think?" She turned once, her grin light and flirty.

It didn't show any cleavage but it was too short and too tight. And the back had a cut out, exposing way too much of her delectable skin. In reality it was perfectly respectable, tame even, compared to what most women wore to South Beach clubs, but he didn't want anyone else seeing all that toned skin. It was totally barbaric but he wanted her all for himself. His ancestors would be proud. Nick stood and forced himself to smile. "Hot."

She let out a short laugh. "That's certainly descriptive."

"You look beautiful," he amended. Hot wasn't the right description for her, even if she was exactly that. The woman was stunning and sweet— and all he could seem to think about was getting her naked.

There went the sexy blush. "Thanks," she murmured. "I'm ready if you are."

The living room was attached to a small foyer so he followed after her. As she started to unlock the front door, he instinctively placed his hand on the small of her back. Something primal inside him simply wanted to touch her, to claim her.

When he did, she looked back at him in surprise. White-hot lust flared in her eyes and the sweet scent of her desire washed over him like a tidal wave. In that instant, he knew they weren't going anywhere.

Her fiery red hair tumbled around her shoulders in seductive waves. Just like in his dream, only the reality was so much better. With a shaking hand, he threaded his fingers through her hair and cupped the back of her head. The desire to completely dominate her surprised him. He'd heard about what happened when other werewolves found their mates, but he'd never completely understood until now. And he really didn't want to fuck this up. Having a human mate wasn't something he'd counted on. If she'd been a shifter, she'd have recognized their connection and would have understood exactly what he needed from her.

"Do you want to stay or leave?" he rasped out.

Her tongue darted out to moisten her pink lips. "Stay," she whispered.

That was all he needed to hear. The second his mouth crushed over hers, he knew that everything he'd previously thought about women and relationships was about to change.

Drastically.

Nick knew Carly deserved wining, dining, and a lot of foreplay, but that would come later. Once he'd gotten his fill of her. Hell, if that was even possible.

He hadn't had a thing to drink, yet he felt almost drunk. Needing to feel more of Carly, he slid his free hand up her leg and under her sexy, lacy dress. His cock surged when he touched more bare skin than material. As he caressed and gripped her ass, she pressed her pelvis tightly against his and started grinding in small little circles.

The feel of her moving against him like that made him crazy.

Nick tore his mouth away from hers and feathered kisses along her jaw. Animalistic urges compelled him to kiss, touch, and claim every part of her body. He continued a trail down to her neck, savoring her sweet taste. A heady scent that was pure Carly enveloped and overwhelmed him, threatening to short circuit what few brain cells he had left.

He might have thought he'd had a clue what this would be like, but his erotic dream paled in comparison to the reality of actually touching her.

CHAPTER SIX

Carly couldn't believe what she was doing. This was her boss. Her very sexy boss, but still, this wasn't the smartest move she'd ever made. It was hard to care when he was touching her, when his hands were gently moving over her bare skin. Hell, it was hard to *think* straight when they were in the same room.

"Nick." His name rolled off her tongue when he pressed her back into the wall.

Every part of her ached with pent-up need. She'd been doing what was expected of her for too long. After her parents died, she'd been such a straight arrow, needing control over her life. It was part of the reason she'd gone into accounting. Numbers could never disappoint her.

Having sex with her boss would definitely qualify as poor decision making, yet she'd never wanted anything more, and she was going to take him.

As his hand glided over her bare skin and tugged at her thong, a shiver skittered through her, surging to all her nerve endings.

"You're so soft," he murmured against her neck.

His hand slid under the elastic of her panties and trailed around her hip until he reached her mound. Pushing the flimsy garment to the side, he gently rubbed a finger over her clit.

The unexpected touch made her jerk against him. She wanted so much more.

As he teased the sensitive bud, he slid his hands up her back and unsnapped the one button holding the keyhole of her dress up in the back. It easily slid down, only to pool around her waist. When she'd said she wanted to stay, she'd known what it meant for them, but being bared to him like this was still unnerving. Nick was such a huge, sexy guy. Sex appeal clung to him like some guys wore suits. It was simply part of his genetic makeup. She knew she was pretty, but it wasn't in that exotic, traffic-stopping way. She couldn't help but wonder if he would be disappointed once he saw all of her.

Nick completely stilled when her breasts were bared. His hand stopped moving over her slick folds and his eyes zeroed in on her chest.

She could feel her face heat up as a sudden wave of shyness overwhelmed her. She was tall and slim, but her breasts weren't much to look at. Instinct took over and she started to cover herself.

Nick grabbed both her wrists and pinned them to the wall above her head. The sudden abrupt action stole the breath from her.

"Don't ever cover yourself in front of me. You're fucking beautiful." His words were a low growl and somehow almost animalistic.

Something she found incredibly hot. She nodded since she didn't trust her voice. Still holding her arms in place, he dipped his head and sucked one of her nipples into his mouth. She moaned at the sharp, erotic action. Arching her back, she tried to give him better access, wanting so much more. Being pinned in place like this shouldn't be so arousing, but she grew damper each second that passed.

With each stroke and lick, an invisible ribbon of desire traveled straight to the throbbing between her legs. Her clit pulsed, aching for him to touch her there again. Pushing her hips forward deliberately, she lifted one of her legs and hooked it around his waist. She wasn't sure if this was a one-time thing and she planned to enjoy every second of their time together.

"Upstairs," she whispered in his ear, feeling a little bolder at his reaction to her. All the rooms in her place were downstairs except her bedroom, which took up the entire second floor.

Thankfully he understood what she meant—as if there could have been a doubt. His pale eyes flared when they met hers. As he dropped her arms, she instinctively linked her fingers together behind his neck. Before she could contemplate the ramifications of what they were about to do, he'd hoisted her up so she had no choice but to wrap her legs around him. He took the stairs two at a time, moving like a man possessed. Standing at five foot eight inches, she wasn't heavy but she wasn't a small woman either. Yet he moved with a grace and strength that surprised her.

As they entered her room she was aware of her feet touching the ground, but when the backs of her knees hit the end of her queen-sized bed, reality crashed down on her. They were moving really fast. Not that she didn't want this, she did. Way too much in fact. But, he was still her boss. "Do you think—"

"No thinking," he murmured before he clasped the bottom of her dress and pulled it over her head.

If she'd felt exposed before, it was nothing compared to standing in front of Nick in a skimpy thong and heels. She could feel her skin warm and her nipples harden as his pale gaze swept over her body. His chest lifted and rose erratically as he watched her.

Carly stood frozen, captured under his spell until it registered that he was still dressed. If she was going to be naked, so was he. She'd been fantasizing about him all week and wanted to see if the reality lived up to what she'd created in her mind.

Grasping his belt buckle, she tangled with it until it came free. As she pulled on the zipper, he lifted his shirt over his head and it was her turn to lose her breath.

She was vaguely aware that he'd kicked his pants out of the way but all she could focus on was his broad, oh-so-muscular chest. A man didn't have the right to look so good.

Dark hair lightly smattered across his pecs. The sharp lines across his chest and down his arms were perfectly defined and cut, as if he'd been chiseled from stone. He was like an incredibly honed machine. Everything about him was solid and sexy.

As her gaze strayed down his ripped abs to the V between his legs her face instantly warmed. His cock was long, thick and so perfect, her mouth actually watered. *Holy hell.* Soon he was going to be inside her. Her inner walls tightened at that thought.

"See something you like?" The deep timbre of his voice jerked her head back up to meet his gaze.

Before she could respond, he came at her fast, his mouth descending on hers with a ferocious, animalistic need.

Instinctively she braced herself for the fall as they tumbled onto the bed but Nick caught her around the waist and gently laid her against the comforter before settling his body against the full length of hers.

This was what she'd been waiting for. Skin on skin. Wrapping her legs around him, she rolled her hips against his. She felt frantic with the need to feel him inside her. After seeing how truly beautiful his thick length was, she wanted to feel every inch of it thrusting into her. Unfortunately he seemed content to take his time kissing her. The way his tongue swirled and danced in her mouth drove her senses haywire.

She'd always been big into foreplay but her body was so hot she felt as if she'd combust at any second. Getting Nick inside her was the only thing that seemed to matter.

When she reached between them and grasped his cock, his huge body stilled and he lifted his head back. His eyes flared with white-hot lust, a mirror of how she felt. "Did I say you could touch that?" he murmured.

A small smile touched her lips at the hint of dominance in his voice. "Do you want me to stop?"

"No, but I don't want to come in your hand." His voice rolled over her like honey as he bent and nipped her jaw.

The small admission told her he was just as turned-on as she was. Her fingers were still wrapped snugly around his cock, but she let go and both her hands trailed around to his backside.

If she couldn't touch that, then she was going to get her feel of the rest of his body. She dug her fingers into his ass and moaned as he continued kissing down her neck and chest. His hot breath on her skin sent tingles scattering over her entire body. She couldn't understand what it was about him that got her so crazy. Normally she had to date a man for a while until she was comfortable enough to take it to the next level. All Nick had to do was look at her and her clothes wanted to fall off.

He left a hot trail of kisses down her body until he reached her breasts. He licked and laved the underside of both, as if he was taking great care to cover every inch of her skin.

He lightly raked his teeth over one of her hardened nipples and began circling it in erotic little circles.

"Nick," she moaned out his name, needing more.

As if he read her mind, he pinched the other nipple between his forefinger and thumb and squeezed. The action bordered on pain, but sent shock waves straight to her pulsing core. Threading her fingers through his thick hair, she clutched onto his head as his tongue and fingers worked their torturous magic.

Her panties were completely soaked, something he had to know. "I want you inside me, now." Somehow she found the strength to utter a few coherent words.

Wordlessly he lifted up and tugged her panties down her hips and legs. She kicked one of her legs, sending the material flying off the bed.

Nick rubbed his thumb over her clit as he inserted one finger past her folds. He pulled it out then gently pushed two inside her. The sensation of him filling her, made another moan tear from her. When he pressed his fingers against her inner walls and slowly dragged them out, she nearly vaulted off the bed.

"You're so wet," he murmured as he withdrew his fingers and nestled between her thighs.

"Condom," she blurted as reality crashed over her. She might want him more than she'd wanted anyone, but they needed protection.

He paused, hovering at her entrance.

Nick inwardly cursed himself. It had been so long since he'd had sex with a woman who wasn't a shifter, he'd completely forgotten about condoms. Shifters didn't need protection because their DNA was completely different. He couldn't get STDs, which meant he couldn't give them. Not to mention female shifters could only get pregnant twice a year. But, Carly wasn't a shifter and she didn't know any of that. He could only hope she didn't think he was an irresponsible jackass.

"One sec." He slid off the bed and grabbed his wallet from the back of his pants. If his emergency condom wasn't in it, he didn't know what he'd do. When his fingers touched the foil packet, all his muscles tightened in anticipation.

His hands trembled as he sheathed himself and he cursed again. Carly was so receptive to his every touch, yet he still worried he'd somehow fuck this up and lose his mate.

By human standards he looked to be around thirty-two, give or take a couple years. In reality, he was almost one hundred and seventy. Losing her because of something so stupid wasn't an option. Never finding a mate was something he'd learned to accept. Or he thought he had. Now that he'd found Carly, he couldn't lose her because he was an idiot.

Gazing down at her, his breath caught. She stared at him with those big blue eyes, making it damn near impossible to breathe. He could drown in that gaze if he let himself.

"Are you ready?" he rasped out.

"Yes." The word fell from her lips without pause. Her eyes slightly dilated, her desire for him sharp.

After settling between her legs again, he pushed the head of his cock against her opening, wanting to give her time to adjust to his size. Even though he was bigger than most, he'd never had a problem in the past since most of his partners had been shifters. She might be taller than a lot of women, but everything about Carly was slim and delicate. And that included her sweet pussy.

Her inner walls clamped around him the farther he pushed. Oh, God, she was so damn tight.

"Am I hurting you?" he whispered.

She shifted her hips, thrust up and completely impaled herself on him with a harsh inhalation of breath. Then she locked her ankles around his waist and held firm. "I'm not going to break, Nick."

His throat was clenched too tight to talk. He stayed deeply buried inside her, savoring the feel of her clenching around his cock. If he moved, even a few inches, he knew he'd come and that wasn't acceptable.

Maybe it was a little superstitious, but he didn't care. When male werewolves mated, it was considered extremely bad luck if their mates didn't climax the first time. He'd been waiting more than a century to find her. He'd be damned if she didn't get off — more than once. Hell, whether it was bad luck of not, he wanted to see that ecstasy playing off her face as she came around his cock.

He cupped both her breasts and rubbed his thumbs over her pale pink nipples. When she let out a breathless sigh and her pussy clenched even harder around him, he knew he was headed in the right direction.

"Touch yourself," he ordered.

Her eyes flashed with brief surprise before she reached between her legs and began massaging her clit. Her lips parted seductively as she watched him. The flush along her cheeks deepened as she continued stroking.

"*Fuck*, Carly." Watching her touch herself was one of the sexiest things he'd ever seen.

Leaning down, he kissed one of her breasts, taking care to lick and kiss all of the soft flesh. When she let out a tiny moan, he took a nipple between his teeth and sucked. Hard.

And that was all it took to push her over the edge.

"Oh!" She cried out, her hands going to his shoulders as she began rolling her hips against his in a frenzy.

Growling, he met her stroke for stroke. He grabbed her hips and searched out her mouth again. Hungrily he tasted her as he started moving in a rhythmic motion. He'd wanted their first time to last a lot longer but it simply wasn't going to happen.

He could smell her dampness and heat as she rode through her orgasm. It felt like a waterfall rushing over his cock as she came. He'd never experienced anything like it.

The combination of her sweet smell and tight body was all Nick needed. He tried to restrain himself but his climax rocketed through him with a roar. Clutching the sheets instead of her hips, he pounded into her. He was afraid of bruising her, even though the caveman part of him wanted her to have his marks on her hips, on her body. He wanted the whole damn world to know this female was his.

Groaning, he emptied himself in long, hard strokes. As he rode through the last wave, he pulled out and collapsed next to her, even if he could have stayed inside her all night.

"Holy shit," she muttered after a few long moments of silence.

"You can say that again."

"Say what again?" Still breathless, Carly propped up on one elbow and stared at him with a confused expression on her pretty face.

Oh shit. He'd heard of mates linking in various ways, but each couple reacted differently. His own parents could communicate telepathically but he'd never expected to experience the same thing. And definitely not with a human. Not to mention they hadn't officially bonded. He still needed to mark her and there was so much he needed to tell her. A healthy dose of worry slid through him at that thought, but he shelved it for now.

He rolled on his side and met her intense blue gaze. Feeling insanely possessive, he clutched onto her hip, needing to feel her soft skin again. He tightened his fingers against her. *Mine*, his wolf said. "I was just talking to myself, sweetheart."

A grin touched her face. *You can talk to yourself all you want as long as we do that again.*

No doubt about it now. She was definitely his mate. He fell back against the pillow and pulled her with him so that her head rested on his chest. Though he hated to do it, he put up a mental shield and forced himself to block out her thoughts. Until she realized what he was and what kind of connection they had, he couldn't invade her privacy. If she found out later that he had, he feared she'd hold it against him. Not to mention, if he could read her, then it was highly probable she could read him. If she didn't realize what was going on, she might think she was going crazy and that was the last thing he wanted.

Sighing, he hugged her tighter against him and inhaled her sweet scent. He loved the way she fit so perfectly against him. "Tell me more about yourself," he murmured after a few minutes.

She let out a sweet, amused laugh and dropped a kiss on his chest, though she didn't move more than that, just stayed curled up against him. "You don't exactly strike me as the kind of guy who likes to talk after sex."

He wasn't, but he wanted to know every damn thing about her. "Indulge me. So far I know you like to knit and that you look good in purple." Hell, she looked good in anything.

"Well that's good because it's my favorite color… All right, what do you want to know?"

"Do you have more family?"

"Ah, sort of. My parents died when I was fifteen. Car accident." He tightened his grip on her, wanting to offer comfort, but she rushed on.

"My Grandma Kendall was my guardian. She was great, taking on a depressed teenager. She moved in to my parents' house so I wouldn't have to move anywhere new and was two parents rolled into one. My mom's parents didn't even come to their funeral. I'd never really thought about it until I lost them..." She let out a short, semi-bitter laugh.

"Why would I because I was a freaking teenager. Anyway, I'd never really thought about my mom being estranged from her parents. She never really came out and said it, but I guess nothing was ever good enough for them. I didn't comprehend what assholes they were until they simply didn't show up for their own daughter's funeral."

"I'm sorry, sweetheart." He rubbed a gentle hand down her spine, hating the pain he could feel rolling off her. The scent of it filled his nostrils, made his wolf edgy.

"It's okay. Well now it is. They mean nothing to me at this point. My grandma helped me through that really hard time and when I graduated high school I got as many scholarships as I could. I stayed living at home to save money and got the degree I wanted. Pretty boring," she murmured.

Not to him. "Is your grandma your only family then?"

"Yeah. When she moved here it was harder than I realized being separated from her. I think she'd planned to move to Florida earlier but then when my parents died, she really stepped up. God, I'm so lucky to have her. I know how differently things could have turned out if I hadn't."

"She's really sweet," he murmured.

"Right, I forgot you've met her. I still haven't met your mom. They play bunco or something together I think."

Nick nearly snorted. His mom was century's old but looked to be in her forties. Still, she preferred spending her time with older generations. "Yeah, my mom adores her."

"So what about you? I didn't realize everyone at that party was related. That's a whole lot of relatives."

Now he did snort. "No kidding. I'm not complaining though. And not everyone was related — just most of us. It could be that sex with you has fried my brain, but I can't even remember how many cousins I have right now."

She laughed against his chest. The sound soothed both the man and wolf. "Your family is loud and fun."

"Loud is an understatement," he murmured, kissing the top of her head. "So how'd you end up with a degree in business?" Considering she knitted she clearly had a creative side.

"I love numbers, always have. No matter what, they don't lie and they don't change." She sat up then and moved until she straddled him, taking him off guard.

The sight of her long, lean body on his had his cock lengthening again. Unfortunately he didn't have any more condoms — but he'd be remedying that soon. She trailed her fingers up his chest, as if she couldn't get enough of touching him.

"You like stability?"

She paused, contemplating her answer. "Yeah, I guess I do. It's probably not very sexy to admit, but—" She let out a little yelp as he moved lightning quick, flipping her so that she was underneath him.

"Everything you do is sexy, Carly," he murmured before capturing her mouth once again. He never wanted her to forget that.

CHAPTER SEVEN

Asha cursed as he pulled down the long circular driveway to his villa. He'd tried tracking the sexy redhead from the party, but he'd lost her scent. That was the problem with living in populated areas. All the smells and noises meshed together. It wasn't as if his extrasensory abilities were as strong as those of a werewolf or other shifters.

It had been sheer luck—or maybe fate—that he'd been invited to a party full of werewolves. And then to meet a woman who was an almost identical version of his first slave? Yes, it had to be fate. Of course the redhead wasn't a shifter, which was almost a pity. He hadn't fucked a lycan in nearly a century.

Thankfully, the partygoers hadn't realized he was Immortal. With the common, fake name of Dennis he'd given them, and the cloaking spell he'd cast, they had no reason to suspect what he was. The spell had been fading near the end, but it had lasted long enough for him to get out of there. Originally he'd gone to the party simply to check out the shifters living in Miami. It had been years since he'd visited the sunny city and last time he hadn't come across any nonhumans.

He placed his hand on the biometric scanner and entered the front door. The house was quiet, just as he'd left it.

"Slave," he bellowed.

Seconds later, the blonde with sharp, exotic cheekbones, that he'd recently acquired, descended the spiral staircase wearing a t-shirt that fell to mid-thigh. She came to stand before him, eyes downcast. A light bruise marred her left cheek.

He fingered the hem of the shirt. "What are you wearing, slave?"

Her head snapped up to meet his gaze. The terror and fear he saw in her blue eyes caused his cock to stir. He loved it when she begged for mercy.

"Don't make me ask again."

"You were gone. I thought...I thought it would be okay." She tucked a strand of hair behind her ear.

"You don't think, whore. You do as you're told." Asha held out his hand and watched her expression as a ball of fire formed in his extended palm.

The orange light reflected in her eyes as she stared at him. "What are you doing?" she whispered.

"I told you what would happen if you disobeyed me. I'll burn that pretty body of yours until you're unrecognizable. Then, I'll let you go."

She took a step back, tears streaming down her face. "I'm sorry. It won't happen again. I promise." Her voice and skinny body shook uncontrollably.

With his other hand he reached out and cupped the back of her skull in a tight, demanding grip. "Since you're new, I'll let it go. *This time.* Now, I'm going to make a drink. When I come upstairs, I want you at the foot of my bed on all fours, wearing nothing."

With wide eyes, she backed away from him and sprinted up the stairs.

Sighing, he headed to his study. Breaking in a new slave was always tedious. Sometimes he hated the twenty-first century. Back when he'd been a prince in Persia, his slaves had never questioned him and never back talked. They did what they were told because it was what they'd been bred to do. Mindless whores. That was all they were.

Which was why he came to Miami every few years. Normally he was able to buy quiet, malleable slave girls from the Russians, but the most recent one he'd gotten cried all the time. For a while she'd tried to insist she had a name. It was nauseating.

Something told him the redhead wouldn't come easily either. She wouldn't be a crier though, she'd probably fight him. He rubbed a hand over his crotch as he imagined her naked and tied to his bed. It had been a while since he'd had a woman with any spirit.

Tracking her down wouldn't be too hard. He already knew her friends. Before he left Miami, he was going to claim her. If she turned out to be as good as he imagined, he might even take her with him when he left for Dubai.

Carly opened her eyes, stretched her arms above her head and let out a big yawn. Oh yeah, she wouldn't mind staying in bed for another hour. But only if Nick spent it with her. Where was he anyway... She rolled over at the sound of her cell phone ringing. Plucking it from her nightstand, she slid her finger over the screen to answer when she saw who it was.

"Hey, Stacie," she said through another yawn.

"Hey, I didn't wake you did I? I assumed you'd be up by now."

"I'm still lying in bed but I woke up a few minutes ago, don't worry. What's going on?"

"Nothing much. Saturdays without you officially suck," Stacie huffed.

When they'd lived together, Saturday's had been their day together. Usually they spent it shopping at a local farmer's market or if they were feeling really motivated, they'd hit up the Navy Pier to have an early lunch and see a movie. "Then you just need to hop on a plane and get down here."

"Trust me, I'm working on it. I should have enough vacation time built up in two months to come stay for a week. That's not why I called though. You'll never guess who I saw last night."

"I haven't even had my coffee yet, I'm not guessing," she groaned.

Stacie sighed overdramatically. "Fine, you're no fun. After work last night I went out with some of the girls for happy hour and I saw none other than your ex, Dan, making out with someone who most definitely wasn't Amanda. When he saw me, he made a hasty exit. What an idiot. As if I'm going to tell your bitch ex-boss he's cheating on her too."

Carly couldn't help the small smile that spread across her face, even if it was a little mean. Karma could be a bitch sometimes. "I'm sure she'll see the light eventually." Or maybe not, Carly didn't really care.

"So how was your first week at work?"

"Ah...interesting."

"What's that tone?"

It was impossible to try hiding anything from her friend so Carly plunged ahead with the truth. "Well, there's no other way to say this except I slept with my boss last night."

"You didn't!"

"Oh, I *did*." And it had been amazing. She finger combed her tangled hair as she sat up. Oh yeah, she could practically feel Nick imprinted on her.

"This is the tall, hot, Greek guy right?"

"The one and only." Though that seemed like such a tame description of the man.

Stacie was silent for a moment then she snickered. "How was it?"

"Amazing. The best sex of my life actually."

"I can't believe it. This is so unlike you!"

"I know, right."

"Well, Miami certainly agrees with you... Crap, that's my other line. It's my sister so I've got to take it. I'll call you back this afternoon though. I want all the juicy details."

"Okay." Carly grinned as she hung up the phone. It was a week after Stacie's sister's due date and her family was just waiting for her to pop.

Easing off the bed, Carly stretched her legs as she stood. Her body was exquisitely sore thanks to Nick. He'd woken her twice during the night. Since he didn't have any more condoms, she thought they'd be through for the night, but he'd had no problem pleasuring her orally again and again. Hell, he'd been insistent. In her limited experience, that was a rare thing for a man. He almost seemed too good to be true.

A healthy dose of anxiety still played in the back of her head that things might get complicated since he was her boss, but it was easy to silence her worries with a man like Nick in her bed. Truthfully, it was easy to forget her own name with him around.

She glanced at the clock as she grabbed the silk robe she'd tossed over the chair sitting at her vanity. It was nine o'clock. After slipping on her robe, she descended the stairs in search of tall, dark and sexy. She didn't hear anything as she rounded the corner and walked toward the living room.

When she found the kitchen empty, her stomach dropped until she saw the spread of food on the round table. There was a box of fresh bagels and cream cheese from a nearby bakery, two bacon and cheese sandwiches, hot coffee—and a new box of condoms—but still no Nick. Laughing lightly, she picked up the box that proudly proclaimed it contained forty-eight lubricated, ribbed condoms. Well, they certainly wouldn't need the lubrication. The man got her wet just by looking at her.

"He must be feeling pretty sure of himself," she murmured to the empty room.

"I am." The enveloping deep timbre of Nick's voice caused her to drop the box. She swiveled to face him.

Pleasure speared through her when she realized he was completely naked. "Where'd you come from?" He'd come from the direction of the back door. Unless he'd been running around in her backyard naked, she couldn't imagine where he'd been.

As if he read her mind, he answered. "Your trash was full so I took it out."

"Naked?"

He shrugged as he walked toward her and ignored her question. "You hungry?"

"Wait, you went to the store this morning wearing clothing, right?" She tracked his long, muscular form as he headed for the bagels. She practically had to bite back a groan watching him move.

"Uh, yeah."

"So you took off your clothes once you got back and decided to go out in my grandmother's backyard, *naked*?"

Nick froze with his hand in the bagel box. "Shit. I didn't think about that."

Part of her thought it was a little odd that he didn't mind strolling around in the buff, but guys were so different. And if she had a body like that, she'd probably flaunt it too. "Thanks for picking up breakfast."

"I've got to keep you fed. Besides, you didn't have anything in your fridge. Want some coffee?"

When she nodded, he continued. "Take a seat. I'll fix it for you."

Carly did as he said, irrationally pleased he was getting her coffee. Watching him move around her kitchen while unabashedly naked was too surreal. She kept expecting to wake up and realize it was all a dream. That she'd just fantasized the whole interlude with Mr. Sexy.

The sound of her doorbell chime made them both pause.

Nick turned to face her, coffeepot in hand. "Expecting someone?"

"No." Shaking her head she stood and made sure the tie on her robe was secure before heading to the front door. After glancing through the peephole, she immediately tensed.

"Who is it?" Nick's voice was dangerously close to her ear.

Her heart jumped as she swiveled to face him. "How do you do that?" she whispered.

"What?"

"Sneak up on me...never mind. It's my grandmother so go hide," she whispered again.

He turned and disappeared down the hallway before she could tell him to go upstairs instead.

Her heart rate had kicked up, but she pasted a smile on her face and pulled the door open. After all, she was a grown woman. It didn't matter who she slept with. "Hey, Grandma."

Her grandmother smiled and kissed her on the cheek. "Hi, sweetie. I'm about to go meet some of the girls for breakfast but I wanted to let you know I saw a big dog running around the yard earlier so be careful. It looks dangerous."

"What kind of dog?"

"I don't know, but it was gray and white and almost looked like a wolf."

A shiver snaked down Carly's spine. "Thanks for letting me know."

"Are you still having dinner with me tonight?"

Crap. She'd completely forgotten. "Uh—"

"If you already have plans, don't worry. Mr. Lancaster asked me out to dinner but I told him I'd have to check with you first."

She placed a hand on her hip. "Who's Mr. Lancaster?"

Her grandmother mimicked her and lifted a haughty eyebrow. "Whose car is parked in the driveway?"

Carly's cheeks heated under her grandmother's knowing stare. "I'll come by later this afternoon, I promise," she mumbled.

"Don't bother, I'll probably be out. If you get a chance though, walk on over tomorrow for breakfast. Bring your friend if you want," she snickered before giving her another peck on the cheek.

Forget retirement, her grandmother had more of a social life than Carly did. After a quick glance around the yard, she shut and locked the front door.

When she returned to the kitchen she found Nick sitting at the kitchen table eating a bagel. She was disappointed to find him wearing boxers.

"Is everything okay?" he asked in between bites.

She took a seat and started smearing cream cheese on the blueberry bagel he'd laid out for her. "Yeah. My grandmother saw a big dog roaming around the yard earlier and wanted to let me know to be careful."

He shrugged. "I'm sure it's harmless."

She fought off a shudder. "I don't care. I hate dogs."

When Nick started choking on his food Carly popped up and rounded the table. She slapped him on the back a couple of times until he was breathing normally.

"Are you okay?" She stared down at him.

He cleared his throat and took a sip of coffee. "I'm fine. Guess it went down the wrong way. Uh, you hate dogs?"

"Hmm? Oh, well, I don't exactly *hate* them, but I don't go out of my way to befriend them." She picked up her bagel.

"Why?"

"When I was eight, a German shepherd attacked me." She stretched out her leg and twisted it so he could see the back of her calf. "You can't really see the scars anymore, but it was a horrible experience. I avoid dogs if I can."

"You don't like *any* dogs then, even puppies?" he asked incredulously.

She rolled her eyes. "Puppies are fine so don't start telling people I'm a puppy-hater. I just don't like the bigger breeds... Why, are you a dog person?"

He shrugged. "So, what are your plans for today?"

"I thought about going to the beach, but if you have something else in mind..." She crossed her legs, letting her robe fall open to expose most of her thighs.

Nick dropped the rest of his uneaten bagel onto his plate and his gaze darkened. "I was going to suggest we go to the Miami Seaquarium, but we can do that another day."

Carly tugged on the tie and let the silky material slide off her shoulders. "If you're sure."

CHAPTER EIGHT

Nick froze as Carly stripped down to nothing. She wasn't even wearing panties. His gaze narrowed in on the soft red strip of hair covering her mound and he could feel a growl begin deep in his throat.

The more he had her, the more he wanted her. He couldn't ever remember being so damn horny. It was as if someone else had taken over his body.

As he pushed up from his chair Carly uncrossed her legs, giving him a perfect view of her pussy. He grabbed her by the hands and hauled her up against him. She fit against his body as if they were two puzzle pieces, as if she'd been made just for him. The thought was ridiculous but he didn't care.

He crushed his mouth to hers while trailing his hands down her back to her perfect ass. He couldn't get enough of touching her. When he grabbed her cheeks and squeezed gently, she sighed into his mouth.

Last night had been torture not being able to fuck her again but now he was prepared. He tore his mouth away from hers and blindly reached for the condom box. After ripping the box open, he grabbed one of the packets and began to open it when she snatched it from his hands.

"My turn." Her smile was wicked as she peeled the packet open. When she fisted his pulsing cock in one of her slim hands, a shudder racked him.

Every time she touched him, he burned for her. It was as if she left a trail of fire in her wake. Instead of rolling the condom on him, however, she set it on the counter behind her and tugged his boxers down.

Before he realized what she planned, she'd kneeled in front of him and had taken the tip of his penis in her mouth. His hips jerked forward at the unexpected contact. When she ran her tongue along the underside of his shaft from the base back to the top, he threaded his fingers through her thick hair and groaned aloud. Ah, hell, it was exactly like his fantasy.

But she was better than any dream.

As she sucked and licked him, his knees started to buckle. God, her wicked mouth. Nick grasped the back of her head, forcing her to look up at him. "I want to be inside you." It was that primal thing driving him; that need to come inside her. It didn't matter that he'd be wearing a condom, he simply needed *in* her.

She moved to snag the condom, but he grabbed her by the hips, turned her around, and pushed her against the counter. It was the perfect height for what he had in mind. His inner wolf wanted to claim this female in the worst way possible.

"Stay still," he ordered, whispering against her ear.

Clutching the counter, she nodded as she looked at him over her shoulder. Then her smile turned pure wicked as she wiggled her ass at him.

It took all his control to get his damn condom on. He loved seeing her like this, bent over, spread open for him. But he needed her legs just a little wider. He spread them farther apart with his feet.

Her breathing became more erratic as he trailed a finger down her back and lower, lower, until he reached the crease of her cheeks. She tensed when he paused by her tight, rosy bud, but he kept going until he reached her slick folds.

With one finger, he probed inside her—and groaned. She was dripping wet and it was all for him. "This for me, baby?" He needed to hear her say it.

"Oh yeah." Her voice was a breathless whisper, the sexual energy rolling off her so damn strong it was like a physical blow.

Slowly, he pushed another finger in, savoring the feel of her clamping around him. A breathless groan escaped when he dragged his fingers against her inner walls. She was so tight.

"This isn't going to be gentle," he rasped out.

"I told you I won't break." She pushed back against him, the scent of her need wrapping around him and pushing him right to the edge of his control.

The lights in the kitchen were off, but there was enough natural light streaming in from the two windows that the room was incredibly bright.

Sunlight bathed Carly's body and reflected off the shiny hair tumbling down her back.

She was already wet enough and he simply didn't have the fortitude for any more foreplay. Last night he'd enjoyed tasting every inch of her but now he needed to feel her again. His entire body ached with the need.

Wordlessly he held onto her hips and plunged inside her.

She let out a yelp and arched her back at the sudden intrusion. He'd been worried about his size earlier, but she had no problem taking the full length of him.

For a moment he stayed where he was, buried balls-deep in Carly, letting her tight sheath squeeze around him.

He kept his hands on her hips and pressed his chest against the length of her back. "Touch yourself," he ordered. Just the thought or the sight of her teasing her clit or her breasts made his cock even harder.

As soon as the order was out of his mouth, she took both breasts in her hands and began palming them.

His cock pulsed with need as he watched her pinch and rub her nipples. From his position he didn't have a great view, but he knew she had the most perfect areolas. Pale pink that seemed even brighter against her ivory skin. And they got darker the more turned-on she was.

Though he was loath to pull out of her by even an inch, he finally began to move, to thrust harder and harder. With each stroke, she let out a purring sound, and it was all he could do not to come.

Each tortured moan she made pushed him closer to the edge. But he needed her to come first, was consumed with the hunger to feel her climax around his cock once again. Reaching around, he cupped her mound and flicked her clit with his thumb. She jerked at the small action, her breathing increasing.

As he slowly pushed in and out of her, he kept the pressure steady on her swollen bud. The harder she panted, the faster he moved his finger and his cock. When the walls of her pussy began locking around him, he clutched onto her hips and increased his pace.

For a moment he let his mental shield down and tapped into her mind. Pure pleasure hit him like a tidal wave. Her thoughts and feelings were too jumbled for him to make sense of anything, but she enjoyed what they were doing.

Her emotions were so strong they nearly knocked him over. He desperately wanted to link with her, to tell her what he was, but it was too soon.

He could bite her and she'd probably assume he was just a little kinky. But that would take away her choice about her future. He couldn't do that, no matter how much he ached to. And damn, he ached for a claiming. Only with Carly though.

Putting the shield back up, he pounded into her with a renewed frenzy. Her pussy fisted around his cock with startling intensity as she surged into orgasm. Her hands dropped from her breasts and clutched onto the edge of the counter. As she let out a low moan, he allowed himself to find his own release. His orgasm seemed to go on forever, her tight body wrenching every bit of pleasure from him.

Breathing hard, Carly leaned over the counter, barely moving. Sweat trickled down his face and back and after a few moments, he pulled out of her. His cock practically protested as he withdrew.

As he disposed of the condom, Carly picked up her silk robe and slid it on before collapsing on one of the chairs. He wished she'd just stay naked, but figured that wasn't going to happen. They'd never leave her place.

"Was I too rough?" He plucked his boxers from the floor.

Her pretty lips pulled up into a smile. "Stop worrying that I'm going to break."

Nick cupped her face in his hands and dropped a kiss on her forehead. "I can't help it. I take care of what's mine."

She might not realize it yet, but she was most definitely his.

"I've gotta say, you look pretty awesome on that bike." Carly snickered as Nick pulled to a stop next to her on the wide open sidewalk stretching down the oceanfront.

She'd convinced him to rent bikes and spend the day exploring the city. Not that it had taken much convincing. Spending Sunday with her like this was fucking heaven.

"I think that guy was lying about not having any other colors." They'd rented bikes at a local stand a few miles back and he'd ended up with a neon purple and blue one.

"It's still an awesome color. You make the purple more masculine."

Laughing, he swung his leg over and nodded at one of the food stands. The salty tinge of the nearby ocean teased the air, mixing with all the spicy aromas. "You hungry?"

"I could go for some ice cream." She got off her bike too and propped it next to his on a bench. "And I'm paying for it."

He ignored the last comment and slid an arm around her as they waited in line. There were only a couple people in front of them so they didn't have to wait long. Once they'd gotten their order they sat on the same bench they'd left their bikes.

"I'm having some dirty thoughts watching you lick that cone," he murmured, scooting closer to her.

"That's because you're a giant pervert." Smiling wickedly, she flicked her tongue over the top of it with slow deliberation.

Once again, he fought a groan. He couldn't walk around with a hard-on for her twenty-four-seven. Well he could, but he shouldn't. "Can't believe you got strawberry." With the ridiculous amount of selections, she'd surprised him with her choice.

"Strawberry is a classic. Plus, red hair? Come on."

A laugh rumbled from his chest as she grinned at him. Yep, he was falling so fast and so fucking hard for her he couldn't stop it if he wanted to. "Is that a rule that redheads like only strawberry?"

"No, but it's my excuse. You know you want some. I've seen you eyeing my ice cream."

"It's not the ice cream I'm watching."

She took another lick, this one slower, definitely more sensual. With her sunglasses on it was impossible to read her eyes, but her grin was all wicked.

"You'll pay for that later," he murmured.

"God, I hope so." She shifted against the bench seat, her navy blue shorts riding up just a bit, showing all that smooth skin he wanted to reach out and stroke. The scent of her desire was more than a little subtle.

He had to consciously ignore what it did to him, knowing she wanted him as much as he wanted her. His wolf clawed at him *again*, telling him to head back to her place so he could claim her. But he was enjoying this time with her.

"I was actually thinking of getting a bike," she continued. "It's too far to bike or walk to work, but it's so pretty where I live I figure I can find some nice places to ride."

"My cousin owns a sports shop not far from here. They've got a good selection of bikes. We can head there when we're done if you want." She would protest, but if she found something she liked, he'd get it for her.

"Let's do it. Would you mind terribly if we stopped by a craft store too? I checked my phone and there's one not too far from here."

If his brothers could see him, they'd laugh. He didn't care. "Sounds good to me. We have no plans today. Why'd you start knitting anyway?"

"Ah, well, it helped with everything after I lost my parents, gave me a creative outlet. At first anyway, now I really just enjoy it."

"Did you do the big throw in your living room?"

She nodded, taking another lick of her ice cream. Nick found himself jealous of an inanimate object.

"Yeah. Back in Chicago I was part of this group who made them for homeless shelters. We knitted tons of blankets and donated them. Eventually I started making baby clothes for a women's shelter near where I was living too. Once I get settled here I'm going to see if there are any knitting groups I can join... What? I know it's kind of a nerdy hobby."

He realized he was grinning when she trailed off and that she'd misunderstood his expression. "I just think it's adorable, that's all."

Her pretty mouth pulled into a frown. "Adorable? That's not what any woman wants to be called."

"Too bad, because you are—though you're still hot too." She was a combination of sweet and naughty. There was definitely something to be said for sweet women, something he should have realized years ago.

"Much better." She slid closer to him.

Without pause, he slung his arm around her shoulders and tossed his half-eaten cone into the nearby trashcan. Today was one of those perfect Miami days. A few white clouds dotted the sky, people biked, jogged, or walked their dogs as they passed by. He couldn't remember the last time he'd come down to the beach and enjoyed himself like this. Never with a woman. "Want to head down to the sand before we hit up the sport and craft stores?"

"You just want to see me in my bikini," she murmured, handing him her half-eaten cone as she laid her head on his shoulder. He tossed that one as well.

"You're not wrong."

She'd worn a tiny bikini under her shorts and tank top and yeah, he wanted to see her in it. Didn't matter that he'd seen her completely naked.

"I love how honest you are. And it doesn't matter to me. I'm enjoying sitting right here with you."

"Me too. My ancestors are originally from Leontio," he said, abruptly changing the subject. He'd actually been born there but he couldn't tell her that.

"That's in Greece I'm assuming?"

"Yep."

"Have you been there?"

"Oh yeah. Leontio's a little mountain village. I've been thinking about heading back for a vacation later this year." And he wanted to bring her with him. He wasn't sure why it was so important, but his inner wolf wanted it as well. By then he hoped to have told her exactly what he was.

"That'll be fun." Her voice was slightly drowsy and though he couldn't see, he guessed her eyes were closed as she leaned against him.

"You should come with me." The words were out before he could think about censoring himself.

She lifted her head. "Are you serious?"

He shrugged. It was too soon to be talking about anything like that, but… "Yeah."

She watched him for a long moment and he wished he could see her eyes. "If anyone else said that, I'd think it was a line."

"I don't need any more lines to get in your pants."

Laughing, she pinched his side and stood. "You're right about that. Come on, let's get out of here before I fall asleep on your shoulder."

He followed suit, getting on his bike when she got on hers. She'd never answered his question. Well, he hadn't actually asked, he'd just said she should go with him. It was too soon for her, especially since she was a human. Not for him though; his wolf and human side were in complete agreement about sexy Carly Kendall. She belonged with him.

CHAPTER NINE

Carly glanced away from the computer screen and shook her head. It was almost noon and she hadn't completed even half of what needed to be done today. All she could focus on was the past weekend with Nick. The sex had been amazing, but she'd also had a lot of fun with him. He was so relaxing to be around—and so incredibly sweet. He'd even bought her a new bike. She hadn't wanted to let him, but he'd been insistent and his cousin had refused to let her pay anyway. It was weirdly awesome to have a guy want to take care of her and be so attentive.

Now she couldn't concentrate on anything. Couldn't keep her mind off the toe-curling sex she'd been having and the wonderfulness of Nick. It almost felt as if she were living someone else's life. A sexy man built like a god who liked giving oral sex more than he liked receiving it did not just fall into her lap.

"Hey, looks like someone's back in the dating game." Alex's voice from the open doorway caused her to glance up.

Carly frowned at the vase of blood-red roses in Alex's hands. There were at least two dozen in the bouquet. "What's that?"

The other woman shrugged as she placed them on the desk. "Someone just delivered them. No note, just your name on a white card."

Carly bit her bottom lip. She and Nick had discussed keeping their relationship private, at least until they figured out where things were going. In reality, she was the one who'd insisted. He didn't seem to care who knew about them but she'd just started working here and didn't want everyone talking about her. She couldn't believe he'd sent her flowers—and freaking roses at that—after the talk they'd had. Even if it was sweet.

Before she could respond, Nick strolled in. A frown marred his face the second he spotted the bouquet. "What's that?"

Alex looked back and forth between Nick and Carly, grinning.

"Someone sent Carly flowers. Wonder who it could be," she sang as she walked out.

"Did you tell her about us?" Carly whispered once Alex was gone and out of earshot.

"No. Who are those from?" he growled.

She blinked. "They're not from you?"

His pale gaze darkened as he stared at the bouquet. "No."

"Oh." She plucked the simple white card from the holder and turned it over. Alex was right, it was blank except for her name. "That's weird." Shrugging, she met Nick's gaze. "I don't really like roses, but they're really pretty anyway."

Instead of responding, he stared at the flowers with a heated gaze, as if he thought he could destroy them with lightning bolts from his eyes.

"Uh, you okay?" she asked.

"Fine. Do you want to take lunch with me today?"

"Do you think it's such a good idea?"

"I told you, Carly. I don't care if —"

"Hey, big brother!" The man Carly had seen at Friday's party, the one who looked similar to Nick, strolled into the office and slapped Nick on the back.

"Hey, what are you doing here?" Nick's entire body was tense, but his expression softened for his brother.

"I stopped by to..." Carly watched in fascination as Nick's brother stopped and sniffed the air. Kind of like a dog would. Then he slapped his brother on the back again. He glanced back and forth between Nick and Carly with a big grin on his face, as if expecting them to say something.

She raised her eyebrows at Stephan, but tried not to stare too hard. Nick's brother might be acting a little strange, but she didn't want to insult Nick.

"Meet me in the garage." Nick's words came out as a tight order.

Chuckling, his brother left the small office.

"What was that about?" she whispered.

Nick shook his head. "Don't worry about it. My brother works odd hours and sometimes doesn't get any sleep for days. He's just tired. About lunch —"

"I don't think it's a good idea, Nick." At his frown she continued. "Not yet anyway. I want to see where this thing goes. I just started working here and people will talk if we start spending lunches together."

"What about tonight?"

"What about it?"

"Do you have plans?"

"No."

"You do now. We can go out or I'll cook for you."

She bit back a grin. "That sounds suspiciously like an order."

He cleared his throat and spoke in much softer tones. "Ah, would you like to have dinner with me tonight?"

"Yes. You can pick me up at seven. And I don't care if we go out or not." That would give her enough time to get home, freshen up and clear her brain. She'd lived and breathed Nick the past couple days and her mind and body needed to decompress. She was falling for him so fast and it was a little terrifying. She could see a real future with the sexy man. When she'd moved here she hadn't even been thinking of dating or men and now she had a perfect one. That just didn't happen.

Nick nodded and left. As she turned her attention back to the computer screen, her cell phone rang. She hadn't given her new number out to many people so she couldn't imagine who was calling.

Even though she didn't recognize the number, it was a Miami area code so Carly answered in case it was her grandmother calling from a different phone. "Hello?"

"Hi, is this Carly?"

The voice sounded vaguely familiar. "Yes, who is this?"

"It's Dennis."

"Who?"

"Dennis Chontos, from Friday's party." His voice held a trace of barely concealed annoyance.

Who? "Oh, right. How are you?" She'd forgotten about him. They'd talked maybe a total of five minutes before Nick had dragged her away. Not that she was complaining.

"I'm great. You left before I got a chance to get your number—"

"Yeah, exactly how did you get my number?"

"From Alex."

"Oh." Annoyance flickered through her. That didn't sound like Alex, but Carly supposed she didn't really know her well enough to make that call.

"Anyway, I wanted to take you out sometime. Are you free this weekend?"

She glanced toward the open doorway, suddenly feeling guilty, even though she'd done nothing wrong. "No, I'm actually seeing someone."

"Alex said you were single." His abrupt, almost rude statement sent a chill down her spine. It wasn't his words so much as his domineering tone.

"We just started seeing each other."

He completely ignored her statement. "Did you get the flowers I sent you?"

"Oh, I didn't realize who they were from. Listen, thank you for the flowers but I'm at work so I have to go." She disconnected before he could respond.

She was probably being paranoid, but she didn't like the fact that someone she didn't know had sent flowers to her place of employment and gotten her phone number without asking her for it first. It was just plain weird. Since she'd practically hung up on him, he'd no doubt gotten the hint.

———————•••———————

Asha clenched his cell phone tightly in his hand. He resisted the urge to slam it against the kitchen counter. The stupid bitch was lying to him. She wasn't seeing anyone. Even if she was fucking that lycan from the party, he hadn't marked her, which meant she was fair game.

His skin practically itched at the woman's rejection. Women never said no to him. She was the perfect blend of innocence and sexuality. As long as he had steady sex, he could keep his power up so it wasn't even that he needed her. No, he wanted this one.

After pouring himself a healthy glass of scotch, he stalked up the stairs. His slave had been unusually quiet all morning. He allowed her to watch television and work out, but in the last hour he hadn't heard any movement. He'd been a little rough with her last night so maybe she'd fallen asleep.

Glancing around his dark room, he frowned to discover it empty.

"Slave, come here!"

When she didn't respond, he headed for the small workout room at the end of the hallway. It was empty.

She couldn't have escaped. Of that, he was sure. With bulletproof, reinforced windows and biometric scanners on all the exits, it was next to impossible for anyone to enter or leave without his knowledge. And none of the motion sensors outside had been triggered.

He walked back to his massive room and opened the bathroom door. His lips curled up in disgust. The woman's head fell to the side unnaturally and her silky blonde hair fell over the side of the clawfoot tub. Splatters of crimson covered the tile floor and white walls.

He cursed when he saw the broken mirror.

Careful to step around the shards of glass, he strode across the room.

Though he hated to get his hands dirty, he reached into the brackish water and pulled the plug. As the water decreased, he could see the jagged wounds slicing across her wrists.

"Stupid bitch," he muttered. Now he'd have to clean up the mess and dispose of her body.

Not to mention he'd be without sex for a few days. If he got desperate, he could find a prostitute, but he preferred his women to look clean and innocent.

Now he knew it was fate that the redhead had fallen into his path. One way or another, the woman would be his.

Nick scowled at Stephan as he stalked across the garage toward him. "What the hell was that? You were sniffing Carly's office like a mangy dog."

His brother simply grinned and leaned against the Mercedes Nick had been working on all morning. "Whatever, I didn't expect to walk in and smell your fucking scent everywhere. Good God man, did you fuck all weekend?"

Nick took a steadying breath. He knew his brother wasn't trying to get under his skin. "It's more than that."

Stephan snorted. "I kind of guessed. Does she know...about the family?"

"No, and I plan to keep it that way for a while."

Stephan nodded. "I understand."

He sighed and scrubbed a hand over his face. "There's more to it than the whole shifter thing. She hates dogs, man."

His brother let out a loud bark of laughter, which just annoyed Nick. "Are you serious?"

"Yep. She was attacked when she was a kid. She's afraid of them."

"Damn."

"I know. It's not that big of a deal but it's going to be hard enough telling her without this added." The world was full of shifters, fairies, Immortals, and even a few vampires were still around, but most humans weren't aware of their existence.

"You going to tell her before you bond with her?"

"Yes." Not only did he have to tell her he was a werewolf, but he also had to tell her that she was his mate. And that would just bring up a dozen other issues they had to deal with. If she didn't run screaming when he admitted what he was, of course. Over the weekend he'd almost bonded with her a couple times, but he'd managed to control his inner wolf. Barely. His freaking wolf was getting cranky and possessive.

"What's the sex like? I've heard that when it's your mate, it's—"

"What's up with all the questions?" he snapped.

His brother shoved his hands in his pockets. "I've been waiting as long as you have, man. I just wanted to know if it's like all the stories we heard growing up."

Guilt swept through Nick. A lot of werewolves found their mates, but many never did. Their parents had been lucky and it was something Nick had wished to experience for longer than he cared to admit. Neither of his brothers had said anything but he knew they felt the same way. They were extraordinarily lucky because they had their family to depend on. Sure they moved every couple of decades to a new city to hide their slower aging, but their pack was large and supportive. Not all shifters had that.

"I'm sorry, my head's all messed up."

Stephan shrugged and pushed up from the car. "I've got to go anyway. Just a heads-up, Mom and Dad will be back tomorrow."

"Thanks," he said as his brother left. That was just one more thing he didn't want to worry about. He and his brothers were born alphas, but as things stood, his father was the current Alpha of their pack so he'd have to introduce Carly. It wasn't a question of not wanting to—or having a choice really—but he knew how pushy his family was and he didn't want them forcing anything on her until she was ready.

Carly waited for the hum of her computer to stop before she pushed her chair back and stood up. She glanced at her flowers as she arranged her desk. Nick had been coming in all day and staring at the stupid arrangement with barely concealed disgust.

Even though they were pretty, she plucked them out of the vase and walked out of her office toward the lobby. She didn't see anyone in the garage so she headed out the front door and rounded the building until she found the Dumpster. Sighing at the waste, she tossed them into the garbage and went back to her office.

The small room had a long way to go before she'd be satisfied with the way it looked, but for now she could at least straighten things.

As she bent over the desk, two hands slid around her waist. For a split second she tensed until Nick's familiar scent tangled around her. She leaned back into his chest, trying to control her erratic breathing while she savored his earthy, spicy, smell. "What are you doing?"

UNLEASHED TEMPTATION | 61

He feathered her neck with kisses before turning her around to face him. "You ready to get out of here?"

"I thought you were picking me up at seven." She tried to take a step back but the desk stopped her.

"I could or we could start right here," he murmured before nipping her bottom lip between his teeth.

As always around him, heat pooled between her legs at his near proximity. "We can't do anything at work. Anyone could walk in—"

"Everyone's gone home and I've already locked up."

Well wasn't he just prepared? She tried to think of another argument, but came up short. It wasn't that she didn't enjoy being around him, because she did—probably too much—but everything was happening so fast. Maybe too fast. It was hard to get a handle on the sudden onslaught of emotions she'd undergone since meeting him. She'd dated her ex for almost a year and hadn't felt one iota of the attraction she had for Nick. It wasn't even in the same stratosphere.

And that scared the holy hell out of her. Even as regret pulsed through her, she lightly pushed on his chest. "Let's do this another time."

"You don't want me to come over tonight?" Though his expression was neutral, there was an undercurrent of hurt rolling off him.

"What...no, I still want you to. I just don't want to do...anything *here*." Okay, she kind of did, but just not today.

The tightness in his shoulders loosened. Nick dropped a chaste kiss on her forehead and took a step back, giving her the space she'd said she wanted. "I'll see you in a couple hours then."

She nodded as she hooked her purse over her shoulder and made her way to the front door. Carly could feel his gaze penetrating her back as she walked, but she refused to turn around. Once she slid into the front seat of her car, she saw him watching her through the lobby window. Thankfully her car started right away. Whatever he'd done to it last week, it now ran better than ever.

She half waved as she pulled out of the parking lot. Once she was on the road, she felt more in control of herself. If she didn't get a couple of hours of time to herself she was afraid she'd fall completely for Nick. And something told her he wasn't the kind of man to be tied down permanently. Sure, he'd made that comment about her going with him to Greece, but it was hard to believe he'd been serious. She needed to gain back some control before she did something really stupid. Like lose her heart.

CHAPTER TEN

Nick put his car in park but didn't get out immediately. He stared at Carly's little one-bedroom apartment and tried to get himself together. He couldn't figure out what had changed between them but it was obvious something had. She'd practically shoved him off her at the office. Okay, maybe it hadn't been that extreme, but human females were a lot more complex than shifter females. He'd scented Carly's desire. Still, she'd pushed him away and he didn't understand why.

More than anything he wanted to get into her head but he couldn't invade her privacy like that. Not if they stood a chance to build a future. He might be relationship challenged, but even he knew that much about women. If he broke her trust now, he'd be screwed for years to come.

Sighing to himself, he grabbed the two overflowing grocery bags and walked toward the front door. It swung open before he'd knocked.

"I saw you drive up. What's all this?" Carly tried to take one of the bags from him, but he held it firm.

"I'm cooking for you." Without staring too hard, he drank in her appearance and tried to tamp down his desire. She'd changed into skimpy pink beach shorts and a white tank top and looked good enough to eat. All that skin on display just for him. His inner wolf flared to the surface, clawing and demanding he claim this female right now.

Her eyes brightened as she peered inside the bag closest to her. "What are you making?"

"Moussaka." It was his mother's recipe and it dated back many years. He'd never cooked it for another woman before. Had never wanted to until Carly.

She grinned as she shut the front door. "I love moussaka. There was a Greek restaurant on the same block where I worked in Chicago. I used to eat there a couple times a week."

That was one thing in his favor. She might hate dogs but at least she liked Greek food. "Have you ever made it before?" he asked.

She snorted as they entered the kitchen. "There's something you should know about me right now. I don't cook. If it wasn't for my grandmother, I'd probably starve."

"I'll just have to teach you then," he said as he set the bags onto the counter.

She shook her head. "It won't help, trust me. My grandmother has tried to teach me. I don't think I have a knack for it."

"We'll see." He pulled out a clear plastic bag full of eggplants and glanced around the kitchen. There wasn't a knife block anywhere. "Uh, knives?"

Carly pulled open the drawer closest to the sink and pointed inside. He frowned at the blunt knives. For now he could use them, but he was getting her some new utensils in the near future. How did someone not have a knife block?

"Is that what you need?"

"This'll work." He pulled out one of the knives and grabbed the cutting board he'd seen hidden behind her bread box.

"So what are you doing exactly?" She peered over his shoulder as he started slicing the eggplants.

"Cutting these into thin enough slices. Then I'll salt them and we'll wait until the salt pulls the moisture out."

Her brows furrowed as she looked at the vegetables. "Do you want something to drink? I've got beer."

"Actually I brought some wine if you don't mind grabbing it from the other bag. It's chilled but it'll need to go in the refrigerator."

She pulled the bottle from the bag and read the label. "Malamatina Retsina."

"It's light. I think you'll like it."

Carly might not use her kitchen for cooking, but she'd still decorated the room. It was set up in a retro style with no overhead cabinets. Instead, shelves displayed bowls, wineglasses and other stemware. She pulled two delicate-looking glasses from the shelf nearest the sink and poured drinks for them.

She set his glass next to him and took a sip from her own as she leaned against the counter mere inches away. His wolf clawed again, wanting a taste of her.

"Was everything okay with your brother? You seemed stressed after he left today."

"Yeah, just family stuff." Talking about his family wasn't something he ever did. The Lazos pack had integrated well into every city they moved to but there was always a certain amount of distance they kept from people. Hell, he hadn't even been able to tell Carly he'd been born in Greece. Instead he'd had to tell her he'd grown up in Miami.

Lying to his intended mate left a foreign feeling of sickness inside him. Of course, he had more important things to worry about. Like figuring out how to tell her he was a shifter. If he moved too soon, he'd scare her away. "Listen, I was wondering if you wanted to have dinner with my family tomorrow night. It'll be like the party on Friday. Lots of food and people."

"Sure." Smiling, she took another sip.

Obviously she didn't understand he meant his parents would be there and he chose not to elaborate. Yeah, it was a total chickenshit thing to do but until he could figure out what had caused her to suddenly pull away from him, he wasn't giving her more ammunition to run. After the weekend they'd had, he hadn't thought she'd have a reason to, but something was off. He wished he could put his finger on what it was.

Slicing the eggplant was the easiest part of the meal. A few moments later, he laid out the pieces onto paper towels and salted them.

"Do you need help with anything?" Carly still hadn't moved from her spot as she watched him.

"Nope. Now we wait."

"Wait?"

"Mmm hmm. For about half an hour. What can we do for thirty minutes to pass the time?" He dried his hands off on one of the dishrags and plucked the wineglass from her hand.

Her cheeks had turned that adorable shade of pink and even though he sensed she was uneasy, desire rolled off her in potent waves. Nick placed both hands on the counter next to her, effectively caging her in. He leaned down until he was a few inches from her face. The sweet smell of wine tickled his nose, but nothing was sweeter than her natural scent. "What's going on in that pretty head of yours, Carly?"

"What do you mean?" she rasped out, her fingers skating over his chest.

His cock jumped when she moistened her lips. "What's changed between us since this weekend?"

"Everything's happening so fast."

"Yeah." *So what?* Everything he knew about her, he liked. Maybe more than just liked. Which sounded stupid in his head, but he didn't care.

"Well, maybe we jumped into this without thinking." There was a note of unease in her voice that sliced at him.

"I don't regret anything."

"Neither do I."

"Then what's the problem?"

She shrugged, but when she nervously tucked a strand of hair behind her ear, he understood what was going on. "I'm not looking for a fling, Carly. Are you?"

"No," she answered quickly, smoothing out some of his raw edges.

Nick leaned a little closer. "Then what else is wrong?"

"Like I said, everything is happening so fast. I don't..."

"You don't what?"

"We haven't known each other that long, but every time you touch me, it's like my body heats up about a hundred degrees and I just can't think straight. You seem almost too perfect."

That was exactly how he felt about her. "And that's a bad thing?"

"No. Definitely not. I've just never had such a physical response to anyone."

"Does it scare you?"

She bit her bottom lip. "A little."

Nick wasn't sure how to respond. Their chemistry was off the charts so he wasn't sure what the problem was. When her bright gaze focused on his mouth, her lips parted slightly. He wasn't sure if she was going to say anything, but he took away anything she might have been contemplating. Hell, she was lucky he'd held off touching her this long.

The need to be touching her, inside her, was all consuming.

Soft lips met his with heated intensity. Whatever her insecurities, they didn't extend to the physical aspect of their relationship. Her heart slammed against her ribs like a jackhammer and he could feel it as clearly as if it was his own pounding heart.

He slid his hands up under the bottom of her shirt so he could feel her bare skin. Skin to skin touching was important to shifters. He shuddered as he wrapped his hands around her ribs. She was slim, but not emaciated like so many of the women that frequented his brother's club. Just enough curves and she fit perfectly against him.

Carly apparently forgot whatever had been bothering her as she hurriedly tugged at the bottom of his shirt. As long as they were touching and she wasn't overthinking, they seemed to be in sync. He stepped back and yanked it off before quickly seeking out her mouth again. If it was up to him, they'd both just go naked whenever they were at her place or his. Not that he'd taken her there yet, but soon.

Her lips were soft and pliant underneath his demanding kisses. His cock pressed painfully against his jeans when she slid her hands up his chest and dug her nails into his shoulders. He'd been thinking about this all day; had been unable to stop himself from dropping into her office just to say hi.

As she moaned against his mouth, her entire body lined up flush against his. That sweet raspberry scent enveloped him to the point he wanted to scrape his teeth across Carly's neck and leave his mark. But he didn't. He couldn't. Not if he wanted to live with himself. She deserved better than that.

Somehow he tore his hands away from her soft skin and tangled with the button on her shorts. As he unzipped them, they slid down her long legs and pooled at her feet. Seconds later, her bright yellow thong followed, revealing the small tuft of red hair covering her mound. He couldn't wait to bury his face between her legs.

Clutching her hips, he lifted her up onto the edge of the counter before using his hands to open her legs further.

"What are you doing?" she whispered.

"What do you think, sweetheart?" Without pause, he knelt in front of her and kissed the inside of her leg right by her knee. He was tall enough that he was at the perfect position to pleasure her this way.

Her legs started to close on his head so he placed a firm hand on one of her thighs. "Relax," he murmured. When he met her gaze, desire burned bright in her blue eyes. Satisfied with her response, he kissed her again, this time higher.

Trailing kisses up her leg, he took his time as he created a path toward her pussy. The folds of her lips were swollen and her pink clit peeked out, begging him to lick her everywhere. After this past weekend, he knew exactly how much pressure to use, how to make her come against his mouth.

The anticipation was almost too much.

Inhaling her sweet scent, he teased her lips, tracing his tongue up the outermost part of her folds. Her breathing hitched as he reached her clit, but he barely flicked his tongue over it. He didn't want to focus all his energy there. Not yet. Not when he knew it would drive her crazy if he prolonged this.

For a moment, he pulled back and simply stared at her. Her pink folds were so fucking perfect it almost pained him to look away. Hell, everything about her was perfect.

Sighing, he leaned forward and delved as deeply as he could with his tongue. Her sweet slickness coated him and it took all his control not to strip off his pants and slide his cock into her. When she moaned and threaded her fingers through his hair his balls pulled up even tighter.

"More." The word was barely above a whisper, but he heard it as clearly as if she'd spoken directly into his ear. That was another sign he knew she was his mate. No matter what he could hear and feel everything she was.

Driving his tongue deeper, he shuddered when he could actually feel her inner walls tremble and contract around him.

By her uneven breathing and the loud thump of her heartbeat, he knew she wanted more from him. All shifters had extrasensory abilities, but as a werewolf, his hearing was even more acute. Her heart sounded as if it would jump out of her chest.

And he knew exactly how to bring her to a quick climax. He'd planned to drag this out longer, but he shifted slightly and inserted two fingers into her tight sheath. He didn't stop kissing her though. As he ran his tongue around her clit, her inner walls convulsed rapidly.

"Right there," she murmured as her hands moved to his shoulders.

He dragged his fingers against her inner walls, earning a shudder from her. She was dripping wet and tight as hell. When she tried to move her hips against his hand, he pushed back into her then pulled out again, increasing his momentum with each stroke.

As he continued thrusting into her wet sheath, he barely grazed her aroused bud with his tongue. Everywhere he licked tasted sweet. The faster he moved, the quicker she contracted around his fingers.

The scent of her arousal and impending release hit him with a startling force. Instead of teasing her, he sucked her clit into his mouth. Her entire body jolted at the tug. When she surged into climax he could actually feel her pleasure shooting through to all his nerve endings. That was how connected they were.

Carly's stomach muscles bunched as an orgasm rocked through her. Somehow, Nick knew every nuance of her body. Knew exactly where to touch and kiss her, guaranteeing she found release every time.

Which only served to confuse her more. He was so intent on pleasuring her all the time, but she was afraid he might be too good to be true. A man who cooked and knew how to bring her to climax with a few strokes was a fantasy. Not to mention she felt this strange connection to him that she couldn't explain, even to herself. It was as if she'd known him forever, and not just a week.

As she came down from her high, he stood and pulled her close to him in a comforting embrace. He was silent as his strong arms enveloped her. She wrapped her legs around his waist and laid her head against his chest. His heart thundered, but he made no move to indicate that he wanted any more from her.

Well, she definitely wanted more. Wordlessly she leaned back and tugged at his belt, but almost instantly he placed his hands over hers, stilling them.

"This was about you, Carly, not me." His deep voice had the oddest soothing effect on her nerves.

Even so, she batted his hands away and finished unfastening his belt. This relationship wasn't one-sided. "The hell it is. Do you have any condoms on you?"

He paused, as if he might argue, but instead he grabbed one from his pocket then let his pants fall around his ankles. As he ripped open the packet, she pulled her tank top over her head. He'd been in such a frenzy earlier he hadn't bothered with her shirt, but right now she wanted to feel his chest against hers. The skin to skin contact with him made her crazy.

With his hand firmly at the base of his cock, he stopped after he'd rolled the condom on and stared at her. The way he seemed to drink her in with his eyes was an aphrodisiac by itself. No man had ever looked at her like that.

Like she was truly special. Beautiful even. He really seemed to care too, wanting to know everything about her.

She scooted closer to the edge of the counter and wrapped her arms around his back. Her hands had a mind of their own as they searched out his firm ass and squeezed. The man had a body so fine-tuned he would put Greek gods to shame.

He didn't need more of an invitation than that. Nick drove into her and at the same time, crushed his mouth over hers in that frantic, now-familiar way of his. Even though she was already slick, an involuntary gasp escaped as he buried his cock in her.

She loved the way he stretched and filled her. She barely had enough time to catch her breath as he pulled out and slammed into her again. His arm and neck muscles corded so tightly she could see the tendons stretch and pulse as he moved. This time there was nothing gentle about their coupling. He grabbed her hips and pistoned into her again and again.

His grip on her was sure to leave bruises, but she didn't care. Carly tightened her legs around him as he moved, meeting him stroke for stroke. Every time he slammed into her, her breasts brushed against his chest. The coarse hair sprinkled across his chest rubbed her nipples, teasing the already sensitized buds.

She could barely breathe as he ate at her mouth, devouring her with kisses. As he tugged on her bottom lip with his teeth she nearly came undone. Her body was undergoing too many sensations at once. All because of sweet, delicious Nick.

When he moved his mouth to her jaw and neck those feelings intensified even more. He scraped his teeth across her neck, the roughness of it pushing her over the edge.

Finally she let go of the small modicum of control she'd been trying to hold onto. A tiny orgasm rippled through her. It was nothing compared to the one earlier, but the pleasant surprise had her clutching onto Nick's shoulders as her pussy clamped around his cock.

Nick let out a loud groan as he buried himself inside her one last time. His groan almost sounded like a roar it was so intense. She wasn't sure how long they held each other afterward, but she didn't mind his solid embrace.

Carly was too tired to move. Hell, too tired to think, really. Two orgasms back-to-back were a bit much. Her toes were numb and her skin was super-sensitized.

Nick eventually loosened his viselike grip on her hips and immediately she missed the connection.

"Birth control." His face was nuzzled against her neck, muffling his words, but she thought she'd understood what he'd said.

"Hmm?"

Still breathing hard, Nick lifted his head and pressed his forehead against hers. "Have you ever been on the Pill?"

She nodded. It had been a while since she'd needed to be so she'd simply stopped taking her pills.

"Will you go on it again? I'll pay for everything."

"Yes, but you don't have to do that." Her words came out as a breathy whisper. How he could talk, much less think was beyond her. She unlocked her legs from behind his waist and stretched them out. She tried wiggling her toes to get some feeling back in them.

"Of course I do," he rumbled.

What? Oh right, birth control. Well, she wasn't going to argue with him. "I'll set up an appointment next week."

He nipped her bottom lip in response.

As her breathing subsided she realized the picture they must paint and a giggle escaped.

"You're laughing while I'm still inside you?" His lips twitched slightly as he watched her.

To her horror, another laugh escaped. "I'm sorry. It's just that I'm naked, your pants are around your ankles and your boots are still on."

An unexpected grin broke across his face, stealing all her breath. God, if he smiled more often, he'd be absolutely irresistible to women everywhere. The smile completely transformed his face. His mouth turned up, revealing an almost perfect row of white teeth and he had a tiny dimple on his left cheek she'd never noticed before.

No longer was he formidable and intimidating. Sure, he still had that authoritative presence, but his relaxed features gave him an almost boyish, charming quality. In reality, there was nothing remotely boyish about Nick. No, he was all man. Every toned, muscled inch of him. Still, that smile…all he'd have to do was turn on the charm and she'd do anything he wanted. A shiver of desire slid up her spine and her nipples beaded even more. Heck, she'd do pretty much anything he wanted right now.

"You should definitely smile more often," she said.

"I smile." The words were almost defensive.

"Hmm. Says you." She poked her forefinger against his chest, forcing him to take a step back so she could hop off the counter. "I need to put some clothes on and you promised to feed me."

A small grin played at the corners of his mouth as he discarded the condom and pulled his jeans back up. "After dinner I hope you're ready for more dessert."

"More?" Her belly clenched as she slid her shorts on.

"You better believe it."

Her legs were weak and tingly but she could handle another round soon enough. Still, they needed to talk about something besides sex or they'd never make it to dinner before she jumped him again. "So, how long have you been working on cars?"

"Since I got my '68 Dodge Charger." His words were laced with undeniable pride.

"Well, that doesn't tell me much because I seriously doubt you got it new off the assembly line."

He glanced at her and for a second he looked confused. The expression disappeared almost immediately. "Ah, since I was a teenager. I'd had it about a year when it started giving me engine trouble. It took a little while to figure things out, but ever since then, I've been a car man."

"It's definitely a hot car. I bet it gave you a leg up with the ladies in school." Not that he would need it.

He just shot her a quick, wicked grin as he started emptying one of the paper bags.

She picked up her glass of wine and took a few sips. She'd never thought watching a man cook would be sexy. Especially not a man like Nick. Everything about him was big and, well, masculine. He should look out of place in her small kitchen, but he moved around as if he'd always been there.

"What about you? You never told me why you moved to Miami other than for your grandmother. I got the feeling there might be more to it." Nick's voice cut through her thoughts.

"Well..." For a second she thought about lying, but then decided against it. There was no reason she couldn't be honest about her ex-boyfriend. It still got under her skin that he'd cheated on her but that was his problem, not hers. "There wasn't one reason in particular. I found out my ex-boyfriend was cheating on me..." She cleared her throat, trying to decide if this fell in the too-much-information-at-once department, but plunged ahead. "With my old boss. Since my grandmother lives here, I figured why not? I needed a change and I had a place to stay. And so far, Miami is kicking Chicago's ass."

His mouth tugged up at the corners at her last statement, but he shook his head as he pulled an onion out of one of the paper bags. "I can't imagine any man cheating on you."

The sincerity of his words touched her in a way she hadn't realized she'd needed to hear. It wasn't a line and he obviously wasn't trying to get anything out of her. He didn't *need* lines to get her into bed. He was just stating a simple fact.

She set her wineglass down and nudged him with her hip. "I'll chop these and you do whatever it is you need to do."

He handed her the knife and glanced around the kitchen. "You have a frying pan right?"

She bit her bottom lip. "I think so."

He groaned as he bent down to pull open the drawer underneath the stove. She cringed when he pulled out an old skillet that she knew wasn't hers. It wasn't dirty, but the plastic on the handle was chipping and it looked like it was about twenty years old. Must have belonged to her grandmother's last tenant.

"Will that work?" She nodded at the pan.

He nodded and chuckled. "It'll work for now, but I'm buying you a new set of pots and pans."

"You can't keep buying me stuff." She'd never been with a man so insistent on taking care of her. When he said he'd buy her pans, she knew it wasn't an empty promise, especially after the four hundred dollar bike. The thought of him spending that kind of money made her cringe a little. Her ex had occasionally paid for her when they went out to eat but he'd been all about splitting things fifty-fifty. It had always bugged her that he'd never taken the time to wine and dine her or even try to impress her really.

He didn't bother turning around from the counter. "We'll just see about that."

Dating a man like Nick Lazos could turn out to be very addictive. She still hadn't decided if that was a good or bad thing.

CHAPTER ELEVEN

Carly sighed as Nick massaged her shoulders and the powerful shower jets pummeled the front of her body. "We're going to be late to work."

"Considering I'm the boss, it doesn't matter." Nick's hands left her shoulders and strayed to her waist. One hand slid around her middle as he pulled her back against his chest. She could feel his heart beating triple time.

Even though they'd already made love once, he was still rock hard, something she should be used to by now. His hips shifted and his cock rubbed against her backside. "You can just forget it," she said without turning around.

"Forget what?" he murmured close to her ear, his voice low and intoxicating.

It was *almost* enough to weaken her resolve but she took a step forward, twisted the shower knob to off and turned to face him. She looked at his cock, then moved back up to his face. "You know exactly what I'm talking about."

He almost looked like a frustrated child as he grabbed her hips. "Who cares if we're late?"

She'd never had sex this amazing and the thought of another bout of lovemaking was more than tempting, but she forced herself to stand her ground. "*I care.* I don't want anyone knowing about us yet. I swear Alex knows anyway and if we both show up late, it'll look strange. Besides, I don't want any preferential treatment."

His lips pulled into a thin line as he dragged the black, white and pink damask shower curtain back. The hooks jangled loudly against the rod, a mirror of his annoyance. Instead of responding, he handed her a towel before grabbing one and wrapping it around his waist.

They hadn't even been seeing each other a week so she couldn't understand why he was upset. Yeah, she liked him a lot, and yes, she could really see this thing going somewhere, but she didn't want to jinx it. She might have had a few twinges of doubt about his intentions but after last night it was obvious he wasn't looking for a fling. Still, that didn't mean she wanted to shout from the rooftops that she was sleeping with her *boss*. Because if things went south it would be beyond embarrassing if everyone at work knew about it.

When he looked at her, his jaw clenched in annoyance before he disappeared into the bedroom. Sighing, she wrapped her towel around her and picked up her comb. As soon as she'd finished brushing the tangles from her hair, he stepped back into the bathroom already fully dressed.

"I'm going to head in now." He had that annoyingly neutral expression in place.

"You don't want to have breakfast together?" It was stupid to feel hurt, but she couldn't help the disappointment in her voice.

"Don't want to be late." She didn't miss the subtle trace of sarcasm in his voice.

"Fine." She turned away from him and faced the mirror. Out of the corner of her eye she watched him pause before walking back out.

Only after she heard the front door shut did she let out a sigh. If she wasn't ready to let everyone know about them, she simply wasn't ready. He'd have to be a grownup and deal with it.

———————————

Nick cursed himself for the hundredth time as he steered into the parking lot of his shop. What the hell was the matter with him?

Unfortunately he knew the answer. The man and the animal inside him wanted to mark Carly and let the world know she was his. She wasn't ready though. So why was he having such a hard time accepting it? And why did she want to hold off anyway? She might not know they were mates but she had to feel the same connection he did. Or at least something similar. The woman was absolute dynamite in his arms. There was no faking that.

He slammed his car door shut and stalked toward the front door of his office but jerked to a halt. The garish roses that had been on Carly's desk were smashed and scattered across the entrance. And he'd seen Carly throw them out yesterday—he'd been irrationally pleased she had too.

His entire body tensed at the possible implication. Why would someone go to the trouble of digging flowers out of a Dumpster? Carly had told him her ex-boyfriend had cheated on her so it was doubtful he'd do something like this. Not to mention he lived in Chicago. Or Nick assumed he did. Whoever had sent them must have done this.

The parking lot was empty, but he glanced around the surrounding area. A few cars sat in the restaurant across the street but he recognized all of them.

As he bent to gather the fallen petals, a new scent accosted him. He took a deep breath, sniffing the air. It was faint, but something foreign pricked his nostrils. There were so many surrounding smells so he focused on what was new.

He couldn't define it but it was earthy, piney, and he detected something acrid and coppery. Almost as if something had been burned recently. The only thing he was sure of, it wasn't human. Or not all human, anyway.

Nick glanced at his watch then unlocked the front door. After grabbing a garbage bag from the supply room he hurriedly gathered the crushed flowers and bagged them. As he was tossing them in the garage's oversized trashcan, Alex walked in zipping up her coveralls.

"Morning, Cousin," she said through a yawn.

"Who sent those flowers to Carly?"

She rolled her eyes. "Well good morning to you too."

"Who?"

Alex shrugged and started rolling up her sleeves. "I think it was that guy Dennis from Friday's party. I felt bad for the guy so I gave him her number."

His hands clenched into balls by his side and he knew his wolf was probably in his eyes.

She immediately held up her hands in mock surrender. "Hey, that was before I realized you were seriously interested. I gave him her number and I'm pretty sure he's the one who sent the flowers. I don't know though, why not just ask Carly?"

Because he didn't want to seem like a jealous asshole. The card had been blank anyway and Carly hadn't seemed to know who'd sent them. He hadn't wanted to push her. Instead of voicing his thoughts, he said, "Where do you know that guy from?"

"I don't know. I think he's one of my brother's friends. They might have met at a club or something." She shrugged again in that typically unconcerned way of hers and he forced himself to bite his tongue.

Nick's generation was so different it was sometimes hard to comprehend the way Alex and her siblings acted. Inviting virtual strangers to family get-togethers was something he would never contemplate. He made a mental note to talk to his father and Thomas about it. This kind of behavior was going to end now.

"Don't give Carly's number to strange men anymore," he ground out.

"Jeez, I'm sorry. Let me get some coffee first then you can yell at me." She stalked past him, flipping her dark hair as she did.

Nick scrubbed a hand over his face and racked his brain. There had been something a little off about the guy at the party, but he couldn't put his finger on why. Not to mention, Nick had been more interested in getting Carly alone than talking to the man hitting on her.

His cell rang, jarring his thoughts. He answered when he saw Thomas' name. "Hey, I've been meaning to call you."

"Hey, little brother. I heard through the grapevine that you've found your mate." There was an unexpected note of sadness in Thomas' gravelly voice.

"And what grapevine would that be?"

"Who else? Mom called and she is not happy with you."

"How the hell does she even know?"

"Alex told her. I expect we'll be meeting her tonight?" Thomas asked.

"No. She's not ready to meet everyone." He hadn't had a chance to cancel with Carly yet, but if this morning was any indication, she definitely wasn't ready. It was apparent she was feeling overwhelmed by their relationship so he couldn't introduce her to the pack. Rules could be damned. If he did, he'd risk alienating her forever. He refused to lose his mate.

"She said that?"

"No. But she's human and I think I'm pushing her too hard…" He shook his head and walked across the garage toward the lobby. Carly would be in soon and he wanted to talk to her. "Listen, that's not important right now. What kind of being or creature smells like earth and fire?"

"Uh, demon?"

"No, it's definitely not that." There hadn't been a trace of sulfur in the air and the scent had been too faint. The scent of a demon was unmistakable and as a rule, they rarely visited this realm in pure form.

"Fire…" Thomas was silent for a moment, then he spoke again. "Was it almost like the forest or a forest fire?"

"Yeah. There was a piney undertone."

"Could be an Immortal."

Nick frowned. He hadn't come across an Immortal in nearly a hundred years. They were a solitary bunch and for the most part, the few he'd met were all a little unhinged. Hanging around for a few millenniums could do that to a person, he supposed. "It's possible, I guess."

Thomas snorted. "Anything's possible. Why are you asking?"

He briefly described what had happened with the flowers and was surprised by his brother's reaction.

"You need to bond with your mate as soon as possible." Thomas' words came out as a harsh, throaty order.

"Don't you think I know that?"

"I'm serious. I'm not saying he is, but if this guy is an Immortal and he's fixated on your woman, he'll stop at nothing to claim her. He won't care that she's technically supposed to be mated to someone else. Until you've marked her, she's fair game. To *anyone*."

"How do you even know this?"

Thomas sighed and Nick could practically see him drumming his fingers on his two hundred-year-old oak desk in annoyance. "Because I paid attention in history class."

"I paid attention." Sort of. When he'd been a randy pup, listening to the history of werewolves, other shifters, and pretty much all other nonhumans hadn't been high on his list of priorities. Not even close. He'd learned what he needed to know about his own kind and that had been good enough for him.

His brother cleared his throat. "Yeah, right. If this guy is an Immortal, it sounds like he might control fire, so be careful. I don't know if it's true, but I've heard they need sex to stay strong. You don't want this guy fixating on your female."

Nick inwardly cursed. He might not remember much from school, but he knew enough that Immortals could be some scary guys if they were powerful enough. He shook those thoughts away and straightened behind the counter when he saw Carly drive up. "I will."

"I don't care how you explain it to her, but you need to mate with her. The last thing our family needs is to tangle with an Immortal."

"I said I'll take care of it," he ground out.

After they disconnected, he slipped his phone into the pocket of his coveralls. He still needed time to make sure Carly was ready, but if a powerful being wanted her, it didn't look like he was going to get the chance.

From what he remembered, there were four different types of Immortals. They either controlled fire, earth, water or wind. The four elements. Some believed Immortals were somehow connected to the earth, because if they died, they turned into whatever element they controlled when they were alive. No one truly knew much about them, however. Unfortunately they were lone beings and it wasn't as if they were going to announce their weaknesses to the world.

The bell dinged as the glass door opened. Carly half smiled at him as she walked in. "Hey."

"Carly, I'm sorry about earlier." He'd felt like a dick leaving like that, knew he shouldn't have.

"Okay." Even if he couldn't smell her annoyance, it was written all over her pretty face when she tried to move past him. Her eyebrows rose haughtily when he wouldn't let her. "You gonna let me pass?"

"We need to talk."

She crossed her arms over her chest. "Fine. Talk."

He glanced toward the inside of the garage before meeting Carly's heated gaze. Most of the guys were arriving, but no one could possibly hear what he was saying to Carly. "I really am sorry about this morning."

"What exactly are you sorry for?"

"For being a jackass."

Her lips pulled up at the corners and the vise around his chest loosened. That was definitely a good sign.

When she didn't respond, he continued. "There are some things I want to talk to you about tonight..." Out of the corner of his eye he watched an oversized, overpriced SUV park next to Carly's small car.

When the man from Alex's party stepped out, Nick's entire body went into battle mode. His wolf clawed at him, demanding he protect Carly. He had to force his canines not to extend.

He could feel his bones start to shift, readying for the change. If Immortals were as dangerous as his brother said, he'd change in broad daylight for Carly and the rest of the world to see if that was what it took to protect her. Even if he didn't want to, if he felt threatened enough, his inner wolf would protect its mate at all costs. Human reasoning didn't even factor into the equation. It had been nearly a decade since he'd fought someone to the death, but if that was what it came down to, so be it.

"Why can't this guy get the hint?" Carly muttered next to him.

Her voice pulled him back to their current situation. Without looking at her, he said, "Go to the office and shut the door."

She placed a gentle hand on his arm. "Nick, I can take care of this myself —"

"Get in the fucking office!" He hadn't meant to shout, but getting Carly out of the way was all he could focus on.

Next to him she gasped, but did as he asked. As soon as the door shut behind her, Nick walked around the counter. He met the man who called himself Dennis as he opened the front door.

The man's green eyes flared an unnatural shade, but he didn't step any farther into the shop.

"What are you doing here?" Nick growled.

"I want to see the woman." His voice was filled with raw possessiveness.

"The *woman* doesn't want to see you." The fact that he didn't even refer to Carly by name riled all Nick's aggressiveness.

"Says who?" Dennis sneered.

Nick took two steps toward him until they were inches apart. "Says me. I know what you are so I'm guessing you know what I am. Stay away from her or I'll rip your fucking heart out with my bare hands." He spoke low enough so it was impossible to overhear.

Even though he didn't step back or flinch, the man's green eyes flared again and Nick knew he'd hit a nerve. If Nick remembered right, he'd have to cut off an Immortal's head or rip his heart out to kill one.

"She is not marked, lycan." His words were just as low and menacing.

Nick gritted his teeth. So the man did know what he was. "She will be."

His gaze strayed behind Nick—no doubt to the shut office door hiding Carly—before returning to Nick. A smirk played at his lips. "We will see." At that, he turned on his heel and left.

When the bell jingled overhead, Nick heard the office door fly open behind him.

Nick swiveled just in time to see Carly marching toward him. "What the hell was that?" She didn't give him an opportunity to answer as she poked him in the chest. "That macho bullshit might work on other women, but don't you *ever* talk to me like that again."

He bit back a sigh. "Carly—"

"I don't want to hear any excuses! Just because we're sleeping together does not give you the right to—"

"Carly!"

She placed a hand on her hip as she glared at him. "What?"

He cleared his throat and nodded behind her. Jimmy and Rodrigo stood in the open doorway leading to the garage, both wide-eyed and not bothering to hide their interest.

She turned then swiveled back to face Nick, her expression murderous. It was probably messed up, but seeing her riled up was insanely hot. Without another word she stalked back to her office.

"Can I help you guys?" Nick asked his two employees, neither of whom had seen fit to make themselves scarce.

"Sorry, boss. We just saw you get in that guy's face and thought something might be wrong," Jimmy said.

"If you see him here again, call the cops." It was doubtful the cops could do much to stop an Immortal, but most nonhumans didn't want to attract any unnecessary attention if they could help it. It was simply the nature of things. And it was all Nick could hope for under the circumstances.

CHAPTER TWELVE

Carly peered through the peephole of her front door and frowned. She'd managed to leave work without talking to Nick. She took a step back from the door, as if he somehow had X-ray vision. For a moment she tried to decide if she should answer. Maybe she could pretend she wasn't home.

He knocked again. "Come on, Carly. I know you're in there. I can smell you."

"Smell me?" she muttered. Grasping the door handle with one hand, she twisted the lock and jerked the door open. "What the hell do you mean you can smell me?"

To her surprise, he was smiling. Well, his version of a smile anyway. "I knew it would rile you up enough to answer the door. Your car is outside, that's how I knew you were here."

Most of her anger dissipated as she stared at him. He stood in front of her with his hands in his pockets and he didn't make a move to enter her apartment.

"Well?" she asked.

He cleared his throat. "Can I come in?"

"Fine, but only because it's humid out," she snapped.

She stepped back and let him pass, then wanted to bite back her smartass words. Arguing with him left a strange, sick sensation in the center of her gut. She might be annoyed with him, but he'd seemed genuinely alarmed when that guy from the party had shown up at work. It had freaked her out a little too, but he shouldn't have yelled at her. "Do you want something to eat?" she asked as she slid the lock back into place.

He took a few more steps into the foyer. "Sure."

"Well, my grandma brought over a shepherd's pie earlier. How does that sound?"

"I really don't care, Carly." He stopped and turned to face her. Before she realized what he was doing, his big hands had settled on her hips, his grip possessive. "I'm sorry about earlier. I shouldn't have yelled at you this morning."

"No, you shouldn't have."

"It won't happen again, I promise... Are we okay?"

"Yeah... Does everyone at work know we're sleeping together?" She'd hidden out in her office most of the day and had only come out to have lunch with Alex. And Alex hadn't breathed a word about anything.

Nick nodded, not looking very torn up about the idea. "Probably."

"At least you're honest."

He tugged her a little closer so that their bodies were touching. And there was no mistaking what he wanted. His cock pressed against her lower abdomen with insistency.

"Do you think I should let you off the hook so easily?" she murmured.

"Probably not." With one hand he threaded his fingers through the curtain of her hair and cupped the back of her head in a possessive grip. Maybe she should stay mad at him longer, but she didn't have the energy. And after she'd had time to think about it, she could tell his reaction had come from a place of fear—for her.

After the cold shoulder he'd received all day, Nick had taken a chance coming over to Carly's place. With an Immortal after her, he hadn't had much of a choice. Even though he'd wanted to wait, Nick was telling Carly what he was tonight. But first, he was going to make her come. A lot.

If he could get her in the right frame of mind, maybe she'd be more willing to listen to what he had to say. Because there was really no easy way to tell her that he could change into an animal.

Her blue eyes brightened with undeniable need as he bent his head to her neck. "You make me crazy," she murmured, a light laugh in her voice.

"Right back at you." He raked his teeth over her skin. His little redheaded vixen tasted sweet and salty. He traced his tongue across her soft neck and his cock jumped. He wanted in sexy Carly right now, but that wasn't going to happen. Considering everything he needed to tell her, she was going to get a lot of foreplay.

As he traced his tongue over her delicate skin, he could feel her moan reverberate through her throat. For a second, he managed to tear his mouth away from her. "Upstairs?" he whispered against her ear.

In response, she clutched his shoulders and wrapped her legs around his waist. Now his cock was really raring to go. Even with clothes in the way, it was like a heat-seeking rocket on a mission.

As he bounded up the stairs, Carly rolled her hips against his, making it increasingly more difficult to focus on giving her foreplay. Once they reached the foot of the bed, he stopped and she unwound her legs from his waist.

Nick took a step back. "Strip." He was barely able to gasp the word out.

A seductive grin played across Carly's mouth as she reached behind her. She'd changed out of the restrictive skirt she'd worn to work. Now she wore a simple sleeveless summer dress the color of her eyes.

He heard the zipper unfasten seconds before the wispy material pooled at her feet. *All mine.* The two words echoed around in his head as he stared at her. Sometimes it was damn near impossible to breathe when he was in the same room with her.

She placed a manicured hand on her curvy hip. "Now what?"

"Lose those too," he murmured, motioning to her black panties.

She hooked her fingers under the thin straps and wiggled her hips as she shimmied them off.

The scent of her desire hit him like a Florida heat wave. It was thick and sensuous and he couldn't wait to taste her. "On your back."

Grinning, she shoved the comforter out of the way and spread out for him on the sheets. Gorgeous red hair pillowed around her, giving her an almost angelic quality. Nothing about her actions or the heat coursing through him was innocent though.

Carly propped up on her elbows and looked at him with an almost glazed expression. Her eyes glittered. "I want you in me, Nick."

His throat seized up for a moment. Tonight was supposed to be soft and gentle and full of foreplay.

"*Now.*" The throaty way she said it was definitely an order. When she spread her legs apart even farther, his cock pushed harder against his jeans.

That sweet raspberry scent of hers enveloped him like a drug. In seconds he'd stripped off his clothes and left a condom lying on the bed next to them. By this point, the foreplay he'd planned was a distant dream, but as long as he didn't put the condom on, he'd be able to hold off a little longer.

Nick grabbed her ankles before slowly running his hands up her inner legs. Her skin was smooth to the touch. Underneath his fingers, her body trembled and hummed with energy.

84 | SAVANNAH STUART

He didn't know if it was because they were mates or if her desire was so potent, but her scent was almost overwhelming. Unable to take the torture anymore he leaned forward and licked the length of her pussy.

Her hips jumped as he stroked her and his body was screaming at him to claim her. To pound into her and take everything she could give him. Then come back for more. He lifted his head for a moment and met Carly's gaze. "Tell me what you want."

"You." Her chest rose and fell rapidly.

"Say the words," he growled.

She pushed up from the bed and grabbed his shoulders with unsteady hands. "I want you to fuck me." The statement was low, almost a whisper, but that was good enough for him.

As Nick covered her body with his, Carly's inner walls clenched with need. His tongue or his fingers just weren't going to cut it. For some reason her skin was super-sensitized. Everywhere he touched her or even looked at her burned.

He settled between her legs, but didn't penetrate her. Instead, he began rubbing his cock over her pulsing clit. The quick movements sent shivers to all her nerve endings, but only increased the ache deep in her womb.

Nick zeroed in on the column of her neck and feathered demanding kisses across her skin before sucking an earlobe into his mouth.

Her breasts swelled under his kisses. She shuddered and wrapped one leg around his back. After the day she'd had, she wanted sex that was hard and fast. Something to take the edge off. She figured they both needed it.

She ran her hands over the bunched, tight muscles of his chest and reached around to his backside. Digging her fingers into his ass, she squeezed. Her pussy spasmed with the need to feel his cock in her. "I want you inside me, now."

"Not yet," he murmured against her ear as if this was all a game.

Nick reached between them and placed a calming hand over her belly before dipping his head to her breasts.

Using his tongue on one, he scraped his teeth over her soft flesh, circling her areola, but never directly touching her nipple. In the same moment, he cupped the other breast and leisurely ran his thumb over her hardened nub. The erotic sensations were almost too much to bear. She shifted and reached between them. Grabbing his thick shaft, she squeezed. "Get on your back."

"What?"

UNLEASHED TEMPTATION | 85

"You heard me," she whispered, suddenly feeling a little unsure of herself. Maybe if her voice was more forceful he'd take her seriously.

She'd never been one to take the reins in the bedroom and Nick was the most dominant man she'd ever been with. The thought of being in control turned her on more than she could have imagined. Cream flooded her pussy at the thought of having Nick at her mercy.

It was almost imperceptible, but his jaw twitched before he nodded and did as she instructed. She inwardly grinned. This had to be killing him, giving up control for even a little while.

She kneeled in between his open legs and ran her hands over his muscular thighs, savoring the feel of the corded, rippling tendons. His cock moved of its own accord, before she'd even touched it.

Unable to stop herself from grinning, she fisted his cock at the base and stroked him. Instantly a bead of pre-come formed at the tip. The small pearl glistened in the dim light.

Without wasting any more time, she bent down and ran her tongue along the underside of his shaft, starting at the base and licking all the way to the tip. He let out a low groan and grabbed onto the headboard above him.

A few more beads of fluid came out of his small slit. She ran her tongue around the head, encircling the engorged mushroom cap. Every moan and slight noise he made, gave her more encouragement and got her even hotter. The fact that Nick liked what she was doing ensured she found pleasure in it.

Keeping his shaft firmly in her hands, she shifted lower against the sheets and briefly teased his heavy sac with the tip of her tongue. Once she'd tasted every inch of his cock, she hovered over the crown before sucking him in fully. It was impossible for her to take him all the way in her mouth, but she used her hands to stroke him as she sucked and licked.

"Fuck yeah," Nick rasped. "Just like that, sweetheart."

Nick's large body trembled underneath hers, his groans pure music to her ears. Twisting her body slightly to the left, she continued stroking him, but positioned herself so one of her breasts rubbed against his thigh. The sensation was purely erotic and she could tell it was making him crazy.

"Keep going." His commanding voice rumbled through her, made something deep inside her flare with need.

She increased her momentum, sucking him harder with each stroke. When he threaded his fingers through her hair, she knew he was close. Could feel it in the stiffness of his body.

Her lungs burned, but she kept going. She could barely hear her own sucking sounds above his harsh moans.

"I'm about to come."

The way he barely rasped out the words and loosened his grip on her head told her that he was telling her for her benefit. The message was clear, if she didn't want to swallow, now was the time to move.

She'd never swallowed before but she'd also never been with a man like Nick. Tasting him suddenly seemed like the most important thing. As she feasted on him she slackened her mouth and ever so slightly scraped her teeth against his shaft. She didn't know why, but she knew he'd enjoy it.

Just like that, his body stiffened and he exploded. As she tasted his saltiness, she continued pumping him with her fist until she'd sucked him dry.

When she raised her head and met his gaze, his eyes were glazed over in pure bliss.

"That was fucking amazing," his words were almost slurred as his head fell back against one of the pillows.

Pushing up, she shimmied up his body and straddled his waist. "I hope you're not too tired because—"

Nick cut her off as he grabbed her hips and pushed her off him. Every line in his body had gone tight. Something was definitely wrong. "Do you smell that?"

She sniffed once. "Smell what?"

Nick pushed off the bed. "Smoke and fire. It smells like—"

Carly followed suit as the overwhelming scent hit her. "I smell it too. I think it's coming from downstairs."

Nick scooped her dress off the floor. "Put this on. I think your place is on fire."

CHAPTER THIRTEEN

"**S**tay behind me," Nick ordered Carly after he'd hurriedly jerked on his pants.

The smell of smoke tickled his nose but if they were fast, they might be able to get out of the apartment. He carefully opened the bedroom door and a wave of smoke accosted them. He was worried more about himself than her. Humans were more fragile.

"Shit!" He slammed the door shut and hurried toward the bathroom.

"What are you doing?" Carly stood right behind him as he grabbed two towels from one of the cabinets.

He shoved one towel at her. "Wet this down."

Without questioning him, she began soaking her towel in the sink while he drenched his using the faucet in the tub. "Wring it out when you're through," he said without turning around.

Seconds later they were finished and standing by her bedroom door. "Stay low and try to breathe normally through the towel."

Carly didn't panic, but wrapped the towel around her face and was following his every move.

Nick tapped the handle with his hand and it still wasn't hot. He opened the door again and smoke billowed in immediately. Taking Carly's hand, he crouched down and they crawled toward the stairs.

It was impossible to guess where the fire started, but if he was a betting man, he'd say the kitchen. And his gut told him this was no accident.

When they reached the stairs, he squeezed Carly's hand and they slid down the first couple stairs. It was too thick to see anything. Even with his extrasensory abilities, crawling through the white smoke was like steering a plane blind.

As they inched down the stairs he realized he still didn't feel any heat. That could mean a number of things. The fire was slow spreading— though that wouldn't explain the thick smoke. Or, someone had set off some sort of smoke bomb. That would be even worse because it meant someone wanted to flush them out of the house.

If it was the Immortal, he wouldn't want any harm to come to Carly so he probably wouldn't risk burning her alive.

Nick's heart rate increased as they reached the bottom stair. They could be walking in to a trap and there wasn't a damn thing he could do about it. He took Carly's hand and placed it on the waist of his jeans. He couldn't hold her hand while they were crawling and he didn't want to lose her.

The front door was the closest, most obvious exit. A few moments later they were by the door. Despite the wet towel, his eyes were watering and he could only imagine how much Carly was suffering.

Closing his eyes, he lifted up on his knees and unlocked the door. As he opened it, a whoosh of fresh air greeted them. Under any other circumstances he would have let Carly go first, but if someone was lying in wait for them, he wasn't taking any chances.

Nick scanned the yard as they tumbled onto the front porch. He didn't see anything out of the ordinary and unfortunately he couldn't smell much. If someone was trying to trap them, the son of a bitch did a good job masking his scent. Either way, he was getting Carly the hell out of here.

Hooking his arm under Carly's, he helped her stand and walk to the middle of the yard.

She wiped her eyes and took off the towel at the same time he did. "What the hell is going on? I don't see a fire."

Smoke billowed out from window cracks and the front door of her two-story apartment, but she was right. No flames. Time to get out of here and ask questions later.

The wind shifted suddenly and all the hair on the back of his neck stood up. The leaves of the surrounding oak and palm trees ruffled and even with the dull city lights, a full moon hung high in the gray sky. "Is your grandmother home?" He hadn't seen her car when he'd arrived.

"No, it's her bunco night. Why are you whispering?" she asked, keeping her voice equally low.

"Whatever happens, promise you'll listen to me without question." He needed to see where the threat was before he got her out of here.

"I don't understand—"

Carly abruptly stopped talking as a figure emerged from around the corner of her apartment.

"Stay behind me," Nick growled as he put himself in between Carly and the man in the black trench coat. Seriously, a fucking trench coat. "Who are you?" he demanded.

The man with the dark hair and flashing green eyes kept a distance of about twenty yards between them. "My real name is Asha. Give me the woman and I'll let you live." His voice reverberated through the trees with an otherworldly growl.

"She's mine." Nick's growl was quieter, but just as deadly.

He found it interesting that the other man started to move to his left and not closer toward them. He obviously had some weaknesses. And his name. Asha? It sounded Eastern. Damn he wished he'd paid better attention in history class.

"Then why haven't you marked her, lycan?"

The scent of Carly's fear tickled his nose but he couldn't comfort her now. And he hated that. He could feel the change coming on. If anything, he was about to scare the hell out of her. Nick ignored the Immortal's question. His answer wouldn't make a difference anyway.

"Carly, start walking backward. Take small steps. When I make my move, run," he murmured under his breath.

It was impossible to know if she would follow his orders, but Nick took a few steps toward Asha. When he did, the other man's hands started to glow a bright orange. It was subtle, but Nick saw him take a step away from him. Interesting. "If you somehow manage to kill me and take my mate, my pack will hunt you to the ends of the earth. You must know that."

"She is not marked! I want the female," the other man growled, ignoring Nick's threats.

Everything around Nick funneled out until his focus was solely on Asha the Immortal. There was a flash of bright light as fire shot from the man's hand.

That was all Nick's wolf needed to change. Even if his human side didn't want to change, he had no choice in the matter. His life and his mate's life were being threatened. No matter how many times he did it, changing form hurt. Flesh tore, bones shifted and snapped, clothes ripped, and fangs extended. It was almost instantaneous.

In the background of his mind he thought he heard Carly scream, but he tuned it out.

Protect his mate. That was his only thought.

He was much stronger in wolf form and he planned to use that to his advantage. His fur burned where he'd been hit, but it was barely an afterthought.

Growling deep in his throat, a savage roar erupted as he lunged at the Immortal. Attack and retreat wasn't an option in this fight.

The Immortal would fight to the death. He went for the throat, but the other man was fast. Much faster than a human. He twisted and Nick's fangs sank into the flesh of his shoulder.

A coppery, bitter taste filled his mouth and he bit down harder, tearing through bone and tendons. A searing pain ripped through his side, forcing him to release his grasp.

Howling in pain, he fell to the earth, landing on all fours.

The stench of burning fur surrounded him, but he continued to circle the Immortal. All he needed was one opening. More than anything, he just needed to keep this guy focused on him long enough so Carly could escape.

One of his opponent's hands burned bright but the arm he'd injured hung lifelessly at his side.

A sharp, piercing scream reverberated through the air. Carly! He didn't turn because he couldn't risk it. But the Immortal did.

For a split second Asha's gaze shifted and Nick saw his opening. Using all his raw energy and rage, he lunged.

Instead of tearing through flesh, he tore through air.

A rush of wind pushed his fur back as a giant mass of black fur and sharp teeth flew past him. Before he could move, the other wolf ripped through the Immortal's throat, severing his head completely from his body.

The Immortal was dead and his mate was safe. His brain computed the thought and he collapsed against the grass. A low pain spread up his side and deep in his belly. Maybe he'd been hit harder than he realized.

Ohmygodohmygodohmygod! Carly clutched her stomach and forced the bile back. What the hell was going on?

The man she was sleeping with turned into a giant gray and white wolf-dog-looking creature, a crazy man was shooting fire from his hands, then two other black wolves showed up.

And one had just ripped the head off the fire-throwing guy. Carly stumbled once before falling on her butt. The grass provided a soft landing and she was too terrified to move. Which was probably stupid, but her entire body was trembling. She vaguely thought she might be going into shock.

Sirens sounded in the distance but she couldn't tear her eyes away from the fallen gray wolf—no, Nick—and the other two wolves. One of the black animals stood over the gray one, licking his face and howling as if it was in pain.

The other stood over what used to be a man but was now a crumbling mass of ash and dwindling flames.

She must have made some sort of noise because instantly the two black wolves turned to look at her. When one started stalking toward her, her flight instinct flared to life and she sprung to her feet. "Uh, nice doggie—wolfie—whatever." Her voice shook as she took a couple steps back.

Instead of advancing, as she expected, the black wolf with the dark eyes started changing before her eyes. There was a cacophony of harsh breaking sounds before a completely naked man—Stephan Lazos—stood before her. Even though she'd just seen the same thing happen in reverse, she blinked a couple times.

"What..." The word barely squeaked out.

"Carly, listen to me. I hear sirens, which means someone probably saw the smoke and called the fire department. You're going to tell the police you don't know what happened, do you understand?"

She didn't *know* what happened so she wouldn't be lying. Unable to find her voice, she nodded before her gaze strayed to the other two wolves.

"Thomas is going to get Nick away from here before anyone arrives," Stephan said, as if he read her mind.

"Is Nick going to be okay?" She wanted to race over to him, but wasn't sure if she should. What if he didn't recognize her in wolf form? And she couldn't believe she was even thinking in those terms.

"He'll be fine. I'm going to stay here. I know a lot of the fire department guys and I'll do most of the talking. Just agree with me. Okay?"

No, it wasn't okay. She desperately wanted to see Nick, but... "Okay."

He turned and nodded. Almost immediately the black wolf pushed the gray one until it stood. The gray wolf turned to her and she found herself staring into familiar pale gray eyes.

Despite everything she'd witnessed, her brain was just starting to comprehend what was going on. When the gray wolf took a step in her direction, she jumped back. Guilt coursed through her at the hurt sound the animal made, but she couldn't help it. It had just been instinct, but she still felt terrible. Seeing the man she was pretty sure she loved change into a scary wolf was a twenty on the Richter scale of crazy. Even so, she hated that she'd just hurt him. "Nick..."

But he turned away from her at the sound of sirens growing louder.

Stephan shot her a desperate look, glanced toward the two animals, then back at her. "Just stay put, okay." It wasn't a question.

Before she could respond, Stephan and the wolves disappeared around the corner of her grandmother's house, leaving her behind.

Wearing her skimpy summer dress and no shoes, she nervously glanced around the yard and wrapped her arms around herself. The pile of smoldering ash had nearly dissipated.

About a minute later Stephan reappeared. This time he wore jeans, a T-shirt, and running shoes.

Before he could say a word she blurted, "Where's Nick going? Are you sure he's okay?"

Stephan rubbed a tired hand over his face. "Thomas is driving him to our parents' estate. He's... Nick is injured and he'll heal faster in wolf form."

The sirens were getting louder so she rushed on. "What exactly are you guys?"

"We're shifters. To be exact, we're werewolves. Or some people call us lycans. Not like you see in the movies though. We *do* have to shift, but we don't shift during full moons unless we want to and we don't run around like uncontrollable monsters."

"So what happened to that guy? And who was he? And what did he want?" She pointed toward the leftover ashes. Her voice rose with each syllable but she couldn't seem to stop herself.

"That guy was an Immortal. I haven't seen one in nearly a century and to be honest, I don't know much about them. They're very territorial and when he met you, he decided he wanted to keep you."

"Keep me? I'm not a piece of furniture!" she shrieked.

Stephan shrugged, and his unconcerned attitude pissed her off even more. "To him, you would have been. He would have used you up until he was tired of you. Then he'd have likely killed you."

She turned at the blaring noises. A fire truck rocketed up the driveway and men spilled from it like ants.

"Are you going to be okay?" Stephan's voice was low and reminded her a little of Nick's.

The thought of Nick hurting somewhere brought a sudden rush of burning tears to her eyes. She shook her head. No, she wasn't okay. Not even a little bit.

CHAPTER FOURTEEN

Carly checked the front of her button-down black raincoat one more time before knocking on Nick's front door. She'd been trying to get a hold of him since everything that happened Tuesday night. Thanks to a smoke bomb, her apartment was currently unlivable and she'd been forced to move in with her grandmother. The police thought it was a couple of kids playing a prank and she was happy to let them think that because she had more important things on her mind. The past couple days had been horrible and Nick hadn't been returning her calls.

It had taken some begging, but she'd gotten Alex to tell her where Nick lived. Considering that Alex had given that crazy fire-throwing guy Carly's phone number, it hadn't been too hard to convince her.

After a few moments, she banged on the solid wood door again. This time harder and louder. She still couldn't believe Nick lived in Key Biscayne. While she'd known he did well for himself, she hadn't expected him to live in such an affluent area. Only a few miles off the coast of Miami, it was like a world away. A virtual tropical paradise. Not that she cared about any of that. She just needed to know that he was okay, to see him with her own eyes — and maybe yell at him for not calling her back.

Nick's car wasn't out front but he had a garage and Alex had assured her he'd be here. Plus, there was a Jaguar sitting in the driveway. She slammed her fist against the door again. She'd had the most insane week of her life and still no answers. If he thought he could hide from her, he was out of his damn mind.

When she raised her hand again, the door flew open. An exotic-looking dark-haired, slightly older woman stood on the other side.

Unexpected jealousy shot through her veins like hot, scorching lava. "Who the hell are you?" she asked, surprised when her question came out as a shout.

Perfect brows rose in amusement as she held out a slim hand. "I'm Alisha, and you must be Carly." There was a slight accent Carly couldn't place.

Carly frowned at the woman's hand and ignored it. "Where's Nick?"

"He's on the back porch sulking. I was in the kitchen getting a glass of wine and I thought I heard some sort of racket," she said, amusement filling her voice.

Years of manners and politeness had been drilled into Carly first by her mother, then her grandmother. In that instant, she threw all she'd learned out the window and stormed past the small woman without another word. Her three-inch heels clacked down the hard wood floor of the hallway.

Expensive pieces of art hung on the walls, but she didn't waste time admiring them. The hallway ended abruptly and she almost tripped in her shoes. To her right was an open kitchen area and to her left was what looked like a family room. Through the glass doors she could see Nick nursing a beer on the back patio.

Her eyes narrowed on his figure. She'd been worried sick about him and he was hanging out with some slut. Taking a deep breath, she hurried through the open room and slung open one of the French doors.

Nick turned at the sound and shot out of the striped lounge chair when he spotted her. He wore casual lounge pants, no shirt, and had a thick bandage running around his rib cage. "What are you doing here?"

She faltered at his harsh tone.

"Shit. I didn't mean it like that, Carly. What…well, why are you here?" he asked.

"Are you serious?" She stared at him incredulously. "I saw you turn into a wolf, your stupid brother gave me some half-assed answers before *disappearing*, everyone at work is saying you're on vacation—*which I know is a lie*—and you won't return my calls."

"You've been calling?" The hopeful note in his voice pulled at her heartstrings.

"Well, yeah, like a billion times. But it kept going straight to voicemail. I wanted to make sure you were okay." *Screw it, she'd come this far*. She crossed the fifteen-feet divide between them until they were standing inches apart. His earthy scent immediately enveloped her. God she wanted to reach out and touch him so badly.

"That night…you flinched away from me. I didn't think you'd ever want to see me again. Hell, I thought you'd be back in Chicago by now," he muttered.

"Give me a break, Nick. I'd just had the shock of my life. I saw you turn into an animal and your brother kill some other guy—who then turned to ash." Screw it, she had to touch him. She reached out and traced a finger across his stubbled jaw. "Stephan told me you were fine. Are you sure you're okay?" she whispered.

As soon as she touched his skin, he covered her hand with his. "Now I am."

Heat warmed her blood at the contact, but she shook her head. He was injured and she recognized that look in his eyes way too well. "I have a lot of questions."

"Come on." He took her by the hand and collapsed back against the chair. When he did, he pulled her with him.

She squirmed in his lap, not wanting to lean too hard against his ribs if he was badly injured. "Are you sure I won't hurt you?"

Nick let out a low groan. "You're going to hurt me if you keep wiggling around."

"Wha...oh." She immediately stilled when she felt his erection pressing against her butt.

"Why are you wearing a raincoat?"

She could feel her face redden but was helpless to stop the heat creeping up her neck and cheeks. "Because I'm only wearing a thong underneath."

His pale eyes darkened and his grip around her waist tightened, but she pulled back.

"Questions first."

He scrubbed a hand over his face. "Okay, ask anything."

"Who's the woman who answered your door?"

His lips curved up into the sexiest grin. "After everything that's happened, *that's* your first question?"

She wasn't sure what was funny about it. "Well?"

"That's my mother."

Carly snorted. "Yeah, right. Maybe if she had you when she was twelve." Instantly she slapped a hand over her mouth and cringed. What if his mother had given birth at a young age?

"Not twelve, darling." The silky smooth voice of the woman who'd answered the door startled Carly.

Carly twisted in her seat to find the woman standing two feet away. The woman was more stealthy than Nick. "I'm sorry, I didn't mean—"

She waved a fine-boned hand in the air. "You two have a lot to talk about so I am leaving. Nicolas, I'll see you tomorrow afternoon. And

Carly, I know I'll see you at my Sunday brunch." It wasn't a question, but a subtle order.

She had no clue what the woman was talking about, but Carly nodded anyway. "Okay."

She turned back to Nick after the woman disappeared into the house. "That's really your mother? She looks so young."

"We age a lot slower than humans."

She bit her bottom lip and tried to formulate her words. Over the past two days she'd had a lot of time to come up with questions. Now she struggled to find her voice. "So…this whole 'turning into a wolf' is a family thing?"

To her relief, he chuckled lightly. "Yes, my entire pack—family—are shifters. Werewolves if you want to get specific."

"Even Alex?"

He nodded. "Yes, but she truly is twenty-one. She's just a pup."

"A pup? Uh, exactly how old are you?"

He cleared his throat. "A hundred and seventy."

She blinked once but pushed past it. There would be time enough later to digest *that*. "What about silver bullets? Will those kill you?"

He shifted underneath her, suddenly looking very uncomfortable. "They're more deadly than regular bullets. If a werewolf is shot with one and the silver isn't removed, we'll die within hours from poisoning."

"Wow."

"It's not something we advertise—"

She cut him off when she realized where he was headed. "Trust me, it wouldn't matter who I told, no one would believe me anyway. So, when were you planning to tell me… Or *were* you planning to tell me?" She hadn't thought about that until right then. What if he'd just wanted a quick fling—

"Don't even think I wanted an affair," he muttered.

"Wha… Can you read my mind?" she gasped, as a hand flew to her throat. Had he been able to read *all* her thoughts? She inwardly groaned. That was beyond embarrassing.

"Yes, I can." His deep voice rumbled.

"Oh my—"

"The only reason I can read your thoughts is because we're mates. And I couldn't do that until after we made love the first time. Even then, I blocked you out. Until today." He took one of her hands and threaded his fingers through hers.

"Oh, well that's…wait, mates? What does that mean?"

"Just what it sounds like. You're my mate. Once I've marked you, if you come in contact with any other shifters or nonhumans, they'll know you're taken and they'll stay away."

"What does marked mean? That man from the other night said you hadn't marked me yet. I thought you said we were mates."

"We *are* mates, but we haven't officially bonded yet. I wanted to wait until you were ready."

She didn't ask the question, and whether or not he could see her thoughts, she guessed what she wanted to know was clearly written on her face.

He cleared his throat. "When we bond, I have to dominate you, take you from behind. While we're making love, I'll bite your neck and mark you. We'll be bonded for life."

Bite her? It was a little kinky, but the thought sent a sudden rush of heat between her legs. Then another thought crossed her mind. "You said you age slower. Does that mean I'm going to grow old and you won't?"

Nick shook his head. "Once we bond — if we bond — you'll develop a similar immune system. You'll age at the same pace I do, you'll heal much quicker, and...if you get pregnant, there is a chance you'll change into a werewolf."

Her throat clenched. "A chance?"

"It's been a couple hundred years since a werewolf and human have mated. At least within the Lazos pack. In the past, pregnant human females change when they bond with their children."

She pressed her free hand to her abdomen. That was a lot to take in at once. A hell of a lot more than she'd even contemplated before coming here. She'd never even thought about having kids.

"I don't care about children. All I want is you," he growled, his throaty words making her pussy clench.

"You've got to stop doing that."

"Doing what?"

"Reading my thoughts. It's not fair."

"You should be able to read mine too."

She narrowed her eyes at him disbelievingly. What was she supposed to do, tap into her Jedi mind control?

When he chuckled, she mock punched him in the arm. "I'm not kidding, cut that out!"

He held up a hand in surrender. "Okay, I promise."

She was silent for another moment as she tried to gather her thoughts.

"I have a lot of questions. Most of them can wait until later, but a second ago you said 'if' we bond. Do you not want to bond with me?"

He laughed aloud, but the sound was harsh. "It's not about what I want, Carly. The answer is yes, but this is your choice."

More thoughts and questions assaulted her mind but she'd asked everything she'd planned. "Okay, I only have one more question. Were you just going to let me walk away from you?"

His jaw twitched before he answered. "I wasn't able to get out of bed until a few hours ago. I was coming to see you after my mother left. There's no way in hell I'd give you up without a fight, woman."

"Right answer," she murmured. Because she wasn't giving this sexy male up. Ever. Moving slightly, she spread her legs and straddled him. The past couple days had passed in a blur, but her body had been aching for his touch.

"What are you doing?" His voice was hoarse and scratchy.

"What do you think?" As she spread her legs farther, her coat pushed up higher, revealing more skin.

She started with the top button, slowly pushing it out of the hole, never taking her gaze off Nick. As his eyes locked with hers, she made a decision. She'd come to Miami to mix things up. Of course, she'd never planned to meet a man like Nick, but she knew what her heart wanted.

There were probably a dozen reasons why this was a bad idea, but a very good one why it wasn't. She loved him. No doubt about it. The thought of losing Nick was worse than the thought of dating someone who could turn into a wolf. That realization had shifted her entire reality. She didn't care that she hadn't known him that long, it was as if he'd been part of her life forever. She wasn't letting him go.

Nick pushed her hands out of the way when she reached the third button. There were eight in all and apparently she was going too slow.

His hands shook as he practically tore the coat off. When the buttons were undone, she shrugged it off, letting it fall behind her. It was a perfect spring evening and since his place was close to the Atlantic, a continuous breeze flowed over them.

He still hadn't made a move to kiss her or touch her really. Wearing a lacy thong, she straddled him, but after he'd gotten her coat off, his hands rested gently on her thighs.

Her skin ached where he touched her and she wondered what he was waiting for. She opened her mouth to ask but he came at her fast, his mouth devouring hers with pent up hunger and need.

There was no time to catch her breath as his tongue teased against hers.

This kiss wasn't tender or gentle. No, his mouth was demanding complete submission. Something she would gladly give.

Carly clutched his shoulders as he started to move. In the back of her head, somewhere in the recesses of her brain, she knew what was going to happen tonight. She wanted it and it was obvious he did too. If she decided to listen to her rational side, it would tell her things were moving too fast.

But deep down she knew she would never meet another man like Nick. Not in a million lifetimes. He'd fought a crazy Immortal for her and had been willing to die for her. He was so incredibly special and she wanted to spend the rest of her life discovering all his secrets and making him feel as amazing as he made her.

As he pushed up from the chair, her legs automatically wrapped around his waist. He might have a bandage around his ribs but he didn't seem remotely bothered as he stood and carried her. With the ease he showed, he might have been carrying a sack of feathers.

Everything around her funneled out. She was vaguely aware of walking into the house. The door made a loud, shaking sound when it shut. He must have used his foot because both hands were latched onto her ass and he was still kissing her with an unrestrained hunger.

They rushed through a living room, a hallway, then suddenly they were in a bedroom. A very masculine room with a king-sized bed. She barely had time to digest their surroundings before he had her flat on her back. The silky sheets chilled her back, but nothing could cool the heat flowing through her.

Nick teased Carly's mouth in the same way he wanted to tease her pussy. There would be no time for that tonight however. At least not the first time.

A couple days without her in his bed had been like a lifetime. His brother had taken his cell phone and he'd had no idea Carly had been calling him. He'd been wounded and disoriented Tuesday night but he remembered her backing away from him. In fear. That image had been burned in his brain but he planned to replace it with a new image.

One of her completely submitting to him.

Now that she was in his arms, he wasn't letting her go. One of his hands found its way between her legs and he pushed her barely there thong to the side. When he covered her mound, she automatically spread farther for him.

The hair covering her pussy was a darker shade of red than the hair on her head. It was so soft and inviting. He slid his middle finger in between her folds, needing to feel what was his. To claim her. She was warm and welcoming—and oh so tight.

Pushing deeper into her, he began moving his finger in and out to the same rhythm his tongue delved into her mouth. Cream and heat coated his hand. She was soaking and ready for him, but he wanted to make sure she came once before he took her the way he planned.

Carly sighed into his mouth when he slid another finger into her warmth.

Somehow he dragged his mouth away from hers. "You like what I'm doing?" he murmured, afraid to break the quiet spell of the room.

She nodded, but he wanted more.

"Say it, Carly. Tell me what you want." He loved it when she was vocal.

Her breathing was becoming more shallow so he stilled his hand, leaving his fingers embedded deep inside her, but not moving. When she tried to shift against his hand, he pulled out.

"Don't stop." Her whisper was a quiet plea.

Experiencing primal satisfaction at her words, Nick pushed back into her, savoring the way her body clenched so tightly around just his fingers. Her sweet pussy was starting to clamp in quicker contractions and he knew she was close to coming.

He was barely touching the rest of her body. His other hand grasped the back of her neck, threading through her thick hair. Their chests rubbed against each other, but he was *barely* stimulating her.

She was that receptive to his touch. The woman was like a tight little package of dynamite and he couldn't wait to see her explode.

A little flick of his thumb over her clit and she began contracting. Sweet, little contractions. He lifted his head back and watched in awe as her eyes glazed over and she reached climax. His entire body reacted in a primal manner to the sight of her like this. Nothing about his release was going to be *sweet*. It was going to be undignified and loud.

His cock felt like a steel club between his legs. Days of being denied built up inside him.

As a pleasant sigh escaped her, he grasped her hips and flipped her onto her stomach. She let out a little yelp, but she didn't struggle. Almost immediately, she pushed up on her hands and knees and looked over her shoulder at him.

Red hair cascaded down her back and over her shoulders. The look on her face was one of desire, but he needed to be sure she was ready.

"Is this what you want?" he growled. The unspoken words were there. Because there was no going back after this.

"Yes." The word wasn't a whisper. It was said with perfect clarity.

That was all he needed to hear. He lost his jeans in seconds and this time he didn't bother with a condom. He'd explain everything to her later and right now, she didn't seem to care that he wasn't getting one.

As he tried to control his breathing, he rubbed a soothing hand down her back before squeezing her hips and plunging into her. The feel of sliding into her slickness with no barrier was beyond anything he'd ever imagined.

There was nothing gentle about his hold or his thrusts. He pummeled into her like a man on death row experiencing his last fuck. He simply couldn't help it. The deepest part of him needed to claim his woman. Make sure everyone knew she was off limits.

His heart beat like a jackhammer, ready to burst from the cavity of his chest as he thrust over and over. Holding onto her, his loud groans intermixed with her quieter ones.

Leaning down, he somehow released one of his hands and brushed all her hair to the side. It fell over her shoulder, and the fresh scent of her shampoo tickled his nose. It smelled like candy. Just like Carly, a sweet treat to be savored.

"If you're not ready, tell me now." The animal inside told him to shut the fuck up. The animal didn't care if she was ready, it wanted to claim what was his. However, the man who loved her sure as hell cared and he wanted to please her in every way possible.

"I'm ready," she whispered.

Holding a hand against her back in an effort to soothe her, he resumed his thrusting. From this position, he went deeper, could feel her inner walls closing around him.

Shadows and light danced through the cracked blinds, bathing her in small ribbons of the glow of the setting sun.

When he felt his release build, he held on to one of her shoulders and nipped her neck. Gently at first, then he sank his teeth into her.

She moaned, the sound one of pleasure instead of pain.

It wouldn't be too painful. At least that was what he'd heard. Just enough to pierce the neck, locking them forever. As soon as he broke through her sensitive skin, he rocketed into orgasm.

Surprisingly, so did she. Her tight pussy fisted around him as they both pushed over the edge. The muscles in his arms and legs tightened and clenched as he let out a shout that reverberated off the walls. Carly was his mate. *His.*

After one last thrust, he collapsed, falling on top of her, even as he tried to roll to the side. They lay intertwined in silence until finally she pushed at his chest with her elbow.

He dug into the recesses of his energy and moved, allowing her to roll onto her back.

"So now we're bonded?" she murmured, rolling into him and throwing her leg over him.

He nodded, wrapping his arm around her. "Yes."

"That was amazing but I don't feel any different."

You sure about that? he asked with his mind. He didn't have any way to be sure she'd understand him, but after what they'd just experienced, he took the chance.

Holy shit! I can read your mind? Her eyes widened as she stared at him.

I told you.

A mischievous grin played across her features. *I like this. Now you'll never be able to hide anything from me again.*

He chuckled and let out a satisfied sigh. Nick didn't want to hide anything from her ever again. "I love you, Carly."

The smile she gave him could have lit up the entire city. He felt the emotions pour from her and wrap around him like a physical caress. "I love you too."

EPILOGUE

Saturday Afternoon

Nick half knocked as he entered his father's study. When he walked in, he found Thomas and Stephan already waiting at the large round table where they usually held pack meetings. "Where's Dad?"

"Uncle Yannis stopped by. They're talking privately," Thomas said.

Nick took a seat in between Stephan and Thomas and glanced between his brothers. "Do we have any idea what's going to happen?"

Stephan shook his head. "So far it doesn't look as if the dead Immortal had anyone close to him, but Dad wants to take all precautions."

"Good." Nick did too. If someone came looking for the Immortal named Asha, Nick wasn't the one who would be hunted.

It would be Thomas.

Even though Nick wanted to be pissed at his brother, he understood why Thomas had delivered the killing blow. Thomas hadn't wanted Carly to see Nick kill someone and as the oldest and next in line to be Alpha, it fell to his shoulders to protect them. Whether they wanted that protection or not. Hell, he knew how lucky he was to have Thomas and Stephan looking out for him. If they hadn't already been out hunting the Immortal, things might have turned out a lot differently.

"How are things with Carly?" Stephan asked, his voice guarded.

"I was going to wait until tomorrow to announce it, but we're officially bonded." He couldn't hold back the smug grin he knew must be on his face. Last night—and this morning—was still fresh in his mind.

After a few moments of congratulatory slaps on the back, Nick turned his attention to Stephan. "Why didn't you tell me Carly had been calling?"

Stephan shrugged, but an apologetic expression crossed his face. "Sorry. I did what I thought was best. She freaked out that night and I wasn't sure what her reaction was going to be. I didn't want anything to interfere with your healing."

Nick opened his mouth to yell at him, but stopped himself from overreacting. He might have done the same thing in his brother's position. The truth was, it would take a lot to kill his good mood.

There were a lot of unknowns in his future, but he'd found his mate and he couldn't ask for more than that.

WORTH THE RISK

One man is getting in the way of her revenge...her mate.

Werewolf Marisol Cabrera has one goal in life: kill the man who murdered her entire pack. When she meets alpha werewolf Stephan and realizes he's her mate, all her carefully laid plans dissipate in seconds. By all accounts, she *should* hate Stephan and everything he stands for. After all, he's a dirty arms dealer doing business with her mortal enemy. Unfortunately, every time the dominating wolf gets close, she can't deny her growing attraction for the last man in the world she expected to want.

But things aren't what they seem...

Undercover DEA agent Stephan Lazos is about to make the biggest bust of his career, but everything that can go wrong, *does*. He never expected to discover his mate while on the job. She saves his life and his cover when he almost shifts in the middle of a crowded Miami nightclub, but that doesn't mean he trusts her. The clock is ticking and if he doesn't figure out what secrets the sexy she-wolf is keeping from him, he might not just lose his job, but his life in the process.

CHAPTER ONE

Stephan Lazos couldn't tear his gaze away from the exotic brunette moving across the dance floor below. From his position in the VIP room, he had a perfect view of almost the entire nightclub. The only thing he could focus on, however, was one woman. The wolf inside him wanted to throw her over his shoulder, take her out of the loudest club in Miami and back to his place for a marathon of fucking.

His skin tingled and burned as he watched her. The unwanted physical reaction was starting to piss him off. She was hot, sure, but she wasn't even his type. At six foot two, he liked his women tall and curvy. Once they got to the bedroom, he wanted a woman who had a lot of stamina and didn't mind the sex a little rougher. The woman on the dance floor looked as if she'd fall over if a strong wind came along.

Long, dark hair fell down her back in waves. It looked as if she wore three-inch heels, and she was *still* short compared to the blonde woman she was dancing with. Everything about her was petite and delicate. Each time her hips swayed in tune with the blaring music, her silky red dress shimmered around her tight body. And each time that happened, his cock jumped to attention. The primal beast inside him wanted to cover every inch of her exposed skin so no one else could look at her.

He liked sex as much as the next shifter, but this was *different* and he didn't understand his reaction. Since he was a pup, he'd never had to exert much mental control to keep his canines from extending. Now it was taking all his self-control not to *change*. And this couldn't have happened at a worse time either.

He was in the middle of an assignment. All his focus should be on convincing Antonio Perez that he was a new arms dealer in town looking to expand to medical supplies and *not* an undercover DEA agent.

"See something you like?" Antonio's voice caused him to step back from the balcony.

"I see a lot of 'somethings' I like," Stephan said as he took a sip of his scotch. The one thing he hated about this undercover role was his playboy image. The expensive suits and drinks were a nice change of pace from playing the role of junkie or hired thug, but the Miami party scene left a lot to be desired. One of his brothers owned a club downtown and Stephan had only been in it a handful of times.

"Anyone in particular?" the other man pressed.

Stephan couldn't afford to show any interest in one woman over another. There was no way in hell he could let Antonio think he had a weakness. "The group of women in the middle."

"I'll invite them up," Antonio said as he motioned to two of his bodyguards.

Stephan shrugged, as if it didn't matter one way or the other. However, his heartbeat quickened when the bodyguards ushered the group of barely dressed women up the stairs.

Her scent hit him with startling intensity. In this crowded, stifling atmosphere, his extrasensory abilities were working overtime. Alcohol, sex, the consistent thump of the bass from the speakers, it was overwhelming. Even so, he still knew the subtle jasmine scent that rolled over him was her.

Whoever *she* was.

As if she sensed him, she glanced around until their gazes locked. Her bright blue eyes widened when they made contact.

Mate.

The word echoed loudly inside his head. His heart skipped a beat at the thought. It was impossible that he would recognize her so soon. *Wasn't it?*

His brother Nick had told him what it was like when he'd met his mate, yet Nick hadn't realized Carly was his mate right away. He'd just been possessive and a little obsessed with her. Maybe in hindsight he should have realized. Of course Carly was human, not a shifter. But even his parents hadn't recognized one another right away. He'd always thought it would take time.

Mate. The word reverberated through him again. His wolf clawed at him, telling him to shut the fuck up; that was his mate. She was a wolf too, he could scent it. *All mine.*

Fuck, no. He refused to believe it.

He mentally shook himself, but his wolf just clawed harder.

Stephan had never imagined something being so physically overpowering that he couldn't think straight. And he definitely hadn't believed that he'd just *know* his mate on sight.

He set his drink on one of the high-top tables and started to make his way toward her. To his surprise, she flipped her dark hair over her shoulder in a haughty manner, turned her back on him and headed for the bar.

What the fuck?

He refrained from growling. Barely.

"Stephan, I have business to attend to." Antonio's voice pulled him out of his trance and back to the present.

The blaring music once again registered as he turned toward the drug-running asshole he needed to do business with. "So do I," Stephan murmured.

A lecherous grin spread across Antonio's face. "Good. Enjoy yourself. I must leave, but everything is still on for tomorrow?"

Stephan nodded. "I'll be there. I already have buyers lined up for most of your products. Your stuff better be as good as you promised."

He waved a hand in the air. "It's better. And I have a surprise for you. Not a product we discussed earlier."

"I don't like surprises."

"You'll like this one. Trust me. I will have women at the party, but feel free to bring some of your own."

Stephan waited until Antonio and his men descended the stairs before stalking toward the mystery woman. He'd been watching her out of the corner of his eye, and she hadn't moved from her seat at the bar. She was aware of him watching too, he was sure of it.

"Leave," he growled to the college-aged guy talking to her.

The blond kid started to say something then he must have recognized Stephan as one of Antonio's friends—or maybe he saw the rabid look in Stephan's eyes—because he mumbled something too low to hear and hurried away.

"That was rude." The blue-eyed beauty narrowed her gaze at him.

"What's your name?" he asked, ignoring her statement.

A small smile played at the corners of her very kissable lips. "Marisol."

Marisol. The name and her voice rolled over him. "I'm Stephan. Why are you out unchaperoned? What pack do you belong to?" Damn it, he hadn't meant to sound so harsh.

For a split second, her eyes flashed a darker shade of blue. She shrugged but he could smell her pain. She was decent at masking it, but it rolled off her in subtle waves. The very scent of it angered his wolf. Stephan had the most irrational urge to comfort her, even though he had no right to touch her. "I have no pack."

"Where are you from?"

She shrugged again. "None of your business."

He leaned in so that his mouth was inches from her ear. It took all his self-control not to nip or lick her soft skin. "It's most definitely my business."

She swallowed and he could sense her fear...and attraction.

Marisol Cabrera forced herself not to tuck tail and run. The wolf next to her was sexy as sin and he radiated dominance, but he was also a piece of shit arms dealer. In truth, she could let that go—and she wasn't sure what that said about her—but he worked with Antonio Perez.

That, she would never let go.

If she wanted to get out of this alive and to also complete what she'd come to Miami to do, she had to play this right. This male was very, very dangerous. Her inner wolf sensed it, even as she wanted to rub up against him. "And why is that?"

"You're my mate." His deep voice was like an unwanted aphrodisiac. Heat pooled in her belly.

Marisol wanted to deny it, but she'd sensed it on the stairs. She'd nearly tripped when she'd comprehended what was happening. She'd given up the hope or desire of finding her mate decades ago. Firsthand experience told her wolves could be just as treacherous as humans. She knew exactly who *Stephan Vasquez* was. She'd been watching Antonio Perez for months, waiting for the perfect time to get close to him before she ended his life.

And now she found out the man he'd been doing business with recently was not only a fucking wolf, he was her *mate*.

Unbelievable.

Fate was a cruel, cruel bitch and she'd certainly had a lot of fun torturing Marisol in the past year. Well, no more. Mate or not, she didn't care. It was only biology after all. Her body might want the man and the wolf, but she didn't love him, didn't even know him.

Considering what he did for a living, it was doubtful she ever would. She threw him a cool look. "So what if we're mates? I have a choice in the matter, you know."

He muttered something she couldn't understand. It sounded Greek, but she thought he was Cuban. Or at least that's what she'd learned through the grapevine. So many of the club-hopping South Beach girls wanted a piece of him. He was obviously rich and powerful, but he got that money through the pain of others. Marisol had only watched him from afar or else she would have known he was a shifter long ago.

She wasn't sure if that would have made a difference in her approach or not. Now she'd never know.

"Have dinner with me," he growled, taking her by surprise with his demand.

"Are you asking or ordering?"

He cleared his throat and she was under the impression that this was incredibly difficult for him. "Have dinner with me tomorrow night...please."

She set her drink down. "Maybe. Where are you going to take me?" She actually planned to say yes. Now that she realized how easy it would be to get to Perez through him, it was her only choice. Still, she wanted this sexy wolf to sweat it.

"I'll cook for you. My place."

She bit back a retort. Somehow she couldn't see this big man wearing an apron. He probably had a maid. But she needed him. "Are your sweaty looking thugs going to be there too?" She tilted her head in the direction of one of the men she'd seen hovering around him earlier.

His head swiveled around then he glanced back at her. It almost looked as if he'd forgotten they were there. "It'll just be you and me, *kardia mou*," he murmured.

She wasn't sure what the foreign words meant, but they sure as hell weren't Spanish. *Interesting.* "If you think you can handle me all by yourself, I guess the answer is yes." She uncrossed, then re-crossed her legs and took pleasure at the low growl she heard start to form in his throat. He had to smell her desire, no doubt about it. "You better watch yourself, *wolf*, or you'll change in the middle of this club."

She'd only been kidding, but his breathing became more labored and when she saw a flash of his canines, her heart rate increased about a hundred notches. Arms dealer or not, he was her mate and something primal inside her shifted at the thought of him in pain. She *had* to protect him. "Come on, let's get out of here." She slid off the stool and grabbed his hand, ready to bolt down the stairs she'd come up not long ago.

He had other plans. Stephan motioned to the men in suits to stay then practically dragged her toward one of the **exit** signs. Once they were in the private stairwell, he finally spoke, but his words were hoarse, animalistic. "I have a car waiting out back."

Something told her they weren't going to make it that far. So she did the only thing she could think of. Pressing her body against the full length of his, she wrapped her arms around his neck. If she could get him to stop from shifting she had to do it.

He didn't seem to need any more motivation than her body against his. His mouth slanted over hers with a rough, hungry intensity. As his tongue rasped over hers in erotic little strokes, she allowed her body to meld against his very hard one. She didn't want to want him, but her mind wasn't listening to reason right now as a rush of heat flooded between her legs.

She could feel the raw energy racing through him. All the hard lines and muscles of his body pulsed with excitement, mirroring her own reaction. The power of it rolled off him and coursed over her. Sometimes the urge to change could be overwhelming, but she hadn't had an issue controlling it since she was a pup. And something told her Stephan rarely had a problem with control either. At least she wasn't the only one so affected by this attraction.

She moaned when he nudged her legs open wider with his thigh. It had been so long since she'd let a man—or shifter—touch her, it was a wonder she didn't combust on the spot. Even though it was ridiculous, he felt somehow familiar, as if they fit perfectly. As their tongues and bodies intertwined, she inhaled his earthy scent.

When his cock pressed insistently against her lower abdomen, she moaned into his mouth. One of his big hands trailed down her back until it settled at the curve of her butt. He shoved the material of her dress out of the way so that he gripped bare skin. She shivered at the feel of his callused fingers.

"Fuck yeah, sweetheart." His voice was still a growl as he pulled back, feathering kisses along her jaw.

An inaudible sound tore from his throat as his fingers dug into her harder. Her inner walls clenched, desperate to be filled by this male, this stranger. She was ready to let him take her right up against the wall in this stairwell. Which was insane.

Before she got completely out of control she pulled her head back and pushed lightly at his chest. He was still breathing hard, but there were no signs of pointy canines and while his gaze was heated, his eyes didn't have that wild, uncontrollable look about them anymore.

"Are you okay now?" she asked. Hell, she wasn't sure if *she* was okay. She felt as if she could crawl right out of her skin and all they'd done was kiss.

"If I tell you no will you keep kissing me?" A trace of humor laced his deep voice, but his words were hoarse and forced.

Despite her desire to feel nothing for this man, Marisol could feel the corners of her lips pull into a smile. "You're not like what I expected," she murmured before she could bite the words back. She hadn't planned to let on that she knew what he did for a living, but now she couldn't take it back. He'd scent it if she tried to lie.

His gaze sharpened. "What do you mean?"

She shrugged out of his embrace and put some distance between them. "I *know* what you do for a living, Stephan Vasquez."

Something indefinable flashed in his eyes, but it was gone so quick she couldn't put her finger on it. Hell, she couldn't even smell the man's emotions. He was obviously very adept at hiding his true self.

"You don't know as much as you think you do, *kardia mou.*"

She rolled her eyes and forced her protective wall to slide back into place. This man was nothing to her. He was a means to an end. Once she completed what she'd come here to do, she didn't care if she lived or died. And she certainly couldn't allow some wolf to get in the way of her plans. "If you're fine, I'm leaving. This club is giving me a headache." Even though they were in the stairwell, the walls reverberated with the thumping music inside.

"I'll give you a ride." He took her by the arm in a possessive grip and started down the stairs.

She had no choice but to follow, but there was no way she was letting him give her a ride. "I'll take a taxi home, but thank you for the offer."

He grunted something under his breath as he held the door open for her. It emptied into an alley where a black SUV limousine with dark tinted windows waited. Before she could attempt to argue, he'd opened the back door and practically shoved her inside. "I told you—"

The door slammed behind him. "You're mine, and I take care of what's mine."

The slam lit the pilot light on her temper. *Arrogant bastard.* "We might be mates, but I haven't submitted to you," she snapped. And it was unlikely she ever would. The words remained unspoken but echoed through her mind. She was prepared to die to kill Perez, and she couldn't allow herself to be mated. Even if he was an arms dealer, to knowingly bond would be cruel to Stephan. Not all shifters mated for life, but werewolves did, and it was very rare to get a second chance if one mate died. If Perez figured out who she was, he would no doubt kill her and Stephan would likely never have the opportunity to mate again.

When she slid a few inches farther away from him, her dress shifted against the plush leather seat and revealed more skin. As if connected by a magnet, his eyes immediately strayed down, his look raw and sexual.

She'd worn the skimpy red dress to get attention. Of course, she hadn't wanted it from Stephan. She'd wanted it from Antonio Perez. The man was almost impossible to get to and she'd known she'd have to flash a lot of skin if she wanted to get invited to one of his parties. Now she had an even better way to get to Antonio and she wouldn't have to pretend to be interested in him. If she was Stephan's woman, he would have no reason to question her. "How long have you been doing business with Antonio Perez? I thought you dealt in weapons." And word on the street was that Perez dealt in drugs—legal and illegal. Guns and drugs were both bad businesses, but they weren't exactly the same beasts. For whatever reason, drugs brought more heat from the law in Miami.

A slight frown marred his handsome face. "How do you know about that?"

She shrugged. "Everyone in the South Beach circuit knows. You've been seen with him at all the clubs."

"Why haven't I seen you around before?"

Marisol inwardly cursed at how smoothly he changed the subject. "I'm not exactly a club girl. I was just out tonight with friends." It wasn't a complete lie. She'd been visiting clubs all over Miami for the past year trying to find a chink in Perez's security. The only time he ever let his guard down was around pretty women. So she'd befriended party girls. She didn't want the focus on her so she asked another question before Stephan could continue. "What pack are you part of? I haven't heard of any Vasquez's living around here."

"What *have* you heard?" He scooted an inch closer so their knees touched.

Her wolf sat up and took notice, wanting to feel more of the sexy male.

She started to answer when the window separating them from the driver rolled down. "Mr. Vasquez, where am I taking you?"

"My place in Key Biscayne," he ordered.

"No—" He pressed a finger over her mouth.

After the window rolled back up, she pushed at his shoulder. "You can't just take me prisoner. And you never answered my question. What pack do you belong to?"

"I'll answer your questions later."

"No. I want answers now. If you're not part of the Lazos pack, who the hell are you?" He was obviously an alpha, but something told her he wasn't an *Alpha*. He didn't run his own pack. No, he seemed like more of a loner. She'd heard that the Lazos pack made their home in Miami, but she'd never formally introduced herself to any of them or even sought them out. Miami was a big place and as a lone wolf, it had been easier than she imagined to blend in. Technically it was wrong, but at this point in her life, she didn't care about breaking some rules.

"You know about them?"

"I know that Miami is their home. I haven't met any of them. Are they okay with you being here?"

A small smile touched his lips. The action immediately softened the harsh planes of his face and she had the most irrational urge to reach out and cup his cheek. "I've spoken to their Alpha and he's allowed me to stay here as long as I respect his territory. Why haven't you introduced yourself?"

"I...truthfully, I hadn't planned to stay in Miami so long and I just never got around to it." Which was just a lame excuse.

"Don't you have any respect for our rules?"

He was one to talk. "Why are you taking me to your home?"

He sighed. "Are you always so difficult?"

"Only when I'm being kidnapped," she muttered.

He was silent so long she wasn't sure he'd respond. Finally he spoke. "Do you want to go home? I'll tell my driver to turn around right now."

She considered his offer for a moment. The truth was, she didn't mind going home with him. The closer she got to Stephan, the easier it would be to make her move against Perez. The nagging voice in her head shouted that betraying her mate was one of the lowest things she could possibly do, but she ignored it. Her family was dead because of Antonio Perez and if it was the last thing she did, she was going to put him in his grave.

Resolved, she hardened her heart and stared out the window. "I'll go with you."

CHAPTER TWO

Stephan shut the office door and fished his phone out of his pants pocket. His boss was going to be pissed when he realized he'd ditched his team, but he didn't want anyone knowing about Marisol. That included *everyone* he worked with. Luckily he'd convinced his boss to hire a private limo company as part of their cover. And that company just happened to be owned by his Uncle Cosmo.

He was taking a big risk bringing her to one of his family's beach houses instead of the place the DEA was using for this operation, but he needed absolute privacy. His cover house was bugged in every room and he'd made sure Antonio Perez knew about its location. Letting the other man think he knew of his whereabouts had gone a long way in establishing trust between them.

Sighing, he dialed the number.

Reuben Woods, Director of the DEA's Miami division, picked up on the second ring. "Where the fuck are you?"

"I can't talk."

"Coleman said you left with a woman. Who is she?"

"I can't say."

"What the fuck does that mean, you can't say?"

"You're just gonna have to trust me. Saturday is still a go, so make sure a team is ready."

"We are. Are you under duress?"

"*No.* Trust me."

There was a long pause. "All right. Check in with me tomorrow morning."

Stephan disconnected then took the battery out of his phone. His phone was already encrypted but he wasn't taking any chances Woods would try to track him. Woods was a good guy, but Stephan had only worked with him a couple times and at this point, Stephan didn't trust anybody. Not with his mate. Most of his assignments had been out of state and that was the way Stephan liked it. Working jobs too close to home made him feel uneasy. His family could take care of themselves, but it lowered his stress level just the same. He'd made an exception for this case.

He knew his boss would be pissed the next time they talked, but hell, Woods was lucky they were even in communication right now. While they'd played this case close to the chest and only a handful of people knew about it, normally Stephan went in undercover with one contact and one contact *only*. It helped eliminate leaks that way.

When he heard a soft knock at the door, he slipped the phone and battery into the top drawer of the desk. All the muscles in his body tightened when he opened the door to find Marisol standing there. The animal in him wanted to strip her naked and fuck for hours. And her outfit wasn't helping matters. The shirt stretched across her small breasts, perfectly accentuating her soft curves and hard nipples. It was too short though, and it exposed the lower half of her flat stomach.

"This sort of fits." She tugged on the hem of the black t-shirt he'd given her.

"It covers more than that dress you were wearing." Stephan heard the possessive note in his voice but couldn't stop himself. Didn't care at this point. All his wolf knew was that she was his mate.

"Whose clothes are these anyway?" She narrowed her bright blue eyes at him, a sudden pop of annoyance rolling off her.

"I've never slept with the woman they belong to if that's what you're asking." The skintight t-shirt and yoga pants he'd given her belonged to his cousin Alex. He knew because he could still smell traces of her in the house. His answer was evasive but it wasn't an outright lie. More than anything he wanted to tell Marisol who he really was, but he couldn't yet. Mate or not, he didn't know anything about her and he sensed she was holding something back from him. The fact that she didn't have a pack — or rather claimed not to have one — set off alarm bells.

The house they were in was one of his parents' extra beach houses they reserved for visiting wolves or friends of the human variety. It was rarely used so he'd known it would be unoccupied and better, it wouldn't have any family photos lying around. His pack was very particular about not keeping personal photos around their own homes, much less a guesthouse.

She placed her hands on her hips and the haughty expression on her face got him hotter than he could have imagined. "So what do you plan to do to me now that you've got me here?"

"Talk." He wanted to do a hell of a lot more than talk, but he needed to know who this sexy she-wolf was and why she hadn't introduced herself to his Alpha sometime over the past year.

"Talk?" Her voice was disbelieving. The sweet jasmine scent he'd noted at the club was more potent and enticing here at the house.

"Do you want a glass of wine?" He needed to keep his hands busy with something other than her. If he didn't, he was likely to take her right on the floor. With the way she'd been grinding up against him in that stairwell, he was pretty sure she'd let him.

Without answering, she turned on her heel and headed for his kitchen. Watching the subtle sway of her hips had his cock on full alert and his brain barely functioning.

He easily caught up to her as they entered the kitchen. Everything in the house was state of the art, but it was also very sterile. It felt like a hotel and probably fit in with his profile as an arms dealer. He hated that she thought he sold weapons for a living.

"Shouldn't you have more security or something?" Marisol asked.

"No one knows about this place. Besides, do you really think I'm worried about getting killed?" Unless someone shot or poisoned him with silver, he was pretty much indestructible.

A soft smile tugged at the corner of her very kissable mouth. "Good point." She slid onto one of the high-top bar stools at the center island while he pulled a bottle from the wine rack along the wall. When she moistened her lips with that perfect pink tongue, he had a sudden vision of her running that tongue over his cock and he nearly dropped the bottle.

"Is red okay?" When she nodded, he poured them both a glass and sat next to her. With his loud family, he normally liked silence, but the quiet room left him nervous.

Nervous.

The word was laughable. He'd never felt insecure around a female—wolf or human—in his entire life. Most of the time he could smell their desire, fear, whatever. People were easy to read.

Not Marisol.

He couldn't tell if she was purposefully hiding her feelings or if she was just private. The only thing coming off her was jasmine and need. Even if she wanted to, she couldn't hide her desire for him. On his most primal level, that pleased him.

The silent tension in the room swelled until the air was thick with his desire mixed with hers. He knew it was biological and he also knew it was what happened when one met their mate, but he didn't like feeling such little control over his body.

After taking a few sips of her wine, she set it down on the marble countertop. Her intelligent eyes studied him carefully. "What are you thinking?"

"You probably don't want to know," he muttered, even as he wondered exactly the same thing. He wanted to know what was going on in her head.

In a surprising move, she slid off the chair and positioned herself between his legs. His cock jutted forward when she lightly pressed her fingertips against his chest. The challenging look in her eyes was unexpected.

Instead of kissing her, he threaded his fingers through the curtain of her dark hair and grasped the back of her head in a tight grip. The strands were silky and cool against his palm. "What are you playing at?" A growl rumbled at the back of his throat.

"You don't want me?" she practically purred. Her hands settled on his thighs and she raked her fingernails teasingly along his legs.

Against his will, his leg muscles clenched under her light touch. God help him, he wanted her. More than he cared to admit. It had been a while since he'd been with a woman. Ever since his younger brother had found his mate, sadness and a touch of jealousy had settled deep inside Stephan. He wanted what Nick had so he'd basically turned down any woman he met. "Don't play games with me."

"I won't let you bond with me, but I want you." The truth was in her words and in her scent. Her desire grew stronger with each second that passed.

He'd been ready to bond since practically the second he'd seen her, but it was the female's right to choose when and where they would bond. He wanted to take Marisol right on the kitchen floor so badly his cock ached, but his human side won out. Unable to voice his intentions, he hooked his hands under her ass and picked her up. Immediately she wrapped her slim legs around his waist. Her erotic scent enveloped him in a thick cloud. Wordlessly, he strode for the master bedroom. They might not be about to bond, but they were certainly going to fuck.

CHAPTER THREE

Marisol knew she was playing with fire, but Lord, she wanted this sexy shifter. If she was going to die, she was going to enjoy life before she did. Fate might have been cruel enough to lead her to her mate now, but that didn't mean she couldn't take some pleasure.

She felt as if she were in heat, she was so hot. She needed relief and she needed it *now*. Rubbing her breasts over his chest, she grinded against his body as he carried her from the kitchen. She sensed he was worried about her sudden change of heart. It wasn't as if she'd planned to sleep with him tonight, but she wasn't going to deny herself what she wanted. Especially when she knew he'd get just as much pleasure. It was a win-win for both of them.

Her surroundings vaguely registered when they entered a large room. Strange, the bedroom didn't smell like Stephan. It didn't smell like anyone. It simply smelled like fresh, clean cotton. She was glad that it didn't smell of another female.

Marisol was more than comfortable with her body, but she was thankful when he didn't turn the lights on. It had been a while since she'd had sex and the last man she'd contemplated letting into her bed had tried to kill her.

The floor-length curtains were drawn back on the wide window, allowing the moon to give them just enough light to see each other. While shifters didn't need a full moon to shift forms, the sight of it always pleased her inner wolf, soothed her.

When her feet touched the floor, she tried to step back but hit the edge of the bed. The heat of Stephan's body wrapped around her was sensual and enticing. Instinctively, she curled her toes into the plush throw rug in anticipation of what was to come. The dark look in his eyes told her she wouldn't be disappointed. He murmured something low and unintelligible as he grasped the bottom hem of her shirt. Her stomach fluttered in response.

Her vision was bathed in darkness for a moment as he lifted the shirt over her head. Cool air rushed over her skin, causing her already hard nipples to pebble even more.

She reached out to touch his muscular chest, but before she realized it, she was flat on her back and he'd pulled her stretchy yoga pants completely off. She'd ditched her thong earlier and by the heated, primal look on his face, he was pleased. He'd be able to scent her desire as well, no doubt.

A strange shyness threatened to overwhelm her, and that wasn't like her. But she was naked and completely at his mercy. The thought was startling.

While she was a lot stronger than she looked, she was no match for this man. In wolf or human form, this man—her mate, could hurt her if he wanted. He wouldn't though. She could feel it straight to her bones. He might make a living peddling weapons, but he didn't hurt women. Somehow, she just *knew* it.

"I don't have condoms," he rasped out, breaking the silence of the room.

She understood what he was asking without him actually having to voice it. Shifters didn't need protection because their DNA was different than that of humans. They couldn't get STDs, which meant they couldn't give them. And female shifters could only get pregnant twice a year. Thankfully, she was three months away from her cycle. "Don't worry, it's not my time—"

Her words were lost as he crushed his mouth over hers. In erotic little flicks, his tongue danced against hers. She briefly wondered what it would feel like to have him kiss her pussy like that. The erotic image that conjured brought a rush of heat to her belly.

As if he read her mind, he tore his mouth away from hers and carved a heated path of kisses along her jaw and neck. Continuing, he moved down her chest and stomach until he hovered at her mound. Oh yeah, he didn't waste any time getting to exactly where she wanted.

Grinning wickedly, he buried his head between her legs. On instinct, she lifted her hips to meet his mouth, wanting everything this male had to offer right now. He dipped his tongue between her folds and licked her slit from the bottom, up to her clit. When he traced his tongue around the sensitive nub, her hips rolled against him.

"Stephan." His name fell from her lips as a ragged moan.

She wasn't exactly sure what she'd been expecting from him in the bedroom, but it hadn't been *this*. Everything about Stephan was big and demanding. The man exuded absolute power. She'd thought he'd take her from behind, needing to dominate her. She'd been so sure that he'd fuck her long and hard in that typical shifter way.

This, however, she could handle. *This*, she wanted more of. With a tenderness she hadn't expected, his tongue stroked between her pussy lips before focusing on her most sensitive bundle of nerves. He gently teased her with his teeth and tongue, the alternating pressure driving her crazy.

She slid her fingers through his hair, digging into his head, and grinding against his face. She felt absolutely possessed. "Oh yeah, just like that."

He growled against her and she could scent his pleasure to her reaction. With each flick against her clit, her hips jerked wildly. He chuckled against her most sensitive flesh. The reverberations skittered over her skin, sending spiraling tingles straight to her aching nipples.

Her legs automatically tried to clench around his head, but he pressed calming hands to her inner thighs. The feel of his touch immediately relaxed her in a way she hadn't expected.

Unexpected tears sprang to her eyes at the gentle way he handled her. It had been so long since she'd let her guard down with anyone and the tenderness from this man was almost overwhelming. The energy coming off him was raw and primal, but he was restraining himself. For her.

She didn't know him, but he was her mate and that obviously meant something to him. It meant a lot to her too. A year ago, she'd have opened her arms to him and bonded with him before falling in love. A year ago she'd been so secure in who she was and her place in the world, that she'd have known that the love would eventually come with the mating — that nature would work itself out. A year ago, she'd been stupid and naïve.

Stephan ran his hands along Marisol's inner thighs and savored the feel of her soft, smooth skin. When he'd first seen her at the club he'd assumed she was delicate. She might be soft and petite, but he could sense the unleashed power humming through her. She was strong. Stronger than maybe *she* even realized, and it made him want her even more. He couldn't believe that yesterday he hadn't known this woman existed and now here she was about to come apart against his mouth. And he'd make damn sure she came, over and over. The need to make sure she was sated consumed his wolf, demanding he take care of his mate.

Dipping his tongue into her pussy once again, he groaned as he tasted her sweet essence. Each time he traced his tongue along her slick folds, her hips jerked. She was so sensitive. Like dynamite.

Mine. The word was loud in his head. Like he needed the reminder from his wolf.

More than anything his cock wanted inside her, but he was going to play this right. Something told him she expected him just to fuck her like an animal, and he wanted to give her enough foreplay so she never wanted to leave his bed. The more he touched and kissed her, the more the desire to bond took over. The need ran deep inside him, coursing through his veins with a rampant, wild intensity. He needed her to submit and accept his dominance.

Something was holding her back though. The fact that they were mates wasn't enough for her. He could sense it.

So he'd bind her with sex until her human side came around if that was what it took. Not that having endless hours of sex with this little vixen would be a chore. Just the thought of that and his hips jolted forward once.

He focused on her pulsing clit. Circling it with the tip of his tongue, he traced it over and over again until her entire body was trembling. He knew she enjoyed it so when she removed her hands from his head, he risked a quick glance up to find her fisting the sheets underneath her. Her head was thrown back, her eyes were closed and her body was stretched out like an offering. And for the moment, she was all his. A low groan rumbled in his chest.

He was thankful he was still dressed or he'd have just pounded into her, claimed her. *Focus.* He looked back at her swollen lips, mesmerized by the erotic sight before him. Her clit peeked out, just begging to be kissed some more. Sucking the glistening pearl into his mouth, he took pleasure when she moaned and arched her back against his kisses.

She was so close to finding release. He could feel it in every tight line of her body. Removing one of his hands from her inner thigh, he teased her entrance with his finger. As he rubbed her, she scooted closer, as if trying to force his finger inside her.

No way, sweetheart. I say when. He withdrew his hand and fisted her hips before tugging her ass closer to the edge of the bed.

Her head immediately snapped up. "Are you stopping?" she gasped. Her blue eyes shone bright in the light from the moon.

His throat clenched as he tried to find the words. *Any* words. "Not on your life," he managed to rasp out. He couldn't have stopped, even if he'd wanted to. She was his mate and his body wouldn't let him forget that.

She looked so beautiful stretched out on the bed. Never before had he felt so possessive, so greedy about a woman. He was possessive by nature, but he'd rarely felt jealous with the women he'd been with. As he stared down at Marisol, he couldn't imagine letting her go. For two werewolves to mate, there was supposed to be a choice. It was against their laws and against nature, but a male could technically impose his wants and take the choice away from the female. Any man who did that was a piece of shit. That was something he could never do to Marisol. She was his mate and even though the wolf inside him wanted to claim her, mark her for his own so the entire world would know she belonged to him, he couldn't take away her choice. He might be part wolf, but his human side ruled him.

He inserted one finger then two inside her wet sheath and shuddered when she clenched around him. She was so tight. It had obviously been a long time for her. His wolf and human side practically growled with satisfaction.

As he slowly dragged his fingers in and out of her, he reveled in the tiny moaning sounds she made. Each time he pressed against her inner wall, she tried to squeeze her thighs around him.

Her legs were bent and her feet were positioned at the edge of the bed, completely spreading her sweet folds open for him—silently begging for more. She painted such an erotic picture it was hard to concentrate on what he was doing.

"Touch yourself," he ordered hoarsely.

Without pause, her hands strayed to her breasts. His balls pulled up painfully as he watched her movements. She cupped both breasts then started strumming her nipples lightly with her thumbs.

Keeping his fingers between her legs, he continued sliding in and out of her then sucked her clit into his mouth.

The sharp, almost abrupt action had the intended effect. Her hips pitched forward so he increased the movements of his fingers. Her inner walls clamped wildly around him.

"Stephan," she moaned.

Just hearing his name on her lips was a turn-on. As he licked and circled her hardened bud, she pushed over the edge.

With a cry, she threaded her fingers through his hair as her body was overtaken with racks of pleasure. He could actually feel her orgasm roll over him. He wasn't sure if it was a mate thing or if they were just physically in tune. Whatever it was, it was hot as hell.

When her climax hit, she came long and hard and clenched even tighter around him, drenching his fingers with her slickness. As she came down from her high, she pushed up on her elbows and met his gaze, her breasts rising and falling with her panting breaths.

Pure satisfaction flowed through him at the blissful expression on her face.

"That was… I don't know…that was…"

"I hope the end of that thought is good," he murmured.

She laughed so lightly it was almost a giggle. Even though she was delicate and feminine and he barely knew her, the sound seemed foreign coming from her. Something told him she rarely laughed.

"Yes. Good. Very good." She got up onto her knees so that he got a full view of her naked body. He wasn't sure what she planned, but when she grasped at his belt and started unhooking it, he tugged his shirt over his head and tossed it across the room.

CHAPTER FOUR

Marisol's breath caught. She'd known he would look amazing, but his broad chest, ripped abdominal muscles and lean waist made her mouth water. She frowned when her gaze rested on a scar across his chest. It took a lot for werewolves to scar. The jagged wound was old but it looked as if it had been painful at one time. She placed a gentle hand over the faded white marking. "How old are you?" she whispered, not wanting to break the quiet of the room.

"One-hundred-sixty-eight." His voice was equally low.

Almost seventy years older than her. "When did you get this?"

He cleared his throat. It was obviously a painful subject for him, but he answered. "Vietnam."

"This must have hurt," she murmured.

He nodded and muttered something under his breath. She wasn't sure what to make of his admission. The man ran guns, but he'd cared enough to fight for his country at one time in his life. Interesting. And confusing.

"Stop thinking." His deep voice brought her back to the present.

She smiled and actually obeyed. He was right, thinking was overrated. She just wanted to feel tonight. Leaning forward, she pressed her mouth to his chest.

His muscles bunched under her touch. Knowing she had the ability to make this huge man shudder was an incredible turn-on.

After tracing her tongue around his small brown nipple, she took it between her teeth and tugged lightly. He actually jumped at the action. Lifting her head, she met his gaze. "You like that?"

"Yes." The word tore from his throat. She bent to kiss him again, but he grabbed the back of her head in a dominating grip and crushed his mouth over hers. He definitely liked to be in control, something she could get used to.

As his tongue danced with hers, her hands wound their way around his neck and she was flat on her back once again. This time, her sexy wolf was on top of her.

She rubbed her breasts against his bare chest. The soft thatch of his dark hair stimulated her already sensitized nipples. The orgasm he'd just given her had been good, but she wanted more. She wanted him inside her and more than anything, she wanted that elusive emotional connection she'd lost during the past year. It had been impossible to let anyone get close to her while on her mission, but being with him now, she realized how lonely she'd been. He'd been so giving and she wanted to make sure he found as much pleasure as he'd already given her.

He pushed up and immediately she mourned the loss of his mouth. He was in tune with what she wanted though because he finished what she'd started earlier and shucked his pants.

His cock sprang free and she involuntarily gasped. It had been longer than she cared to admit since she'd let a man in her bed, and he was long and thick. So very thick.

Before she had too much time to dwell on his size, he covered her body once more as he sought out her mouth. She knew it was crazy, but kissing him somehow felt familiar. Right even. She really *really* didn't want to care or think about the future, but allowing a man like Stephan into her bed was something she could get used to.

Pulling back from her just a fraction, he smoothed a hand over her hair. "Where'd you go just now?" he murmured against her mouth.

"What?" she whispered back. His tenderness tangled her up inside.

"You're thinking of something else." His breath tickled her skin.

She wanted to deny it, but the words stuck in her throat. Luckily, he didn't expect a response. He feathered light kisses along her jaw and earlobe until he centered on her neck.

She shuddered when he raked his teeth over her skin. Her neck tingled and burned with a desire to be claimed. Her entire body was screaming that this was her mate, but she simply couldn't submit to him. If she allowed him to pierce her skin, marking her as his own, they would be bonded for life and—no! She couldn't allow her thoughts to drift in that direction. It was pointless and it wouldn't be fair to him anyway.

When his head dipped to her breast, all those thoughts fled like dry leaves in the wind. He traced his tongue around her nipple in the same erotic motion he'd teased her clit. She was helpless to stop the way her entire body quivered. Instinctively she wrapped her legs around his waist and arched her back, lifting into him.

For a moment, he raised his head. "Are you ready?"

She nodded because she didn't trust her voice.

"Say it," he persisted, his gaze locked on hers. Oh yes, he was very demanding.

"Yes."

He briefly tested her pussy with a finger then pushed his cock into her with one hard thrust. Her inner walls expanded and tightened around him as she adjusted to his size. Instead of pounding into her, as she'd expected, he stayed immobile and bent his head back to her breast.

Why did he have to be so damn nice? So tender and gentle? He was making it much harder to think of him as an arms dealer who just happened to be her mate. Her heart squeezed.

She tensed as thoughts of a future with him entered her mind. They could have a family. She wouldn't be alone anymore. She could love someone and they'd love her back. Her life could be different. A burst of hope surged through her, but it was quickly doused with reality. She wasn't going to get a chance to have a family or a future. She didn't deserve it.

He must have sensed her distress because he lifted his head again. "Am I hurting you?"

"No, not even close."

In response, he began moving inside her. He kept his movements fluid and controlled. His neck muscles corded tightly and the raw energy rolling off him was unmistakable.

The man was definitely controlling himself and she found that it pleased her immensely. She locked her ankles behind his back and met him stroke for stroke.

His cock hit her deep inside and each time it dragged against her G-spot, she thought she'd explode. She was so close to climaxing again, she couldn't believe it. She just needed a little more stimulation.

Propping up on one elbow, he hovered over her and flicked and teased one of her nipples with his thumb. When he took her other hardened bud between his teeth and tugged, she lost it.

Her entire body felt overly sensitized. On one level she understood that they were mates but she couldn't understand how this virtual stranger had learned what her body needed so quickly.

The sweetest sensation surged through her. She ran her hands down his smooth back and clutched his backside in a tight grip as a forceful climax built and peaked. When she dug her fingers into his taut skin, it was as if she set him free.

Clutching the sheet next to her head, he shuddered as he emptied himself inside her. Over and over, he thrust until he finally spent himself. With a loud shout, he collapsed on her, melding his body to hers.

She threaded her fingers through his hair with one hand and gently stroked along his back with her other. His muscles clenched under her soft touch and she could feel his erratic heartbeat against her chest.

After a long moment, he groaned and rolled off her. Before she could protest, he disappeared into the bathroom.

Sighing, she lay against the pillow and stared at the ceiling. Getting tangled up with this wolf was probably the dumbest thing she could have done, but it was so hard to care when her body was completely satisfied.

She glanced up when he returned. Frowning, she nodded at the cloth in his hand. "What's that?"

"I told you I take care of what's mine." He sat on the edge of the bed and before she could guess what he meant to do, he reached between the juncture of her thighs and cleaned her. The soft stroking was soothing and as pleasurable as it was unexpected. Her whole body sighed at the consideration he showed her.

No! She refused to fall under his spell or to even dream about a future.

When he was finished he tossed the cloth onto the floor and slid into the bed next to her. Without a word he pulled her so that her back was against his chest. The curve of his body was so warm and strong. His breathing was slightly labored and she could feel his cock lengthening against her back.

Thanks to biology, shifters were able to have sex for hours on end. He was obviously ready to go again, but she wasn't, and it surprised her that he wasn't pressing her for more. It made her throat tighten.

If someone had asked her a day ago what she thought about Stephan Vasquez, she would have had a sure answer. Now she realized she didn't know anything at all and that terrified her.

CHAPTER FIVE

Marisol's eyes flew open with a start. She glanced around the foreign bedroom and frowned when she realized she was alone. The espresso colored silk sheets were rumpled next to her, but the bed was otherwise empty. And Stephan wasn't in the connected bathroom either. She knew because she couldn't smell his scent. Last night had been amazing and it surprised her that she wanted to see him again so soon. She'd been waking up alone for the past year with no one to care if she lived or died.

She slipped out of the huge bed and walked to the window. Her eyes widened as she took in the landscape. The night before she'd been too wrapped up in Stephan for her surroundings to even register. In addition to a private dock, a boat—scratch that, *a yacht*—a perfectly manicured lawn and an Olympic sized pool, Stephan had a completely unobstructed view of the ocean. Calm, glistening and expansive—the teal-blue water seemed to stretch out forever.

It was a little chilly out, but she'd love to try his pool. Then her stomach rumbled, and she realized how hungry she actually was. Casting a backward glance at the pool, she tugged on the clothes he'd given her the night before and went in search of Stephan. She still couldn't believe she'd found her mate in a Miami nightclub of all places. Even though she wanted to call what they'd shared the night before simply sex, she couldn't.

He'd taken such gentle care with her, it was frightening. She didn't want to care for this man. Didn't want to feel anything. Somehow he'd gotten under her skin without even trying.

Her feet were quiet along the hallway runner, the stairs and the wood floor that led to the kitchen. The aroma of rich hazelnut coffee and something—*someone*—tickled her nose. Whoever she scented was female.

Her canines tingled in annoyance. Marisol frowned as she stepped into the kitchen. "Hello?" She nearly jumped back when a tall—very pretty—redhead popped up from behind the large island in the middle of the room.

The redhead's blue eyes widened. "Hi...who are you?"

Marisol didn't sense any danger from the woman, but she was surprised at the jolt of jealousy that shot through her. Why the hell was another woman in Stephan's house? Before that thought had fully formed another scent hit her with startling intensity. This woman was marked by someone and it most definitely wasn't Stephan. Marisol's jealousy instantly dissipated.

"You're human," she blurted out before she could censor herself. She hadn't even realized humans and werewolves could mate.

A curious smile played across the woman's face. "A few months ago, I might have thought you were crazy if you'd said that to me... I'm Carly by the way. Are you friends with Nick's parents or something? Alisha said I could stop by, but she didn't mention anything about anyone being here."

"Uh, who are Nick and Alisha?"

The redhead's mouth pulled into a thin line and a wave of blatant distrust rolled off her. "Who are *you*?"

Marisol opened her mouth, though to say what, she had no idea. The sound of a door handle jiggling stopped her. She turned to find a completely naked Stephan walking in from the backyard.

"Oh my Lord! I don't want to see that!" Faster than Marisol would have thought possible, Carly threw a dishtowel at Stephan and covered her eyes. "For the love of God, cover yourself!"

To Marisol's surprise, his neck and face turned four shades of red. "What the hell are you doing here?" he muttered.

"Your mom sent me over to grab candlesticks for Nick's birthday thing. Which by the way, you still haven't responded to... Are you covered yet?"

He shot Marisol a guilty look and cleared his throat. "Yeah."

Carly dropped her hand and glanced back and forth between Stephan and Marisol with narrowed eyes. "Why are you staying at the guesthouse? I thought you were out of town or something."

"Guesthouse? You don't live here?" Marisol asked.

"Not exactly," he muttered.

"Are you related to him?" Marisol directed her question to Carly because she had a sneaking suspicion that Stephan had been holding back a lot from her.

Carly nodded. "He's my brother-in-law—"

"Damn it, will you just stop?" Stephan thundered.

Both women turned to stare at him.

"I'm sorry, I didn't mean to yell. I just...ah, damn it." He raked a hand through his dark hair and cursed under his breath.

This woman was mated to a werewolf and as far as Marisol knew, only *one* pack lived in Miami. If Stephan had lied about where he lived... "What's your last name?" she asked Carly.

The pretty woman bit her bottom lip and cast a nervous glance at Stephan, but she answered. "Lazos."

Marisol swiveled to Stephan who held his hands up in defense. When he did, he dropped his towel.

The redhead averted her eyes again. "Oh for the love of... I'm leaving...it was nice to meet you, uh, what was your name?" she asked Marisol.

Despite the barely leashed anger humming through her, she gave the other woman a tight smile. "I'm Marisol."

"It was so nice meeting you. Sorry about barging in. I didn't mean to interrupt anything...okay, then, I'll..." Oversized candlesticks in hand, she brushed past her and hurried from the room. Her heels clacked against the tile of the kitchen and echoed as she moved throughout the rest of the house.

When Marisol heard the front door slam, she blindly reached for one of the coffee mugs on the counter and hurled it at Stephan. She'd had enough wolves lie to her to last a lifetime. "You lying son of a bitch! Is this some kind of game?"

"I can explain!" He ducked out of the way and the mug smashed against the wall.

Before the broken shards had even hit the floor, she picked up another mug. As she hauled back to throw it, he grabbed her and held her arms by her side. Using the extra body weight he had on her, he shifted positions and pinned her against the island counter.

Despite his strength, she struggled against him. "Let me go, you bastard!" she shrieked. Against her will, a sob tore from her throat and tears started to fall. Everyone was a liar! *Even her mate.*

"Don't cry! Shit, *kardia mou*, don't cry." He started to loosen his hold but when he did she got an arm free and punched at his chest.

There was no give to the broad expanse of his muscles, but it made her feel better. Since he wasn't holding her legs, she lashed out and kicked him in the shin. He winced but she doubted it even fazed him. "You lying piece of shit! I'm leaving." She tried to kick him again, but he hooked his much larger leg around the back of her knees, immobilizing her. She wiggled again. In that instant, she hated how short she was. If she could just get a leg free…

"I'm an undercover agent for the DEA!" he shouted in her ear.

She stopped fighting and her head snapped up at the admission. "What?"

"Fuck. Fuck, fuck, fuck!" He released his grip and pushed away from her.

Stephan turned his back to Marisol. He was in such deep shit he couldn't even wrap his mind around it. This woman might be his intended mate, but that didn't matter. He didn't know anything about her. It was doubtful, but for all he knew, she was a mole for Perez.

When she'd said she was leaving, something inside him had snapped. He couldn't lose her. Not when he'd just found her.

He swiveled back to face her. She still stood next to the island. Her hands were clasped so tightly in front of her, her knuckles had turned white. They faced off, neither saying anything. Hell, he didn't know where to start.

Finally she broke the silence. "So, you're not an arms dealer, huh?" Her quiet voice seemed overly loud in the even quieter room.

"Nope."

"How do I know you're telling the truth?"

"Why would I bring you to my family's home? When I realized who you were, I wanted to keep you safe. Stephan *Vasquez* doesn't care about women, but Stephanos *Lazos* cares about his mate. I couldn't let Perez know you meant anything to me so I brought you here. I sure as hell didn't plan for you to meet my sister-in-law."

She stared hard at him for a moment then nervously rubbed her hands over the front of her pants. Even though she held his gaze, a light blush of pink stained her cheeks. "Sorry about your coffee mug."

"That's the least of my worries," he muttered. He might have just screwed up one of the biggest takedowns he'd ever been involved with. It had taken decades to find a job he enjoyed. Hiding the fact that he was a werewolf was hard enough. He wasn't even sure how he was going to tell his boss that his cover was blown.

"I'm not going to tell anyone." Her voice was barely a whisper.

"What?"

"I won't… I'm not going to tell anyone who you are if that's what you're worried about. There's no one I could tell even if I wanted to."

Her last statement caught his attention. "What pack are you from? No lies."

"Tell me about yours first...please." The pleading note in her voice tore at his gut. Standing in front of him, she suddenly looked lost and impossibly young. By shifter standards he guessed she was close to a hundred, but she looked to be about twenty-two. Without the makeup she'd had on last night, she *barely* looked that.

"My real name is Stephanos Lazos. I hail from Leontio, Greece, though I haven't lived there for over a century. My father, *my Alpha*, is Lucas Lazos, my mother is Alisha, and my two brothers are Thomas and Nicolas—Nick for short. You just met his new wife, Carly. She's one of the few humans who know about us. For now we call Miami home but we'll probably move in a decade. I have a lot of cousins, but there are too many to name. Your turn."

She bit her bottom lip as she assessed him. He felt as if he were under a microscope, but if it got her to talk, he didn't care about the scrutiny. "My last name is Cabrera and my entire pack is dead. I'm originally from Asuncion, Mexico, but my Alpha moved us to northern California when I was a pup. We moved around but I had never left the state...until a year ago when I came to Florida. I literally have no one in my life so you have nothing to worry about from me."

"You have me." The words slipped out.

Disbelief flitted across her face, but it happened so fast and then her protective mask was back in place. Her pain and loneliness tore at his insides. He couldn't keep his distance any longer. Closing the gap between them, he wrapped his arms around her and pulled her into a comforting embrace.

At first she tried to pull away, but finally she wrapped her arms around his waist and laid her head against him. She was quiet, but he could feel the wetness of her tears on his skin. His chest tightened as the thick shroud of her emotions surrounded him.

A dozen questions raced through his mind—like why the hell was she in Florida and why had her entire pack *died*? Even though he needed to ask them, he knew *she* needed to be held. Whether she admitted it or not. His protective instinct kicked into overdrive as she pressed her lean body against his.

He searched for a way to distract. "You want to go for a run?" he murmured into her hair.

"Is it safe?"

"My pack owns a private stretch of beach here. That's where I just came from."

She pulled her head back to meet his gaze. Her eyes glittered with unshed tears but there was a hopeful spark in her eyes. "I'd love to."

She stepped away from him and stared at him expectantly. His older brother, Nick, had connected telepathically with his mate after the first time they'd had sex, but Stephan couldn't link with Marisol. Or maybe she was intentionally blocking him out. Either way, he wished he knew what was going on in her head at that moment.

"Uh, it's this way." He motioned toward the back door.

Tentatively she followed him. When they were outside on the stone patio and she didn't make a move to shift, he realized she might be shy about undergoing the change in front of a stranger.

He didn't have a lot—or any—modesty, but she was in a new area with someone she barely knew. Hell, she'd lost her entire pack. That was something he couldn't even fathom. Without his family, he'd go crazy. It was a wonder she hadn't.

Wordlessly he turned and changed forms, hoping to give her some privacy and to let her see him at his weakest moment. As his bones shifted and broke, then realigned, the pain hit with the intensity of a tsunami. While the pain was inevitable, it was always fleeting. It quickly faded until he felt nothing more than pleasurable tingles along his spine.

In wolf form, his auditory senses were amplified a hundred fold. Behind him, he could hear her clothes hit the ground then he heard her sharp intake of breath before she made the change herself.

Before he could turn, he felt a cold nose against his fur. When he turned to look at her, he growled protectively. It shouldn't surprise him, but she was a small wolf. Maybe seventy-five pounds and her shifted form was that of a brown and white Alaskan malamute. She was...cute. It was the only word to describe her.

She nudged him again and yipped playfully. In response, he trotted across the patio toward the open stretch of sand. Instead of following, she ran a few feet ahead then turned to face him. With her paw, she kicked up the grains in his direction and yipped again.

Follow me, he projected with his mind, but she didn't seem to understand. His pack could communicate telepathically in wolf form and while it was just a pack thing, he'd thought it might be possible with Marisol since they were mates. Hopefully after they bonded they'd be able to communicate that way.

She crouched down on all fours as if ready to attack but her tail wagged playfully. When he bounded toward her, she leapt away from him and ran toward the ocean. Keeping his pace slower so he wouldn't scare her, he followed suit and let her lead the way. He liked this side of her. She was definitely easier going in wolf form.

As they ran along the beach, he let go of his earlier worries. He'd have to face them eventually, but for now he let the salty essence of the ocean envelop his senses while he enjoyed this time with his mate.

CHAPTER SIX

Marisol forced herself to relax as the shower jets pummeled her shoulders. She guessed the bathroom had been custom designed because everything in it was higher and wider than normal and very expensive looking. The marble shower—which was big enough for four people—and matching oversized tub had the splendor of the old-world. Combined with the dark cabinets and warm fall colors of the room, it was actually very inviting. Traditional in style.

The run with Stephan earlier had been exhilarating, but now she had a bigger dilemma. Stephan wasn't the asshole she thought he was.

He was a freaking DEA agent. He was one of the good guys.

Which meant he wanted to arrest Perez. She didn't want the man behind bars though, she wanted him six feet under. He was an absolute monster. Now she wasn't sure what to do. One part of her wanted to tell Stephan what Perez was capable of, but she worried he'd try to keep her away from him. What was she thinking, of course he would. He was a male shifter and her mate. Males were always so damn protective.

She couldn't afford that. Not when she'd come so far. Not when she was so close.

Stephan's earthy scent tickled her senses. He must be close by. As soon as they'd returned from their run she'd changed back to her human form then darted off to take a shower. She knew he had questions but she wasn't prepared to answer them so she'd run away like a coward. She should have known he'd follow.

Her eyes were closed as the water rushed over her body, but she knew he was in the bathroom now. He wasn't making a sound, but she could practically feel him in the room with her. Maybe it was the mate connection because she swore she felt him caressing her skin. "Why don't you just get in here?" she asked.

"I am." She opened her eyes at his deep voice. He was right in front of her and she hadn't even heard him approach.

"You're very quiet," she murmured.

"That's because I'm the big bad wolf," he growled playfully.

She liked this side of him, even though part of her wished she could still view him as an arms dealer. Still holding the sudsy loofah in her hand, she shifted out of the way so he could join her under the water.

As he stepped under the steady stream, he reached for her hips, but she swatted his hands away and swept the loofah over his chest and stomach.

A soapy river trailed down his chest and her gaze couldn't help but follow it. His cock twitched as she drank in the sight of him.

"Are you just going to stare, or are you going to touch?" His deep voice brought her gaze back up with a start.

Stephan's dark eyes glittered with barely contained lust. Without responding, she set the loofah on the built-in bench and knelt in front of him. She was most definitely going to touch all she wanted. He was like a tasty piece of candy and she was going to savor the time she had with him.

Grasping his cock at the base, she ran her clasped fist up the length of him, then back down again.

"Marisol." Her name tore from his throat on a groan as he pulsed in her tight grip.

She risked a quick glance upward. His eyes were closed and his chest rose and fell rapidly. She loved being able to make him pant. Grinning in satisfaction, she leaned forward and licked the underside of his thick shaft. She kissed and nibbled along his length. Each time her lips or tongue touched his cock, she could feel almost imperceptible tremors racing through his body.

All the muscles pulled tight in her body as she licked him. Knowing she could bring him pleasure made her ache with an undeniable need. He'd taken so much care the night before making sure she found release, she wanted to do the same for him.

Keeping her hand tightly around the bottom of his cock, she wrapped her lips around his crown and sucked lightly. Thick and long, the man was a freaking fantasy.

"Oh yeah," he murmured, sinking his fingers into her hair and tightening on the strands with a gentle pull.

Those two words were all the incentive she needed. She traced her tongue around the crown before taking him fully in her mouth and sucking hard. With her free hand she played with his balls, lightly tugging on them while she continued working his cock with her mouth. When his hips started gently thrusting, and he moaned out her name over and over in a sort of prayer, her nipples hardened in response.

Water rushed down her back and over her chest but she could barely feel it. All she cared about was getting him off. Bringing him pleasure was suddenly the most important thing. It was totally primal, but this was her mate and she wanted to hear him crying out her name. She didn't have to wait long.

His cock jerked in her mouth and she realized he was close to coming. When his grip tightened on her hair, she increased her movements.

Her fist squeezed and pumped faster as she sucked him harder. And that was all it took.

"Gonna come." His voice was hoarse. "Marisol, shit…" Another groan wrenched from him.

She rarely swallowed, but she wanted — no, needed — to taste him. It wasn't lost on her that he gave her the opportunity to pull back either. But moving away was the last thing she wanted. She placed a hand on his thigh for support as he exploded in her mouth.

His come hit the back of her throat in long, hard jets. Keeping her lips firmly around his cock, she continued sucking and kissing him until he sagged against the wall.

She lifted her head and couldn't stop the smile spreading across her face. He looked so satisfied, it was hard not to feel pleased with herself. His dark gaze sought hers out and before she realized what he planned, he hooked his hands under her arms and lifted her up.

As his mouth crushed over hers in a demanding, erotic dance, he fisted her hips and pulled her roughly against him.

She clutched his shoulders for support and when he tugged her bottom lip between his teeth, she arched her back. Tingles shot down her spine and the ache between her legs grew with each second that passed.

It had been so long since she'd been with a man and she'd thought last night would quench her thirst. Instead she was primed and ready to go for hours and hours. Even her breasts were heavy with need, every single part of her body over sensitized.

His hands began a slow trail up her waist until they settled right under her breasts. He cupped them and in unison, rubbed his thumbs over her nipples.

Desire coiled in her belly. She desperately needed to find release; her wolf was clawing at her in demand. When she groaned into his mouth, he pulled his head back a fraction.

"What do you want, *kardia mou*?" His breath was a whisper over her swollen lips.

"I want you inside me." She spoke softly, not wanting to break the intimacy of the moment.

His eyes flared with white-hot lust at her declaration. Immediately, his hands strayed from her breasts and around her back. He grasped her ass and squeezed lightly. When he did, her inner walls tightened. She savored the feel of his fingers caressing her wet skin, even as she wanted more.

"Hands on the wall," he murmured, sending more shivers skittering across her skin, straight to her toes.

"What?"

"Now." The word was a subtle order.

She instinctively clenched her legs at the command that resonated through his voice. Slowly, she turned around and placed her hands on the cool tile.

"Now spread your legs." He hadn't shaved that morning so his stubble tickled her neck when he spoke close to her ear.

His cock pressed against her back and when she did as he ordered, a cool draft rolled over her slick folds. They were already swollen with need and he hadn't even touched her.

When she felt his mouth on her shoulder, she tensed for a split second as she wondered what he would do. But he didn't attempt to mark her. He simply feathered kisses along her back.

The trail led straight to her ass. He pulled away so that neither his mouth nor hands were touching her. She couldn't see him, but she knew he had to be kneeling behind her. He was able to see every little imperfection about her. She was spread open for him and she was suddenly very aware how much at his mercy she was. If he wanted to claim her, bond with her, he could. Her instinct told her he wouldn't without her permission, but a sudden dose of fear poisoned her thoughts and her muscles tightened.

She started to close her legs when he dipped a finger inside her. At the same time, he raked his teeth over her behind and her body pushed her insecure thoughts away. So far Stephan had been nothing but giving and kind. She was so wet it was almost embarrassing. Her slickness flowed freely over his hand and down the inside of her thighs.

His finger felt good, but she wanted a lot more. She needed his cock to fill her, stretch her, take her. "I want *you* inside me."

WORTH THE RISK | 141

"Soon." He continued teasing her sheath for a moment before trailing his finger back to her tight rosette. She clenched as he pressed his finger against it. The thought of letting him touch her there was surprisingly erotic. Especially since they barely knew each other.

"Relax." Again, his voice was commanding.

Braced against the wall, she trembled. He wouldn't hurt her. She was sure of it. If she told him to stop, he would. Forcing her body to listen, she imagined what it would feel like when he once again filled her. When she exhaled a long breath, he slipped his finger into her hole. Her head fell back on a soundless cry at the foreign, yet erotic sensation.

In her hundred years she'd never let a man touch her back there. She'd never had the desire to. Now she wondered why she'd waited so long. The slight stretching filled her with indescribable pleasure.

He continued pushing into her with slow measured movements. Her body clenched around his finger and her inner walls spasmed out of control, wanting to be filled. This male knew exactly how to make her crazy.

"You're so tight." His deep voice sounded strained.

Her breath caught as he penetrated deeper. The building ache threatened to make her lose her mind. Desperate for relief, she reached between her legs and touched herself. Gently rubbing between her swollen folds and over her pulsing clit eased the ache some, but she still needed more. She needed Stephan.

Without warning, he withdrew his finger and seized her hips. Before she had a chance to prepare herself, his cock plunged inside her. Her inner walls stretched and expanded, but in this position it was easier than the night before to take his size.

He reached between them and ran his callused palm over her ass, tracing a finger down her cleft. This time she wasn't nervous when he slid a thick finger inside her tight rosette. A soft moan escaped her lips. "Stephan…"

With wild and almost uncontrolled thrusts, he rocked into her. The rougher movements were different from their first time yet her body felt on fire. It was almost as if her skin burned for his touch everywhere. Her ass clenched around his finger as her pussy clamped around his cock.

It was too much to take. Bending forward a few more inches, she moved her hips back against his, meeting his insistent strokes. Every time his shaft slid into her, she pushed closer to finding her release. Combined with the steady probing of his finger, she finally pushed over the edge in a soundless wave of ecstasy.

Her mouth opened, but no sound came out as a violent jolt of pleasure rippled through her core. It started between her legs and pushed outward, moving across her belly and breasts. The climax built and built until it felt as if she could actually explode from the pleasure. She reached out to hold onto something but the tile was too slick and her knees felt like rubber.

Stephan could feel Marisol's body contracting around his finger and cock simultaneously. It took all the willpower he had not to come again. She might not realize it, but he wasn't done with her yet. Not by a long shot.

He needed to bind her to him and he planned to do that in the most primal way possible.

As she rode through the last part of her orgasm, her legs gave way. Hooking his free hand around her waist, he pulled her up so that her back pressed against his chest.

Slight tremors raced through her body. Strange that he could feel the tremors almost as if they were coursing through him. He bit back a groan as he slowly withdrew from her. His own body screamed for release, but this was about her. She turned around on unsteady legs so he kept his arm hooked around her waist.

"Are you okay?"

"More than okay." She laughed lightly. "That was...amazing."

Pure satisfaction filled him. He didn't know how he knew, but she'd never allowed a man to touch her the way he had. Later, when they knew each other better and she completely trusted him, he wanted to use more than his finger. "I'm not through with you yet."

"You're out of your mind." She pressed a weak hand to his chest, but he turned off the shower and grabbed a towel.

She was silent as he rung the dampness out of her hair. When he finished drying her, he picked her up and carried her to the bedroom.

Before her back had hit the sheets, he claimed her mouth in a possessive, demanding kiss. He loved taking her from behind, but he loved kissing her even more. She had a distinct, sweet taste that was something purely hers.

Even though he'd just been inside her, he wanted more. As he stretched out on top of her, he covered her mound with his hand and played with her clit. She'd just come, but he simply wanted to touch her, bring her as much pleasure as she could handle.

She arched her back against him so he bent toward her chest. When he drew her ripe nipple between his teeth and pressed down, the doorbell rang.

Marisol tensed underneath him. "Are you expecting someone?"

Sighing, he stopped sucking her breast and laid his head on her chest. "No."

He wasn't expecting anyone, but that didn't mean his family wouldn't stop by unannounced. Now that they knew he was here and that he'd brought a woman to one of the family homes, they'd be stopping by to check her out. His pack was just nosy like that. If he had to guess, he'd say one of his brothers was at the door.

Or his Alpha.

CHAPTER SEVEN

Antonio Perez pressed his hand to the biometric scanner and waited for the solid steel door to open. Seconds later, it drew back with a whoosh.

Dr. Reed looked up as Perez entered the sterile room. "You're just in time. This latest strain is showing more promise than the others."

Antonio looked through the glass at the two subjects chained down. "How are the subjects fairing?"

"These two are stronger than the other werewolves. The small one is doing the best. She's...different. Her blood is different from the other one. It's working better with the mutation."

Antonio narrowed his gaze at the petite Spanish woman chained down. *Woman.* That word was laughable. The werewolf before him had so much unleashed power and he planned to share that power with governments willing to pay enough. If it wasn't for the sedatives pumping through her system, he had no doubt she'd be able to break through her restraints.

With the right formula, he was going to create super soldiers. But first, the drugs needed to be perfected. "How did the human test subjects fair with this strain?"

"It's only been a week but one male subject is adapting perfectly. His DNA is bonding with the formula and his strength has tripled. No side effects either. He's the exception though. The others...weren't so lucky. However, it's my opinion that the current group of humans is too weak. If we're going to truly examine the possibilities, I need men who are physically above average. Their bodies will go through an extreme transformation and they need to be able to handle it."

"You'll have your men. Vasquez is coming tonight. Will everything be ready?"

The doctor shifted from one foot to another. "Possibly."

"What the hell am I paying you for? You've had years to perfect this! We've finally found the perfect werewolves. Vasquez has the contacts I need. If I renege on this, he'll kill all of us! Maybe I should find someone more willing—"

"No, no, everything will be ready." He shuffled away, mumbling to himself as he peered into one of his microscopes.

"It better be." Perez dealt in heavy quantities of drugs but as a very lucrative arms-dealer, Vasquez had the contacts he needed and Perez couldn't afford to make him wait. It wasn't as if he could call up third-world dictators or other heads of state and schedule a meeting. No, something like this would require a go-between. Someone respected and feared would need to introduce him and Stephan Vasquez was just the man.

Antonio had no clue how the doctor's mind worked and he really didn't care, so long as he gave him what he wanted. Before leaving the lab he strolled to the thick two-way window and raked his gaze over the two naked subjects. They were different in physical appearance but both equally stunning. One was a petite brunette with perfect round tits any man would enjoy. The other was tall, blonde with a body made for modeling. That was what she'd done at one time. Now she was just another missing person.

The two before him were his favorites so he was thankful they hadn't died during the experiments. Kidnapping them had been time consuming and expensive, but after he'd killed the males of their packs and poisoned the females with smaller doses of silver, it had been easy enough. Even though they couldn't internally ingest it without getting sick, for some reason, silver bonds had a calming effect on the werewolves. In addition to the drugs he was giving them, they were helpless.

As if she knew she was being watched, the petite brunette with the midnight black eyes turned to stare at him. It was impossible that she could see through the mirrored window, but she glared directly at him nonetheless. He walked a few feet to the left and her eyes followed his movements.

His skin crawled under her scrutiny and he could actually feel himself getting weaker. It made no sense, but he had the strangest desire to open the door to her cell. An intoxicating sluggishness flowed through his arms and legs, as if he were stoned. Antonio walked toward the door, but the doctor's nasally voice dragged him back to reality.

"Yes, yes. We are almost ready," he muttered.

He looked back at Doctor Reed who was mumbling to himself as he jotted down notes.

"I'll be back this afternoon. Make sure the drug and the video is ready." Without waiting for a response, he hurried from the room. Anger hummed through him as he strode through his house. He wasn't sure what the hell had just happened in there, but he knew one thing. Once they'd gotten what they needed from the pretty werewolves, he was going to fuck that dark-haired one long and hard before he killed her. He might even keep her around as his slave for a while. He'd give the blonde to his men. So many of them had already shown interest, it would be a shame to let that body go to waste.

Stephan didn't bother looking through the peephole. He knew who was on the other side before opening the door. He pulled the heavy oak door open to find Thomas waiting.

"Hey, little Brother. I hear you've got company." A tired smile lit up Thomas' normally unreadable expression.

Stephan stepped back to let his brother inside. "I guess the whole family knows I've got a she-wolf here?"

"Nope. Just me." Thomas' shoes were silent as he stepped onto the tiled foyer.

"Carly didn't tell everyone?"

"Nah. She told Nick, who called me."

Relief rolled over him immediately. "I thought for sure she'd have called mom by now."

"I think she wanted to, but Nick stopped her."

Stephan bit back a smile. He couldn't be certain, but he was fairly sure Carly was still pissed at him for keeping her mate away from her all those months ago. It had been necessary at the time—and only a couple days—but she hadn't seen it that way.

Thomas continued. "So who is she?"

He glanced back at the stairwell. It was empty. "Her name is Marisol Cabrera... She's my mate."

Thomas' dark eyebrows shot up. "You're sure?"

"Yes."

His brother's lips pulled into a thin line. "Cabrera, why does that sound familiar?"

"I still don't know much about her, but she's without a pack. She said her pack died."

"How?"

"She didn't say."

"And you didn't ask?" Thomas' gravelly voice was incredulous.

"It's complicated."

"*I'll bet.* You stink of sex. Is the reason you haven't asked because you haven't come up for air?"

Stephan growled at his oldest brother who only laughed.

Just as suddenly, Thomas' face sobered. "Cabrera... Dad said their Alpha wasn't at the last Council meeting and no one has been able to contact any of their pack since."

Stephan frowned. The last Council meeting had been almost six months ago. Packs from around the world met twice every year to get updates on one another, to hold trials for rogue werewolves and to handle any general business. It wasn't unusual for some Alphas to occasionally miss a meeting, but they always sent someone in their stead. "I'll speak to her about it today."

"See that you do. Dad will want to meet with her soon."

Stephan bit back a sharp retort. The protectiveness humming through him was expected, but if what his brother said was true, Marisol would have to come up with an explanation for why her pack had suddenly died and she was still alive. He'd just been avoiding the fact. "I know."

"Why not bring her to Nick's birthday party on Wednesday? It'll give her a chance to meet everyone. She can talk to dad before the party starts."

It was Saturday. Four days should be enough time to convince his intended mate to tell him the truth about what had happened to her pack. It wasn't that she'd outright refused, but it had been obvious she hadn't wanted to tell him. While he didn't want to push, he had no choice. "We'll be there...if you could keep it under wraps that I'm staying here —"

"I won't let mom find out."

"Thank you." With the exception of his cousin Phillip who'd driven him the night before, no one knew he was staying at the guesthouse. Well, now Carly and his brothers knew too, but that didn't bother him. The one person he really didn't want finding out was his mother. She'd been hounding Carly to have children for months and if she discovered he'd found his mate, there would be no end to her interference. It wouldn't matter that it was loving and with good intentions, it would still drive him insane.

After his brother left, he started up the stairs only to find Marisol descending them. "I was just coming to find you. That was my brother."

"Oh." Her cheeks tinged a dark crimson and from her guilty scent, he guessed she'd been eavesdropping. "I need something to wear other than this." She motioned to the t-shirt and yoga pants.

Even though all he wanted to do was strip her naked and *keep* her naked, he knew she was right. She needed clothes and he needed to call his boss. "Grab your dress and shoes. I'll call my driver and we'll head to your place in a few minutes."

Wordlessly she nodded and hurried back up the stairs. Once she was out of sight, he headed to the office and called Reuben.

He answered on the second ring. "Hey." He definitely didn't sound as angry as he'd been last night. That had to be a good sign.

Stephan just hoped his boss was feeling generous this morning. "Listen, I know I acted unprofessionally last night but I ran into a family friend at the club. She was about to blow my cover so I had to leave with her."

"Shit," Reuben muttered.

"I've explained things to her and she'll be staying with my family the next couple days so there's no chance of her relaying the information to anyone—not that I believe she would anyway. Still, it's a risk so if you want to call off the operation, I understand." He couldn't tell his boss the entire truth, but it pacified his conscience somewhat to tell him they'd been compromised.

"No, we've worked too hard to bring Perez down. You sure she'll keep her mouth shut?"

"Positive—and she won't make any unsupervised phone calls anyway. She's tight with my family, it won't be an issue." He cringed at the lie, but there was no other way.

"Do you think we should put her under protective custody?"

"No. That'll just scare her. Besides, the meet is tonight—and it's my ass on the line. I trust her." The fact that his boss had even asked as opposed to telling him, meant he didn't want to go through the hassle of putting someone under protective custody. If they did, more people would be privy to their operation and that meant a greater chance of a leak.

"All right. As soon as you hear from Perez, contact me and you better get back to your cover house. He's got men watching the place and it'll look odd if you don't show up."

"I've got a few things to take care of but I'll be there this afternoon." He needed to explain to Marisol why he needed her to stay at his family's beach house tonight as opposed to her own place. They had a good security system and more importantly, he was going to have one of his brothers stay with her to keep an eye on her. It wasn't as if he could bring her to Perez's home.

"See that you are."

As soon as they disconnected, he scrubbed a hand over his face and sighed. He'd finally met his mate and it couldn't have come at a more complicated time in his life.

CHAPTER EIGHT

Marisol glanced over her shoulder, worried that Stephan would check on her. After tossing half her closet into her suitcase, she grabbed her pistol, extra ammunition and the printed layout of Perez's home she'd acquired. She quickly tucked the weapon into the bottom of her bag.

She'd tried telling Stephan she'd be fine staying at her apartment, but he'd been absolutely unwilling to listen. Not that she was actually complaining about that part. The sex with Stephan was like nothing she'd ever imagined.

She rolled her luggage into the living room to find him sitting on her couch. The tufted loveseat hadn't been made for comfort and with his big size, he looked incredibly uncomfortable.

"I've got all my stuff." For some reason, having him scrutinize her place made her nervous. When she'd moved to Miami, she hadn't planned to stay as long as she had and decorating hadn't been high on her list of things to do.

He stood and immediately reached for her suitcase. Instinctively, her grip on it tightened, but she forced herself to let go. She reminded herself that he wasn't planning to dig through her things, he was just being a gentleman. He was acting like a mate.

As he started to roll it toward the door, she cleared her throat. Even though she desperately wanted to get him out of her place, she still had unanswered questions. "Why can't I stay here tonight?"

"I'll tell you once we're out of here."

"No. I want to know *now*." She sat on the edge of the couch and crossed her legs. The temperature had dropped considerably since yesterday so she'd put on a tight turtleneck sweater dress with knee-high boots with four-inch heels. She didn't miss the way his gaze lingered on her legs and she also couldn't help the way her panties dampened at the evident lust in his dark eyes. This mating pull was insane. She'd never really believed the attraction could be as intense as this. Whatever she'd thought in the past, she hadn't even come close to the reality.

"I can throw you over my shoulder, Marisol." His voice was wry.

"You could, but I won't make it easy for you. Do you really want people paying attention to you? Remembering you were here?" She couldn't bite back a grin at his annoyed expression. He might be an alpha wolf but so was she. She didn't take well to orders, even if they were from her mate.

He swore softly under his breath and released her luggage. "I'm meeting with Perez tonight and in case things go wrong, I don't want you here alone. It's doubtful he even knows we left the club together, but I won't take the chance."

"You're meeting with him? What does that mean?" Her heart quickened.

"I... I can't tell you."

"Why can't I go with you?" she persisted. If he was meeting Perez, this was the perfect opportunity for her to get to him.

"You just can't."

"So you're going to go party with him and a bunch of his whores and you want me to stay home? If that's how you treat your mate—"

"Damn it, Marisol! You know that's not what I meant. This is my job."

Wordlessly she stood and strode past him. Something told her that no matter how much she gave him the silent treatment, it wouldn't matter. She needed to devise a plan to make him listen to her. It sounded as if tonight's meeting was important and it might be the only chance she ever got to kill Perez. If only she could convince Stephan to let her go with him. No, that would never work. He was in protective mate mode. She'd just find another way to get to Perez.

She was silent as they made their way to the elevator and once they were cruising down the road in his dark SUV, she finally broke the silence when it was obvious he wasn't planning to. Apparently this male was stubborn. "Is tonight's meeting important?"

"Very." A simple, one-word answer.

She tapped her finger against the center console and gritted her teeth. If he didn't want to talk, that was fine with her. She'd been living by herself for the past year with no real friends. It was a little depressing, but she'd gotten used to silence.

Palm trees and cars whizzed by as he headed toward Key Biscayne. She hadn't realized how close downtown Miami was to the barrier island. Before she realized it, they were pulling down the long private driveway of his beach house. He hadn't said it outright, but his pack had to have a lot of money to own a private stretch of beach in south Florida. *A lot.*

Hers had done well enough for themselves and she'd managed to leave California with a large chunk of funds but nothing compared to what the Lazos pack must have. She couldn't help but wonder what Stephan's real place looked like and what he must have thought of hers. All the furniture she'd gotten at second-hand stores and she didn't live in the best part of town—

"Stop, you're killing me," Stephan muttered.

"What?" She shot him a quick glance.

"Whatever you're feeling insecure about, just stop...please. It hurts."

"You can read my mind?" She'd heard of mates being linked telepathically, but they hadn't bonded so she'd assumed it wouldn't happen.

"No. I can feel your insecurities." He reached out and squeezed her hand.

Of all the things he could have done or said, that surprised her the most. She froze for a moment but didn't pull away. Touch was something she'd desperately craved over the past year. Her pack had been big and loud and often obnoxious, but she'd loved them. She missed her oldest sister's laugh more than anything. Marisol had been the youngest of three girls and her sisters had always looked out for her. She hated that she hadn't been there for them. Hadn't been able to stop what that monster had done to her whole family. She didn't know where that bastard wolf who'd betrayed them to Perez was, but she knew where *Perez* was and that was good enough for her.

"Fuck," Stephan growled as he threw the SUV into park.

"What?" she gasped as his hold on her hand tightened.

Stephan unstrapped his seat belt before releasing Marisol's restraint. Whatever was going on in her pretty head was nearly killing him. His chest tightened in absolute agony. She was such a mystery but now he knew without a doubt that she kept a lot of pain and misery locked inside. He didn't know much about comforting the opposite sex. Sure, his younger cousins sometimes came to him for advice, but this was different. He wanted to take all of Marisol's pain and just make it disappear.

"Come here," he murmured, reaching for her.

Without having to explain his intentions, she understood. She was surprisingly agile for wearing those fuck-me boots. Within seconds she straddled him, stretching her petite body over his.

Her dress rode up over her legs, pushing up high enough that he could see a peek of bright red panties. His hands settled on her thighs. She tensed under his touch, but her hips rolled once, her own response to him clear. Even with clothes on, he could feel the heat of her rubbing over his cock.

Like a mindless animal, his body wanted to fuck, but the pain he'd sensed from her still lingered in the air. "Tell me what happened to your family," he murmured.

"I can't. Not yet," she whispered. More than anything he wanted to push and force her to tell him, but he didn't have the heart to. Not when he could sense her emotional distress. His wolf clawed at him, telling him to comfort her, not talk.

Her dress was some sort of turtleneck thing so he clasped the bottom hem and lifted it upward. With her legs tightly clasping around him, she rose up and allowed him to pull it over her head. He was a little surprised she didn't protest since they were in his SUV, but he could sense her hunger as strong as his own. The mating pull was beyond intense.

Somehow he managed to get the dress free of her body. When he finally got to view what he'd been craving all morning, his cock jerked against his pants, begging to be set free.

Wearing a lacy cherry-red matching bra and panty set with knee-high boots, she was a wet dream come to life. Everything about her drove him wild. Not wanting to remove her bra completely, he shoved the straps then lace cups down to reveal perfect brown nipples tipping her full, round breasts. She shivered under his gaze, but the pain he'd sensed earlier had subsided.

Now all he felt was her desire. It shined from her eyes in white-hot lust and emanated from her body in potent waves that made him and his wolf a little bit wild. And all he wanted at that moment was to be inside her. He wanted to ease her ache as much as he wanted her to ease his own.

Taking him off guard, she reached down and clasped her fingers around his belt buckle. Her hand slipped once so he took over, unwilling to wait. He hadn't bothered with boxers because he didn't want the extra barrier. He wanted to fuck Marisol when and where he wanted with as little trouble undressing as possible.

When he lifted his hips, she loosened the grip she had with her thighs and helped him tug his pants down. His movements were constrictive and it was surprisingly hot. Normally he liked to be completely in control of everything. He cupped the back of her head before devouring her mouth. Kissing and teasing her tongue in much the same way he'd teased her pussy earlier, he tried to remind himself to give her *some* foreplay, but his cock wasn't listening. He loved the way she tasted, couldn't get enough of it.

She rolled her hips against his, and each time her lace-covered mound rubbed against his dick, he moaned into her mouth.

"You make me crazy, female," he murmured against her.

"Back atcha."

He felt as if his body was on fire and Marisol was the only thing that could douse it.

Dipping his head, he sucked one of her nipples into his mouth. As he traced his tongue around the hardened bud she arched her back, pushing herself deeper into his mouth.

She made tiny gasping sounds as she rubbed her body against his. Her fingers clutched his shoulders tightly and each time he tugged on her nipple, her body trembled.

He continued his assault on her breast and at that moment, he wished he had more hands. He wanted to touch all of her at the same time. His hands trailed up her thighs around to her ass. Smooth, tight skin greeted him. Dipping his finger underneath the stretchy material of her thong, he pulled it back and let it snap against her soft skin.

"Ah," she moaned, her body jolting at the action, and threaded her fingers through his hair.

Even through the lace barrier, he could feel how wet she was. Keeping one finger under the strap of her thong, he trailed back to the front of her body before pushing the flimsy material to the side. He cupped her mound and rubbed his middle finger over her soaking folds without penetrating. When she surged against him he grasped her hips and lifted her so her opening hovered over his cock.

"You ready?" he asked.

Wordlessly, she nodded.

"Say it." Because he fucking needed to hear it, needed to hear her say she wanted him.

"Yes."

"Say you want me in you."

She wiggled against his grip, but he held firm. This was torturing him as much as her. He would hear her say it. "Stephan," she rasped out.

He pushed up slightly, teasing her.

"Damn it, in me now." Her words were a rough growl.

Without pause he surged into her, pushing balls-deep with one long thrust.

"Stephan," she groaned.

He wanted more. He wanted his name on her lips at all times. He wanted her to think of him whenever she touched herself, whenever he couldn't be with her. Thrusting forward, he didn't give her time to adjust as he stretched and filled her.

Her pussy spasmed and tightened around him as he thrust forward again. When she moaned loudly he froze, worried he'd hurt her. At his pause, she lifted up and slammed down onto him again and again. She took him to the hilt and still wanted more.

Mesmerized, he stared at her as she rode him and had to force himself not to come. He was so close, but he wanted to make sure she came first. Her eyes were closed and her dark hair tumbled around her face and shoulders in thick waves.

"Touch yourself," he murmured. He could easily do it, but he was desperate to see her teasing herself.

Without opening her eyes, one of the hands that had been clasping his shoulder so tightly found its way between her legs. He stared at the vision of his cock driving into her sweet body while she rubbed herself.

It was too much to bear. Leaning forward, he kissed her other breast, licking and laving the top and underside before zeroing in on her rock-hard nub. The second his tongue touched it, her inner walls clamped tighter around his erection.

It was as if her pussy was connected to what he was doing with his mouth. Lashing his tongue over her nipple again, he groaned when she began spasming around him.

"Just like that, Stephan," she whispered.

He cupped her breasts, pushing them up and alternating between which nipple he sucked. The more he teased her, the faster she rode him. She abandoned her clit and clutched the seat behind him. Moving up and down, faster and faster, until her back bowed and she cried out his name, gripping him like a vise until her cream flooded over him.

As soon as her climax started, he allowed himself to let go. He released her breasts and gripped her hips. Letting his head fall back against the headrest, he slammed his cock upward into her tight sheath.

His balls pulled up painfully tight, but it was the sweetest pain he'd ever experienced. Looking at her, touching her, being inside her was fucking heaven. He wanted to claim her so badly he could feel his canines start to extend, but he forced them back.

He might be ready but she sure as hell wasn't. With a loud shout, he jerked upward completely emptying himself. Even as he rode through his orgasm, his cock blindly jutted into her until she'd completely sucked him dry.

She didn't attempt to move away from him and for that he was thankful. He tightened his grip around her back, encircling her waist so that she was snug against him. Their labored breathing and the heady scent of sex overpowered the interior cabin. Traces of sadness lingered around her, but so did satisfaction and something else he couldn't quite put his finger on.

They needed to clean up and he had a lot of explaining to do before he left her with his family, but he didn't want to tear himself away from her just yet. And he really didn't want to leave her alone tonight. His job meant a lot to him, but this case paled in comparison to finding out what had caused her so much pain.

He'd give up taking down Perez for her and that thought alone terrified the holy hell out of him.

CHAPTER NINE

Marisol tried to control the anticipation humming through her. She didn't want Stephan's brother to sense what she had planned. It wasn't as if he could read her thoughts, but Stephan had sensed her emotions in the vehicle earlier and she had no doubt his brother, Thomas, was just as astute. Maybe more so.

She was smart enough to realize that Stephan was blinded by his lust enough that he hadn't wanted to push her by asking questions about her family. She'd overheard his conversation earlier with Thomas and she knew her grace period was coming to an end. After tonight he'd no doubt want answers, but it probably wouldn't matter after what she was about to do.

She quickly shoved her cocktail dress, stilettos, phone, gun and purse into her backpack then tossed it out the bedroom window. Thomas had already canvassed the yard once so she crossed her fingers that he wouldn't see her bag lying in the bushes.

Once she'd shut and locked the window, she hurried downstairs. Luckily, she found Thomas in the kitchen. "Hi." She hovered by the doorway, unsure how he'd react to her request.

He nodded politely at her as he pulled a beer from the refrigerator. He had the same muscular build as Stephan. "Hi. Would you like a drink or something?"

She shook her head. "No, uh, I was wondering…would you mind if I went for a quick run along the beach?" He frowned so she rushed on. "I ran with Stephan earlier and he said it's private, right?"

"My family owns most of the houses for miles in each direction."

"I'm just a little worried about Stephan. He obviously couldn't tell me what he was doing tonight, so I thought it would be okay if I just stretched my legs and worked off some of my tension." *Lord, she was rambling and couldn't seem to stop herself.* He was going to say no. She could feel it in her bones.

158 | SAVANNAH STUART

"All right. Just don't go far."

Surprise bowled her over, but before he could change his mind, she hurried toward the back door. "Thanks. And uh, would you mind not looking while I uh..." Most wolves were unabashed in their nudity, but she didn't relish the thought of Stephan's brother seeing her nude.

He frowned for a moment until understanding dawned on his face. "Oh right. Of course. I'll give you privacy." He cleared his throat and strode from the room.

She rushed out the back door and changed as soon as she'd stripped. The pain rushed over her as her bones cracked and realigned, but the adrenaline pumping through her overrode most of her normal discomfort. She scanned the back of the house just to make sure Thomas wasn't watching through one of the windows — not that she'd actually expected him to — before grabbing her backpack between her teeth and bounding across the yard.

Her time was limited and she had to hurry or her friends wouldn't wait for her.

———————◆◆———————

Thomas cursed as he glanced at his watch. Marisol had been gone long enough that he knew she wasn't coming back. Something had been off about her scent, but he'd pushed his instinct aside because she was his brother's mate. Stephan had been so damn protective about her; Thomas hadn't wanted to spook or offend her.

He wasn't sure what she was up to, but if she planned to hurt his brother, he'd take care of her himself. He tucked his clothes and cell phone into a small bag before changing.

Picking up her scent wasn't hard. She wore a distinctive jasmine perfume and there was something else about her that was solely hers. Not to mention she had his brother's scent all over her. Being a wolf definitely had advantages.

After trailing her a mile down the beach, her fragrance shifted back toward the mainland, away from the water. According to Stephan, Marisol was a small dog so it would be easier for her to blend in. He, on the other hand, weighed about one hundred twenty-five pounds and he *looked* like a wolf. Whereas some of the others in his pack had softer qualities and looked more like pets, nothing about him was soft. He knew he looked ferocious in his shifted form so he had to be careful.

Sticking to the shadows, he managed to blend in as he raced through neighborhoods. It wasn't late, but the sun had set and most people were in for the evening. The few cats he came across scurried when they saw him.

Her scent started to fade when he spotted her in human form, waving at someone. She stood on a sidewalk in front of a modest sized house. She was half bent over, slipping her foot into a high-heeled shoe. After straightening her dress, she shoved something under a cluster of bushes.

He wanted to change and stop her, but by the time he shifted he wouldn't be able to put clothes on and catch her. Since running naked wasn't an option, he was screwed. Sticking to the shadows, he watched as she got into the backseat of a luxury car and slammed the door. As the car sped away, he ducked behind a cluster of oversized elephant ear leaves and changed. After the pain subsided, he called his brother.

* * *

Marisol fought the guilt coursing through her. She was a complete and total asshole. No doubt about it. Not only had she lied to the man she was falling for, she'd lied to his brother too.

"I'm so glad you wanted to come out tonight. This party is supposed to be amazing." Talia, the tall blonde Marisol had gone out with last night, glanced at her in the rearview mirror from the driver's seat.

Marisol plastered on a big smile. "I wouldn't miss it."

"I can't believe Antonio Perez is actually having a party at his house. I've never been before but I heard the place is absolutely sick. Three stories, a tennis court..."

As Talia and the other two girls in the car droned on, Marisol managed to answer their questions and laugh when appropriate. Still, it was impossible to fight the nausea threatening to overwhelm her. This was supposed to have been easy. All she needed to do was get Perez alone and she'd kill him. One shot. That was all she needed. Then all the guilt and suffering she'd experienced over the past year would go away. Even if she died. Especially if she died. It was her fault her family was dead anyway. Maybe she didn't deserve to walk away after killing Perez. Just a week ago she wouldn't have cared. Now...all she could seem to think about was Stephan and how this would hurt him. It was the last thing she wanted to do but her pack deserved justice.

When she thought about her family, her skin felt too tight for her body. It was almost impossible to breathe. She actually had to focus on *not* changing. Her thoughts strayed to Stephan and even though her heart rate increased, the desire to change decreased. If she could just keep her attention on him and what they'd shared together, she could control her body. Of course if she did that, she also had to focus on her guilt at lying to her mate, but that was just the price she had to pay.

When they finally pulled down Perez's long, winding driveway, two armed men stopped their car. After checking the trunk, the men waved them through. Marisol had been banking they wouldn't check their purses. If they had she would have been screwed. Or she'd have just explained it away. After all, who was going to hide a gun in a small clutch. Besides, no one was dumb enough to try to kill Perez when he was surrounded by armed guards.

Well, no one but her. It was why she was using a gun and not her shifter strength. It would be easier to get to him this way.

After they'd parked, Talia hooked her arm through Marisol's. "Come on, let's head around back to the pool area."

The other woman was a little flighty, but she was incredibly sweet and Marisol was thankful she'd been willing to pick her up as late as she'd called. Blood rushed in her ears as they walked along the stone path leading to the backyard. Loud music and voices trailed around the palatial monstrosity.

Almost as soon as they rounded the corner, a man carrying a tray of champagne greeted them. Just to keep her hands busy, she took one. Scantily clad women, men in suits and armed guards milled around the backyard. White twinkle lights were strung up around the gazebo and waiters with trays of food and drinks casually mingled with everyone.

Scanning the crowd, her gaze automatically landed on Stephan. With his height and size, he stood out anyway, but now that they'd slept together, she'd be able to pick his scent out anywhere. It was almost as if his scent had grown stronger, been etched in her memory.

As she drank in the sight of him, his head turned and his dark, penetrating eyes locked on hers. He looked at her as if he'd like to swallow her whole. But he didn't look surprised to see her. No, he looked angry, as if he'd been expecting her.

"Shit," she muttered under her breath. Thomas must have called him.

"Oh isn't that Stephan Vasquez?" Talia cooed. "I heard you went home with him last night, naughty girl." She said something else, but Marisol zoned out as Stephan stalked toward her.

She was on the other side of the yard, but he moved effortlessly through the mix of people. His dark eyes were practically gleaming as they zeroed in on her. When a tall brunette touched his arm, he glanced to his side and Marisol took the opportunity to hide.

Ducking behind Talia, she grabbed her friend's hips and used her as a shield. Talia was slim, but she was tall.

"Oh my God, what the hell are you doing?" Talia laughed.

"Hide me. Let's get inside," she whispered.

Talia giggled loudly but did as she asked. Sidestepping a few people, they hurried toward the back entrance of the house. "I take it you don't want a repeat of last night and he does. Was he bad in bed?" She laughed again, seeming to think the whole situation was hilarious.

Marisol peeked around Talia's lithe form and spotted Stephan talking to the woman who had grabbed his arm. Unwanted jealousy sparked through her like a brush fire, but the fact that he looked annoyed and bored went a long way to soothing her annoyance. Not that she should be focusing on her jealousy anyway.

"We're almost there," Talia muttered under her breath.

Once they ducked into Perez's house, Talia plucked the champagne glass from Marisol's hand. "This is my payment for helping you out. And you better not think you're getting away without telling me what's going on with Mr. tall, dark and dangerous. Come on, spill…was he bad in bed?"

She opened her mouth with a lame excuse when a shriek from a few feet away interrupted them. A girl Marisol vaguely recognized ran up to Talia and embraced her in a drunken hug. She knew it was crappy to abandon her friend, but Marisol skirted through the thick throng of guests until she was able to duck into one of the downstairs bathrooms. It was down one of the hallways and away from the crowd. She hadn't seen anyone come this way so she figured she was safe for a few minutes.

Once inside, she locked the door and dumped the contents of her purse onto the counter. She unfolded the printed layout of Perez's home and pinpointed where she was. Getting this had cost her a lot of money, but it had been worth it. Apparently he'd had an additional room built and a steel door with biometric security installed. She wasn't sure what was behind it, but whatever it was, it was important to him.

Now all she needed to do was find a place to hide and wait for the party to end. Once she got him alone—or relatively alone—she was going to do what she had to. She re-folded the paper and shoved it and everything else back into her small purse. As she stepped out, ready to ease the door shut behind her, a large hand clamped over her mouth and another hand snaked around her waist, pulling her flush against a strong body.

She started to scream when Stephan's scent slammed into her. Lord, she hadn't even smelled him coming. She'd been too caught up in her plans. Before she could think about struggling, Stephan opened the door and practically toppled over her into the bathroom.

Grasping her by the shoulders he swiveled her around so she was facing him. His fingers bit into her skin through the thin material of her dress. "What the hell are you doing here?" The question was asked calmly, but there a deadly edge to his voice that, while it shouldn't have surprised her, scared the hell out of her.

"I, uh..."

"Don't lie to me, Marisol."

She swallowed at the way he said her name and tried to take a step back. When she did, her butt hit the counter and he simply advanced on her, moving like the lethal predator he was. He leaned forward and placed his hands on the edge of the counter, caging her in and forcing her to arch her back against him. She gasped when she felt his erection pressing against her lower abdomen.

"I'm waiting for an answer." There was a slight rise to the pitch of his voice.

"I..." She couldn't say it. The words refused to come. Nervously, she tried to shift her weight, and when she did, her purse clattered to the floor. She darted a quick glance at it and couldn't help the surge of nerves that skittered through her.

Stephan narrowed his eyes and looked at her purse then at her. Her lungs squeezed as he stared at her. Without giving her a chance to react, he snatched it off the floor and jerked it open.

"What the fuck is this?" he rasped out, his voice deadly quiet. He withdrew her gun and stared at her.

Unable to meet his gaze, she focused on the floor. She couldn't explain it to him and now she'd screwed up her one chance to take down Perez. Not only that; she'd ruined everything with her mate. Her throat seized as she tried to fight the sudden onslaught of tears coming. Oh God, she hadn't cried in forever. She couldn't have a breakdown now. Not here.

A stray tear slipped down her cheek. Before it even reached her chin, Stephan cupped her jaw and tilted her head upward. Anger radiated from him, but his expression was a little softer. And a lot less intimidating. Which was somehow worse. Dealing with his anger seemed like a better option.

"Why do you have a gun?"

She took a deep breath, steadied herself. "I came here to kill Antonio Perez."

Her shallow breathing and the blood rushing in her ears were the only sounds she heard and they seemed to permeate every nook of the otherwise silent room.

The hand that embraced her jaw slid around until he cupped her head in a harsh grasp. It didn't hurt, but it left no room for doubt who dominated the room. He opened his mouth, but a familiar male voice called his name from the hallway.

It was Perez.

Marisol froze, unsure what to do, but Stephan stripped his shirt off then grabbed her by her hips and lifted her onto the counter. She barely had time to blink before he'd spread her thighs wide, forcing her dress up to her waist. She had no choice but to wrap her legs around him.

"I saw him go in here, boss," someone said.

Stephan covered her mouth with his in a possessive claiming. His kisses were harsh and angry and incredibly passionate. As he stroked her tongue with his, her fear gave way to desire. His fingers threaded through her hair on either side of her head so she clutched onto his shoulders. Her panties dampened when he shifted and ran one of his hands up her thigh, trailing under her dress and under the thin material covering her mound.

The sound of the door opening tore them apart.

"Get the fuck out of here!" Stephan barked.

Through a haze, she made out the figure of Perez and someone else, probably one of his bodyguards. The door shut immediately, no doubt because they realized what Stephan was doing.

"Meet me in twenty minutes," Perez shouted through the door.

Stephan grunted a non-answer then resumed his assault on her mouth, but not before locking the door. As his tongue rasped against hers, she moaned and locked her ankles behind his back.

With each stroke of their tongues, his cock surged against her. He pulled his head back and muttered a string of obscene curses that probably shouldn't have turned her on—but kind of did. She was sure he was going to yell at her or haul her out of there, but instead, he grappled with his belt until his pants slid down his legs.

His very muscular legs.

"What are you doing?" she whispered.

"I'm going to fuck you." That deadly edge was back to his voice, but it was laced with something else.

Desire.

Need.

Hunger.

The command of his voice and the man behind that voice caused every muscle in her to pull taut. She started to slide off the counter so she could shimmy out of her panties, but he stopped her.

He covered her mound with his hand and pushed the flimsy material to the side. Without any warning or foreplay, he buried his cock inside her with a hard thrust.

Her inner walls stretched to take him but he didn't give her any time to adjust. He kept his gaze locked on hers as he pulled out of her then slammed into her again.

In and out. In and out.

Her pussy spasmed each time he drove into her. She wanted to look away from his penetrating gaze but she couldn't. His dark eyes seemed to have some sort of hold on her.

While he didn't make a move to take off the rest of her clothes, he palmed one of her breasts through the silky material of her dress. She hadn't worn a bra and the dress was thin. Her nipples were already hard, but they pebbled painfully under his insistent teasing. He tweaked and rubbed her in erotic little strokes. It was as if an imaginary string was attached to her aching nipples and pulsing clit. Each time he touched her, her clit throbbed.

She was so close that even a little more stimulation would push her over the edge. "I'm so close, Stephan," she moaned.

Her words had the opposite effect of what she wanted. He drove into her. Hard. Then he remained buried, balls-deep and refused to move.

She tried to roll her hips against his but he simply grabbed her and held her in place.

"What are you doing?" she rasped.

"Why do you want to kill Perez?" he demanded, his words so low she might not have been able to hear him if she'd been human.

"You want to know *now*?" His cock was buried to the hilt and ripples swelled through her pussy like the aftereffects of an earthquake. If he'd just move a little, she could come.

"Tell me," he whispered before leaning forward and grasping her earlobe between his teeth. He pressed lightly and tugged.

His breath was hot against her neck. She arched her back against him, but he remained immobile inside her. Scorching, singing heat radiated from him with unbelievable force. She could actually feel the warmth coming off him it was so potent. "I can't."

He shifted his hips and pulled out of her by a couple inches. She immediately mourned the loss. "Tell me, she-wolf." His voice was still a whisper.

She was so close to climax. Her body hurt. It ached. And she just needed release. And she desperately needed to tell someone her secret.

The words were on the tip of her tongue. She wanted to trust Stephan with this.

"Tell me or I walk out of here," he rumbled.

She believed him. "He killed my entire pack and it's my fault. I want him to pay for what he did." The words tore from her chest with a sob.

He tensed for a split second and some foreign emotion rolled off him. She couldn't place what it was, but before she could even think, he pushed into her and he didn't stop.

His thrusts were rough, shaky, and she couldn't catch her breath before an orgasm rocked through her. Her inner walls clenched around him with ferocity as her climax took over. Not wanting to give anyone a show, she bit into his shoulder to keep from crying out. Pleasure emanated out of her every pore as the waves swept through her.

His corded muscles bunched underneath her teeth but he didn't push her away or show pain. Instead, his grip on her hips tightened and his thrusts increased. He moaned low and deep, but he didn't cry out either as he emptied himself into her. Clutching onto her hips, he kept thrusting until he was completely sated.

She pressed her forehead to his bare chest, unwilling to look him in the eye. To her horror, tears started leaking from her eyes. Stupid, stupid tears. She swallowed against the lump in her throat and tried to force herself not to show weakness, but it was no use.

The harder she tried to control herself, the more she cried. She bit her bottom lip so she wouldn't sob, but Stephan wouldn't let her go. He cupped her face and feathered kisses all over her. Across her jaw, her cheeks, even her nose. The sweeping motion was sweet and unexpected and it wrenched even more tears from her. He was being so kind and she didn't know why.

"Don't cry, *kardia mou*," he murmured over and over.

She wasn't sure what the endearment meant, but every time he said it, her stomach did a strange flip-flop. Swiping at her errant tears, she met his gaze. "Do you hate me?" She didn't even want to ask, wasn't sure she could handle the answer.

His jaw tightened as he shook his head. "Never."

An awkward silence descended on the room and she suddenly realized how exposed she was. Glancing down, her breath caught at the sight they made. He was still buried inside her and both their juices covered her thighs. Her underwear cut into her skin from being shoved to the side.

He must have understood her discomfort because he slowly pulled out of her and began cleaning her. Once he was finished, she tried to adjust her dress but her hands were too shaky. She'd just admitted her darkest secret to him and he hadn't said anything about it.

Thankfully Stephan was still a gentleman. He helped adjust her clothing before hooking an arm around her waist. He opened the door, then when he was sure the hallway was empty, he stepped out into it and dragged her with him.

"What are you doing?" she whispered.

But he didn't answer. As he strode down the hallway she had no choice but to keep pace. Instead of heading back toward the party, he led her down another hallway that emptied into a foyer. Two large faux Corinthian style columns encased a sturdy looking front door.

A few men with guns stood casually by. When they saw Stephan they nodded at him but didn't make a move to stop them as he opened the door. Her breath hitched when she saw the same tinted SUV from the night before. He opened the back door and practically shoved her inside. "You're going back to my place. I'll see you later." He turned toward the window and muttered something in a foreign language to the same driver as the night before. The young wolf responded then rolled the window up, giving them privacy.

Stephan leaned forward and pressed a soft kiss to her lips. Her mouth still tingled from his previous more demanding kisses and the change of pace was unexpected.

"I'll see you later." His voice was hoarse and raspy. Without giving her a chance to respond, he shut the door and the driver pulled away a second later.

Glancing out the back window, she couldn't help the sinking sensation forming in her gut. He didn't seem as angry as he had earlier, but she really didn't know him well enough to make that observation. A shiver snaked down her spine so she wrapped her arms around herself and leaned back against the leather seat.

There wasn't much she could do now other than wait.

CHAPTER TEN

Stephan barely contained the rage flowing through him as he walked back inside Perez's house. He had to play this carefully or he was going to rip the man's throat out and ruin the entire operation. He was used to schooling his features, but the thought that Perez had hurt his mate was about to send him over the edge. It wasn't something she'd have lied about. Stephan might not know the details, but the truth had been written in every line and curve of Marisol's body—and in her pained scent.

The moment he entered the house, Perez, his men and two of Stephan's teammates were waiting for him. "Everything all right?" Perez asked with a smirk on his face.

"It would have been better if someone hadn't interrupted me." His voice was dry.

A lecherous grin spread across Perez's face. "I'm glad you're having a good time, but now it's time to get down to business."

"Agreed."

"I want to talk to you privately." Perez glanced at his personal guards then at Stephan's men before returning his gaze to Stephan. "Just the two of us."

Stephan nodded. "That's acceptable, but if you try to double-cross me, I'll cut your heart out."

Perez cleared his throat, but nodded. "This way."

Stephan fell in step with the other man as they headed for one of the many hallways in Perez's mansion. He kept track of how many turns they made until they stood in front of a steel door that seemed out of place among the oak-paneled pictures and ornate crown molding lining the hallway.

When Perez placed his hand on a biometric scanner, Stephan could feel the energetic charge rolling off the other man. Just what the hell was behind this door that had him so excited?

As they stepped into a laboratory of some sort, Stephan frowned as he scanned the room. When he saw two naked women strapped down behind a glass window, his gut roiled. "I don't deal with slave girls. I thought that much was clear." But he'd sure as hell come back and rescue these females.

Perez snorted. "These aren't whores. They're...werewolves. And I've managed to duplicate their abilities in regular humans. We will be able to create super soldiers."

Stephan's heart rate increased. *Was Perez testing him?* "Is this some kind of fucking joke? Werewolves? I thought you were serious about doing business with me."

"I am! This is why I called you in here alone. Watch." He picked up something that looked like a PDA and pressed a couple buttons. A flat screen against one of the walls flashed on.

The date stamp on the screen was six months ago. It was near dusk, somewhere close to the ocean. What city or state though, he couldn't be sure. Stephan watched as a team of masked, armed men surrounded a barking dog. The dog yapped and growled but someone shot it with something—*a tranquilizer gun*. The light brown and white Akita yelped in pain before it fell on its side. Then it shifted into a naked blonde woman who looked vaguely familiar.

"What the hell?" He tried to act as astonished as he could.

Perez beamed at him proudly. "So far we've only found two females able to undergo our testing. She is one of them."

"How do I know this isn't staged?" Stephan asked.

"They both have too many drugs in their system now. We've already started reducing their dosage. Once you guarantee me the contacts I require, I'll set up a live demonstration in a very controlled setting. It will be for your eyes only, *before* we meet with any of your friends. I don't have a death wish and I wouldn't try to cross or embarrass you. We can both make a lot of money."

The girl on the video cried out as they threw a net over her. Stephan's hands fisted at his side. *Do not change, do not change, do not change.* His wolf was raging pissed, demanding he unleash all his rage on this piece of garbage who'd chained up wolves for monetary gain. "Why does she look familiar?" He needed to keep the other man talking and he desperately needed to keep his mind off the sight of one of his own kind being hunted.

He shrugged dismissively. "She's a model—*was* a model, for some international clothing company."

Stephan tore his gaze away from the screen. "Who's the other woman in there?"

"Her name isn't important. I got her a year ago. She's the only one of her pack to survive."

"Pack?" Stephan asked while imagining himself ripping Perez's head from his body. He'd do it slowly too, make this fucker suffer.

"That's what they call themselves, if you can imagine." He turned his attention back to the screen and pressed another button.

A new video popped up dated two days ago. The setting was in a warehouse. That much was clear. A man wearing camouflage fatigues lifted a two-door car off the ground. "We'll need to conduct longer studies of course, but so far, the results are what we were hoping for. The human we injected is almost a hundred times stronger and his healing capabilities are like nothing the world has ever seen before. I know this must be a shock to you—"

"How did you find out about these...creatures?"

"One of their own kind betrayed them for a lot of money."

Betrayed. Marisol had said it was her fault—no! His mind immediately rejected the thought. She'd been distraught and she'd come here to kill Perez. She couldn't have done it.

Perez continued. "This is why I wanted to do business with you. You have the contacts I need. If you back me and provide introductions, we can make a fortune."

Stephan's lips pulled into a thin line. "How many of your men know about this?"

"The four in the first video and the doctor who created the serum are the only other people who know about this."

"Good. I need a few days to think things over, but this is between you and me. My men will not be privy to anything you've shown me here." Stephan's heart beat erratically and his blood rushed loudly in his ears. The only thing keeping him from changing was the knowledge that he was going to burn Perez's home to the ground. Possibly with Perez in it.

Stephan braced himself as he entered the beach house. As soon as he stepped inside he was hit with an array of emotions.

Anger, hurt, fear, pain. And he wasn't sure what was coming from whom. A low murmur of voices trailed from the kitchen so he made his way there.

His father, Nick, Thomas and his Uncle Cosmo stood around the center island, deep in conversation. Marisol and his mother sat at the table near one of the windows. Marisol's eyes were red and puffy. The wolf inside him cried out to comfort her, but duty prevented him. He risked a quick glance at his mother. She didn't look necessarily angry, but her dark eyebrows rose questioningly at him.

The men became silent as he entered the room. He could feel Marisol's gaze bore into him but he couldn't look at her again. If he did, he was likely to take her into his arms and drag her upstairs to take care of her. The need to take care of his mate was all-consuming.

"You should have told me you found a mate," his father said.

Stephan nodded at the same time Thomas spoke, "He was going to after he wrapped his case up. A day or two would *not* have made a difference."

As next in line to be Alpha, Thomas had more leeway than any other male in the pack, but Stephan didn't want his brother to stand up for him. Not now. He'd fucked up and he deserved the rebuke. Still, he appreciated his brother's loyalty.

"It doesn't matter. The pack comes first." His father didn't raise his voice because he didn't have to. His command and presence enveloped the entire room. At two-hundred years old, he looked barely forty-five. Standing over six feet, there was no sign of gray in his dark hair and his dark eyes had an unmistakable air of insight—and deadliness.

Stephan knew there would be time enough later to discuss his mistakes. "We have more important problems to worry about." As quickly as he could, he explained everything he'd seen at Perez's house. When he was finished, an eerie silence descended on the kitchen.

His father was the first to speak. He focused on Marisol. "Did you know Perez was doing experiments on shifters?"

Eyes wide, she shook her head. "No, I swear. He killed all the males of our pack and most of the females. I thought... I just thought he hated our kind." The truth was there in the shakiness of her voice.

"What did you tell your boss, Stephan?" This time Thomas spoke.

Stephan paused at his brother's question. Thomas had been looking out of him and Nick since they were pups. It wasn't lost on him that his brother cared about Stephan's job—something his father didn't concern himself over. "I lied to my team. They think Perez wants time to think about doing business with me. I managed to buy myself a week at the most."

"We cannot wait a week. We'll move against him tonight," his father said.

WORTH THE RISK | 171

The others murmured in agreement with the exception of Nick. "We need a plan first. If this guy is experimenting on shifters, he's going to have proper weapons to hurt us. I think half of us should go in human form, the other half, shifted."

His father and the others nodded. That still didn't alleviate the fact that they didn't have the schematics of Perez's house or know how many men they'd be up against, but they'd make it work. Stephan knew the layout of the first floor so that would have to be good enough.

"I might be able to help," Marisol's soft voice silenced the rest of the room. Her hands shook as she opened her small purse. "This is the design plan for Perez's house."

Stephan was across the room before anyone could move. He frowned as he scanned it. The DEA hadn't been able to get this because it hadn't been recorded online anywhere. "How did *you* get this?"

"Luck and money. I met the architect a few months ago at a club in South Beach. It took a lot of sweet talking and cost a small fortune, but he gave me a copy."

He held out his hand to her. She stared at it for a moment before placing her much smaller one in his then stood. Stephan glanced at his family. "Give me a second." He didn't wait for a response as he led her from the kitchen. He kept walking until they were upstairs and out of earshot.

Once they were alone, he placed his hands on her hips and pulled her close. Touching her soothed his wolf on so many levels. "Are you okay?"

She tensed under his touch and shrugged, the action jerky. "Your family is *not* happy with me."

"They'll get over it." Because he wasn't letting this female go.

She swallowed hard. "I don't really care about them…no offense. I just care what you think."

He wasn't exactly happy she'd lied to him either, but that wasn't what she needed to hear. Part of him wanted to shake her senseless, but more than anything he just wanted to take her in his arms and comfort her. "Why didn't you tell me about Perez?"

"I… I didn't think I'd even get out of his house alive. I just needed one shot to kill him and…" Tears rolled down her cheeks as she trailed off.

And she'd been willing to die to do it. The words hung silently in the air. He wasn't sure how to even digest her words. The thought of her willingly going into a situation like that without backup…it sliced him up. He gently wiped away her tears. "I have to go, but we *are* going to talk about this."

"I know," she whispered.

So many things still needed to be said but time wasn't his friend. They needed to catch Perez unaware. His guard would be down tonight. Stephan had seen the greed in his eyes earlier. Perez was ready to deal and he thought he had a sure thing with Stephan *Vasquez*. He'd made his first big mistake by settling in Miami.

Stephan was going to make damn sure that son of a bitch didn't make it out of his house alive tonight. Then he was going to hunt down whoever had betrayed Marisol's pack.

CHAPTER ELEVEN

In wolf form, Stephan edged along the perimeter of Perez's expansive backyard. He'd already knocked out two armed guards using brute strength. Thomas, his father and he had opted to shift because they were stronger in wolf form and looked a hell of a lot more intimidating than the other two who'd stayed in human form. Using the overgrown foliage and gazebo as cover, he blended in with the shadows.

The males of his pack had spread out and they were converging on the house from all angles. It would give them the element of surprise.

With his heightened senses, everything around him was clearer. In addition to the men he'd knocked out, a guard or someone not of his pack was nearby. He could smell the individual. Tobacco and a specific body odor accosted Stephan's senses. As he peered around one of the bushes, he spotted a man sitting on one of the lounge chairs by the pool smoking a cigarette.

Stephan could sense other bodies, but he couldn't make out anyone else that was closer than the lone guard. He hoped his brothers had already immobilized the outside guards.

Crouching as low as he could, he inched toward the outside stone fireplace that sat between him and the guard. He just wanted to stun the guy, not kill him, so he had to be careful.

After the guy tossed his cigarette to the ground and stepped on it, he bent to pick up his M4. In that moment, Stephan made his move.

Using all his momentum and strength, he pounced from his hiding position and tackled him from behind. His paws slammed into the man's back. The guy let out a shout as they tumbled over the chair, but his head struck the stone tile and his entire body stilled. Which was exactly what Stephan had hoped for. Fighting for even minutes wasn't in the game plan. They needed to immobilize these men and take the house.

Stephan nudged him with his paw, but the man didn't move.

174 | SAVANNAH STUART

"He's out cold," Nick murmured as he bent next to the man and secured his wrists behind his back. He tapped his ear. "Cosmo says it's clear out front and I took out three other armed men. I guarantee Thomas and Dad have taken out more."

Stephan understood his brother, but he couldn't respond. In shifted form, he could project thoughts with his mind, but his brother would only understand him if he was in wolf form too.

As they continued toward the back patio, Thomas rounded the corner. Once they were all together by the French doors, Thomas ordered him to shift to human form.

Pain rippled through Stephan until he was on his knees and groaning. Changing back to human form always hurt worse.

Nick had already pulled most of their clothing from his backpack by the time he and Thomas had changed. Wordlessly, they slipped on black fatigues and long-sleeved black shirts. With the weapons they'd brought, there hadn't been enough room to include shoes.

"Dad and Cosmo are going in through the front," Thomas whispered.

The back door was locked so instead of wasting time picking it, Stephan broke the glass and unlocked it manually. A piercing alarm sounded as they rushed inside. Before leaving their family's beach house, they'd all studied the layout of Perez's house. Everything on the diagram corresponded with the layout he remembered from his short visit.

Now they simply needed to make it to the lab and figure out a way to get inside before any cops showed up.

"We've got two minutes," Thomas shouted above the noise.

As they fanned out across the open living room, two guards appeared from around the corner. Both men raised their pistols.

Stephan fired at the one on the right. The man fell at the same time his partner did. Either Thomas or Nick had taken him down with one shot. It had been decades since he'd been in an all-out gunfight, but the last time had been with his brothers in Vietnam. After almost two-hundred years of living and fighting together, it was only natural they knew how to work as a team.

Sidestepping the fallen men, Stephan crouched low then rounded the corner. The hallway was empty so he motioned to his brothers. As werewolves, regular bullets wouldn't kill them but they would still cause excruciating pain.

When they neared the end of the hallway a loud explosion ripped through the air so Stephan and his brother picked up their pace. They rounded the corner and into the hallway leading toward the laboratory.

Stephan nearly stumbled at the sight in front of them.

"What the hell?" Nick shouted above the alarm.

The steel door leading to the lab was blown off and smoke billowed out from the room. As they neared the door, the petite brunette he'd seen strapped down appeared in the open entrance.

She was completely naked but a bright blue ball of—something, maybe energy or lightning—crackled in her hands. She lifted a hand as if to fire at them but paused as she smelled the air. As she looked at the three of them, it was as if all the energy was sucked from her body. Her eyes rolled back in her head and she collapsed in a small, lifeless heap.

"I'll grab the girl. Torch the lab!" Thomas said as he sprinted ahead of them. He scooped her up as Stephan and Nick headed inside.

Glass shards covered most of the tiled floor, the television screen was cracked and the beakers and test-tubes he'd seen earlier were smashed on the floor. Three guards and an old man in a lab coat lay dead on the floor with giant holes burned through their chests. What had once been a two-way mirror was now shattered open. Stephan spotted the blonde woman huddled in a corner. She was naked and dirty, but her eyes were open and terrified.

"I got her." Nick tossed the bottle of lighter fluid to Stephan before bounding over the glass. His boots made crunching sounds, even above the siren.

As Stephan started spraying everything with the accelerant, his father and uncle ran into the room, both in human form.

"Everyone is down but Perez isn't here." His father flipped open his silver lighter and tossed it into the middle of the room.

Flames erupted with a loud whoosh. Bright orange fire licked its way across the floor, eating everything in its path with a hungry intensity. Stephan had wanted to gather some sort of records, but there was no time.

The cops—or worse, the DEA—would be arriving soon and Stephan knew he couldn't be anywhere around.

They all rushed from the room and sprinted back the way they'd come. An explosion ripped through the house, rocking the foundation, as they emptied onto the back patio.

The familiar blare of a fire truck siren screamed through the night.

"Shift!" his father ordered.

Regardless of their state of dress, they all changed. Thomas and Nick were already long gone with the women.

If they wanted to get away from the cops, they couldn't be in human form. Stephan stayed close to his father and uncle as they ran across the backyard. Shouting humans sounded around them, but no one tried to stop them and Stephan didn't pause to see who had arrived. Considering the growing fire and the potential problem that caused, a couple of loose dogs roaming around wouldn't even register on Miami PD's radar in a situation like this.

The farther they ran, the more his paw ached. A piece of glass must have embedded itself in his foot, but that was the least of his worries. When his father slowed, so did Stephan and his uncle. They neared the quiet dead-end road where his father had left his SUV.

Luckily, the back hatch was open and Nick stood guard. The three of them dove inside and Nick slammed the door shut behind them. Moments later, the vehicle jerked to life. Only then did Stephan allow himself to think about what they'd just done. Everything had happened so quickly and they hadn't had adequate time to cover their tracks. If they made just one slip-up, it could send their entire pack on the run and into hiding.

CHAPTER TWELVE

Marisol's eyes flew open at the sound of familiar voices. She pushed the afghan throw off and rubbed her eyes. She and Stephan's mother must have fallen asleep in the living room. Glancing around, she groaned when she saw the clock on the mantle. *Four o'clock.*

"They're here," Alisha murmured as she pushed up from the loveseat.

Stephan's mother had been strangely quiet since the males of the Lazos pack had left hours before. Of course she hadn't let Marisol out of her sight, but she also hadn't drilled her with questions.

Footsteps across the tiled entryway and the front door slamming jerked Marisol out of her daze and into action. In addition to all the familiar bodies she scented something else. Something—*someone*—very familiar. But it couldn't be. Hope bloomed inside her, so sharp she was afraid to believe what she scented.

She hurried out of the room and almost ran directly into Stephan. He wore tattered shorts and no shirt or shoes. She instantly reached for him, wanting to comfort him. "Are you okay?"

He stepped back and kept about a foot of distance between them. "We're fine. The lab is destroyed and probably Perez's entire house."

"What about Perez?" Marisol was vaguely aware as Alisha passed them and headed toward the kitchen. Her heart hurt at Stephan's rejection so she wrapped her arms around herself.

"We didn't find him, but there were two survivors. Both female werewolves. He's been experimenting on them, but they seem physically fine. One of them is different…"

Instinctively she tensed at his guarded tone. Maybe what she'd scented was real after all. "What do you mean?"

"I'm not sure. Most of the lab was destroyed when we got there. One of the she-wolves we saved harnessed some sort of blue light in her hands."

"Blue?" Marisol's heart skipped a beat. Oh God, could it be her?

"Yes, almost like lightning—"

Marisol sidestepped him and raced for the kitchen. Her bare feet smacked against the cool tile. She tried to control the hope that surged through her, but it was useless. As she entered the kitchen, that hope blossomed with the intensity of a hurricane.

"Paz!" Her sister's limp form was stretched out on the center island of the kitchen, covered by a large towel.

Thomas stood next to her sister, wiping soot and dirt from her face, but she ignored him as she took Paz's hand.

It was warm. A good sign. If her sister used too much of her powers, she drained herself of energy. But she was alive. That was all that mattered.

"You know her?" Stephan's voice sounded close behind her.

"Paz, she's my sister. I thought... I thought she was dead." Something in the back of Marisol's mind taunted her that this was a dream, but in her heart she knew it wasn't. Clasping her sister's hand, she breathed a sigh of relief when Paz's fingers tightened slightly.

Experience told her it would be hours before Paz woke up, but Marisol didn't care.

"What is she?" Stephan asked.

Mindless of everyone's gaze on her, she focused on Stephan. She could lie and tell him she didn't know what he meant. Of course if she did, everyone in the room would know she was a liar and she was tired of lying to him anyway. "She's half werewolf, half-fae."

"*Faerie?*" Alisha gasped from the other side of the room.

Marisol nodded and tried to force down the burst of fear that bloomed in her chest. Stephan was her mate. He wouldn't harm her or her family. Or at least she hoped he wouldn't. Technically Paz was more powerful than everyone in this room—the Alpha included—but she was passed out and helpless. "Her mother was full-blooded faerie, but she wasn't evil, like the Council seems to think faeries are. My father and her mother fell in love, but Selena—that was her mother—died giving birth to Paz. Decades after her mother died, he met and mated with my mother. My father never told the Council about her and the entire pack was sworn to secrecy because..." Marisol swallowed and glanced away from the penetrating gazes of the Lazos pack.

She didn't need to say it aloud because they would understand. The Council of Werewolves would have ordered Paz to die simply because of the magic that ran through her blood. The Cabrera pack wouldn't have listened and it would have begun a bloody war. Millennia ago—long before any of them had been born—faeries and werewolves had been at war. Of course, werewolves had also been at war with vampires, Immortals and any other being that was different. Their history was just as violent as the humans.

"What are her powers?" Lucas asked. His voice was calm, but it didn't stop a tremor of fear from snaking down Marisol's spine.

She risked a quick glance at Stephan. His face was an unreadable mask, but at least he stood by her side. That felt like something. "She...she has the ability to draw energy—life force, I guess you'd call it—from most living beings. It usually manifests in the form of blue light. Basically she turns kinetic energy into a blast of power...it looks sort of like lightning. She's never killed anyone though and from the time she was a child our father helped her to control her powers."

"She killed the men in the lab." Lucas's voice was wry.

"Then they deserved it!" Even though Lucas was an Alpha, she couldn't stop the rising pitch of her voice. She would die for her sister if need be.

Lucas nodded once. "They certainly did. For now, your sister is under the protection of my pack. However, no one outside of this room will know that she's more than a werewolf."

Relief flooded Marisol's veins until her gaze fell on a tall blonde woman leaning against one of the counters. A black t-shirt fell to mid-thigh, but she was dirty and otherwise naked. "Who are you?"

The blonde cast a nervous glance at Lucas, who simply nodded. The she-wolf wrapped her arms around herself defensively. "My name's Shea Hart. I've been held captive with your sister for about six months. She kept me sane and she saved my life. I won't tell a soul about her. I swear it. I owe her so much..." she trailed off with a broken whisper.

The truth of the woman's words rolled over her along with a healthy dose of grief and sadness. Marisol could only imagine what the pretty blonde had been through. Apparently the woman's emotions hit the other wolves in the room too because Lucas immediately took charge.

"Shea, you're coming home with Alisha and me. Stephan, I'm sending over Caro to look at your mate's sister. Everyone else, go home, get a few hours of sleep, we meet at my house at noon." He turned his dark gaze to Marisol. "If your sister is awake, she comes too."

Without a word, Marisol nodded as everyone filed out. She noted that Thomas lingered by Paz, but he eventually made his way toward the door. Once everyone had gone, Marisol made a move toward Stephan but he averted his gaze. "I'll carry your sister upstairs. My aunt should be here soon."

Before she could respond, he'd scooped Paz's small body in his arms and strode from the room. Marisol had hoped his annoyance with her would wane with time, but evidently not. Sighing, she followed him up the stairs but stopped in their room first. And since when did she start thinking of it as *their* room anyway? Rolling her eyes at herself, she grabbed one of her favorite pajama sets and hurried to the guestroom.

She found Stephan tucking the comforter around Paz. Her heart warmed at the sight. As a werewolf, Marisol was more uncomfortable than most with her nudity, but Paz would die if she knew others had seen her naked. For a half-fae, she was incredibly insecure. Maybe because she'd grown up feeling like an outsider. It was ironic that considering how powerful she was, Paz had more human attributes than anyone Marisol knew.

"Thank you," she murmured.

He grunted one of his non-responses and disappeared from the room. It took some work, but Marisol dressed Paz in the silk pajamas and tucked her back in. By the time she was finishing, an older female wolf carrying a black bag appeared in the doorway.

"Hi, you must be Marisol. I'm Caro, Alisha's sister." The tall, dark-haired woman waited by the door until Marisol nodded for her to enter.

"Thank you for coming. This has happened to her before and I'm sure she'll be fine." Or Marisol desperately hoped so. She wasn't sure if Paz had drugs or something in her system. "Are you a doctor?"

Caro nodded. "For the better part of this century. I spoke to the other rescued werewolf, Shea. She told me they weren't sexually assaulted, but when your sister is awake, I'm going to speak to her about it."

"Okay." Marisol sat on the bed next to Paz and held her sister's hand as Caro examined her. She was thankful the woman was being so gentle.

After a few minutes, the pretty werewolf stood. "You're right. She's sleeping, but she's okay."

On one level, Marisol had already known that, but hearing someone else repeat the sentiment gave her peace of mind. She stared at the other wolf expectantly and when she didn't make a move to leave, Marisol frowned. "Did you need something else?"

"I'd like to stay and keep an eye on her if you don't mind. You can go sleep with your mate. I'll make sure your sister is safe." It wasn't a request.

Marisol's eyes narrowed. "Did Stephan's father put you up to this?"

She shrugged. "More or less."

Marisol wanted to argue with her. Every fiber in her being wanted to throw a tantrum and insist on staying by Paz's side, but she knew when to pick her battles. Her sister was passed out for at least a few hours and this wolf wasn't threatening to her. Besides, she desperately needed to talk to her mate. "If she wakes up, you'll get me?"

The woman nodded. "Of course."

"Immediately?"

A ghost of a smile touched her lips. "Yes."

She placed a quick kiss on her sister's forehead before searching for Stephan. When she entered the bedroom they'd been using, she found the main lights off and he was lying on his side, with his back turned to her. A twinge of pain sliced through her chest, but she knew she deserved his anger. She'd done nothing but lie to him since they'd met.

If she had to go back and do things over, she wasn't sure she'd tell him the truth though. Sighing, she slipped under the sheet and comforter and closed her eyes. She had hoped they'd be able to talk, but it didn't appear he wanted to.

"So that's it?" Stephan's voice cut through the quiet room.

Her eyes flew open. "Is what 'it'?"

"You're just going to go to sleep?"

She sat up in bed. "Do you want to talk?"

The sheets rustled beneath him as he turned to face her. The light from the bathroom streamed in, letting her see the harsh lines of his face.

When he didn't continue, she clutched the sheet tightly in her hands. "I wanted to thank you earlier. I can never repay you for saving my sister...it seems lame to just say thank you, but it's all I can offer."

He sat up fully. "Why did you lie to me?"

"I wasn't sure if I could trust you." It pained her to admit it out loud.

"I told you who I was, what I did for a living."

She bit her bottom lip. "I know, I just... I don't know. I thought if I told you I was going to kill Perez you would stop me."

"Damn right I would have stopped you!" He cleared his throat and his tone softened as he continued. "How's your sister?"

"She must have used a lot of energy, but she'll be fine. This has happened to her before... Is your father going to tell the Council?"

"We'll find out for sure in a few hours, but I think I can safely say no. You're my mate; he won't do anything to betray family."

She sighed and collapsed against the pillow. Her sister was alive and safe for now. Just knowing Paz was still alive dulled the desire to kill Perez.

Stephan stayed sitting and stared at her, far too many emotions in his watchful eyes. She shifted under his intense gaze. "What do you want to ask?"

"You said it was your fault your pack died. Did you betray them?"

"No!" She jolted upright, unable to believe he could ask that. "I made a stupid decision, but I would never betray them. *Never.*"

He reached out and took both her hands in his. She tried to tug away, but he was relentless and the truth was, she needed his support.

"Tell me what happened."

"I was stupid. So, so stupid. I met a lone wolf, Preston Morales, and invited him into our pack. I was..." She cleared her throat, wondering how she was going to tell Stephan this. Mates could get really jealous and territorial and she certainly wouldn't want to hear about him being interested with another female.

"You were involved with him?" he prodded.

"Not physically, but I was attracted to him and I was thinking about sleeping with him. He was charming and good looking and it had been so long since I'd been with a man who—"

"I get it," Stephan cut in.

"Uh, sorry, I'm just trying to explain the history of what happened. I don't know exactly how he did it, but he poisoned the males of our pack and most of the females. He kidnapped me—apparently he wanted to keep me alive—but I escaped. By the time I made it back to my pack's estate, everyone was dead or missing. For months I searched for the missing, but it was useless. After a while, I assumed everyone was dead."

"How did you find out about the connection between him and Perez?"

"I hired an investigator to tear apart Preston's life. That led me directly to Antonio Perez. I found out that my pack's death wasn't the first. It wasn't like I knew for sure, but Perez and Preston were connected all over the states. Each time they did business, werewolves turned up dead or just disappeared. The Doyle pack in northern New York, the Harrington Pack in Montana, and I'm assuming that Shea's pack was killed or she was kidnapped."

"Kidnapped."

She nodded and continued. "When Perez settled in Miami, it appeared he was going to stay for a while. There hasn't been a sign of Preston anywhere so I've just been waiting to make my move...until you came along."

Stephan dropped her hands and scrubbed a hand over his face. "Why didn't you go to the Council?"

"I was scared and to be honest, I didn't want their help. My sister has had to hide who she is her entire life because of them." She had a lot of anger stored up for the Council.

"Fair enough," he muttered.

She could actually feel his anger dissipate and in that instant, she simply wanted to make things right between them. "I never wanted to lie to you, Stephan." She gently cupped his face. His jaw tightened under her touch, but he didn't back away.

Her inner wolf let out a sigh of relief, right along with her human side. They could make things work, she was sure of it.

CHAPTER THIRTEEN

The little vixen had him tied up in knots. He wanted to be angry with her, but he couldn't find enough energy to hold onto it. Not when she looked so dejected and tired…and lost.

When she touched him, he felt the touch all the way to his groin. Need burned deep in his belly, but after the way he'd roughly taken her in the bathroom at Perez's house, he wanted to wait until they made love again.

He was embarrassed at the way he'd lost control. He'd just started fucking her like an animal. She might have come, but it didn't matter. She deserved better than that. "You need to get some sleep." The words tore from his chest, but he had to take care of his mate.

"I don't want to sleep." The dark circles under her eyes told a different story.

"Don't argue." He lay back against his pillow and tugged her with him so that her head was against his chest. Barely seconds passed before her body stilled and her breathing was steady.

"Marisol," he murmured.

She didn't move.

He tightened his grip on her and savored her sweet, jasmine scent. His cock was painfully aware of the sexy woman in his arms and he was slightly pissed because he couldn't do a damn thing about it.

Even if they were mates, they'd started sleeping together before they'd gotten to know one another. If he could go back in time and do things differently, he wondered if he would. Hell, if he *could*.

Just being near Marisol and his normally tight control loosened. Sighing, he closed his eyes and tried to think of anything but her lean body pressed up against his.

Stephan's eyes flew open as a scream pierced the air. Instinctively he reached out to protect Marisol. She jolted upright at the same time he did but didn't push him away.

"My sister," she said, terror lacing her voice.

They both jumped off the bed, but he placed himself in front of her as they entered the guestroom. His aunt Caro was trying to calm Marisol's sister down, but the small woman had backed up against the headboard and was clutching a pillow in front of her body in self-defense.

When her gaze fell on Marisol, she dropped the pillow. "Marisol? Where am I?"

"You're safe. This is my mate's house. His pack is going to protect us." Marisol hurried to the bed and sat next to her sister.

Stephan's heart squeezed at the way she said mate without hesitation. Her sister glanced over Marisol's shoulder and looked at him. "I remember you."

"I was at Perez's house the night you escaped. We came to rescue you."

"Where's Shea?" Her voice rose as she asked the question.

"She's safe at my parent's house," he said.

Paz let out a sigh of relief. "Good... What about that bastard, Perez?"

"We don't know where he is...yet. But we're going to find him."

"Not if I find him first," Paz muttered.

"How did you escape your bonds?" He knew he should probably wait to grill her, but his father was going to have questions later. If something could help them to find Perez, they needed to know now.

"I built up an immunity to his drugs."

Marisol cleared her throat and glanced back and forth between them. "Stephan, can I talk to my sister alone?"

"Of course." He glanced at his aunt who silently walked out of the room. As he shut the door behind him, the sound of his cell phone ringing made him hurry to his room.

When he saw his boss's number on caller ID, he instantly tensed. "Yeah?"

"Hey, you okay?"

"Yeah, why?"

"I guess you haven't heard. Perez's house was torched sometime early this morning and his body was found mutilated in an abandoned warehouse. Whoever killed him did a real number on his face. It looks like an animal ripped him apart."

"Shit." Stephan didn't have to feign surprise.

"Since I know you're not at the cover house, I want you to stay wherever you are. Lay low for a few days."

"What?"

"I don't know what's going on or if your cover's been blown. You need to stay out of sight. I've already got the rest of the team doing the same thing. Keep your phone close to you. I've also got an outside team investigating Perez's death. As soon as I'm convinced it's safe, I'll bring you and everyone else back in."

"All right, boss." Under normal circumstances he would've fought his boss to come to work, but right now, he needed the down time with his pack and his mate. They needed to regroup and now they needed to figure out who had killed Perez. It wasn't any of them. Of that, he was positive. That left a lot of questions.

When they disconnected, he started to head back to check on Marisol but changed his mind. After a quick shower and shave, he figured he'd given them enough time alone. It was close to noon and he needed answers from her sister before they headed to his parents' house.

As he started to knock, the bedroom door swung open. Marisol nearly stumbled when she saw him.

"I was just coming to find you." She sounded nervous and out of breath.

"We need to leave soon."

"I know she's awake but... I was thinking Paz doesn't need to come. She's been through a lot and she needs to rest. Meeting the whole pack now will be too much. Especially since they know...what she is."

"Okay." The word was out before he could stop himself.

The megawatt smile Marisol gave him was completely worth the anger he might incur from his father. It lit up her face and eyes. Before he realized what she meant to do, she threw her arms around his neck and held tight.

"Thank you," she whispered in his ear.

Her breath tickled his skin, sending unwanted desire shooting through him. He was an idiot. His Alpha had given him a direct order, but if it made his mate happy, he'd sell his fucking soul. Yeah, he was totally screwed where this female was concerned.

She pulled back and glanced over her shoulder at her sister. "There's food in the kitchen. Hopefully we won't be gone long."

Paz stood near the edge of the bed clutching a pair of jeans and a sweater—no doubt clothes from Marisol. "Thanks. And Stephan, thank you...for everything. I promise to meet with your Alpha in a couple days. I just need some time to adjust."

He nodded and pulled the door shut behind them. "They're going to have a lot of questions, Marisol."

"I know. I'm ready to answer all of them. I just can't believe my sister's alive. That monster's been holding her for a year. She thought all of us were dead too."

"Your sister can sleep easier because Perez is dead."

"What?" She jerked to a halt in the middle of the hallway.

"I got a call from my boss this morning. He was found dead in an abandoned warehouse."

"Who killed him?"

"Don't know yet." But he planned to find out.

"Wow." Marisol shook her head as they entered their bedroom.

"What?"

"It feels sort of anticlimactic. I've been hunting him for the better part of the year. I expected to feel, I don't know, different. Now that I have my sister back..." She shrugged and pulled her pajama top off.

He forgot to breathe for a moment as she started to strip out of the rest of her clothes. Braless and wearing only a skimpy thong, she knelt in front of her suitcase and started rummaging through her things.

Stephan sat against the edge of the bed and drank in the sight of her. Even though she was a werewolf, he'd noticed her apprehension at getting naked in front of him before. Now it seemed she had no such hang-ups. His cock jerked when she shimmied into a pair of jeans. There was nothing intentionally sexual about what she was doing, but his body tingled with excitement as he watched her. This was his mate.

His.

When she pulled a black bra from her clothes, he stopped her. "Don't wear a bra."

Her eyes widened. "What?"

"Please," he rasped. He loved the thought of her wearing nothing under her top. Loved knowing he could slide his hand right under her shirt and touch flesh.

A small smile pulled at the corners of her lips. "Okay." She let the bra slip from her fingers, but instead of putting on the sweater she clutched in her other hand, she dropped it too.

Her hips swayed seductively as she walked toward him. He still sat on the bed so she positioned herself in between his open legs. Wrapping her arms around his neck, she leaned forward and pressed her breasts against his chest. He could feel her hardened nipples through the fabric of his shirt.

Groaning, he grasped her hips. "We don't have time," he murmured.

"I know. I just want you to know how grateful I am for everything you've done. I've lied to you at every turn and that's not who I am. I know we're mates, but I want to get to know the real *you* and I don't want to hold anything back from you anymore."

Relief coursed through him at her words. "I can live with that."

"I'm not sure how to say this, but I want to bond with you," she said quietly.

Her calm declaration punched through him. He wanted to bond with her too. He'd been aching to claim her as his own from the moment they'd met. But..."I don't want your gratitude."

Her full lips pulled into a thin line. "This isn't about that."

Another thought formed in his mind. "Are you saying this because you think my pack won't protect your sister otherwise?"

"No!" Her grip around his neck tightened. "I want this. There's a lot we don't know about each other, but if I'd actually had a choice in my mate, I couldn't have picked anyone better. I *want* to be with you."

He leaned forward so that their faces were inches apart. "Once we do this, there's no going back."

The pupils of her eyes widened as she nodded. "I know."

He pressed a light kiss to her lips but released her hips. "Get dressed or we're never going to make it to the meeting." His words were hoarse and uncontrolled.

Grinning, she stepped away from him and tugged the black sweater over her head. Disappointment rushed through him when the sight of her perfectly rounded breasts and light brown nipples disappeared under her clothing, but the rational part of his brain knew it was for the best.

He needed to call his father and tell him everything he knew *before* the meeting. It would go a long way in calming his father's annoyance at Paz's absence.

Stephan settled into his chair around the table in his father's study. Normally he sat next to one of his brothers, but Nick had given up his seat for Marisol. She darted a nervous glance at him as his father entered the room. Everyone else had already taken their seats around the table and a few hovered near the built-in bookcase. The she-wolf, Shea, was one of the ones that hovered. She obviously felt as uncomfortable as his mate. Not that he blamed either one of them. While he wasn't sure what his Alpha planned, he knew his father would take care of her too. He and his father didn't always see eye to eye on things, but he was a fair leader.

His father glanced in their direction and frowned, no doubt because Paz wasn't with them, but at least he didn't comment. Instead, he took his seat at the round table. "I hope everyone was able to get a few hours of sleep. We have a lot of things to discuss, but I'd like to keep it brief. First things first, my son's new mate has informed me that Preston Morales is the name of the wolf who betrayed her pack. I've contacted the Council and they're already aware of Morales' existence. He's been on their radar for the past couple years but they haven't been able to hunt him down. They didn't realize he had anything to do with taking out the Cabrera pack, but now that they're aware, he's moved to the top of their priority list. Even though he's being tracked, if anyone hears anything from friends—shifter or human—it doesn't matter how unimportant the detail might seem, come to me immediately."

A low murmur of agreement rippled through the room.

His father waited until everyone quieted. "Second, Antonio Perez is dead. I don't think I need to ask, but did anyone have a hand in that?"

The room was silent.

When no one responded, his father continued. "I didn't think so. My sons and I will be investigating his death, but if you hear anything, you come to me first. This leads me to the most important thing. According to Stephan, before Perez died he injected a human male with some sort of serum derived from werewolf blood that gave him super human strength. Everything in Perez's lab, including the doctor doing the experiments, was destroyed, so we don't know who the human is, where he's gone, or even what the exact effects are of the drug he was given. Keep your ears low to the ground for any strange activity here in Miami or elsewhere. The Council is aware of what happened and if this man is discovered, it could send us all into hiding. Before I turn the floor over to Thomas, there is one more thing. Shea Hart and Paz Cabrera are officially under our pack's protection. Until we get them set up with jobs and a living arrangement, they'll be staying at the spare beach house."

Stephan could feel Marisol tense next to him. He cleared his throat, drawing his father's attention in his direction.

His father tilted his head slightly. "Yes?"

"I'd like Paz to stay with Marisol and me." He didn't need to give a reason or excuse. His father should understand why. His mate had been alone for a year. It might cramp his needs a little, but he couldn't take her away from the only family she had left.

"That's acceptable. If Shea is uncomfortable living alone, we'll work something else out." His father glanced at his oldest brother and gave a brief nod.

Next to Stephan, Marisol reached under the table and grabbed his hand. She threaded her fingers through his and squeezed. The show of simple affection wasn't something he was used to, but he squeezed back. In fact, he couldn't remember a time he'd ever held hands with someone. It was a small thing, but it made something warm and foreign swell in his chest.

Truth be told, he hadn't technically dated in the past hundred or so years. When he found a willing female, they carried on a sexual relationship until one tired of the other. Not that he'd actually had that sort of arrangement in a long time. Growing up, he knew what his parents had was special. He'd never wanted to invest too much time with anyone when he knew it wouldn't last.

As Thomas stood, the room seemed to grow even quieter. His father rarely yielded the floor to anyone. Whatever his brother had to say was no doubt important.

"We're going to make a formal announcement to the entire pack, but for now, everyone in this room needs to be aware that Adam Tucker will be arriving in a week. The Council thought it prudent to send him here until Morales is caught and until we figure out who the infected human is."

A small wave of fear vibrated across the room and even Marisol shifted in her seat next to Stephan. Adam Tucker was the Council's enforcer, for lack of a better word. Whenever there was a problem with any pack, they sent him to keep things in line. Stephan had met the lone wolf once or twice, and on a personal level, he really liked the guy. Still, he understood the fear of everyone in the room. He was at least two hundred fifty years old — yet looked about forty-five — he had no pack to speak of, and when he came to town, werewolves often died.

"He's not coming here to cause trouble for our pack. The Council wants an independent assessment of the situation. If anyone has a problem, don't cross him. Come to your Alpha or me. Any questions?"

No one said a word. Probably because their Alpha and his second-in-command had just laid out a lot to digest. For so many years, they'd lived peacefully all over the globe. Dealing with outsiders wasn't something their pack was used to.

Times were changing and they'd just have to deal.

"Good. Enjoy the rest of your Sunday everyone." When Carly loudly cleared her throat, Thomas stopped everyone. "Don't forget, Nick's birthday is Wednesday and Carly will have everyone's hide if you don't RSVP to her invitations."

His last minute announcement broke the tension in the room. As the meeting broke up, everyone broke off into different conversations. Carly and his mom immediately pounced on Marisol, so he took the time to speak to his brothers and father privately. They convened in the far corner of the huge study.

"Is this serious? The enforcer coming?" Stephan asked. He'd spoken to his Alpha before the meeting but he hadn't mentioned anything about Tucker visiting.

Thomas shook his head. "It's serious but not for us. We have nothing to hide and once he sees that, he'll focus on what he came here to do."

"So when are you bonding with your mate?" His father effectively changed the subject.

Stephan was rarely embarrassed about anything, but even discussing his bonding brought out every protective instinct inside him. What went on between him and Marisol was their business. "Soon...tonight, most likely."

"Good. I'll introduce her to everyone at Nick's birthday." He glanced over his shoulder then nodded at the three of them. "I'm going to take your mother and Shea home, but I want to see the three of you tomorrow after breakfast. We have a lot to discuss."

Once he walked away, Nick spoke. "This is insane. First that crap with the Immortal, now this."

Thomas shook his head. "Go home to your mates, have a lot of sex and get this shit out of your system. If the rest of the pack senses fear from *any* of us, they'll worry. Besides, we've got each other. No one fucks with the Lazos brothers."

Stephan couldn't help but chuckle at that. "You're right about that."

After Nick walked away, Thomas briefly clamped Stephan on the shoulder. "How's your mate holding up?"

"Now that she has her sister back, she'll be fine." He loved his brother, but he didn't feel like divulging anything else about his mate. She hadn't said it outright, but he knew she was worried enough about her privacy and he didn't want to discuss her without her being there.

"I didn't want to say anything in front of the pack, but when Tucker arrives, we'll make it a point to keep Marisol's sister away from him."

Potent relief slid through his veins. "Thank you."

Stephan glanced at Marisol who was deep in conversation with Carly and Nick and grinned. Carly might be human, but she fit right in with their pack and if anyone could bring Marisol out of her shell, it was the tall redhead.

Marisol turned and when their gazes locked, fire and need erupted in a flash. He muttered something to his brother and strode toward her. If he didn't get her home soon, he was going to behave like the animal he was.

CHAPTER FOURTEEN

Marisol's heart rate had increased since the meeting and it hadn't stopped now that they were back at the beach house. She was finally going to bond with her mate. Maybe not this instant, but it was going to happen very soon. Considering the heated looks he'd been throwing her, she guessed tonight. Equal doses of excitement and nerves flowed through her.

After Stephan's declaration that Paz could live with them, she'd had no doubt in her mind that he was the wolf for her. He understood how important family was. That much was obvious. Having her sister live under the same roof as them would restrict his style, something he knew, yet he'd offered anyway. And it hadn't been a half-assed offer either. He'd been completely sincere.

As they neared the front door, she noticed a piece of paper taped to it. Stephan grabbed it before she could reach it. He grinned as he read it.

"What?"

Wordlessly, he passed it to her.

Your clothes are too big and after a year of being kept naked, I want something that fits. I've gone shopping with Caro. I know I freaked before, but she's cool so don't worry. We'll be gone for hours. Enjoy your mate, little hermana. Love, Paz. P.S. I want details.

She folded the note and tucked it into her jeans as Stephan opened the door. When she walked past him, his lust rolled over her like a heat wave. Suddenly, she felt nervous.

They'd had sex. Lots of it. And it had been mind-blowing. Bonding was different though. What if they didn't do it right? What if she somehow screwed it up? Werewolves were superstitious and if the bonding didn't go well, it was supposed to curse the mates for life. That was a long freaking time.

"Stop," Stephan growled close to her ear.

She swiveled to face him. "What?"

"Stop worrying." He shut and locked the door behind him, the click almost ominous sounding. Before she could think about what the next step should be, he advanced on her like a predator stalking its prey and lifted her up so she had no choice but to wrap her legs around his waist.

His mouth descended on hers with little finesse. Hungrily he ate at her lips, stroking his tongue over hers with such fervor, her pussy contracted with the need for him. She could taste the remnants of his toothpaste—sweet and minty.

Scrambling for the hem of his shirt, she tugged at it while he carried her up the stairs. After she peeled it off, she ran her hands along his muscled chest. She dug her fingers into his hard flesh and groaned into his mouth.

Most werewolves stayed in shape, but this man—her man—was absolute perfection. All hard lines and muscles and just a smattering of hair across his chest, he was the kind of man who turned heads. And he was all hers.

That made her feel ridiculously proud. Her wolf wanted to strut around and freaking preen that this was her male.

Until now she'd forced herself to keep her feelings at bay, but letting them free was liberating. She was free to want something again, to claim something as her own. Stephan was hers and every wolf and woman in a hundred mile radius was going to know. She was no longer alone in the world and that in itself, unchained her.

Her nipples pressed painfully through the fabric of her sweater. As she rubbed herself against him, the hardened tips stroked against the material, begging to be released.

Suddenly she was falling. She tensed for impact but her fall was cushioned by the rumpled comforter of their bed. Shirtless, and breathing hard, Stephan stood above her. His chest rose and fell and the heated look in his dark eyes was enough to curl her toes.

He quickly shucked his pants and she was pleased but not surprised that he'd gone commando. His cock jutted forward proudly. She couldn't wait until it was buried deep inside her. His pubic hair had been trimmed before but she noticed he'd shaved and cut almost all of it. The realization that he'd done it for her made her stomach clench. Not to mention, the effect made his cock look even bigger.

When she reached for the hem of her sweater, he stopped her. Like lightning, he straddled her on the bed. His strong thighs encased her in a tight grip, making it impossible to move her legs. Grasping her wrists, he held them above her head.

She was completely caged in. The reality of being dominated turned her on more than she could have imagined.

"This time, you don't do anything unless I say," he rasped.

She nodded and her hair swished against the covers. "Okay."

With one hand, he held her wrists in place, and with the other, he pushed her sweater up. As his hand trailed up her skin, tingles trailed across her entire body. When her breasts were bared, she fought off an involuntary shiver. Cool air rushed over her, but before she could blink, he covered one nipple with his mouth. Kissing and teasing, he trailed moist circles around her areola.

Arching her back, she tried to get closer to him. When she attempted to spread her legs, his thighs tightened around her.

His head lifted slightly. "I don't think so," he murmured against her breast. His hot breath sent tantalizing shivers skittering across her skin.

The hand keeping her wrists captive loosened and he worked a slow trail down to her other aching breast. Cupping it, he lightly stroked his thumb over the distended tip while continuing the assault with his tongue. The male was way too talented for his own good.

Her pussy clenched and unclenched with the need to be filled. She'd assumed he'd want to get straight to business and mark her but it appeared he was taking his sweet time.

Of all times, she did not want foreplay. After the rough coupling they'd had in that bathroom, she hadn't been able to get it out of her mind. She'd always thought she liked her sex a little softer, but when he'd taken her like that, almost in anger, it had been hot as sin.

And she wanted more of it.

Since he'd released her hands, she was free to do as she pleased. Threading her fingers through his thick hair, she clutched his head. What he was doing to her breasts felt amazing but unless he eased the throbbing between her legs, he was just a damn tease.

"Enough," she muttered.

He chuckled against her skin and lifted his head. When their gazes locked, there was no laughter in his eyes. He looked...feral.

And hungry. *For her.*

The dark glint sent her senses haywire. She was his meal and that was more than fine with her. His hands dipped south and in a few movements, he'd unzipped her jeans and pushed them down. Somehow, he managed to get her almost fully undressed without losing that skin on skin contact.

While he tugged her pants off, she finished shimmying out of her sweater. Now the only barrier between them was her barely there thong.

With one of his large hands, he covered her mound. Teasingly, he pushed the flimsy material to the side and played with her clit. Strumming the hardened bud with his middle finger, he kept his eyes locked on hers.

She could come simply from the light stroking and his white-hot gaze. But she wanted him inside her when that happened. She wanted their bonding to be perfect. For a year she hadn't had anything good or pure in her life, and she wanted this to be everything she'd ever hoped for. More importantly, she wanted it to be perfect for him. He deserved it.

"I'm ready." She almost didn't recognize her own voice as she spoke. Her hoarse words sounded sensual and seductive.

Without a word, he removed his hand, grasped her hips and flipped her over. The sudden show of power made her entire body light up with need.

As he clutched her hips, she was already pushing up on all fours. The need to feel him inside her was overpowering. He pulled her panties down so they were at her knees and spread her thighs apart a little more.

Her thong added a bit of restriction to her movements and when a brief thought of what it might be like to be tied up by him flashed in her mind, heat pooled between her legs. She could definitely get on board with that idea.

He ran a callused palm over her back and ass then reached between her legs. Tracing a finger over her folds, he kept going until he skated over her clit, just barely teasing her. Before she had time to protest his slowness, he moved back and pushed inside her. She couldn't bite back a moan.

She clenched around his finger and tried to push back, needing to feel him deeper. He removed his finger before bending forward over her. His chest rubbed over her back and she could feel his cock pressing against her opening. Still, he didn't try to push into her. Instead, he placed his hands over hers and feathered kisses along the back of her neck.

Apparently he was determined to make her crazy.

"You sure you're ready?" he murmured in between kisses.

"Yes." More than ready.

That was all he needed to hear. Pushing up, he placed his hands firmly around her hips and thrust into her, filling her completely. Without giving her a chance to adjust, he pulled out then pushed in again. This time with more force.

Her inner walls clenched and contracted around him with a fervor. She was so slick and wet, she had no problem taking him. Gasping, she clutched the sheets and tried to ground herself as he thrust in and out of her.

"Who do you belong to?" His voice was raspy.

"You," she whispered.

"Who?" he growled.

"Stephan." The word tore from her throat like a prayer.

The declaration seemed to do something to her. As she said it, she realized it was true. Her life had changed drastically after finding him and now they had a whole mess of things to worry about, but she finally felt like she belonged somewhere. With someone.

The harder he pushed, the more she propelled toward that edge. Her inner walls contracted wildly until that sweet release was just within her reach.

"Let go," he murmured before raking his teeth over the area where her neck and shoulder connected.

So she did. Her fingers dug into the sheets as a powerful climax ripped through her. Her pussy pulsed around him as she rode through her orgasm. The desire in her belly uncoiled with a burst as the pleasure expanded and coursed through her entire body. Even her toes tingled with the release.

Before she could come down from her high, Stephan scored his extended canines into her neck. The sharp feel of his teeth imprinting her make her cry out in a mix of pleasure and pain. "Stephan."

He growled against her neck, the sound completely primitive. The knowledge that they were bonded overrode the fleeting pain.

After marking her, his grip on her hips tightened as he continued to drive into her. With a shout, he emptied himself inside her and when he finished, he lightly squeezed her waist before collapsing on the bed. Instead of falling on top of her, he rolled to the side and dragged her with him. He stroked his hands all over her, as if he couldn't get enough of touching her. She felt exactly the same.

She curled up against him, savoring the feel of their bodies intertwined. She wasn't sure if she should feel different now that they were bonded. Glancing down at herself, everything looked and felt normal. Propping up on one elbow, she looked at Stephan. "Do you feel…different?"

"Yeah, I hope you do too. If not, I seriously fucked that up." He chuckled under his breath as he reached out and stroked her neck. "Are you okay? I didn't hurt you, did I?"

"I'm fine, but that's not what I meant." She bit her bottom lip. Narrowing her gaze at him, she tried to project her thoughts. *What does kardia mou mean?*

"My heart," he murmured as he stroked his thumb over her tender neck.

Oh...hey, it worked.

We should also be able to communicate in wolf form now too, he said.

"So, my heart, huh?" she asked aloud.

His eyes flashed a darker shade as he nodded. "That's right, vixen. You're mine now."

She scooted up a few inches and pressed her lips against his. All the external stuff in their life melted away for a few seconds as his hand strayed to her waist and he pulled her closer against him. The skin on skin contact was exactly what she needed.

The fact that the Council was sending their enforcer to Miami was a little scary, but she had no doubt the Lazos pack—now her pack—would protect her and her sister. Stephan's father hadn't hesitated in his commitment to take them in. In her experience, that was a rare quality. She'd loved her pack but they'd been wary of all outsiders. The Lazos' had not only taken them in, but the blonde werewolf from the lab as well.

While there weren't any declarations of undying love between her and Stephan, she knew it was only a matter of time before she told the big wolf she loved him. Hell, she was half in love with him now. Maybe more than half. Saying it now wouldn't feel right though. Sighing contentedly, she snuggled closer to him.

It would be nice if everything in their lives could be fixed and wrapped up with a pretty red bow, but that wasn't going to happen. Still, even with all the external forces against them, she felt incredibly lucky and safe in the arms of her mate.

EPILOGUE

Two Days Later

"**W**hat the hell is that?" Stephan growled and tightened his grip over Marisol's bare stomach.

"I think it's my cell phone." Chuckling, she swatted his hand away and rolled over. Scrambling for her purse, she found it where she'd tossed it on the floor earlier. When she saw the number on the caller ID, she frowned. It was a Miami area code but she didn't recognize it. "Hello?"

"I left a present for you." A familiar voice chilled her veins.

"Preston Morales," she spat his name.

"So you remember me?" His voice was low, mocking.

Of course she remembered the wolf who'd helped betray her pack. She turned around to find Stephan sitting straight up in bed. His jaw was tense, the rage rolling off him potent. She tried to ignore it and focus on Preston. He was calling her for a reason. "What present are you talking about?"

"Antonio Perez of course."

"*You* killed him? Why?" It made no sense considering they'd been business partners.

"Sniveling human tried to double-cross me."

"What do you want?" She tried to fight the nausea swelling in her stomach. Despite the fact the last couple days with Stephan had been absolute heaven, a dark cloud had been hanging over her head. Whoever had killed Perez was still out there and now she knew who that someone was.

"What I've always wanted. You."

"*What?*"

"I've been trying to track you for months but you're a sneaky little bitch."

200 | SAVANNAH STUART

Her throat clenched. She opened her mouth but no sound would come out. She'd been extra careful over the past year because she'd known he'd been out there, but she hadn't realized he'd been hunting her.

He continued, "Perez was your first gift. Until you give yourself over to me, I'll keep delivering more presents."

The way he said "presents" sent a chill slithering down her spine. "Why'd you poison my pack?"

"Your father didn't want us together. No one did. I thought that once they were out of the way we'd be together. But you had to run away from me." His voice trembled manically.

"You're insane!"

"Watch your tongue, little bitch. You've got something to lose now. Either come to me willingly or I'll kill that wolf you've been fucking."

He'd been watching her.

As if he read her mind, he said, "That's right. I know you've shacked up with that Lazos wolf. You've got twenty-four hours to make a decision. Come to me willingly or I'll get you myself." The phone died.

Her hands trembled as she laid the phone on the bed between her and Stephan. "That was Preston Morales. He just admitted to killing Perez. Said it was a present for me. Either I give myself over to him in the next twenty-four hours or he's threatened to kill you."

A dark shadow crossed Stephan's gaze. "Sweetheart, we're going to catch this bastard and put him in his grave. He just made his first mistake by contacting you. If he knows we're together, then he's in Miami."

Another tremble raced through her. "Why the hell is that a good thing?"

"He's one wolf. My family is strong and we have ties all over the city. Hell, the world. Now that he's on our radar, he's dead. I'll keep you and your sister safe, *kardia mou*, I promise." There was a dark edge to Stephan's voice that left no doubt in her mind, he'd keep his word.

Fear still trickled through her body, but she had an entire pack of fearless wolves to back her up. She was still a little scared for her mate, but she had to believe that they'd kill Preston. If the evil wolf had been half-smart he wouldn't have contacted her. Now he'd shown all his cards and it was simply a matter of time before her mate ended his pathetic life.

"I love you, Stephan." She didn't care if it was too soon, that they were still getting to know one another. She felt the love for him bone deep and it wasn't going away. Ever.

With a sigh that sounded a lot like relief, he gathered her into his arms. "I love you too."

POWER UNLEASHED

She has a big secret...

After a year in captivity, werewolf Paz Cabrera is trying to figure out her place in the world. While her sister's new family is welcoming, Paz still doesn't feel like she belongs to the Lazos pack. She has a *big* secret that could harm them all and give The Council ammunition to kill her. When The Council sends their legendary enforcer to hunt a rogue werewolf terrorizing Miami, she makes a shocking discovery about the one man she's supposed to be avoiding. He's her mate and she's terrified he'll uncover her secret.

He'll stop at nothing to uncover the truth...

As enforcer and one of the oldest living werewolves on the planet, Adam Tucker had fated himself to a lonely life. After centuries by himself, he never expected to meet his mate while on the job, but now that he's found her, he won't let her go. Paz denies their connection, but she can't escape the sizzling heat between them. No matter what it takes, he plans to uncover the truth behind her resistance and bond her to him forever.

CHAPTER ONE

Adam Tucker stared at the palatial guesthouse from the front seat of his rented SUV. The Lazos pack was one of the few who had done incredibly well for themselves over the years. Most packs were well-off, but this family lived in luxury. The fact that they owned a private stretch of beach in Key Biscayne spoke volumes. That was in addition to their other holdings across the country. Not that any of that would matter to The Council if they'd gone against their laws.

When the front door opened and Thomas Lazos stepped out, Adam realized he might have been sitting outside too long. Without pause, he got out and strode over to one of the alphas of the pack. More distinctly, the next-in-line to be *Alpha* of the Lazos pack. "It's been a while, Thomas."

The dark-haired wolf nodded politely and held out a hand. "I wish it was under different circumstances, but welcome to our guest home. My Alpha sends his regards, but—"

Adam grasped his hand and brushed away the apology with a shake of his head. "Your father called. No apology necessary."

"Good then. Do you have many bags?"

He shook his head. "I'll get them later. For now I'd like to get down to business."

Thomas stepped back and held out his arm toward the open front door. They were silent as they strode across the tiled floor and entered the kitchen. That was one of the things he liked about the other wolf. Thomas didn't reek of fear as so many others did in his presence.

Adam understood that as The Council's enforcer, it was only natural that wolves would be wary around him, but it made for a lonesome existence. He'd long ago adapted to the idea of never finding a mate. Even if it tore him up inside.

Thomas surprised him by grabbing a beer from the refrigerator. "Want one?"

It was instinct to say no to any food or drink offered, but he nodded as he took a seat at the granite top center island. "Sure."

As he popped open the beers, Thomas glanced over his shoulder. "You can start firing away if you're ready."

Adam waited until Thomas slid the beer across to him and took a seat. "It's a formality because the business with the Immortal has already been settled. Asha was on The Council's radar for years and it's officially been ruled that your kill was justified."

Thomas shrugged and took a sip of his drink. "I wasn't worried."

Adam hadn't expected him to be. When a crazed Immortal had tried to kidnap Thomas' brother Nick's mate, Thomas had no choice but to kill the Immortal. As a rule, they were a lone bunch and Asha's reputation for abusing human women had been growing. He wasn't going to tell Thomas, but The Council was relieved Asha was dead. Any supernatural beings that couldn't follow the laws of man and nature put *all* of them in danger from the humans. "So what have you learned so far about the rogue werewolf, Preston Morales?"

"He's in Miami. That much we're sure of. He contacted my brother Stephan's new mate yesterday and told her that if she didn't turn herself over to him, he was going to start leaving more presents for her."

"More?"

"He said Antonio Perez was his first gift to her."

The body of Perez, the human who'd tried to genetically alter werewolf DNA to create super-soldiers, had been found bloody and mangled in an abandoned warehouse a few days ago. It was good he was dead, but there was still a missing human who'd been injected with some sort of serum and now had super strength. No one knew where he was or how big of a threat he posed. "What about the human?"

Thomas shook his head. "No leads."

"And your brother can't use his resources with the DEA?" Stephan, the youngest of the Lazos brothers worked for the DEA and if it hadn't been for him, they might not have found out about Perez's plans.

"No. Since Perez's death Stephan's boss has him and his entire team on indefinite leave until they figure out if their cover was blown. It's not as if Stephan can admit he knows who killed Perez so until then, he's working with us to bring Morales down."

Adam nodded. "Good." Thomas wasn't lying to him. It was obvious in his scent and body language. No doubt the Lazos pack wanted this settled as quickly as The Council. "I'd like to speak to the two she-wolves who were held captive by Perez."

Thomas' entire demeanor changed in an instant. His back straightened and his gaze became shuttered. "Tonight is Nick's birthday. His new mate is having a party at my Alpha's house at six and everyone will be there, including Shea and Paz. It's your choice but I thought it might be easier on…everyone if you spoke to them in a relaxed setting. They're both still adjusting."

Adam could imagine they'd be "adjusting" for quite a while after what they'd been through. The report on Shea Hart and Paz Cabrera was sketchy at best. The two very different she-wolves came from different parts of the country and were just two of the wolves who had been kidnapped and sold to Antonio Perez for experimentation. Out of all the males and females the madman had kept captive, only these two women survived. They had to be exceptionally strong, both mentally and physically. "That's acceptable."

After draining his beer, Thomas stood. "If there's anything else you need, you've got all our numbers. The house is yours so feel free to choose any bedroom upstairs. Do you want a ride to the party tonight?"

He shook his head and glanced at his watch. He only had a couple hours to get settled in and review his notes on the entire pack. "No. I think I'll be able to find my way."

"All right then. I'll let myself out."

Adam scrubbed a hand over his face once Thomas was gone. Some days he hated his job more than others. He said a silent prayer that the Lazos pack wasn't hiding anything from him. For the most part he kept his distance from all wolves, but this was one pack he wanted to be above reproach. After all the shit he'd seen over the past few decades, he was getting tired of dealing with liars.

Paz glanced at her sister Marisol as the sound of male voices grew closer. "I think we have a visitor," she murmured.

"Do you want to go rest or something?" Marisol asked, concern etched on her pretty face.

It was weird having her little sister constantly checking on her. If Paz hadn't been missing for a year and presumed dead, she might have been annoyed with Marisol's constant concern, but she understood where it was coming from. And it was hard to be mad at someone who loved you and wanted to look out for you. "I'm not going to fall apart just because we have unexpected company."

Marisol rolled her eyes and threw a dishtowel at her. "I know that. I'm just—"

206 | SAVANNAH STUART

"Worried. I know. And I appreciate it, but I'm fine." And she was. For the most part anyway. It had only been a few days since she and Shea had been freed. Not a lot of time to actually process everything.

"Okay, I swear I'll stop bugging you...eventually." Marisol placed the knife next to the eggplants she'd sliced and reached for a bottle of wine. "Feel like a drink?"

"Yes, please." Despite saying she was fine, tension prickled the back of her neck. In a few hours she'd be seeing the entire Lazos pack for the first time. Sure, she'd met a bunch of them over the past couple days, but she didn't relish the thought of being in a crowded room.

"Hey, Paz, Marisol." Thomas' voice drew her attention to the archway between the kitchen and hallway. The tall, dark-haired shifter stood halfway in the room but was obviously keeping his distance.

She nodded politely and took the glass her sister handed her. "Hello."

"You got a sec to talk?" he asked.

"Ah—" Marisol interrupted.

"Yes." Paz dropped a kiss on her sister's cheek. "I finished the trifle. I think you can handle the eggplant parmesan by yourself." Without giving her sister a chance to protest, Paz followed Thomas through the back door onto the lanai.

"So what's up?" She collapsed on one of the wicker armchairs.

He sat next to her on an ottoman and leaned forward. His dark eyes flashed with unease and that surprised her. Thomas was next in line to be Alpha should that day ever come and the male never seemed to be ruffled by anything. A good quality in a leader. "Adam Tucker is here."

"I figured as much. So why are you worried?" Paz had been staying with Marisol and her new mate Stephan, and for the past couple days Thomas had been stopping by for obviously made up reasons. Not that she minded the company, just the opposite. But now she wanted to know why he kept making excuses to see her.

He shook his head. "I'm not. As long as we stick to the story, we'll be fine."

She took a sip of her wine and regarded him carefully. They'd been over the story only a hundred times. The Lazos pack had broken into Perez's home and saved her. She hadn't used her "wicked blue-juice" powers, as Marisol liked to call them, to blast everyone away. Or at least that was what they were telling The Council's enforcer. If anyone found out she was half fae, half-werewolf and that it had been she who'd killed Perez's men by herself, they'd sentence her to death simply because of the magic that flowed through her veins. It was a barbaric and antiquated law, but there wasn't much she could do about it. Well, except hide her true heritage and she'd been doing that since birth. Adam Tucker was simply one more person to lie to.

"That's not why you're here. You've been acting weird since yesterday so spill it." The truth was, out of everyone — excluding her sister — she felt more comfortable around Thomas than anyone. Not in an 'I'd-like-to-get-you-between-the-sheets' kind of way but more brotherly.

"I want to ask you something, but it might be too personal."

Her heart skipped a beat. "What?"

"Do you know other...faeries? Or half faes like yourself?"

She lifted her eyebrows. That was certainly an interesting and unexpected question. "Why?"

He cleared his throat, but he held her gaze. "I just wanted to know if you knew anyone by the name of Nissa?"

There weren't many faeries living in the United States, but she had heard of *a* Nissa who lived somewhere in the United Kingdom. She was part of some royal line or something. It was probably bad, but Paz knew little of that piece of her heritage. Her entire life she'd been so worried about hiding the magic in herself, sometimes it was easy to pretend she was full-blooded werewolf. If she believed it, others would too. That was the code she'd lived by for so long. "I have heard the name whispered. Why?"

To her surprise, a faint stain of crimson crept up his neck. "No reason."

"Oh. My. *God.* You fell in love with a faerie." It wasn't a question. She could smell the truth roll off him when she said it. And that surprised her. As next in line to be Alpha, he'd have learned to hide his emotions as a pup.

She took a sip of her wine and shook her head. "No wonder you didn't have a problem with me. Holy hell, Thomas. That's insane."

"The Council needs to rethink their laws. Those wars were over long before any of us were even born. It's — "

"Archaic. Trust me, *I* agree." She would love to be able to admit exactly what she was instead of hiding her heritage. "But don't think you get off that easy. What happened with her?"

Thomas' spine straightened at her question, but surprisingly he answered. "I fucked up."

"How long ago?"

"A century."

She let out a low whistle. "Dang."

His dark eyes flashed briefly with pain, but just as quickly that mask was back in place. "That about sums it up."

Her heart twisted for him. A century was a long time to pine over someone. In the hundred plus years she'd been alive, she'd never met a man or wolf who held her interest for very long. Not wanting to cause him further pain, she decided to change the subject. "So tell me who's going to be at this party. Any cute wolves?"

To her surprise, he let out a bark of laughter. "How the hell am I supposed to answer that?"

"Hey, you've got cousins, right. How old are they?"

He rolled his eyes and stood. "Too young for you. You'd probably eat them alive."

"I've literally been under lockdown for a year, so you're probably right." It felt weird but refreshing to joke about it. When she was around Marisol, it was hard to joke because her little sister had been through her own version of hell the past year in her quest for revenge.

"I've got to get out of here, but I'll see you tonight."

She nodded and started to follow him inside.

"Paz…" He paused, his hand on the door. "No matter what happens, even if The Council finds out about you, our pack will protect you."

Her throat seized at his words and unexpected tears stung her eyes. Thankfully, he must have sensed her discomfort because he muttered a quick goodbye and was gone before she'd taken two steps into the kitchen.

Marisol looked up from the stove. "Everything okay?"

"Yeah, he just wanted to let me know that Adam Tucker has officially arrived. Hey, does Thomas remind you of anyone?"

A funny smile played across her sister's face. "Dad?"

"Yes! It's weird, right?"

Marisol shook her head and dipped a finger in the top whipped cream layer of the trifle. "Not the way he looks or anything, but yeah, I've thought that since I met him."

Paz had too, which made being around this new pack a lot easier. Paz grabbed the big bowl and slid it away from her sister. "Hey! I want to make a good impression and that's not going to happen if your paw prints are all over my dessert."

Marisol just grinned and turned back to the stove.

After putting the dessert in the refrigerator, Paz made her way to the guestroom. Marisol and Stephan had set up the room as hers and she savored having her own private haven. It had been so long since she'd done anything social she wasn't sure what to wear. Especially since the enforcer was going to be there. That was such a dumb title too; *enforcer*.

She was pretty curious what he looked like though. Probably a big, jackass Neanderthal-type werewolf who was alpha to the bone. Sighing, she trudged up the stairs. If she had to deal with the inquisition tonight, she was going to take a bubble bath beforehand.

CHAPTER TWO

Adam parked his rented truck behind an older muscle car near the end of the winding, private driveway. When Thomas said they were having a party Adam hadn't realized he meant the entire pack. And from the looks of it, half of Miami.

As he walked up the stone drive he took in the vehicles. They were all a little older but in good shape. The family obviously didn't like to show off, which made sense. Drawing attention to yourself was never a good idea, especially for shifters. He started to knock on the intricate—probably custom carved—wood door when it flew open and two younger she-wolves nearly ran him over.

"Sorry!" one of them yelled over her shoulder as they raced toward one of the cars.

Something foreign twinged deep in his chest. He might work for The Council but he didn't consider any of them his family. He had no pack, no real friends, no real home. Not anymore. His life was fucking lonely and something told him that spending time with the Lazos pack would only remind him of what he was missing and would never have again.

Shaking his head, he stepped farther into the foyer. To the right was a giant dining room with a huge spread of food. A cake sat in the middle and there was a smorgasbord of other food surrounding it.

"Hungry?" Thomas asked as he joined him.

"I'm okay for now. Could go for a beer though."

Thomas grabbed his shoulder in a light, almost brotherly grip. "Come on, we'll get you settled." The action was unexpected and it also reminded him that he couldn't get too close to these wolves. He was there to do a job and if anyone had acted against The Council's code, he'd have to turn them over for judgement.

The dining room connected to an even larger kitchen. A sea of mainly dark-haired wolves mingled around in groups of two and three. Only a few stood out. A tall, pretty redheaded human. From his files, he knew she was Nick Lazos' mate and new wife. And of course Marisol, Stephan's mate. She was a brunette like most of the Lazos' but she was Hispanic, not Greek. When he met Shea Hart's gaze, the tall blonde wolf he needed to question, she quickly averted her eyes and said something to the much shorter brunette she-wolf she was talking to.

The petite wolf swiveled to look at him and when their gazes locked, his heart actually stuttered in his chest. It was Paz Cabrera. He'd recognize those midnight eyes anywhere. The dossier he had on her didn't do her justice though. He couldn't tear his gaze away from those intoxicating eyes. She was pretty, yes, but it was those damn eyes that drew him in. Dark, exotic and full of passion and life. After what she'd been through, the fire he saw there surprised him.

When she turned away from him, he mourned the loss like a physical blow. It seemed as if he'd been staring an eternity, but in reality only seconds had passed.

"Here ya go." Thomas handed him a beer and nodded toward Paz and Shea who stood by themselves near a glass door that lead to a back patio. "I'm sure you already know, but those are the she-wolves we rescued. I've spoken to them and they're ready to talk to you when you want."

"Now's as good a time as any." The truth was, he could have waited. Would normally have preferred to wait and acclimate to his surroundings, but the wolf inside him was desperate to be alone with and talk to Paz. Hear her voice, draw in her scent. Something. Anything. He spoke low enough for only Thomas to hear him as they approached the women. "I'll speak to Paz first."

A burst of primal protectiveness rolled off Thomas and nearly bowled Adam over with its intensity. He had to stop the growl that started in the back of his throat. He had no claim over Paz and even the thought was ludicrous enough that he almost laughed at himself.

"Shea, Paz, this is Adam Tucker," Thomas said.

Both she-wolves nodded politely, but he didn't miss the light sheen of sweat that had formed on the blonde's brow.

He pulled the sliding glass door open and kept his attention on Paz. "If you don't mind, I'd like to ask you a few questions and just get them out of the way now."

She shot a quick, guarded look at Shea before returning his gaze. "Of course."

Adam slid the door shut behind them. He'd never been in Florida in the fall and the weather was mild and perfect. A light breeze pushed up from the Atlantic. The salty smell rolled over him with a subtle freshness and he realized why they'd chosen to settle in Miami.

Before he'd taken two steps, she blurted, "I thought you'd be taller."

He couldn't help himself. A sharp bark of laughter escaped at her words.

Horror immediately covered her pretty face and her very full lips formed a perfect O. "I'm so sorry. I can't believe I said that. I...I haven't been out in public in a year. That's my only excuse."

Grinning, he motioned toward two of the Adirondack chairs near the pool. "It's okay. I think you just said what most people usually think when they meet me." At five foot ten, he was probably the shortest out of all the male wolves in the house, but in a fight, he had no doubt he could take any of them. Thomas and his Alpha included. Size didn't mean shit to him. He was older, faster and stronger than all of them. A reason he'd held his job for so long.

"Still, I'm sorry." She perched on the edge of the elongated chair so he sat across from her. She shifted against her seat. When she did, her yellow dress slid up to reveal smooth, perfectly bronzed skin. She cleared her throat and he realized he was staring. Averting his gaze to her face was worse. He felt as if he was falling when he stared into her dark eyes.

Mentally shaking himself, he got down to business. "For the record, I just need to know what happened with Preston Morales and Antonio Perez. When you were taken, where you were held, any little details you can think of."

Paz stared into the greenest eyes she'd ever seen and tried to concentrate on his words instead of his sinfully sexy voice. There was the slightest trace of an accent, but she couldn't place it. No, Adam Tucker most certainly wasn't a jackass Neanderthal. He was approachable and sexy to boot. And that little dimple that appeared in his left cheek every time he spoke was going to drive her crazy. Not to mention the sleek, muscular lines of his forearms and broad shoulders straining against his shirt. Things she should *not* be noticing. She needed to keep her distance from this male more than anyone. And more importantly, keep her cool.

"My pack lived in a very tight community, but I'm sure you're already aware of that. Somehow Morales poisoned our water system with silver. Not with copious amounts at first. I think he must have started small to weaken us. I don't really know much after that though. I've been informed that he killed most of the pack and only kidnapped some of us, but that's not from first-hand knowledge. I woke up in a lab with ten other wolves. By the time Perez and his doctor were finished…" She didn't finish because she didn't need to. Thomas knew only two of them walked out of that lab.

"Do you know what he did with the other bodies?"

Swallowing hard, she shook her head. She'd watched too many of her packmates slowly die—writhing in agony from all the injections and experimentation. If she thought about it too long, she knew she'd fall into a pit of depression and she couldn't allow that to happen. Not until Morales was caught. Only then could she truly grieve.

"Do you know what he was doing with your blood?"

Again she shook her head. As the questions continued she tried to compartmentalize her thoughts. *Where is the human he injected? Were you ever allowed outside? What kind of experiments was he performing?* The questions were never ending and her head was starting to hurt. Memories flooded back in a sickening rush. No, she wasn't allowed outside. She hadn't seen sunlight in over a year and that disgusting doctor had touched her however and whenever he'd wanted. At least he hadn't raped her. Paz pressed a hand to her stomach.

Frowning, Adam sat up straighter. "Are you okay?"

No. "I'm fine. Do you think we could finish these questions later?"

He paused, nodded and stood. When he did, he held out his hand to her. She stared dumbly at it until she realized what he wanted. For some reason the thought of touching him scared her, but she placed her hand in his. An unexpected electric zing shot through her like lightning. It coursed up her arm and through her body all the way to the knot in her stomach.

She met his gaze and what she saw there startled her. It was lust. Plain and simple. That surprised the hell out of her. Tucker had such a reputation for being scary, but maybe the way he got his information from she-wolves was by seducing them. She yanked her hand away and wrapped her arms around herself. "I think you should wait to question Shea. She had a worse time of it than me and it's too crowded for her right now. Question her tomorrow morning. I'll bring her over to your house." It came out like an order. As she spoke she realized it was stupid to bark orders at him of all wolves, but she couldn't help it. She was worried about her friend and the truth was, Paz had lost a lot of her social skills and couldn't seem to rein in her big mouth.

His lips quirked up slightly as he regarded her, but he nodded. "That's fine. Make it early and maybe we can go for a run in the morning."

The request startled her. "Oh ah…okay."

His gaze softened on her face as he held open the door for her. She couldn't help but wonder what the hell was wrong with him. He was an enforcer. Why was he being so nice?

He cleared his throat and suddenly looked nervous as they stepped inside. "Would you mind introducing me to everyone?"

She wasn't sure if his nervousness was an act. If it was, it pissed her off. "I don't exactly know everyone either."

"All right. Want me to refill your drink then?" He plucked her wineglass from her hand without waiting for a response.

She frowned at him. She hated that her insides had turned to mush around him since he was no doubt trying to use her. "I don't know what this nice guy routine is, but I know who you are and why you're here so if you think you can seduce me for whatever reason, you're out of your mind. And you better not think you can try that crap with Shea. I will claw you to ribbons."

His emerald eyes darkened until they were practically black. He leaned closer until he was inches from her ear. She tried to ignore his earthy scent but found it impossible with his hot breath against her neck. "I do want to fuck you, long and hard, but not for any other reason than I want you. For the record, I haven't been with a woman—wolf or human—in over two decades." He shoved the glass back into her hand before stalking away.

Blinking, she stood there staring after his very tight backside. *Well, hell.*

CHAPTER THREE

Adam raked a hand through his hair as he strode through the house. Ignoring the curious stares, he continued until he was outside. He wanted to kick himself for speaking to her like that. He might be The Council's enforcer but he sucked at talking to women. Or at least he did tonight. He'd sounded like a complete dick.

He fished his keys out of his pocket and headed toward his truck. All his questions for Shea could wait until tomorrow. Lucas Lazos, the Alpha, wasn't even here so it wasn't as if he needed to stick around to speak to him. Lucas and his mate were on a trip to speak to Shea's pack about allowing her to live with them indefinitely. That was something Adam needed to speak to the blonde about too, but that would just have to—

"Adam! Wait."

He turned to find Paz hurrying toward him. Her heels clacked loudly against the stone driveway. When she reached him, she placed a light hand on his forearm. He felt her touch course throughout his entire body. "I'm sorry. I swear I'm not usually such an ass, I just... I think I've forgotten how to talk to people, especially people I don't know."

Her apology surprised him. And so did the fact that she wasn't afraid of him. Normally an aura of fear surrounded others when they were around him. But she wasn't afraid. Hell, none of the Lazos pack seemed to be.

He shook his head. "I think I should apologize for the way I spoke to you. Normally I don't lose control like that. I'm not so rude."

Her brow furrowed. "I didn't think you lost control... Did you mean what you said?"

"Ah... About what?"

Her cheeks flushed a bright shade of crimson. "Are you going to make me say it?"

His cock hardened painfully when he realized she wasn't offended by his graceless words. Just the opposite in fact. "I meant everything I said."

She moistened her lips nervously and when she did, all he could picture was that pink tongue running the length of his cock. He had to bite back a groan of frustration.

Slowly, he reached out and cupped her cheek. When she didn't step away, he rubbed his thumb over her skin. It was soft, smooth and perfect. Just like the rest of her. Paz's breath hitched when he stepped closer, but she *still* didn't pull back.

He was giving her plenty of time to tell him to stop, but she simply stared at him with those dark, inviting eyes. Leaning forward, he didn't stop until his mouth covered hers. He ordered himself to take it slow, but his body wouldn't listen.

Threading his hands through her hair, he lightly gripped the back of her skull. With his other hand, he grabbed her by the waist until she was flush against him. His body's reaction to her was pressing against her abdomen.

She moaned against him, the sound lighting the match on his desire for her.

Her tongue rasped against his in a hungry fervor. She tasted sweet and fruity. When he tightened his grip on her ass, she wrapped her arms around his neck and pressed harder against him. Her moans were so damn erotic. She started grinding against him and it took all his control not to push up her dress and just start fucking her the way he wanted to. But he wasn't a fucking animal. Not like that anyway.

Somehow, he drew his head back with restraint he hadn't realized he possessed. "We've got to stop. Now. Or I'm going to do something stupid."

Looking dazed, she stared up at him, lust and hunger bright in her eyes. Her fingers dug into his shoulders and she didn't make an attempt to move away from him. "Wow," she murmured.

The man and wolf inside him experienced a surge of primal satisfaction. It had been so long since he'd let his guard down around anyone. After just one kiss, he was ready to bed her. That hadn't happened to him in...ever. His body screamed at him to do something about the dull ache spreading through him. "Do you want to take a walk along the beach?"

Paz opened her mouth but was cut off.

"Paz!" Marisol's voice broke them apart. She hurried across the drive toward them. She looked between them accusingly. "What are you doing?"

Paz looked at Adam then at her sister. "What does it look like?"

Marisol's mouth opened and she stuttered for a second. "Well, whatever you're doing, just stop it and get inside. There's something on the news you both need to see." Without waiting for a response, she turned on her heel and rushed back in.

Paz was a little embarrassed at the shameless way she'd basically wrapped herself around Adam and started grinding against him. She barely knew him and if she wanted to do what was good for her—what was smart—she'd stay away from him. If he found out she was half fae, he'd probably turn her over to The Council. Hell, if he didn't kill her first. She had no clue what his views on mixed-bloods were. For all she knew, he was just as prejudiced as the majority of werewolves. Taking a step back, she put some distance between them and averted her gaze. "I guess we better get back in," she muttered.

"Paz—"

Whatever he was going to say, she didn't want to hear it. She followed her sister and hurried inside, effectively cutting him off. She was a complete and utter idiot. After a year with no human contact her brain had apparently turned to mush.

Adam waited until Paz disappeared inside before following. He wanted to give her space and he needed to get his body under control. As he entered through the front door he was immediately hit by the silence. No music, no chatter. Once inside the foyer, he followed the sweet scent of Paz down a short hallway until he found everyone in a spacious living room.

Everyone was packed inside and watching the news on a flat screen television against the wall. He spotted Paz immediately. She leaned against the arm of one of the loveseats where her sister and Shea sat. It was slight, but he didn't miss the imperceptible change in her stance. She was aware that he'd entered the room. He tore his gaze away from her and focused on the screen where a petite Asian woman delivered the news.

According to police, this is one of the worst animal attacks the city has ever seen. And it's not the first. A few days ago, reputed drug-dealer Antonio Perez was found mauled to death in an abandoned warehouse. Police are speculating that whatever killed this couple was the same animal that killed Perez. Until both families are notified, names are not being released.

218 | SAVANNAH STUART

A low murmur broke out as they cut to a commercial break. Thomas stood and flipped the television off. "All right, everyone. We know what this means and who this probably is. No one goes anywhere unless they're chaperoned, especially the younger wolves." He looked pointedly at a group of three younger she-wolves. They couldn't be more than fifteen or sixteen. "We stick together like we always have. Until your Alpha is back in town, you come to me with any problems. If no one has any questions, go back to the party, enjoy yourselves." When no one spoke up, he nodded at Adam, then looked at his brothers and motioned for them to follow him.

Adam maneuvered around everyone and followed the three brothers through another door into what was likely their Alpha's office. He waited until they all sat then took a seat next to Nick, who he hadn't officially met yet. He knew Nick was mated and married to the redheaded human, that he owned a few auto body shops and that it was his birthday, but that was it.

Nick gave him a brief nod. "I'm Nick, nice to meet you."

He took his outstretched hand. "Likewise."

"Before anyone asks, I left a message with my boss and he still hasn't gotten back to me so I don't know anymore about those attacks on the news than you do," Stephan said.

A sharp knock on the door had all four of them turning toward the sound. Before anyone could speak, it flew open and Marisol and Paz stormed in. Actually, Marisol was the one doing the storming. Paz trailed after her but hung back.

"What the hell do you think you're doing excluding us?" Marisol growled at Stephan.

"Damn it, woman!" He started to rise, but Adam took the opportunity to cut him off.

"I think they should be here for this," he said quietly. The rogue wolf they were hunting had personally threatened Marisol. She had a right to hear everything discussed.

Thomas lifted an eyebrow, but he nodded. "I agree. Ladies, have a seat."

Adam refrained from smiling when Marisol didn't sit next to her mate but next to his brother instead. Yeah, someone was in the doghouse tonight.

Thomas took over the floor again. "As far as we know, the couple attacked tonight is not related to us in any way, but once their names go public, we'll know for sure. All the males in our pack are ready to start hunting Morales. As soon as the police clear out of the park, I think we should start there."

Adam cleared his throat. Normally he liked to stand back and handle an investigation by himself, but this was a different situation. They needed to work as a team and while he realized it, it still went against every fiber of his being. "I have a friend who works for the DOJ. I'll call him and see if he can get us access to the traffic cameras around the park and throughout the city. If we can get an idea of where Morales went, we can narrow down where he's living." No doubt Morales was masking his scent. A traitorous bastard like that would have been hiding his true self for years. It would be second nature to him. And Miami was big. They needed to shrink the playing field.

"And I'm getting Marisol the hell out of town," Stephan interrupted.

"I'm not going anywhere!" she shouted.

Adam ignored her outburst and focused on Stephan "I agree. You need to take her and her sister away from here. It'll be easier to hunt him down if they're gone." Despite wanting nothing more than to finish that kiss with Paz, he wanted her safe. Some primal part of him he hadn't been aware existed until right this moment, demanded it.

"I'm not leaving," Paz said. Maybe it was because Paz was quiet or maybe it was because she rarely spoke—Adam couldn't know since he'd just met her—but the room went silent at her soft-spoken declaration.

Marisol was the first to break the silence. "If I'm leaving, you're sure as hell leaving."

"I thought you said you weren't going anywhere." Paz's voice was wry.

"I...I..." She turned to Stephan and glared. "This is your fault." She stood and pushed the chair back with startling force before striding from the room.

Stephan muttered a string of curses under his breath before following after her.

"I take it this isn't their first discussion about leaving?" Thomas directed his question to Paz.

She shook her head. "Ever since Morales called Marisol with that taunting message, Stephan has been trying to get her out of town. And I agree with him. She's just too stubborn."

"No, she doesn't want to leave you." Thomas' expression softened when he spoke to Paz and Adam had a very real, very violent urge to lunge across the table and kick the other male's teeth in. What the hell was wrong with him?

The rage he expelled sent a wave over the room and all three turned to look at him. "I'm ready to catch this bastard," he muttered. The explanation pacified everyone, but he wanted to kick his own ass for letting his emotions get away from him. It rarely happened and certainly not with strangers. He shifted in his seat and caught Paz's gaze. "Why don't you want to go with your sister?"

She darted a quick look at Thomas then back at him. "Thanks to being held captive for a year, I've built up an immunity to silver. I'm stronger now and I'm older than him so if he attacks me one on one, I can hold my own. Plus...I think we can bait him out into the open. Besides her new mate, he knows I'm the one person Marisol will do anything for. We can use that against him."

"No!" Adam surprised himself and everyone else in the room with his outburst, but he didn't care.

Thomas' eyebrows arched for the briefest moment, but he shook his head at Paz. "We're not going to use you as bait."

"I'm just saying it's an option if we can't catch him. I'm more than capable of handling myself." Her head cocked slightly to the side and something passed between her and Thomas. It wasn't a look of lust, or desire but something else. Adam couldn't place his finger on it, but he didn't like it.

"Well, I can't make you leave," Thomas muttered.

Technically he could. Something everyone in the room knew, Adam included. Adam wondered why Thomas wasn't pushing the issue but let it slide. It seemed he now had more to investigate. Unfortunately, all he was interested in was finishing that kiss with Paz.

Stephan walked back into the room. "Paz, will you *please* talk some sense into your stubborn sister?" he growled before sitting back at the table.

Wordlessly, she nodded and left. Finding Marisol wasn't difficult. She was outside on the back patio, alone and practically spitting fire. As Paz opened the sliding glass door, her sister stopped mid-pace and glared at her. "You're insane if you think I'm leaving you."

"Will you please sit down and listen, little *hermana*?"

Marisol pushed out a long breath and lost most of her steam as she collapsed onto one of the lounge chairs. "I don't want to leave."

Paz sat next to her. "It doesn't matter what you want. Your mate can't think straight if you're in constant danger. If his head isn't on right, then that puts you and his brothers in danger. Heck, the whole pack." She knew guilt would work on her sister so she used it to her full advantage.

"Then why don't you want to come with me?"

"It's not that I don't *want* to. I'm not going to run away from anyone ever again and I want him to pay for what he did to me, Shea, *you*, our entire freaking pack and all those other packs he betrayed."

"But what if something happens to you?" The desperation in her sister's voice pulled at her heartstrings.

Even though it killed her, she stayed firm. "It won't."

"What if you kill him using your powers and Adam finds out what you are?"

That was something she'd already thought of, but there wasn't anything she could do about the possibility now. "You can 'what if' yourself to death, Marisol. Preston Morales needs to be stopped. If he isn't, the death toll is going to keep rising in Miami, and our existence—your mate's existence—will be threatened." Paz wouldn't allow that.

"I don't understand why you won't come with me."

Paz had her own demons to face and she'd be damned if she ran away when she knew she had the ability to stop a monster like Morales. Thanks to her heritage she was more capable of killing Morales than any of the werewolves in the house, Adam included. They might not all realize the extent of her gifts, but her sister certainly did. The drugs she'd lived with for a year were completely out of her system and while she hadn't tested her powers yet, she planned a little test run tonight once everyone had gone to sleep. "You know why I'm staying, Marisol. I can help. Besides, you *just* bonded with your mate. You deserve some alone time."

"I don't give a shit about that. I don't want to leave you again."

"One week. That's all I'm asking for. It's not long." She scooted closer down the seat and wrapped her arm around Marisol's shoulders then used her most sickly sweet voice she knew would annoy her sister. "Pretty please? Don't make me beg, little *hermana*."

She rolled her eyes. "Ugh. If you stop, I'll say yes."

Chuckling, she dropped her arm and nudged her sister with her elbow. "By tomorrow morning you'll be thanking me for letting your mate whisk you away."

"We'll see." Then Marisol's eyes narrowed. "What on earth were you doing outside with Adam Tucker, *the enforcer*?"

Paz could feel her cheeks flush. "Ah, I'd rather not talk about it."

"Seriously, of all people, why him?"

Paz shrugged. "I like him. He's not a pig and he's not very good at talking to people. Something we have in common."

"Yeah, but, are you still, you know…"

"A virgin? You can say the word, Marisol. And yes, I am." She was probably the world's oldest freaking virgin — literally — but after her year in captivity she planned to make some serious changes. Life was much too short.

Marisol shook her head and stood. "Please be careful with Adam. He's not one of us and you know what could happen if… I better go find Stephan and stop him from sulking."

Paz raked a hand through her hair and leaned back against the lounge chair. The sound of the ocean waves crashing against the shore was incredibly soothing. As she closed her eyes and stretched her legs out, the sound of the sliding glass door and Adam's unmistakable scent greeted her senses. He was all spicy and earthy, his scent completely primitive.

A second later, he sat on the edge of her seat. Leaning back the way she was, her dress had ridden up against her thighs and was exposing a lot of skin. She wanted to tug it down but didn't want to draw any more attention to herself. And okay, she didn't mind baring a little skin to Adam.

"How'd you get your sister to listen to you?" he asked.

She shrugged. "I'm older. It's not too hard."

"Why aren't you going with her?"

It would be impossible to explain to him why without revealing her true nature. So she changed the subject. "After one kiss you're already looking to get rid of me?"

His green eyes darkened to storm clouds. Taking her by surprise, he leaned forward until their noses were almost touching. "Not on your life," he murmured before closing the rest of the small distance between them.

The porch and the decorative column obstructing them offered a certain amount of privacy from those in the kitchen. And thanks to the angle of the chair and the dim lighting, no one could really make out what they were doing. Kissing him was stupid and it could get her into trouble. It was just so hard to care when he was slipping his tongue inside her mouth.

CHAPTER FOUR

As Paz opened her mouth to him, Adam placed a hand on her exposed thigh. Underneath his callused fingers, her leg clenched, but she didn't pull away—much to his relief. Her tongue danced against his, almost shyly and in complete opposition to her personality. Something told him she hadn't been with many men. Wolf or human. The knowledge pleased him more than he cared to admit.

When he swept his tongue along her teeth, she gripped his shoulders and scooted a few inches closer. His hand automatically slid up her leg. Instead of stopping, as a gentleman would have, he kept going until he covered her mound. What he wouldn't give to sink into her.

"What are you doing?" she whispered as she pulled back from his mouth. The pulse point on her neck was going crazy.

"I want to touch you here." He kept his voice just as low as hers and slid a finger underneath the material of her panties. He could feel her soft thatch of hair and he'd bet anything it was just as dark as the soft espresso-colored curls framing her face.

"I'm not going to have sex with you," she blurted.

Despite every fiber inside him wanting to flip her over and mount her, his human side wanted to learn what made her tick. What her body liked. And he desperately wanted to please her until she was coming against his mouth and cock. "That's okay. I just want to touch you."

Confusion rolled off her, but when he pushed the flimsy fabric completely to the side, a new expression covered her face. Her lips parted slightly and her breath hitched erratically.

With his middle finger, he rubbed gently against her clit. Each time he did, her hips arched against him. She let out little moans that almost sounded like purring.

Instead of kissing her, he watched her expressive face while he became more intimate with her body. Rubbing lower, he slid his finger inside her pussy and wasn't able to restrain a small groan. She was tight and incredibly wet. And it was all for him. The knowledge made that primitive caveman inside him do a fist pump. Hell yeah.

"Do you like that?"

She nodded and clutched the side of the chair. "This is crazy," she whispered.

As if on cue, the sliding glass door opened and without looking he knew who had stepped outside. *Thomas.* Adam bit back a growl. Paz immediately closed her legs, forcing him to remove his hand. He leaned closer as he pushed up and stood. "Meet me tonight by my beach house. Eleven o'clock." Without waiting for a response, he nodded once at Thomas before brushing past him.

It was definitely time for him to leave the party. He spotted Marisol and Stephan arguing in one corner of the kitchen and Nick and his human mate, Carly, kissing by the mini-bar. No one else paid him much attention as he exited the house. While he wanted nothing more than to stay and talk to Paz, he knew it would be impossible with so many people around.

Her sister didn't like him talking to her — that much was obvious. And something was going on with her and Thomas. He didn't think it was physical because Paz didn't seem like the kind of woman to stray, but he planned to find out what secrets she was keeping from him.

Despite the cool breeze blowing in from the Atlantic, fire burned through Paz's system as she stripped her dress and panties off. She felt guilty lying to her sister about wanting to go for a run alone, but she brushed those feelings away. It was embarrassing how much she wanted to see and talk to Adam again. And she wasn't quite sure why she was so interested. He wasn't suave or even very charming like so many of the wolves who'd tried to get into her pants before. And, more importantly, he didn't know what she was. The wolves from her old pack had known she was half fae. The ones who'd tried to bed her had made her feel as if they were doing *her* a favor by wanting to sleep with her. She snorted at the thought.

Adam was different. He wanted her for her. She wasn't certain that she was going to sleep with him, but he didn't seem to care about that. Taking a calming breath, she prepared herself to change form. Even though she was half fae, shifting into her wolf form still hurt just like any other full-blooded werewolf.

As her bones broke, shifted and realigned, a rush of adrenaline

POWER UNLEASHED | 225

pumped through her with lightning speed. It had been a couple days since she'd stretched her legs and the sensation was refreshing. She was smaller than most shifters, maybe because of her faerie heritage, she couldn't be sure.

Bounding across the sand, she let the salty essence of the ocean rush over her. Running over the softer surface forced her to exert her muscles more. As she headed toward the beach house where Adam was staying, she slowed her pace when she scented him. The closer she got to the house, the stronger his scent grew, but she couldn't see him. For a brief second, a trickle of fear raced down her back until he jumped out from behind a sand dune.

She paused and took him in. He was a perfect snowy white. She'd never seen an all white wolf before, and he was beautiful. Unlike so many shifters who took on various canine forms, he was truly a wolf. Her sister was an Alaskan Malamute and she was a fairly small, brown Cocker Spaniel. Not exactly terrifying or even majestic.

He kicked up some sand in her direction and motioned for her to follow. She did, but when she got closer, she nipped his side playfully. They didn't know each other well and she knew she was taking a chance, but she wanted to feel out his personality. It was easiest for her to do that in her shifted form. Not being able to talk was always easier for her. It meant she couldn't say something stupid. When she nipped him, he rolled on his back and bared his neck for her.

The way he made himself so vulnerable touched something deep inside her. She jumped at him but didn't show her teeth as she attempted to tackle him. When he playfully growled she pushed off him and ran toward his place.

She jerked to a halt when she spotted a blanket spread out on the sand just in front of the patio by the pool entrance. He continued past her and before she realized what he intended, he shifted. She glanced away even though it was obvious he didn't care about a little nudity. Out of the corner of her eye she watched him pull on a pair of pants then sit on the blanket.

"Aren't you going to change?" he asked.

She crouched down on her stomach and covered her eyes with her paws for a moment, hoping he'd get it. She didn't even like it when her sister watched her shift. It was such a personal thing and she completely understood why so many werewolves didn't care, but she was different than most. And she wasn't going to apologize for embracing her human side.

"Ah, I see." He turned his back to her.

When he didn't attempt to peek, she changed. He had to have known she'd shifted form but he still didn't turn around. As she neared the edge of the blanket she scooped up his T-shirt and slipped it over her head. His earthy scent immediately enveloped her like a cocoon.

"You can turn around now," she said as she sat a couple feet away.

She sucked in a deep breath when he faced her. His chest and abs were sleek, muscular lines of perfection. He was a lot leaner than the men of the Lazos pack. Where they were bulkier, he was trim and completely ripped. What surprised her most were the scars covering his chest. It took a lot to scar a werewolf, but it was apparent someone or many "someones" had tried to kill him.

"You look good in my shirt," he murmured.

The quiet words drew her gaze back to his face. "Then why do you look disappointed?"

His shoulders lifted slightly. "I was hoping you'd be wearing nothing."

She could feel her cheeks heat up, but she held his gaze. At least the man was honest. Under the moonlight, his green eyes were darker, smokier. Almost midnight black. "Did you ask me here so you could grill me with more questions about my captivity?"

He shook his head. "No."

One word answer. *Okay.* Getting him to talk was going to be interesting. "Is this your first time in Miami?"

"No."

Sighing, she stretched out next to him and propped up on one elbow as she faced him. When she did, the shirt rode up dangerously high. "Are you going to keep giving me one word answers?"

The corners of his mouth quirked up slightly in what she assumed was his version of a smile. "No."

She rolled her eyes and lay on her back. The glittering stars scattered across the sky seemed to be winking at her. "Fine. When you want to talk, I'm here."

The blanket shifted as he moved closer. Her stomach flip-flopped when he stretched out beside her. Supporting himself on one elbow, he stared down at her and all she could think about was his very kissable lips. From what she'd seen of him, he rarely smiled and definitely didn't laugh, but when he'd kissed her before, she'd felt it straight to her toes.

"Is something going on with you and Thomas Lazos?" he growled.

The unexpected question—and the intensity of it—jerked her out of her thoughts. "What? *No.* Lord, no. Not that he's not attractive, but...no." She bit her bottom lip to keep from rambling and frowned at him. "Why?"

"I just wanted to make sure you weren't taken." His deep voice rolled over her like warm honey. Smooth and sensuous, it stirred and heated her blood.

"Well, I'm not." The words were barely a whisper.

"Good." His neck muscles corded tightly and she knew he was restraining himself from kissing her. She wished he'd stop holding back.

"Would you have invited me here if I was?" She didn't know why she asked.

"Yes." His answer was immediate.

When he moved closer, she pressed a hand against his chest. Underneath her fingertips, his muscles clenched and tensed. "Can I ask you a question?"

He nodded, as if talking were too difficult.

"Has it really been…two decades for you?"

"Yeah." His voice was hoarse and scratchy, but he didn't hesitate.

Something strange fluttered in her stomach. If it had been that long for him, it meant he valued sex as much as she did. The knowledge went a long way in pacifying her nerves. Before she'd come to meet him she hadn't been sure what her own intentions were, but now she had no doubt. By the time the night was over, she was going to sleep with Adam.

CHAPTER FIVE

Adam stared down at Paz and hated the way his entire body ached for her. It had been over a century since he'd allowed himself to get close to any woman. He was in Miami on a mission. Find the rogue werewolf, the escaped human and destroy them both if necessary. Getting tangled up with a sexy she-wolf wasn't part of his plan. If anything, it was one of the dumbest things he'd done in a long time.

Something about Paz drew him in though. He should be more wary considering he knew so little about her. There wasn't the scent of another man on her and all he could focus on was making sure his scent *was*. He wanted everyone to know she belonged to him. The truth was, if she'd been with someone else, he didn't think that it would have stopped him. And that scared him. The animal inside him craved her with a desperation that shook him to his core.

By nature he was possessive and protective, but he'd never felt such a dominating need to claim a woman. To mark her as his own.

As her vanilla scent tickled his nose, his canines extended. When she placed a hand on his chest, the action immediately soothed him. For how he felt, that shocked him.

Before he could react, she pushed up on her elbows and met him halfway. Without pause he closed the distance and covered her parted lips with his own. Tasting her once hadn't been enough. He wasn't sure that tasting her now would be enough either. The way his body burned, he was certain the fire humming through him would never be quenched.

Her taste was sweet and it was hers alone. As he ran his tongue across hers, he sucked her bottom lip between his teeth and tugged. When he did, she arched her back against him, making that sweet moaning sound, and he nearly lost it. He wanted to taste more of her. All of her.

After he settled between her legs, he skimmed his hands over the hem of the shirt she wore. When he pushed it up to her waist, she stilled and her eyes opened. She watched him carefully.

"I want to see you," he murmured against her mouth. Her only response was an increase in her heartbeat so he continued sliding the shirt up until her breasts were bared. "Can I take it off?"

Jerkily, she nodded. He quickly pulled it over her head. Under the moonlight and stars, her silky skin seemed to glow. He almost forgot to breathe as he drank in her naked body. She was perfection. Her slim waist flared into surprisingly curvy hips. Hips he'd like to hold onto as she rode him. His stomach clenched at the thought. She squirmed under his gaze so he forced himself to focus on her face. "Are you cold?"

"No. Just..."

"Just what?" he pushed.

She shook her head and her dark hair swished against the blanket. "Nothing."

"Are you nervous?" Of course she was, what the hell was he thinking? Paz was beautiful and confident but she'd also been through a lot.

"A little."

"Do you want to stop?"

"No, just go slow."

"I can do that." He could do any damn thing she asked of him.

Wordlessly he dipped his head to her neck and grazed his teeth along her jaw line. The last thing he wanted was for her to feel insecure. He planned to worship her body the way it deserved.

As he spread kisses down to her neck and shoulders, she moved her hips against his in sensual, erotic thrusts. His cock ached between his legs. Thick and swollen, it felt like a heavy club, but right now wasn't about him. The woman beneath him was all that mattered. He was still trying to wrap his mind around why she'd suddenly become so important to him when a potent wave of awareness rippled through him.

Mate.

The word sounded loud and clear in his head. Pausing above her left breast, he looked at her to see if she'd felt it too.

Her eyes flew open. "What's wrong?"

A jagged twinge of disappointment struck him that she hadn't experienced the same realization as him, but he brushed it aside. "Not a damn thing," he murmured before clasping her already hard nipple gently between his teeth. When he tugged, she moaned and he restrained himself from flipping her on her knees and taking her the way his body demanded.

Her fingers threaded through his hair as she gripped his scalp. "That feels so good." The words were barely a whisper on her lips.

He continued licking her pebbled nipple and tweaked the other between his finger and thumb. He wanted to know everything she liked, wanted to make her crave him so all she thought about was him being inside her. When he squeezed, a barely perceptible tremor raced through her and her grip on his head tightened.

He'd lived centuries longer than most werewolves and he'd never scented anything as intoxicating as the heat and desire rolling off her. It made his head spin. Trailing a path of kisses around her light brown areola, he savored covering every inch of her soft skin.

Unable to control himself any longer, he reached between their bodies and slid a finger across her slick folds. She was hot and inviting. He inserted one finger and shuddered when she clamped down on him. Damn, the woman was tight and wet. When he imagined what it would feel like to slide his cock into her, his hips rolled once.

"That feels good," she murmured, her voice thick with pleasure.

Exactly what he wanted to hear. Lowering himself, he raked his teeth over her soft mound and her hips jerked upward, inviting him to bury his face between her legs. He pressed her thighs open wider and sucked in a deep breath at the sight of her glistening folds.

Waves crashing behind him and the unsteady beat of his heart were the only sounds he was aware of as he stared at the perfection before him.

"Are you going to taste me?" There was such a mixture of curiosity, innocence and arousal in her voice that it touched something inside him he'd forgotten existed.

Spread out before him, she was so trusting. He wasn't sure what he'd done to deserve her. Over the years he'd made so many enemies and though he had little regrets from the battlefield, he'd always thought maybe he didn't deserve a mate. To find her after so long seemed impossible. Their first time together was more important than anything he'd done in his life. He tilted his head down and nipped her inner thigh.

She trembled under his touch, the scent of her desire unmistakable. Inching even closer, he dipped his tongue between her folds.

"Adam." Her hips jolted slightly but she scooted down closer to his face.

Biting back a smile, he stroked between her folds again, then centered on her clit. The pink nub peeked out from beneath her swollen lips, begging to be kissed.

He circled her clit with his tongue over and over. With each teasing motion, he earned a heated cry from Paz. Her body trembled beneath him and her moans filled the quiet night. Although he didn't know her well, he knew she was close to coming. She was that reactive to him.

But he wanted to extend their time together. Wanted her to writhe beneath him as long as possible. His cock ached for release but the desire to keep her with him overrode those feelings. He didn't want this moment to end.

As he teased her clit, he slowly slid one finger inside her hot sheath. She was tight but much wetter now. Her juices coated his finger so he glided another finger inside. When he did, her hips moved against him, rocking in a slow rhythm. He didn't need more encouragement than that.

Slowly at first, he dragged his fingers out of her then pushed them back in. Her inner walls clenched around him so he continued the action and increased his movements. The faster he moved, the tighter she clasped around him. He wanted her to come at least once before his cock was inside her; felt possessed with the need.

Her hips raised up again and she fisted the blanket beneath her. "Oh my…"

Though he was loathe to stop watching her, he tilted his head forward and sucked her clit into his mouth. The sharp tugging action pushed her over the edge.

Foreign but fabulous sensations spiraled through Paz's entire body. She'd masturbated before but nothing compared to what Adam was doing to her. She felt as if she could actually burst from the pleasure.

Each time he pushed his fingers into her, she wanted him to go deeper, wanted to take more of him. She wanted his cock. Even thinking it sent tingles skittering across her skin. Her fingers tightened against the blanket. After waiting so long for this moment, she couldn't understand why she wasn't more tense. Part of her wondered why everything about being with him felt so natural. So right. She barely knew him and by all standards she should be avoiding him, but her mind and body were drawn to him with a surprising intensity.

As he took her clit between his teeth then lashed his tongue over the sensitive bundle of nerves once more, the building need inside her exploded. She wanted to restrain herself, but it was too much. The tightness in her belly loosened and she let go as her pussy spasmed out of control.

She clutched the blanket beneath her as the climax pulsed through her. The tiny shots of pleasure overwhelming her body seemed to shoot to every direction. They hit all her nerve endings in an explosive, erotic sweep that had her crying out his name. The slight embarrassment she felt at being so loud dissipated when Adam slowly withdrew his fingers and met her gaze.

The look on his handsome face was one of primal satisfaction. Not that she blamed him. He should be proud. She just hoped she could make him feel as good.

She started to sit up, but with the sleek movements of a lethal predator, he slid on top of her, stealing her breath. She wanted to keep her head on straight around him, but when his strong chest covered hers, it was impossible.

There was a light thatch of blond hair covering his chest and it tickled her hardened nipples. Involuntarily, she arched her back against him, wanting to feel more of him. More skin on skin. She wrapped her arms around him and smoothed her palms down his back. His muscles rippled underneath her touch.

It was as if an uncontrollable hunger had taken over her. She wanted more of Adam. "That was amazing," she whispered against his cheek when he bent to nip her ear.

"We're just getting started, sweetheart." His voice was just as low, but there was an underlying bit of dominance in it that turned her brain to mush.

After a year of captivity, being dominated was the last thing she should be thinking about, but her mind and body told her that Adam wouldn't abuse her. She might not trust him with her secrets, but she knew he wouldn't hurt her body. The man could quickly become like a drug to her.

Inhaling his addictive scent, she slowly raked her teeth along his stubbled jaw. Everything about him was so clean cut and put together. She liked the scruffy bit of hair covering his face.

"I don't have condoms. Are you…protected?" He murmured close to her ear.

She understood his question. Shifters normally didn't need protection such as condoms because they couldn't get or give STDs. But there were two times during the year a female could get pregnant. Luckily, now wasn't one of those times. "My cycle doesn't start for another month."

It was as if her words set him off. He reclaimed her mouth in a fervent, hungry kiss. She parted her lips willingly as she drank in all he had to offer. She guessed the foreign, sweeter taste from him was her. The realization created a burning low in her belly. She wanted to taste him too, but knew there wasn't time for that now.

He was ready to fuck. Probably had been since they'd started kissing. Despite the cool breeze, his body was hot to the touch. As his tongue made erotic little sweeping motions inside her mouth, she slipped a hand between them and under his pants.

She clasped his cock in her hand and squeezed. The male was definitely blessed, something that pleased her immensely. He immediately stilled and pulled his head back.

Her eyes flew open. "What?"

"I don't want to come in your hand." His voice was hoarse and strangled.

"Wh...oh." His admission surprised her. Something told her Adam could last for hours, but right now he was as on fire as she was. Feeling very powerful, she removed her hand and raked her fingers down his perfectly honed chest. "Why don't you come in *me* then?"

The seductive question surprised the hell out of Paz, but Adam didn't need to be asked twice. She was already wet and primed for him. A tiny part of her brain wondered if she would be able to take him. Shifters were more endowed than humans and her body was made to allow for that, but the muscles in her stomach clenched involuntarily as he sat up and shimmied out of his pants.

After he kicked them away, he sat on his knees and settled between her spread legs. She swallowed once as she stared at his pulsing cock. It was definitely big. Longer — and thicker — than she'd expected. That tiny trickle of fear turned into a river, but her worries were doused when Adam leaned forward and covered her body once again.

He used his elbows to support his weight as he stared down at her. His cock rested between her legs, but he didn't make a move to thrust into her. Their faces were inches apart. "Let's just get used to feeling each other. There's no rush, sweetheart."

Sweetheart. No one had ever called her that. Something warm and unexpected blossomed in her chest. He was nothing like she'd expected and she was very thankful for that.

As he moved between her thighs she automatically wrapped her legs around him. The muscles in his back tightened underneath her and his eyes immediately darkened. He might have said there was no rush, but she ached for more than just his fingers.

She sought out his mouth as she ground her hips against his. More than anything, she wanted him inside her, wanted to feel what he had to offer. After so long without any real human contact, she needed this. Needed Adam.

He shifted slightly and in one fluid motion, he pushed deep into her, completely filling her. All the air whooshed from her lungs, but just as quickly she caught her breath. The stretching sensation was foreign but welcome. She unhooked her legs from around his back and planted her feet on the quilt underneath them.

Adam was motionless inside her, letting her get accustomed to him. When he gently caressed one of her breasts, she managed to relax. The feel of him touching her so sweetly, grounded her.

All the tendons in his neck were pulled tight and his expression was strained so she knew he was holding back. At that moment, she was happy she'd waited for someone like Adam. He had to be in agony but it was obvious he didn't care and that he'd rather put her needs first.

Now she wanted to make sure he found just as much pleasure as he'd given her. When she started moving her hips, he pushed up higher on his elbows and started driving into her with barely controlled thrusts.

CHAPTER SIX

If Adam died tonight, he'd definitely die happy. The thought scared the shit out of him, but he was so far beyond caring about anything but Paz's pleasure. She was an odd mix of sensuality and innocence and he wanted to lose himself in her.

Her pussy wrapped around him like a tight, hot, glove. He was so close to coming but refused to embarrass himself. She was going to climax again before they were finished.

Balancing on his elbows, he continued thrusting. Her inner walls were clenching around him tighter and tighter. Her dark eyes were slightly glazed over and the muscles in her body were all drawn tight. It was simply a matter of time before she came again.

She was spread out before him under the moonlight and he didn't think he'd ever seen anything so beautiful. Her dark hair feathered around her like a soft curtain and those dark eyes were practically sparking fire.

"Adam," she groaned his name and he nearly lost it. Every time she said his name, he felt it all the way to his core.

Gritting his teeth, he slowed his pace to make it last for her, but she locked her ankles around his back and gripped him.

"Faster," she murmured.

He did as she commanded and reached between them. When he tweaked her clit, she arched her back and her cream rushed over him. Her climax was more intense this time. Her back bowed and her mouth opened in a silent O as her sheath tightened around him. Only when her slick sheath spasmed out of control, did he allow himself to let go.

A jarring, pulsing climax ripped through him as he poured himself inside her. Crying out her name he thrust into her again and again until the explosive eruption subsided into calmer waves of ecstasy.

Her mouth was parted and she didn't break his gaze as he settled on top of her. He knew he'd eventually have to move, but buried deep inside her was the only place he wanted to be.

The soft smile playing across Paz's swollen lips sent an unexpected jolt straight to his cock. When it stirred inside her, her eyebrows rose. "I'm not ready for another—"

"I know." His words were practically a growl as he dropped a kiss on her forehead.

When her breathing became faintly labored, he forced himself to move. Though he hated it, he slowly withdrew from her and rolled onto his side.

Paz stared at the sparkling sky above her as her heart rate returned to normal. She felt stretched, sore and absolutely wonderful. Sex had been a lot better than she'd expected. She wasn't sorry she'd waited so long to experience it though. In her heart she knew that if she'd slept with someone from her old pack, it wouldn't have been like this. Adam was completely giving and wonderful. Of course he had no idea what she was. She shelved that thought for now, not wanting anything to ruin her mood.

"Paz?" His deep voice sent shivers spiraling over her skin.

She rolled on her side to face him. He was lying on his back with his head propped up underneath his arms and looking completely at ease.

She curled up against him. "What?"

There's something I need to tell you.

When his lips didn't move, she realized he was projecting with his mind. Which likely meant he could read her thoughts. Her throat seized and her elation transformed to terror. Not caring that she was naked, she scrambled away until she was standing in the sand a few feet away from him. "You've been able to read my mind this whole time?" she whispered. *Oh god, oh god, oh god!* Did he know what she was? Had he simply been using her? Nausea swirled in her gut and she barely tamped it down.

He jumped to his feet with surprising agility. "No!" He took a step toward her, but when she backed away, he held up his hands in a defensive gesture and stilled. "No, I swear. I think...I think we're mates. Try projecting your thoughts."

"No!" she shrieked. Was he insane? She wasn't going to project anything! Her body temperature started to rise and she knew she was working herself up, but she couldn't stop. "We are *not* mates. We're not! That's the most ridiculous thing I've ever heard." No, this couldn't be happening.

She took another step back. Something pricked the back of her mind. If he could link telepathically with her, it was probably true they were mates. It would certainly explain her drugging need to be near him, to be with him. If he discovered what she was...a shudder snaked down her body at the thought, but she shoved it out of her mind. She couldn't let him find out.

He kept his hands up but took another step closer. "I didn't mean to scare you. We're mates, Paz."

"No, we're not!"

"Why? Am I not good enough?" Hurt glinted in his emerald eyes and her first instinct was to wipe that pain away, but she stopped herself.

She needed to get away from him. *Fast.* The Lazos pack had protected her. She couldn't endanger them. Taking another step back, she pushed aside her insecurities and let the change overcome her. The adrenaline pumping through her overrode most of the pain as her bones twisted and broke. Without waiting to see his response, she sprinted back toward her sister's home. If she could just make it back, she'd be fine.

And safe.

Her heart pounded wildly as she kicked up sand and it didn't settle when she skidded to a stop on the stone steps of her sister's back patio. After she changed into her human form, she slipped her dress over her head. As she did, she saw Adam in wolf form on the beach barely ten yards away.

He just stood there, watching. It felt as if a fist was squeezing her heart. She wanted to talk to him, give him an explanation, but she couldn't. She was too afraid. If she admitted what she was, he'd have no choice but to turn her in to The Council. They might be mates, but they hadn't officially bonded and they didn't know each other that well.

When she bent to grab her panties, he started trotting toward her. Even though she knew she was being a total chickenshit, she stumbled back and raced for the back door. Paz had no doubt her sister was still awake and probably waiting to ream her out, but she'd rather face Marisol than an angry Adam.

Adam stared helplessly at Paz's retreating figure. Anger and humiliation hummed through him. They were mates. He knew it and no doubt, she did too. Whether she wanted to admit it or not. He loped up the stone steps to see what she'd left behind. When he saw the scrap of black lace material that definitely belonged to her, he grabbed it in his mouth before running back to his beach house.

After he'd shifted and settled back into his house, he was still angry as

238 | SAVANNAH STUART

hell. As he went through what had just happened in his mind, nothing made sense. He'd said they were mates and she'd run like a scared rabbit. Sure, he was feared and respected as The Council's enforcer, but apparently his position in the hierarchy wasn't good enough for her.

Maybe she'd just been interested in a fling? No. He quickly brushed that thought away. She hadn't admitted it, but he was fairly certain she'd been a virgin—and the thought humbled him that she'd chosen him to be her first. At the most, she had little experience with the opposite sex. He wasn't even sure how he knew that. Everything had just seemed too fresh to her.

That left one thing. She just didn't *want* him to be her mate. Whatever the reason, it didn't matter.

Grabbing a beer from the fridge, he frowned when he saw the time. It was after midnight, but it wouldn't be that late on the West Coast. He grabbed his cell and scrolled through the list of names until he landed on the one he wanted. Jacob Freeman.

After four rings Adam was about to hang up when his old friend answered. "Adam Tucker, holy shit. How are ya, brother?"

Despite his foul mood, he smiled. Freeman was one of the few wolves he actually trusted. Relatively speaking, he was a newer Alpha of his own pack, but he was wise for barely being a century old. "Can't complain. How about yourself?"

"I'm in the fucking desert right now freezing my nuts off."

Adam frowned. "I thought you were living in Washington."

"I was…I am. Currently, I'm hunting someone," he growled.

"Everything all right?" He hadn't heard that the Freeman pack had any problems lately.

"It will be. Shit man, this isn't Council business if that's what you're worried about. I'm trying to track down my stubborn-ass mate."

"What?"

He sighed. "She's…you know what, don't worry about it. It's under control. I know you didn't call me to bullshit so tell me what's on your mind."

At least he wasn't the only one with mate problems. The thought was somewhat comforting. "You still got that contact at the Florida Department of Transportation?"

"Yeah. Got one in New York and in Illinois too."

"I need access to some traffic cameras in the greater Miami area."

"Tell me exactly what you want and I'll see what I can do."

Adam quickly ran through the dates and times of the attacks in addition to requesting video feeds of all the surrounding areas.

"This sounds like heavy shit. You need any help?" Jacob asked when Adam was finished.

It shouldn't have, but the offer surprised him. "No, but thanks. I'll call you if I need anything else."

After they disconnected, his mind was still racing. He wouldn't get the information he wanted until at least tomorrow. While he could scour the city at night randomly looking for Morales, the chance of finding him in a place this size was minimal. Until he knew if there was a pattern to his attacks, or could at least narrow down his hunting ground, trying to track him would be pointless.

At the moment, that didn't matter as much to him as talking to his mate. He slammed his beer down on the center island and cursed under his breath. If Paz thought she could run away from him, she was out of her damn mind. There was no way he could rest until they'd at least talked. And if he couldn't sleep, she didn't get to either.

As he started for the back door, his cell rang. When he saw the number, his heart rate tripled. It was the number to Stephan Lazos' house. "Yeah?"

"Uh, Adam? It's me." Paz cleared her throat nervously.

"What the hell were you thinking—"

"Marisol got another call from Preston. He told her that he left another present for her but wouldn't say where. Stephan is packing the both of them up and they're planning to leave soon. She wants me to go with her and I think maybe she's right. I know what I said before, but—"

"I'll be there in a few minutes." He disconnected, and without bothering to shift into his wolf form, he simply locked up and jogged down the beach. Something foreign—fear maybe—spiked through him. He couldn't let Paz out of his sight.

He didn't scent any other wolves except those he knew as he neared the back door to Stephan's house, but his body was on alert and ready for battle. All the muscles in his legs were pulled tight in anticipation. If he had to change at a moment's notice, he would.

As expected, the back door was locked and fortified with extra security. He rapped on it once. A few seconds later it swung open. Paz stood before him wearing loose jogging pants and a hoodie sweater with the Miami Dolphins logo on the front. She bit her bottom lip and eyed him warily.

Sighing, he stepped in and shut the door behind them. For now, the mate discussion would have to wait. "Where's your sister?"

"Upstairs with Stephan. They're packing."

Without a backward glance, he strode through the Tuscan-themed

240 | SAVANNAH STUART

kitchen and found the stairs. As he bounded up them, he announced himself. "Stephan, Marisol, I hope you're both decent."

The first door on the left was open, but by the scent he knew it was Paz's room. He found the second door open also. And it was occupied.

"Stephan, what's going on?" He knocked on the open door as he stepped inside.

Stephan looked up from his suitcase. "I was going to call you once we'd packed up." He nodded in the direction of a closed door, probably a connecting bathroom. "Preston called Marisol and told her he was coming for her. I have no doubt of my abilities to protect my mate, but I don't know what kind of firepower he has or what he's planning. I want her out of this house as soon as possible. She's a sitting duck here."

Adam nodded. "I agree. What else did he say?"

"He told her he left her a 'present'. After the news last night I can only imagine what that means. Marisol did say she could hear the ocean in the background when he called. She said she could distinctly hear water crashing against something."

Adam started to respond when the bathroom door swung open and Marisol walked out carrying a small bag. She narrowed her dark gaze at him. "I don't care what she says, my sister is coming with us." Her words were a growl, as if she was challenging Adam to defy her.

He would show respect for his mate's family, but Paz belonged with him. Whether she wanted to be with him or not was another matter. "I would have agreed with you a few hours ago, but Paz is staying with me. Under my roof and under my protection." He'd planned to give her some space but after this development, he didn't give a shit if she wanted to stay with him or not. She was *his* to protect. His wolf would allow nothing less.

"That's crazy! She's —"

"She's my mate." His quiet declaration stilled the room.

Stephan's hand hovered over the open suitcase and Marisol's eyes widened in...horror. That was the only word Adam could think to describe it. *Shit, was he that bad of a catch?* He'd never thought about it before. He'd just assumed that if he found his mate, she'd want him as much as he wanted her. Something tightened around his chest, but he pushed past it. Emotional bullshit could get him killed. He needed to start thinking with his head. "That's right. And she's not leaving my sight."

Marisol's gaze strayed past him and without turning he knew Paz had stepped into the doorway. He could scent and feel her.

"Is this true, *hermana*?" Marisol asked.

He didn't turn because he couldn't bear to see her embarrassment.

"It's true." Paz's voice was quiet, remote.

Stephan cleared his throat as he zipped up his suitcase. "Adam will have no problem taking care of your sister, Marisol. We're leaving in five minutes so make sure you pack everything you need."

"But—"

"No buts. I would fight anyone to the death to protect you. Do you think it will be any different for him? Pack. Your. Stuff." Stephan plucked his luggage off the bed and skirted past his angry mate. Adam turned and watched as Stephan linked his arm through Paz's. He practically dragged her from the room.

Frowning, he waited a moment before trailing after them. They were at the end of the hallway.

"If you're truly mates, give him a chance before condemning him," Stephan murmured.

Adam knew he wasn't meant to overhear, but like so many of his kind, his hearing was exceptional.

"I want to, but what if..." Paz trailed off as she met his gaze. Just as quickly she turned and hurried away from Stephan and into her bedroom. The door shut behind her with a resounding thud.

What the hell was going on? Before he could voice anything, Stephan motioned to him. "Will you speak with me in private?"

Gritting his teeth, he nodded and followed the other wolf down the stairs.

Stephan was silent until they entered his office and shut the door behind them. He turned to Adam immediately. "Give Paz time to adjust to the fact that you're mates."

"Excuse me?"

Stephan lifted a dark eyebrow. "She wasn't very receptive to the fact that you're mates, was she?"

He didn't answer since it was pretty damn clear to everyone in the house.

"Look, I know you didn't ask, but my mate is cut from the same cloth as yours so I'm giving this advice for free. Paz had a rough year. A year that would have likely broken most wolves. She's just figuring out who she is again and then she meets you, *the enforcer*. She has a right to be wary of you. If—when—she puts her trust in you, don't break that trust. If you do, I don't care who you are, you'll have to deal with the entire Lazos pack."

He wasn't exactly sure what Stephan was getting at, but this was the kind of conversation friends had and he couldn't afford that type of relationship. Adam digested what Stephan said but veered the conversation in another direction. "Do you know where you're taking your mate?"

Stephan's gaze narrowed for a fraction of a second before he nodded. "Yes. And I'm not telling anyone where, including you. I've already contacted my brothers and my Alpha so they're aware of the situation."

"Good. Leave both your phones." He might have use for Marisol's phone. If he could bait Morales out into the open with it, he would, but he didn't voice that.

Stephan reached into his pocket then handed both phones to Adam, as if he'd been prepared for the request.

"Call as soon as you get settled in. I'm sure Paz will want updates from her sister." Even though he was hurt by his mate, he still wanted her happy. For the second time that night, the knowledge scared the shit out of him.

CHAPTER SEVEN

Paz risked a glance at Adam as they strode up to the front walk of the beach house. He hadn't said more than a few words to her since she'd said goodbye to her sister and packed up what few clothes she had.

His jaw was clenched tightly as he held open the front door for her. She nearly jumped when he secured it behind them. The lock clicking into place sounded so ominous, but she fought off a shiver. She understood why he was angry, but it still sucked, especially now that they were going to be stuck under the same roof.

"I'm not sure how long you'll have to stay here so tomorrow morning we'll go back and grab more of your clothing," he said as he strode toward the carpeted staircase. Even though he was angry with her, he still carried her bag. The action wasn't lost on her and made her feel even worse for the way she'd reacted.

"I don't own any more clothes." Considering she'd been in captivity for a year, did he really expect her to have much? Her little suitcase was sad, but hell, she'd only been free less than a week. Extensive shopping hadn't been high on her list of things to do and even though her sister had given her money she wanted to save it.

He paused at the foot of the stairs and turned. His eyebrows rose as he lifted her bag. "*This* is all you have?"

She could feel her cheeks heat up, but she nodded and averted her gaze.

"Come on. I'll show you to your room."

She trudged up the stairs after him, feeling as if she was headed to her execution. She needed to clear the air but was unsure what to say. He opened the second door on the right and motioned for her to enter. She tried to ignore his scent as she passed him but failed miserably. She wanted to lean into him and rub her whole body against him. The spicy richness of sandalwood would forever be seared into her brain as part of him.

As he dropped her bag at the foot of the four-poster queen-sized bed, she grabbed his forearm. "I'm sorry about earlier. I acted like a total freak and I don't know what else to say other than I'm really *really* sorry."

"Why'd you run?" His arm tensed under her fingers so she dropped her hand.

"I..." She bit her bottom lip and decided to plunge ahead. "I don't want you reading my thoughts. I don't care if we're mates, you have no business in my head. Okay?"

"Okay."

She frowned. "That's it?"

"You want me to argue with you and tell you I'm going to hijack your thoughts?" His voice was wry and his expression unreadable.

"Well, no." She crossed her arms over her chest and took another step back from him. She didn't like this cold side of Adam. At least when he'd been awkward before, he'd been endearing and approachable. Having him give her the cold shoulder hurt more than she could have imagined. It didn't matter that it was her own fault.

"Just because we're linked doesn't mean I can jump into your head anytime I want. I can project my thoughts, yes, but I don't think I can read your mind unless you allow me to."

"You're sure?"

He shrugged. "As sure as I can be without trying. Once—if—we bond, we'll likely link completely, but that's neither here nor there."

Crap. She hadn't even thought about bonding. If they were mates, of course he'd want to bond. But then he'd definitely be able to read her thoughts whenever he wanted. Or at least that was how it was for her sister and her mate. An icy shiver rolled over her. She couldn't have him in her head digging around her innermost secrets. "Okay then." She stood there feeling incredibly awkward, but she wasn't sure what else to say. It was late, she was tired, she'd lost her virginity to the mate she couldn't be with, and she already missed her sister desperately. With the exception of the mind-blowing sex, this night sucked.

"Maybe not tomorrow or even this week, but later I'll take you shopping."

She frowned at the sudden change of subject. "What? Why?"

He stared at her as if she'd grown two heads. "Because I take care of what's mine."

Subconsciously she smoothed her hands over her pants. When he shut the door behind him, she let out a long breath she hadn't realized she'd been holding. The house was a lot warmer than her sister's so she changed into a slim-fitting T-shirt and matching navy sleep shorts. Then she slid under the silky sheet and plush comforter. With high ceilings and custom crown molding, the guestroom was devoid of personal decorations, but everything was crisp and clean. There was even a spacious sitting area near one of the windows complete with a chaise lounge and a small bookshelf full of recent fiction releases. She felt like she was in a bed and breakfast or a really nice hotel.

As she closed her eyes, she tried to force sleep to come, but it was annoyingly elusive. She kept picturing Adam's face, and each time, she felt guilty as hell. Not to mention, lonely. After what they'd shared together, she'd hoped to at least cuddle with him for a while, but then she'd freaked out like some sort of maniac. There was no question she could have handled things better and now she was worried she'd done irreparable damage. What if he got curious about why she was so insistent he stay out of her head and started digging deeper into her past?

When an hour had passed and she still couldn't sleep, she punched her pillow once more for good measure and slipped from her bed. Peeking out into the hallway, she found it empty. She listened for a moment and when she didn't hear any noise, she hurried toward the stairs, which were also empty. At the bottom stair, she realized she hadn't asked Adam where anything was but figured she'd find what she wanted. She walked across the foyer and through an archway that led into an expansive kitchen. Everything was state-of-the-art stainless steel and spotless. Most of the appliances looked new.

There was enough moonlight streaming in through the skylights so she didn't bother with the overhead lights. Not to mention she had supernatural night vision. The refrigerator creaked open, but before she'd pulled it out all the way, she was aware of another presence. She swiveled to find Adam standing in the archway wearing boxers and a grim expression.

Her throat seized as she stared at his ripped stomach and chest muscles. That body of his made her positively stupid. She quickly shut the door. "Hi..."

"I heard you get up and wanted to make sure everything was okay." He turned to leave, and even though everything inside her told her to shut up, she called out to him.

"Wait."

He paused but stayed turned away from her. Yeah, he was pissed and she didn't blame him. Smooth lines and tight muscles accentuated his back and calves. His body was drool-worthy and her mouth instinctively

246 | SAVANNAH STUART

watered as her gaze narrowed on his ass. If only he didn't have those boxers on.

"Are you going to stay mad at me forever?" she asked.

At her question, he turned. It wasn't anger she saw there but confusion and desire. He let out a short sigh. "I'm not mad, Paz. I...shit...I don't even know what to say. You find out we're mates and you run away." His jaw clenched tightly as he abruptly stopped talking.

Did he think she'd run because she didn't want him? Maybe if she let him think that, it would be easier to keep her distance. Staring into his green eyes, she could feel herself losing the battle in her head. She needed to stay away from him, but there was an inexplicable pull every time she was near him. Separation physically hurt. Okay, so maybe it wasn't that crazy. Her sister had told her that was what it had been like when she'd found her mate. It was supposedly just biology but the deep ache was low in her belly and it pulsed throughout her entire body. She *needed* to be near him. Needed to feel his hands on her again. "I'm not embarrassed you're my mate if that's what you think. The opposite in fact."

His gaze narrowed as he assessed her face, but some foreign energy rolled off him and nearly bowled her over. *Hope?* She couldn't put her finger on it. Before she could change her mind she walked toward him until they were barely inches apart. "Can I sleep in your room tonight?"

At her question, mercurial storm clouds swirled in his eyes, but he nodded. When he didn't make a move, she brushed past him and was surprised when he placed his hand on the small of her back. She was even more surprised that he left it there as they ascended the stairs all the way to his room. It was almost as if he was making a statement, but she wasn't exactly sure what it was yet.

She knew she'd been the one who had screwed up so it would be up to her to get him talking again. The lights were off, but the curtains on the broad window were drawn back, giving them plenty of illumination. She frowned when she realized the bed wasn't even rumpled.

"Have you gone to sleep yet?" She looked at him as he shut the door behind them.

"No." He shook his head and nodded at the small desk by the window. A laptop was on and papers were fanned out.

A sudden wave of apprehension threatened to sway her, but she forced her legs to move toward the bed. "What side of the bed do you like?"

"Doesn't matter." Short, curt and to the point.

A knot formed in her belly as she pulled back the chocolate-colored comforter and equally dark silky sheet. She slid under the covers and turned on her side as he shut down his computer. When he got in next to her, she reached out to touch him, but he tensed so she pulled her hand back. It was obvious he didn't want to talk so she rolled onto her other side and stared at the huge curio cabinet against the wall. Asking to sleep in the same room as him was a dumb idea, but she'd wanted to touch him. Her wolf needed the connection as bad as she did.

The bed moved suddenly and before she realized it, he'd slipped his arm around her waist and pulled her back flush against his chest. She sank into his hold. "You want to start over?" he murmured against her ear. His hot breath sent shivers to her toes.

She nodded and shifted so that she was on her back instead of facing away from him. "I'm sorry—"

He placed a gentle finger over her lips. "No more apologies. We're starting over."

His expression was still unreadable, but his eyes filled with undeniable lust. He might be mad at her, but he still wanted her.

"So we really are mates, huh?" she whispered.

"Afraid so." He pressed a soft kiss to her forehead and lay back against the pillow but still stayed turned toward her. And he kept that hand across her stomach in a clearly possessive hold. Not that she minded.

Her shirt was pushed up and she was very aware of the bare skin his fingers idly caressed. She had no clue what the future held for them or if they'd ever bond, but if he was her mate she wanted to know more about him. Stephan was right. Before she condemned Adam, she needed to find out what kind of man he was. Because so far, he'd been pretty amazing. "So how did you get the job as The Council's enforcer?"

His fingers stilled and tightened against her. He was silent for so long she doubted he'd answer, so he surprised her when he spoke. "Centuries ago when The Council formed I handled a few skirmishes between packs and since I don't have a pack to speak of, the job fell to me."

The sadness that rolled off him sent a dagger through her chest. Maybe it was because they were mates or maybe it was because she'd never fit in well anywhere. Whatever the reason, she ached for him. "Do you like what you do?"

He shrugged. "It's my job."

Not exactly an answer, but she let it slide. For now. She decided to ask something else that had been weighing on her mind. "Exactly how old are you?"

His lips pursed. Under the moonlight streaming in, his face was all harsh lines and angles. "Roughly five hundred."

248 | SAVANNAH STUART

She gasped. He barely looked forty years old. And that was stretching it. "How is that possible?"

He shrugged again, but this time he didn't answer at all.

"Does anyone else know?"

"The members of The Council."

"Wow." She had more questions, like what had happened to his pack, but suddenly nothing else seemed that important. *How the hell was he that old?*

"I'd appreciate it if you didn't tell anyone my age. It's not a secret exactly, but I don't spread it around."

She nodded and stared at the ceiling. She was barely a hundred, but she'd thought werewolves only lived to be four or five hundred years old. Since she'd never actually seen one that old, she'd assumed they'd look older. Adam looked younger than Lucas Lazos, the Alpha of the Lazos pack, and she was pretty sure Lucas was only two hundred years old. It didn't make sense. Unless Adam had different magic running through his blood. Just like her. *Interesting.*

"I can see those wheels turning in your head. Shut your eyes and get some sleep. We'll talk in the morning," he murmured.

Technically it was already morning, but she didn't comment. When he lay on his back, she shifted and stretched out across his chest. His heartbeat was steady and true. She could also see his cock was hard as a rock underneath the sheet, but he didn't make a move to touch her other than wrapping his arm snuggly around her.

For the first time in over a year, she felt safe. Ironic that it was in his arms, but she didn't care. As she listened to the thump of his heart, she allowed the blackness of sleep to engulf her.

CHAPTER EIGHT

Adam opened his eyes as the increasing sunlight crept up over the sheets through the window. Paz still lay across his chest and every so often, she let out a soft cry that clawed at his insides. His wolf demanded he fix whatever was wrong, but he didn't want to wake her. Even if it killed him not to.

He knew she was battling something in her sleep and needed to get it out. Despite the wet tears on his chest and the protective need that nearly overwhelmed him, he held back. Barely. If she could fight her demons while asleep, it would be good therapy.

"No—" Breathing hard, she jerked up and met his gaze. Her hand was still on his chest as her breathing slowly evened out. "Was I dreaming?"

"Yeah." He tried to catch his breath as he stared at her. Her dark hair was mussed around her face and her eyes were still hazy with sleep. He rubbed his thumb across her cheek, swiping away some of the wetness. "Are you okay?"

She nodded, but she didn't look okay. Those dark eyes were haunted and full of so much sadness. His belly ached as he looked at her. No matter what had gone down between them yesterday, he couldn't stand to see her in pain.

Sliding his hand through the curtain of her hair, he cupped the back of her head. "Come here." He wanted to give her a chance to say no.

Her lips parted slightly as she realized what he wanted and without pause she leaned forward and pressed her mouth to his.

That was all it took to settle his inner wolf. He'd gone to sleep with a hard-on and he'd woken up with one. And it was all for her. For centuries he'd had complete control of his body. He loved sex as much as the next wolf, but his fist would do just fine. Hell, it had been all he'd had over the past couple decades. Now he couldn't imagine using his rough hand when he had Paz's sweet body.

As he teased her lips open, his hands strayed to her waist. He shifted so that he was half sitting and he pulled her so she straddled him. Rolling his hips, he rubbed his bare cock over her covered pussy. Without wasting time, he tugged on the hem of her tiny top and drew it over her head.

When her breasts were bared he had to restrain himself from burying his head against them. She was still coming down from the memories of whatever nightmare she'd been having and he wanted to take things slow, to give her back some control.

She clutched his shoulders and he could tell she was nervous. Maybe it was because it was daylight. She definitely didn't have anything to be worried about. Everything about her was perfect.

"Can I ask you something?" he asked, never averting his gaze from her eyes.

"Yes." Her voice was breathy and seductive and sent a jolt straight to his aching cock.

"Was last night your first time?"

Her cheeks tinged pink, but she nodded. "Yes."

He wanted to ask why she'd chosen him, but he wasn't sure he wanted the answer. All he knew was that even though she'd run from him, she'd still chosen him as her first. *Him.* The knowledge sent a primal surge of satisfaction through him. That had to mean something. Now that he'd had her, he planned to make sure he was the first and last man she ever slept with.

Wordlessly he ran his palms over her breasts. An almost imperceptible shudder rolled over her as he rubbed his thumbs over her hardening nipples. She moistened her lips and her eyes glazed over in undeniable desire.

Seeing her like that had all his possessive instincts flaring to the surface.

Needing to taste her, he reclaimed her mouth as he teased her breasts. Every so often she made little moans and he worried he'd come on the spot from those noises alone. Barely moving his hips, he started rubbing his cock against her covered folds. The skimpy shorts she wore offered little barrier to him. Even if he couldn't smell her heady desire, he could feel how soaked she was.

Though he hated to stop kissing her, he wanted to taste her more. Pulling his head back slightly, he dropped a kiss on her cheek then forehead. "Your shorts need to go," he murmured.

Jerkily, she nodded and pushed up on her knees. He grasped the waistband and helped her shimmy out of them. Now nothing was between them. She settled back on him, but he didn't make a move to penetrate her — even though that was all he wanted to do.

As she slid her soft, wet folds over him, a shudder weaved through him. His cock jutted up between their bodies. She had a soft thatch of neatly trimmed dark hair between her legs and no tan lines anywhere. Her skin was a perfect caramel and an erotic contrast to his. Where he was tanned from the sun and rougher from spending time outdoors, she was soft and all his.

Leaning forward, she wrapped her hands around his neck before pressing her body against him. The feel of her rock-hard nipples against his chest made the muscles in his stomach bunch. He couldn't imagine ever getting tired of the feel of her against him.

He gripped her hips and warred with himself. It would be so easy to plunge deep inside her. Bury himself in her warmth. His cock demanded it, but he wanted to give her more. If he wanted to keep her in his bed, he couldn't fuck her like an animal every time he got near her. Even if that's what his body wanted.

Keeping his hands securely around her hips, he scooted down so that he was flat on his back and she was on top of him. When he moved, her eyes flew open and she drew her head back a fraction.

"What are you doing?" she whispered.

He wasn't sure why she was whispering, but he kept his voice just as low. "I want to taste you."

Her eyebrows pulled together in confusion for a split second until she understood his meaning.

"Just hold on to the headboard and kneel over me. If you don't like what I'm doing, we'll stop." No matter that he wanted to take her from behind, give her his mark and completely dominate her, he wanted her to take back some control in her life. Stephan's earlier advice had given him a lot to think about. After a year in captivity, she was handling herself remarkably well, and although it went against his nature, he wanted her to be on top. Just this once.

Her cheeks were flushed, but she pushed up on her knees and shimmied up his body until she straddled his face.

As she moved over him, he delved his tongue into her wet folds and groaned against her wetness. She was sweet and like nothing he'd ever tasted. Just like her scent, there was something about Paz that was special and belonged solely to her.

"Ahh." The headboard shook slightly under her touch and her thighs quivered when he probed deeper with his tongue.

252 | SAVANNAH STUART

Reaching up, he grasped her ass from underneath and held onto her as he stroked her pussy. With the exception of last night, it had been so long since he'd tasted a woman and even longer since taking a woman this way. Despite his need for dominance, he loved the position and the angle. And he loved her sweet taste.

Taking his time, he circled his tongue around her clit, knowing the stimulation would make her crazy. When he did she jerked above him but maintained a fairly steady stance. He licked her from her clit to as far back as he could go. When he ventured into other territory, she tensed so he returned his focus to her swollen nub. There would be time enough later for anal play when she was more comfortable.

Touching and kissing her was all that mattered. As he swirled his tongue around her slick folds, her body rocking against his face, he could practically feel her orgasm coming on.

"Adam?" His name on her lips was breathy and sexy.

Somehow he stopped himself from what he was doing. "Hmm?"

"I want you inside me." There was no trepidation in her words. Just longing and need.

It mirrored how he felt and there was no way in hell he could argue with her request. Since the moment he woke up, his cock had been aching with the need to feel her sweet pussy wrap around him again. Sliding down the bed, he sat up and turned around so he was facing her back. When she started to move, he pressed his chest against her back and placed his hands over hers.

Wordlessly, she leaned forward a fraction and pressed her backside against him. The small submissive gesture did more to turn him on than anything else she could have done. Smoothing his hands down her waist and hips, he clutched onto her as he grounded himself. He almost felt as if he needed to prepare himself before entering her. Last night had been like nothing he'd ever experienced.

He kept one hand on her hip and slid the other over her ass and between her legs from behind. Her pussy immediately clenched around his finger like a vise, but she was wet and ready for him.

After withdrawing his finger, he brushed her hair to the side and kissed her neck and shoulder. She shuddered as he raked his teeth over her delicate skin and it took all his self-control not to mark her. The wolf inside him might want to brand her for the world to see, but his human side won out. If he did it without her permission, it would cause irreparable damage between them.

When they bonded, it would be for life and he wanted to know her better when they did bond. Possibly love her. Most mates eventually fell in love and despite the fact that he'd been alone for so long, he found himself longing to have that connection with someone. Well, not just anyone. With her. Maybe then he could quit his job and start a life with her.

Paz trembled under Adam's kisses. Her skin felt over-sensitized as he covered her exposed shoulder with kisses. The experience of his tongue licking her pussy had been amazing but she wanted to feel his cock inside her again. She already missed the pleasure of being completely filled by him.

She might have run from him the night before, but what they'd shared was seared into her brain and she desperately craved more. She could barely explain it, even to herself, but she *needed* him inside her.

Clutching onto the headboard, she bit back a moan. She wanted to demand he start thrusting into her, but it had taken all her courage to ask him to stop what he was doing moments before. So far he'd been incredibly giving, but he was also unreadable. Every so often she'd sense something from him or she'd be able to read his expression, but the man was a mystery. A really, sexy one.

"Please." The word tore from her lips before she could stop herself.

"Please what, sweetheart?" He tugged her earlobe between his teeth.

"Do *something*."

The chuckle in her ear was positively wicked. He was intentionally torturing her. Before she had time to prepare, he grasped her hips again and thrust, long and hard. The action was abrupt but welcome. Her inner walls expanded and clenched as she adjusted.

When he didn't move, she tried to, but he snaked an arm around her waist and held her fast. Her pussy pulsed and spasmed, begging for relief. If he would let her move, just a little, she'd push over the edge. She was so close. Had been close when he'd simply been licking her. But she'd wanted to feel him inside her when she came, had wanted that extra connection.

"Don't move," he whispered into her ear as he removed his hand.

Her body listened to his command even though nothing was stopping her from moving. One of his hands slid up her side and over her rib cage until he cupped her breast. She sucked in a sharp breath and he flicked her hardened bud before lightly pinching it between his fingers.

The erotic action had her involuntarily jerking against him. When she did, he slid another hand over her stomach and down between her legs. He didn't waste any time finding her clit.

His fingers expertly and playfully strummed her aching bundle of nerves. He knew the right pressure, the right tempo. It was simultaneously torture and heaven. The faster he tweaked her, the tighter her pussy contracted.

A pulsating wave of pleasure started deep in her belly. Finally she couldn't take it anymore. She moved forward then back. And he didn't try to stop her. Just the opposite.

His hand dropped from her breast and he pounded into her with a fierce rhythm. In and out. He slammed his cock into her with no restraint. "You like that?" The question was little more than a guttural growl.

But she couldn't answer. The feel of his cock moving in her was too much. Her climax hit with shocking intensity. Her inner walls spasmed out of control as he slammed into her again and again.

She grabbed onto the headboard for support, but Adam's arm was once again underneath her stomach, giving her balance. He held her through her racking orgasm. Her toes and fingers felt numb as she came down from her high.

Behind her, a loud shout exploded from Adam as he plunged deep into her with one final thrust. As he emptied himself inside her, he growled her name and reality wiggled its way into her brain. She couldn't have sex and keep herself separate from her emotions. The more they did this, the closer she felt to him. And the more likely it was they'd bond and finalize that they were truly mated. He hadn't mentioned anything about bonding, but he was biding his time. She sensed it straight to her core.

She shoved those thoughts from her mind as he collapsed onto the bed and pulled her on top of him. Stretched over him, she couldn't fight the giggle that erupted when his cock began to harden again. "You're a machine," she murmured when he swept kisses across her jaw and over her cheek.

"Only for you, sweetheart." His deep voice enveloped every part of her.

Even though she tried to keep thoughts of the future out of her head, she realized that before they bonded she'd have to be honest with Adam about what she was. Maybe she should give him the benefit of the doubt before assuming he'd discard her once he knew the truth, but certain prejudices ran deep. If he rejected her, she didn't think she could bear it. With that rejection would come betrayal because he'd no doubt turn her over to The Council. She wouldn't go willingly and she knew the Lazos pack would never let him take her without a fight. There would be bloodshed and she couldn't stand the thought of that hovering on her conscience either.

CHAPTER NINE

Adam stared out the expansive window as he tried to figure out what was going on in Paz's head. She'd enjoyed herself in bed, of that he was sure, but when they were finished, she'd emotionally withdrawn from him again. And he had no idea why.

The sound of running water stopped and he realized she must be done with her shower. He'd contemplated joining her, but she'd seemed as if she needed time alone. Even though he wanted to try linking with her telepathically and delve into her thoughts, he couldn't break that trust. He'd promised to stay out of her head and he had to do just that. If—when—they bonded, he doubted he'd be able to stay out though. According to most shifters, once the bonding was official, mates linked telepathically and permanently.

As he turned from the window, something near one of the sand dunes caught his eye. "What the hell..."

"What's going on?" Paz asked.

He turned to find her wrapped in a towel looking good enough to eat. She'd twisted her wet hair up into an oversized clip and without any makeup on she practically glowed. He mentally shook himself. He couldn't afford to be distracted now. "Stay here and keep the doors locked."

Without waiting for a response, he headed downstairs. He didn't bother with any weapons because he was faster and more powerful than most werewolves realized. The Council knew some of his secrets, but not all of them.

The salty air slid over him the second he stepped outside. He didn't waste time hiding or trying to stalk the werewolf on the beach. The man had been visible from the window and it was obvious he wasn't trying to hide. Or if he was, he was doing a shitty job.

The sand shifted between his toes as he stalked across it. "What the hell are you doing?" he demanded when he spotted the naked human curled up next to a small sand hill.

The dark-haired man focused on Adam for a split second before writhing in agony. "Fuck, this hurts! Help me, please." He started to shift. His bones cracked but only halfway realigned before he reverted back to his human form.

"Adam!" He turned at Paz's voice. Wearing jeans and a T-shirt—and no bra—she hurried across the patio and down the short wooden steps.

"I thought I told you to stay inside," he growled. Didn't the fact that he was known as the enforcer carry any weight with the stubborn woman?

She rolled her eyes and tried to brush past him, but instinct kicked in and he blocked her.

"Don't go near him."

"This is the human that doctor injected. I recognize him from Perez's video scans. They didn't tell the subjects what they were giving them. I swear I've seen him before."

Doctor Reed, the monster experimenting on his kind, along with Antonio Perez had been killed in the explosion that saved Paz's life. It would stand to reason Paz recognized him. "You're sure?"

"Yes." She glanced at the man still writhing, then back at Adam. She placed a gentle hand on his forearm. "He's just another victim. We need to help him."

Sighing, Adam turned and crouched next to the man. "I'm going to help you inside. If you try to attack this woman, you'll regret it. Do you understand?"

All the muscles in the man's body were pulled taut, but he nodded. "Yes," he gasped out.

Even though the man was taller and heavier than him, Adam lifted him up with ease and strode past Paz. All his protective instincts told him to kill this human or get him far away from his mate, but he knew he had to act rationally. They needed to find out who he was and who else knew about him. Adam could sense that he was a shifter, yet somehow different. It was an intriguing, foreign scent.

Paz hurried past him and opened the door to the kitchen. Once inside, he stretched the man out on the center island. He didn't care about nudity and Adam seriously doubted the other man did either, but Paz grabbed a towel and threw it over his lap.

Before he could move, Paz elbowed past him and took the man's face in her hands. "Can you hear me?" she asked.

"Yeah," he rasped out.

"What's your name?"

"Ethan Connell." His voice was slightly stronger this time, as if Paz's presence had a calming effect on him.

"How did you find us?" Adam interjected.

"I could feel you." Ethan looked at Paz when he answered.

She glanced back at Adam, then back at him. "What do you mean?"

"I don't know...they put something in my blood...told me it would make me stronger, not turn me into a fucking animal." He howled in pain and curled up in a fetal position.

Paz brushed his shaggy hair back from his forehead. "Listen to me, Ethan. Take a deep breath and relax."

Adam was surprised when the man did. His legs and arms went slack at her words.

"Take another breath and close your eyes. Now go to sleep. You want to shut your eyes and go to sleep. You'll feel better when you wake up." Her voice was like a lullaby.

And Ethan did exactly as she said.

There was more to Paz than met the eye. Adam was now convinced she was keeping something from him. "How did you do that?"

She stepped away from the island and turned toward him. "I didn't do anything. He's tired and stressed. He just needed to ground himself. I'm going to call Caro and have her come over to check him out."

Adam frowned as he racked his brain. "Caro?"

"Oh, Caro Angel. She's Alisha Lazos' sister. She was at Nick's birthday party before you arrived, but she got called to the hospital."

"Right." He'd read Caro's file. She was a pediatrician at one of the hospitals in Miami, specifically in the oncology department. When Paz said the she-wolf's name, her voice softened. It was a small thing, but he guessed they were likely close.

"She should be home by now. Would you mind carrying him to one of the bedrooms so he's more comfortable?"

Adam nodded as Paz hurried from the room. Now he was more than intrigued. Once again she was all business. The only time Paz let her guard down was during sex so if he had to use that to get close to her, so be it.

Paz waited until she was upstairs to let out the breath she'd been holding. As she'd been calming that man down, she'd forgotten about Adam's presence. Well, not completely but enough that she let her defenses slip. And that couldn't happen again.

As a half fae, she had the ability to influence people. Not all people, of course, and usually not supernatural beings, but the man downstairs had been near his breaking point. His subconscious had been begging for help. He'd wanted to listen to her. And Adam had seen her use her abilities. Of course she could deny it, but he'd still seen her in action.

She shook her head. That was something she'd just have to worry about later. When she found her cell, she dialed Caro.

Thankfully, she answered on the second ring. "Hey, sweetie."

She didn't bother with niceties. "Caro? I need your help. We found that human the doctor injected. From what I can see he's having a hard time controlling his ability to shift, but I got him to go to sleep."

"Did you use your *influence*?" Caro was one of the few people who knew about most of her abilities.

"Yes. I don't think Adam realized though." She whispered the last part.

"I'll be right over."

"Thanks." As soon as they disconnected, Paz slid her phone back into her bag and collapsed on the bed.

She was still a little nervous being alone with Adam so she was thankful Caro was coming over. When Paz had awakened directly after her year-long nightmare, Caro had been one of the first people to help her. She'd gone shopping with her and had told her to stop by the house anytime she wanted to talk. Hell, she'd treated her normal, not like some victim. Although she was one hundred and ninety, Caro was still unmated. In human years, it meant she looked like she was in her thirties, but for a shifter, it was a long time to be single.

Not that Paz blamed her for not settling. It would be horrible to mate, then to find out your true mate was still out there. Hell, she was still shocked she'd found her mate and even more shocked by who he was. Growing up she'd heard rumors about the enforcer and how badass he was, but she'd been more terrified of him than anything else. He represented The Council and they represented death for her.

A sharp knock on her open door jerked her gaze up. Damn! She hadn't even scented him coming up the stairs. She needed to get a grip on herself.

Adam stared at her for a long moment then spoke. "I put him on the couch in the living room. Is Caro on her way?"

She nodded and stood.

"Good. Thomas and Nick will be here soon too. Once they arrive, I've got something to do, but you'll be in safe hands."

She started to ask where he was going but stopped. If she didn't know what he was doing, she wouldn't worry. At least that's what she told herself. "Okay, I'll wait downstairs."

Adam gritted his teeth as he drove away from the beach house. He hated leaving Paz alone, but his DOJ contact had called while she'd been upstairs and he now had a meeting he couldn't break. Leaving her with Thomas and Nick should ease his mind, but it just pissed him off. He hated how at ease she was with Thomas.

He actually liked Thomas and under different circumstances, might even throw back a couple beers with him, but as it stood, until he and Paz bonded, he didn't want her around him — or any males. His human side knew his attitude was archaic. His other side didn't give a shit.

Once he reached the local transportation department, he parked in the main lot as he'd been instructed, then waited. After a few minutes, he spotted a middle-aged man wearing a white dress shirt and dark slacks weaving through the various vehicles. And he looked agitated.

Adam got out of the SUV and shut the door, waiting to be approached.

"Are you Adam?" He stood back a couple feet and Adam could scent his nervousness.

"Yeah. And you are?" Adam knew the man's name, he just wanted to be sure.

"I'm Frank. You ready?" Despite the cool breeze, he wiped his palms against his slacks.

"When you are." Adam fell into step with him and didn't bother making small talk. Since the Department of Justice was a virtual umbrella over so many agencies, his contact with them was technically this guy's boss. But Adam understood his friend was doing him a huge favor by allowing him unlimited access to the traffic videos.

After using his keycard to open a side door to the two-story building, Frank glanced at him as they headed down a hallway. "I've already got the videos set up for the day you requested, but you have only ten minutes, so make sure you get everything you need because I can't let you in again." As they came to stand in front of a plain, blue door, Frank used his keycard again. "I'll be back in eleven minutes and I expect you to be gone."

"Will do. Thanks." Adam nodded as he ducked into the room. There were four oversized monitors displayed in front of a desk and each screen was paused. It would take more than ten minutes to get what he wanted, so he pulled out two flash drives and inserted them into the two computer towers. He was fairly good with computers, and his contact had told him exactly how to upload all the files he'd need to view later.

Once he finished he glanced at his cell phone. Five minutes to spare. He tucked the flash drives into his pocket and left the way he'd come. When he had time and privacy, he was going to dissect every part of the video feed. Then the hunt was officially on.

CHAPTER TEN

Paz grabbed a bottle of water from the refrigerator, but paused after she shut the door. She couldn't be sure, but she sensed Adam was back. The sound of the front door opening then shutting confirmed it. She waited a moment, and when he didn't enter the kitchen, she headed back to the living room.

Nick Lazos had already left, but Thomas and Caro were still there watching over Ethan with her. As she passed the stairs, she caught Adam descending them. She'd assumed he'd already be in the living room with the others. "Hey, how long have you been here?"

"Just got here. Had to put some stuff upstairs."

"Okay, well Ethan is probably going to be knocked out for a couple hours, but he woke up for a while."

"What did he say?" Adam asked as he reached the bottom step.

"He told us his name again. Supposedly he's ex-military and he's done a lot of contract work since he got out two years ago. He heard through the grapevine—I'm assuming an illegal one—that Antonio Perez was working on something to create super-strength or some crap like that. He signed up for a clinical study and he was the only one who survived the treatments. At first, he really did just have above average strength, but then he started changing."

"Changing?"

"Like us. He can't control it, but he's able to shift into a wolf. And he's just as strong as werewolves."

"What else did he say?" Adam asked.

"That's it." Thomas answered before she could.

She glanced up to find Thomas walking down the hallway toward them. When Adam immediately put his arm around her shoulder in a clearly possessive gesture, she bit back a smile. Not very subtle but she doubted he cared.

His grip on her tightened and he pulled her a few inches closer to his side. Her instinct to keep her mate happy kicked in. She stepped into his embrace and wrapped her arm around his waist, wanting him to know that he was the important male to her. The sensation was foreign, but she found she liked it. More than she wanted to admit. She'd never been touchy-feely with anyone other than her family, but especially not with a male. Touching Adam this way brought up all sorts of feelings she wasn't sure she was prepared to handle. Sex she could deal with, but the public displays of affection were weird if not nice.

"I took his fingerprints once he finally fell asleep again. I'm going to have one of Stephan's contacts run them and see if his story checks out. In the meantime, in case he's unstable, I think it's best if I keep him at my house where I can keep an eye on him. Unless you want him here...around your mate?" Thomas lifted a dark eyebrow.

Paz refrained from rolling her eyes. She wasn't sure why Thomas was practically goading Adam, but it was childish. If Adam wanted to keep Ethan under his supervision, it was his right as the enforcer. She knew it wasn't jealousy on Thomas' part though. Maybe it was just a stupid thing alpha males did to one another.

Adam's grip on her tightened a fraction. "That's fine. As soon as he's awake, call me. I want to talk to him."

"How did your meeting go?" Thomas asked.

"Good. I got the video feeds I needed. Now I just need to view them."

Paz wasn't sure what he meant, but it was obvious Thomas did.

Thomas nodded once. "All right. Caro and I are about to head out with Ethan. I'll call as soon as I get a hit on the fingerprints or when he wakes up. Whichever happens first."

Next to her, she could feel Adam relax. "We'll be here."

Thomas disappeared down the short hallway and into the living room. Paz turned toward Adam but kept her arm around him. She found she wanted to maintain their contact. "I'm going to say goodbye to Caro, okay?"

"I'll be in my room if you need me." He dropped a quick kiss on her forehead and headed back up the stairs.

She felt the loss of touching him as soon as he'd gone and couldn't help but wonder if that was something mates naturally experienced or if it was just because she missed him.

After saying goodbye to Thomas and Caro, she locked the front door and set the alarm. They'd be able to scent someone coming into the house, but everyone was being extra careful. No one knew exactly how devious

Morales was and if he found a weakness he'd exploit it, no matter how small.

When she opened the door to her bedroom, she froze. Shopping bags covered her bed. Most were from stores she didn't recognize, but two large bags were emblazoned with the very recognizable Victoria's Secret logo. She couldn't even pretend not to be interested. After shutting the door, she dug into the first pink bag.

Then she just dumped everything onto the bed. Her eyes widened as she took in everything Adam must have bought for her. It wasn't just lingerie. There was a plush robe, a few dozen panties, bras—she wondered how he'd figured out her size—pajamas and a whole mess of other stuff.

She swallowed when it hit her how much he must have spent. With shaking hands, she peeked into the other bags and found stacks of jeans, sweaters, sexy tops, summer dresses and even a couple bathing suits. When she spotted one of the receipts, her eyes widened. He'd spent almost a grand. *At one store.*

Leaving everything on the bed, she headed to Adam's room. She knocked on the half-open door as she entered. He wore a pair of jeans— with the top button undone—and nothing else. She lost her train of thought as her gaze followed the dark thatch of hair that disappeared under his pants.

He immediately stood and took a step toward her. "Is everything okay?"

"What? Yes. I, uh, just saw my bed."

"Oh. Is everything okay? I left the receipts in there in case something didn't fit."

"How did you manage to get all that stuff so quickly?"

He shrugged and she didn't miss the way his neck slightly reddened. "I told the saleswomen your size and told them to pick stuff they thought a woman would like."

"Thank you doesn't seem to cover it, but thank you—so much. That was really thoughtful. I can't believe how much...I mean, it feels weird talking about money with you, but are you sure you didn't get too much? My sister and I have some money from before our pack was... Anyway, once I get a job I can pay you back."

He snorted. "You're *not* paying me back. You're my mate and I wanted to do something nice for you."

"We haven't even bonded yet though." The words just slipped out and she immediately wanted to kick herself. She'd been hoping to avoid this

264 | SAVANNAH STUART

conversation for at least another week and then she went and brought it up. *Way to go.*

Adam took a few steps closer and immediately she was hit with the intensity of the desire he was putting off. Instinctively, she wrapped her arms around herself as she waited for him to respond.

"Do you want to bond with me?" And there it was. Right out in the open.

Her throat closed off for a second and she wondered if she deprived her brain of oxygen long enough, maybe she'd pass out and wouldn't have to answer the question. She'd already hurt him by running away after the first time they made love. How the hell was she supposed to answer this?

She cleared her throat. "We don't really know much about each other yet." *Okay, that was a safe answer and one he couldn't argue with.*

His gaze narrowed for a fraction of a second, but then he surprised her by sitting on the end of the bed and patted the area next to him. "What do you want to know?"

She could listen to that deep voice of his and never get tired. It was liquid sin rolling over her. Somehow she ordered her feet forward. Instead of answering his question, she decided to take the plunge and ask something that had been weighing on her mind. "Do *you* want to bond with me?"

"Yes." The answer was strong and immediate.

Well, damn. "But...*why*? You barely know me."

"We'll get to know each other with time." He reached out and traced a gentle finger down her cheek. The small action sent a shiver to her toes.

She didn't understand how he could be so sure. "But what if I have a deep dark secret that you can't live with? Wouldn't you want to know before we bonded?"

"I want to know anything you want to tell me."

"That's not an answer!" She knew she shouldn't get angry, but she could feel a bubble of annoyance pushing to the surface. Why wasn't he more concerned about this? When mates bonded, it was forever. He should want to ask her a million questions. Lord knew she wanted to know everything about his past.

He sighed. The sound was long and heavy. "Listen, Paz. I don't care what you've done in the past. It can't be any worse than the things I've done. I've... I've been alone for a long time and I like you. *A lot.* I'm not going to change my mind about bonding, but take all the time you need to make a decision."

She bit her bottom lip and eyed him suspiciously. "Fine. How is it that you're five hundred years old but you look younger than those half your age?"

His jaw clenched once. "My father was an Immortal."

A gasp escaped before she could stop herself. "You're a mixed-blood?" His eyes darkened and she immediately realized her mistake. Before he could respond, she grabbed his hand. "I didn't mean that as an insult, I swear. You just surprised me."

Tension still hummed through him, but he didn't pull away. "No one else knows."

"I thought Immortals needed sex to stay strong. Or is that a myth?" Immortals had always fascinated her. And if she was really honest, they'd also terrified her a little too. Compared to the other supernatural beings on the planet, so little was known about them.

"It's a combination of both. Immortals don't need sex, but it does make them stronger. I'm…different."

"What do you mean?" If anyone understood being different, she did.

"It doesn't matter. Just know that I don't need sex to survive or to keep up my strength."

"Well what about my life span if we bond? And what element do you control?" As far as she knew, Immortals controlled one of the four elements and when they died, they reverted back to whatever power they'd possessed when they'd been alive. Adam scrubbed a hand over his face and she wondered if she should have held back some of her questions. "You don't have to answer me if—"

He shook his head. "It's fine. I should have expected this. I'd rather not talk about my abilities…yet. If we do bond, you'll age at the same pace as me. I guess that's something I probably should have told you sooner."

She swallowed hard at his words. "How do you know I'll become like you?"

"My mother was a full-blooded werewolf and when she became pregnant with me, her aging process changed to match my father's. Besides, I wouldn't be the first mixed-blood to mate. Nature has a way of working things out."

The inflection in his voice when he mentioned his parents told her they were likely dead. Even though she wanted to ask, for once she made herself bite her tongue. If he wanted to talk about them, he would. She was still holding his hand so she linked her fingers through his and scooted a few inches closer.

Maybe if she opened up to him now it would be easier later to tell him the truth about what she was. As a mixed-blood, he wouldn't have the prejudices so many others did. Or she hoped he wouldn't. "So why do you work for The Council when they denounce so many different supernatural beings?"

He frowned at her words. "What are you talking about?"

"Their laws are archaic."

The lines around his mouth and eyes deepened. "Which laws in particular are you referring to?"

A cold sweat blossomed across her forehead, but she forced herself to answer. "The law that says any werewolf with other magic in their blood will be put to death."

"That hasn't been implemented in centuries. And it was only put in place for those who had mated with faeries, not Immortals."

"And you don't see a problem with that?" Anger more than fear started to boil inside her as she waited for his answer.

"I've never met a faerie who didn't deserve to die." His words were laced with loathing.

Feeling as though she'd been burned, she dropped his hand and stood. "Well, it's nice to find this out about you now." Without waiting for a response, she strode from the room and slammed her bedroom door with startling force. The frames on the walls shook dangerously, but nothing fell. She knew she should have contained her anger better, but it was as if someone had embedded a knife in her chest. Tears stung her eyes, but she angrily brushed them away. She thought he'd be different.

Her door flew open as she was pushing the bags of clothes off her bed.

"What the hell was that about?" He stood in the doorway, hands balled at his sides, anger pulsing off him in waves.

"Get out of my room," she said through clenched teeth.

"Not until you answer my question. What could I have possibly done to set you off?"

"Other than supporting The Council's antiquated laws and judging an entire group of people based on nothing more than their heritage?" Her hands shook so she shoved them into her pockets.

"You're too young, but I was there during the end of the Great War. I saw firsthand exactly how devious those faeries are. They came under the guise of peace and killed my parents right in front of me. And they didn't do it quickly either. So yeah, I fucking hate them." His words were a low growl that sent shivers snaking throughout her entire body.

More tears burned her eyes so she turned away from him and reached into one of the bags to keep her hands busy. "Please leave my room."

Maybe it was the please that did it, but a few seconds later, she heard the door click shut behind him. Letting her tears fall, she collapsed onto the bed. The fact that faeries had killed Adam's parents left little room for debate. Some faeries were definitely evil. But so were some werewolves. As the crazy werewolf they were hunting right now proved. Once they caught Morales, she was leaving Adam. Hell, she had no choice. She couldn't mate with him knowing he hated her kind and she couldn't hide who she was for the rest of her life.

CHAPTER ELEVEN

Stephan watched his mate through the sliding glass door that led to the porch of their rental house. Marisol stared out at the beach but he knew she was aware of his presence. She was just ignoring him.

He understood her need to protect her sister, but Paz needed room to breathe and figure things out for herself. Something Marisol couldn't understand. He did though. Paz was strong and more than anything, she deserved to get to know her mate without her little sister interfering or trying to coddle her.

Sighing, he opened the door and stepped outside. The beach in Saint Augustine looked pretty much like the beach in Miami. Instead of heading too far up the eastern seaboard, they'd stopped in north Florida. In case the pack needed them, they wouldn't have too far to travel back home. "Still mad at me?" he asked as he sat at the foot of her lounge chair.

Scowling at him, she moved her feet so they wouldn't touch him. "What do you think?"

"I think you need to get over yourself."

Her eyes widened. "Why you—"

"*Kardia mou*, don't say something you'll regret."

Her mouth snapped shut, but at least she was silent.

"I have brothers so I know what you're going through. You can be a bit of a bulldozer sometimes." When her eyes darkened, he quickly continued. "A very sexy bulldozer. Listen, Paz is strong. You know that."

"We left her with that Adam guy." Guilt and anger threaded her words.

"That Adam guy is her mate."

She crossed her arms over her chest. "I don't care. What if he finds out what she is?"

"It won't matter. He'll die protecting her."

"How do you know that? What if he hates faeries? We don't know anything about him." She leaned forward and grabbed his hand.

Now that she was touching him, he knew he was almost out of the doghouse. "Even if he does hate them, he won't harm her. I sensed how much he cares for her. He might not even realize it yet, but that wolf is over the moon for your sister. Remember how much you loathed me when we first met?" When they'd first met, she hadn't known he was an undercover DEA agent. She'd thought he was a bottom-dwelling arms dealer.

"Yes." She sniffed in that haughty manner of hers that made his cock stand at attention.

"You still protected me when I almost lost control in that club. It's what real mates do. I know the lengths I'd go to save you and it's true with every mated male in my family. It's biology, baby. He will *not* hurt her. And right now, my only concern is keeping you safe."

She pushed up from her chair and sauntered toward the rail lining the porch. He bit back a groan as he watched the soft sway of her hips. With her back to him, she leaned forward on the railing, but he could tell he was almost forgiven.

He crept behind her and slid his arms around her waist. She didn't fight him so he pulled her tighter against his chest. His erection pressed insistently against her backside, but he doubted she was surprised.

When she didn't say anything, he brushed her hair to one side and nibbled at her earlobe. Her sweet scent nearly bowled him over. Sometimes he couldn't believe he'd finally found his mate. And she was a constant fireball of passion, surprising him every day.

As he started to spread kisses across her neck, she twisted to face him. "I shouldn't let you off the hook so easily," she murmured.

The scent of her desire was unmistakable. "You want me as bad as I want you."

She bit her bottom lip and he could tell she was fighting a smile. Instead of responding, she grabbed the bottom of his shirt and started tugging upward.

His entire body tensed with anticipation. Didn't matter how many times he'd had her, she was an addiction. After he finished shrugging out of his shirt, he gripped her hips and lifted her onto the railing. The rental properties on either side of them were empty and he couldn't scent anyone else along the deserted stretch of beach. She let out a little squeal when he pushed her short summer dress up to her waist.

"I thought I told you to stop wearing panties." He frowned at the red material covering her pussy.

"It does you good to work for it a little." She grinned as she grappled with his belt.

Today was going to be fast and hard. He could feel it. Pent-up energy buzzed through both of them. They'd barely said two words to each other on the drive up and he was tired of fighting with her.

As she worked on his pants, he plucked the tie at the back of her neck and let gravity do its job with the straps to her halter. He loved it when she wore the sexy halter-style dresses. Easier access for him and she knew it.

The muscles in his stomach tensed as he stared at her. He stepped out of his pants as they fell, but all his attention was on her perfect light brown nipples. He'd kissed and licked them so many times, he had all her curves memorized. And seeing any part of her bared got him hot every time.

"You gonna stand there staring all day?" Her question jerked him into action.

Her sweet, exotic scent surrounded him as he leaned down and captured one of her already hardened buds between his teeth.

Teasingly, he painted the underside of her breast with his tongue then swirled around her areola before centering on her nipple. When he gently raked his teeth over the hardened point, she let out a tiny moan and arched her back, pushing herself farther into his mouth.

She clasped onto one of his shoulders for support and reached between them with her other hand. Fisting his cock at the base, she slowly stroked upward once, twice—it was too much. Panting, he lifted his head. He needed to be inside her now.

Through a lust-induced haze, Marisol stared into Stephan's eyes. She loved it when he got all hot and bothered like this. His eyes were like storm clouds, dark and intense. All she had to do was lightly touch him and he was ready to go.

Having that kind of power over a man was a strong aphrodisiac, especially when he had the same control over her. His hands, which had been on her hips, suddenly grasped the slim strap of her panties and snapped the material apart.

"You owe me another pair," she gasped.

"Stop wearing them and it won't be a problem." His words were a low growl that sent shivers skittering over her.

Cool air rushed over her bared pussy, but only for a moment. He quickly covered her mound and pushed one of his thick fingers inside her without giving her any warning. Not that she needed it. She was soaking wet for him. And had been for quite a while.

As he slid his finger into her, he feathered kisses along her neck and jaw. She wrapped her legs around his waist, trying to entice him to use his cock instead, but he refused.

She'd been hot for him their entire drive and that had just pissed her off more. Even when she was mad at him, she wanted him. Now she desperately needed relief and he was the only one who could give it to her. Maybe he was trying to tease her for keeping him at arms' length.

He pushed into her again, knuckle deep, and slowly pulled out, dragging his finger against her inner walls with practiced precision. Then he added another finger and thrust into her. Instead of moving, he stayed inside her and strummed her clit with his thumb. Gently and much too slowly.

Oh yeah, he was torturing her for giving him the silent treatment, that had to be it. The man knew what kind of rhythm she needed and he was holding back.

"I don't want your fingers," she gasped out.

"Too bad," he murmured against her neck. "I've been wanting to do this for hours."

Jerking against his fingers, she met him with insistency, forcing him to give her what she wanted.

Chuckling against her skin, he pulled his head back. "You have no patience."

Her entire body was pulled as taut as a hunting bow. Her leg and stomach muscles tightened in anticipation as she waited for him. She held onto his shoulders and finally, her stubborn mate dragged his fingers from her and drove his cock into her.

She sucked in a deep breath as he stretched and filled her. As her body adjusted to him, he came at her fast, invading her mouth with his tongue and hours of pent up energy. He kissed her deep and hard, flicking his tongue against hers in tantalizing strokes.

His cock pulsed inside her, yet he barely moved. Just rocked his hips slightly against hers. Still, she was about to come. Usually they fucked hard and fast, but this was different. He was eating at her mouth with hunger, but everything else was so subdued. So gentle. It surprised her.

The points of her nipples ached painfully. Luckily Stephan could literally read her mind. Cupping one of her breasts, he covered it and stroked the throbbing bud. Each caress brought her closer and closer to climax.

It was as if the pleasure points in her nipples were connected to the growing heat between her thighs with an invisible wire. He fondled the other breast and paid it just as much attention. The pads of his thumbs rolled leisurely over the hard buds, drawing more moans from her.

If he would just move a little, she'd come. Her body and mind screamed. Just a little—

No patience whatsoever, kardia mou, he projected with his mind.

She locked her ankles around his waist and held on tight as he pulled out of her, then slammed his cock back into her.

The sharp action was exactly what she needed. She savored the feel of the cool air rushing over their bodies as they joined together. Stephan fastened onto her hips as he drove into her with wild, uneven thrusts.

Her inner walls tightened around him with each stroke. She clamped onto his shoulders but he didn't seem to notice how hard she dug in. "Ah." She could barely think let alone speak any coherent words.

In and out.

Harder and faster.

Her legs gripped his waist as tight as her pussy wrapped around his cock. She arched her back as the explosion rippled through her. Her legs already felt weak as she released control and let her erotic hunger dominate her. Tiny shocks of pleasure swelled like waves across her entire body, sending zings to all her nerve endings. The pleasure that was becoming so familiar was almost too much to bear.

As she allowed her legs to fall from around him, Stephan pounded into her with one final thrust and a loud shout. If they'd had neighbors nearby, there would have been no doubt what they were doing. Not that she cared.

Panting, he reached behind her back and tugged the zipper on her dress the rest of the way down.

"I think we're a little late for that, sweetie," she murmured.

He grunted something before tugging it over her head. The cool breeze chilled her bare body.

"What—"

But he didn't let her finish. Gripping her behind, he hoisted her up in one swoop. As he strode across the long porch she realized he was heading toward the hot tub. She might be able to handle the elements better than humans, but jumping in a freezing tub wasn't her idea of fun, even if she could stand it. "I think it's too cold."

"I turned on the heat when we got here." He didn't break stride as he descended into the water.

The steam hit her before she actually touched the water. Without letting go of her, he sat on the step then stretched back and flipped on the powerful jets.

Bubbles and heat surrounded them. She shifted her position so that she was stretched out across his lap instead of straddling him. Then she laid her head against his shoulder. "Thank you," she said against his neck.

"For what?"

"For putting up with me."

He chuckled against the top of her head. "As if I could live without you."

CHAPTER TWELVE

Adam stared at the ceiling, trying to contain his annoyance and confusion. He still wasn't quite sure what had happened between him and Paz but he knew he'd fucked up. Big time.

It wasn't that much of a shock considering he sucked at talking to most people. He'd simply been honest about what he felt, but maybe he *had* been a little harsh. The truth was he hadn't actually seen a faerie since the Great War. They mostly lived in the United Kingdom and some were scattered throughout Australia now.

Thinking about what had happened to his parents, much less talking about it, had brought back too many memories. Memories that needed to stay buried. Hearing his father's roar of anguish when they'd found his mother's broken body was a sound he'd never forget. And seeing his mother with a giant hole in her chest was something else he'd never scrub from his memory. His father had managed to kill most of the faeries that night before someone had gotten in a lucky shot and taken off his head. Adam had been a boy then, barely in control of his powers and he hadn't been able to help. He shook his head, ridding himself of the bloody visions.

No matter what was in his past, he needed to make this right. He pushed up out of the bed and headed for Paz's room when a bright orange ball of fire exploded in his line of sight through the second story window.

He crept toward the window but stayed in the shadows. Glass was shattered across the patio near the pool and a few pockets of fire dimly burned against the cement. It looked as if someone had thrown a couple Molotov cocktails. A dark shadow darted down the beach in the direction of Stephan's place. Looked like a wolf.

If it was Morales, he'd only done it to get their attention. By now he must realize that Marisol was gone. Maybe he thought she was staying here. Or hell, maybe he wanted to hurt Paz as a way to get to Marisol. That was more likely.

Morales was already at the top of Adam's shitlist but now it was personal. He moved away from the window as Paz rushed into his room. She jerked to a halt just inside the doorway.

"What's going on?" Her eyes were wide. Not with fear exactly, but she looked panicked.

"It looks like someone threw Molotov cocktails on our back porch."

"*Morales,*" she growled.

In that moment he was proud of her anger. He wanted a mate who wasn't afraid to take care of herself. He nodded and pursed his lips together. Adam had spent hours reviewing those security tapes and he had a fairly decent idea which area of the city Morales was staying in. He'd managed to track him to the warehouse district. Which made sense. If he wanted to avoid the police and everyone else, he'd just hole up in an abandoned warehouse or dilapidated home.

"Will you call Thomas and spread the word what happened here?" he asked.

"Uh, sure." Her eyebrows shot up in surprise.

It was obvious she wondered why he wasn't making the calls, so he answered her unspoken question. "I need to check outside and make a couple calls myself."

She hovered by the door for a moment before darting from the room. When she did, he couldn't help but watch the way her ass swayed. His cock stirred as he watched her and he wondered if the burning need inside him would ever subside. Scrubbing a hand over his face, he sighed. It was time to get down to work.

After checking outside and dousing the rest of the smoldering embers, he scouted the beach in both directions. It was easy to ascertain which way Morales had left. There were faint traces of his scent, but he was definitely gone.

Tonight he'd made his first mistake. He was getting desperate. Showing up and revealing himself in this way meant he was coming unhinged. The rogue werewolf wasn't thinking clearly. Once he was sure Morales was truly gone, he hurried back inside.

Upstairs in his room, he found Paz sitting on the edge of his bed. "Everyone is accounted for."

"What about your sister?"

Her cheeks flushed pink. "What do you mean?"

"I know she wouldn't have left without giving you a way to contact her."

Her cheeks darkened even more, but she nodded. "I called. She and Stephan are both fine."

"Good." He pulled a small bag from underneath his bed that he'd prepacked and hoisted it over his shoulder. If he could help it, this was going to end tonight.

She stood and placed her hands on her hips. "What are you doing?"

"I'm going after Morales."

"By yourself?" Despite their earlier fight, there was concern in her voice.

His throat tightened. That had to mean something. "I've been doing this a long time, Paz. There's no guarantee I catch him tonight, but I can't pass up this opportunity to track him."

"Call Thomas, or take me with you."

He snorted. It wasn't that he didn't think she was capable, but he didn't know what tricks Morales would have up his sleeve and Adam could never knowingly put his mate in danger. Morales had poisoned and killed packs all over the country and Adam would never underestimate an opponent like that. "I'll be back soon. Keep your phone on."

She muttered something under her breath about stubborn alpha wolves as he strode from the room. Once he took care of this problem, he was going to figure out a way to get back into Paz's good graces. Then he was going to bond with her. His body and mind demanded it.

Whatever differences they had could be worked out. He was certain of it. He refused to let his mate go.

———————•:•———————

Paz shifted from foot to foot as she waited for Thomas to pick her up. When she spotted the high beams of his SUV, she raced across the driveway before he'd made it halfway up the drive.

After he stopped, he leaned over and opened the door before she could. With nerves racing like wild horses, she jumped in. "Go!"

He hit the gas and the vehicle jerked to life once again. "How are you certain where he's gone?"

"I looked over some of his notes and...I can feel him."

Thomas spared her a glance. "What does that mean?"

"I don't know. I just can. Maybe it's because he's put himself in a dangerous situation, but I know where he's going."

"You two haven't bonded, though," Thomas said.

Thomas and every other wolf within a hundred-mile radius would have been able to scent that they were officially mated. "I know that. It doesn't seem to matter. For whatever reason, Mother Nature has a screwed up sense of humor and I can sense him as sure as I can see you right now."

For the next fifteen minutes Thomas followed her directives without saying much. Neither of them felt the need to fill the silence and for that she was grateful. No matter what had passed between them earlier, Adam was her mate and something deep inside her called to her to save him. Biology or whatever it was burned a hole in her gut at the thought that he might be in harm's way.

"Stop here," she ordered as they passed an abandoned building on the outskirts of the warehouse district.

Thomas pulled up to the curb and parked. As they stepped out of the vehicle she noticed a group of three young men loitering near a flickering streetlight. She could sense an aura of danger around them, but they wouldn't be able to harm her. Without bothering to tell Thomas what she intended, she strode toward them.

The dark-haired one with two gold chains and a few gold teeth straightened when he saw her. She rolled her eyes when he grabbed his crotch and made an obscene gesture. "Hey, mama, watcha doing in this part of town?"

"My friend and I are here to take care of some business. You *want* to watch our vehicle and make sure nothing happens to it, don't you?" She lowered her voice and used a small reserve of her power as she projected her influence over them.

Mutely they all nodded.

"Thank you. We will back soon and pay you for your time." She hated exerting her influence over humans, but she felt it was necessary. It wasn't as if she were harming them. And the subtle command she'd used wouldn't last forever. In about an hour it would wear off and if she and Thomas weren't back, they'd likely strip the vehicle and sell the parts. Or they'd just steal it.

"I forgot you could do that," Thomas murmured as they headed down the nearly deserted sidewalk.

Trash littered the street and there were a few homeless people loitering down some of the darkened alleys they passed, but the area was otherwise empty. She and Thomas were in no real danger. Not yet anyway. She wasn't sure how powerful Morales was. Even though she'd tested her powers, she wasn't at full capacity yet.

As they came to the end of the block, she grabbed Thomas' arm and tugged him against the wall. Peering around the corner, she pointed toward an oversized warehouse right on the bay. "They're in there."

"You're sure?"

She nodded. Her mate was definitely inside that building.

"Let's go then." He stepped in front of her and led the way.

As they crossed the street, she inhaled something sickly and sweet. Blood. Her mate's blood. Instinct kicked in. Without thinking, she raced across the street then the abandoned parking lot. Behind her she could hear Thomas shift, but she stayed in her human form. Her feet pounded against the pavement and she cursed when Thomas' dark form flew past her. He was a big wolf and incredibly fast. A few moments later she joined him by the wall of the metal building.

She crouched down and pointed at the broken window. He couldn't respond but she knew he understood what she meant. Standing, she peered through the opening. In the middle of the abandoned warehouse, two wolves circled one another.

Adam's beautiful white coat had a streak of red smeared against his side, yet the black and brown wolf in front of him was unscathed. Before she could stop herself, she grabbed the edge of the window. Jagged glass shards that still stuck into the pane of the window dug into her palms, but the pain barely fazed her. She hoisted herself up and over. No one was going to hurt her mate.

When her boots hit the concrete floor, both wolves turned. Adam reared back and Morales took the opportunity to strike.

No!

He went for her mate's neck and a flash of rage lapped through her like a wildfire. Not caring about the consequences, she drew on the life force of everything in a half-mile radius. All the energy would be replenished and she wasn't hurting anyone, but at that point she didn't care. The only thing that mattered was keeping Adam safe.

Her palms tingled and burned as energy formed there. She pulled her arm back and threw a ball of crackling blue fire toward Morales. When she grazed his back, he yelped and rolled to the floor but just as quickly jumped to all fours. She cursed herself. A year ago she wouldn't have missed.

Adam still stood near him. Too close for her comfort. "Back away, Adam!"

He didn't listen. He bared his teeth at Morales and growled.

The black and brown wolf snapped his teeth when she took another step closer. She was powerful, but in her still-weakened state, if he got close enough, he could hurt her. It was unlikely he'd kill her, but she didn't relish getting mauled. Unfortunately she was out of practice with her aim and she desperately needed to make this shot count.

She narrowed her gaze on Morales and forced herself to block out her mate's existence. She needed to taunt Morales, needed to make him lunge at her. If he bared his underside, she could strike him hard and fast in the heart and this would finally be over. If she blew a hole through his chest, it would destroy his heart and that was what she needed to do to kill him. "My sister is with her mate right now. Can you guess what they're doing?"

Morales growled again. The deep and eerie sound bounced off the metal walls.

"You're the last thing on her mind you piece of shit. Why she ever talked to you in the first place, I'll never know. You're nothing but a pathetic mongrel. She's probably fucking her mate right now."

That was all it took. He threw all caution and common sense to the wind as he launched himself at her. But she was ready.

Hauling back her arm, she started to unleash another blast of energy when a white blur of fur hurled through the air. With a giant, angry snap, Adam ripped Morales' head from his body as if it was nothing.

The sound of flesh tearing and a surprised yelp tore through the air. She managed to stop herself from blasting Adam and sent her aim wild toward the roof. Metal ripped apart and a chunk of the ceiling collapsed a few yards away.

Unable to speak, she stared at the gory scene before her. She couldn't believe how quickly Adam had taken him down. Morales' head lay in a pool of blood a few feet from his lifeless body.

And Adam stared at her with blood dripping from his mouth.

Fear spiked through her. She took a few steps back when reality set in. He knew what she was. And he hated her kind. Turning away from him, she brushed past Thomas. She did the only thing she knew to keep herself safe.

She ran.

CHAPTER THIRTEEN

Two Days Later

Adam tossed his phone onto his bed when what he really wanted to do was throw it against the wall and watch it smash into a tiny thousand bits. But if he did that, he might miss a call from Paz.

Not that she was eager to contact him. That much was clear. For the past two days he'd been going crazy trying to hunt her down, but she'd covered her trail. Occasionally he thought he scented her along the beach but knew his mind was playing tricks on him. She was long gone. And now he'd likely have to scour the country trying to find his errant mate. When he'd realized what she was, her earlier anger at him had made sense.

And he wanted to kick his own ass for not seeing that sooner. The faeries he'd dealt with in the past were evil, but she sure as hell wasn't. She was one of the bravest she-wolves he'd ever met and he couldn't believe he was lucky enough to have her as his mate. When she'd shown up at that warehouse, he felt as if he'd lost a hundred years of his life. He'd been baiting Morales, making him think he could win before he killed him. Adam had wanted that bastard to suffer for all the harm he'd caused.

Then she'd shown up. He had no doubt she could have killed Morales, but Adam hadn't wanted her to deliver the killing blow. She'd been through hell over the past year and he knew the burden it sometimes cost to take another life. Not that he was sorry the crazy wolf was dead. He simply didn't want Paz to carry that burden.

When the doorbell rang, he nearly jumped out of his skin. The sexy vixen had him all sorts of twisted up and if he didn't find her soon, someone was going to pay. Hell, he still couldn't believe she'd managed to outrun him the other night. Disappointment coursed through him before he swung the door open because he knew who would be on the other side.

"Have you found Paz?" he growled at Thomas. The other wolf had been avoiding his questions the past two days and he was about to get his ass kicked.

Ignoring him, Thomas brushed past him. "My father just got a call from The Council. Seems that everything here is settled, but they want to call an emergency meeting. All Alphas must attend. *Apparently*, there's going to be a vote on some new laws regarding mixed-bloods and other supernatural beings."

Adam shrugged as he shut the door. "Tell me something I don't know." He was in a foul mood and the last thing he wanted to do was talk to this son of a bitch who no doubt knew exactly where his mate was — yet refused to tell him.

"Oh I know a lot you don't." Thomas was positively smug as he stepped farther into the foyer.

He refused to take the bait. "Why are you here?"

Thomas' eyes narrowed. "I want to know if you had something to do with this emergency meeting."

"I might have said something to The Council."

Thomas snorted. "I refuse to believe it's a coincidence that in the past five hundred years they haven't seen fit to reexamine their laws and now all of a sudden, they're calling an emergency meeting."

"I don't give a shit what you believe. Tell me where my mate is or get the hell out of here."

"Technically you're still in my family's beach house and your mission is over. I should be telling you to get out." Thomas crossed his arms over his chest and that annoying smirk of his grew even wider.

Lightning fast, Adam crossed the distance between them and wrapped his fingers around Thomas' neck. Not hard, but he put enough pressure to show his intent. The other wolf's eyes widened, but he didn't struggle.

"Where. Is. She?"

"Give me one good reason why I should tell you." Thomas' words were strained as he gasped for air.

Adam let his hand fall. "I love her." The words came out before he could stop himself. His head told him it was too soon, but his heart knew it. They were kindred spirits. His wolf side had recognized it before his human side had. Now both sides were on the same page and they wanted the missing piece of their soul back.

Thomas stared at him for a moment with a curious expression. Finally he spoke. "She's at her sister's house. If you hurt her... Shit, I'll just send Marisol after you." Then he turned and left.

Adam stared at the door after he'd long closed it. Paz was a few houses away from him. *This whole time.*

He'd scented her along the beach but had assumed he'd been going crazy. Without wasting any more time, he hurried out the back door and jogged down the short stretch of sand. He opted not to shift because he didn't want to scare her if she was actually there. And damn it, he'd checked this house. The last time she'd seen him, she'd looked terrified and he couldn't blame her. He'd just killed another wolf and had been covered in blood.

As he raced up the steps to the back porch of Marisol and Stephan's house, he jerked to a halt when he saw Paz lounging in a bikini on one of the chairs by the pool. He'd been going insane scouring the entire city trying to find her and she was tanning? He slammed the small gate behind him and stalked toward her stretched out figure.

"What the hell are you doing?" he shouted, then immediately cringed at himself. He was supposed to be making things right between them, not yelling at her.

She lifted a hand to block out the sun as she looked up at him. "Baking cookies."

His mouth opened then snapped shut. She sounded pissed. *At him.* He'd been trying to track her down the past couple of days and apologize. "You're mad at me. *You've* been hiding from me, and you're mad." He collapsed onto the lounge chair next to her and scooted it closer. God, he wanted to touch her, to pull her into his arms and stroke his hands over her everywhere.

"Does it look like I'm hiding?" she muttered as she turned her face away from him.

No, she definitely wasn't. Her entire body was practically exposed to anyone who wanted to see. Werewolves were usually unabashed about their nudity. Hell, he usually was. Now he wanted to cover his woman up so no one could get a peek at her smooth, tanned skin. The tiny blue triangles covering her breasts and the small scrap of material covering her pussy was practically nonexistent. His cock hardened at the sight even as he tried to force himself to calm down.

"I've been trying to find you for the past two days."

"Why?" She still didn't look at him.

"Because you're my mate."

Now she turned toward him and her gaze burned. "I'm half fae, did you forget that?"

"I'm sorry about what I said to you. More than you'll ever know. I didn't realize what you were." His apology sounded stilted and lame but he didn't know how to tell her how truly sorry he was. Maybe when she found out that he'd talked to The Council it would make a difference.

"Thank you for the apology, but it doesn't matter. You can't change the way you feel and I can't change what I am. If you're going to turn me into The Council, I won't go easy." She abruptly sat up and reached for the towel she'd draped across the chair he was sitting on.

He snatched it and held it away from her. Frowning, she lunged for it and he snaked his hand around her waist. Before she had a chance to react, he hauled her up and onto his lap. He wasn't letting his mate go anywhere. "I *can* change the way I feel. I love you, Paz. And if you think I'd turn you over to anyone, you're out of your pretty little mind."

All the fight left her body. Her eyes widened as she stared at him. "What?"

His gut twisted when she didn't return his sentiments but what could he expect. At least she didn't try to run away from him. "You really fucking think I'd let someone hurt you?" When she didn't respond, he continued. "Nothing's official yet but I've spoken to The Council and there's going to be a major overhaul of all our laws. They've called an emergency meeting. You don't have to hide who you are anymore and I wouldn't want you to."

"Oh." She squirmed in his lap and his grip on her tightened.

The feel of her skin beneath his fingers made him itch to take the rest of her skimpy clothes off. "Is that all you have to say?" He'd assumed she'd be ecstatic.

"I've spent the past two days mad at you. It feels wrong to let go of all that pent-up anger now." The corners of her mouth pulled into a small smile.

"And I've spent the past two days going crazy." His heart still beat an erratic tattoo at the thought of losing her. And he still couldn't believe she thought he'd actually turn her over to anyone. He'd kill and die for her.

"So...what does this mean? You *like* faeries now?" She eyed him warily and he didn't miss the not-so-subtle sarcasm in her voice.

He racked his brain, trying to think of the right words. It didn't help that his tongue naturally got twisted in her presence. He really didn't want to fuck this up. "After meeting you, I realize there's a lot I don't know about your kind. I'm not too proud to admit I was wrong. More than anything I'm sorry by how much I upset you the other night. I was angry thinking about my parents, but...I was wrong."

He still hated those who'd killed his family but Paz was right, he couldn't lump everyone into the same group. If he did, he'd lose his only chance at happiness. Holding onto that kind of hatred wasn't worth it if he lived without Paz.

"So what does this mean for us? You're the enforcer and you live in Chicago. Do you...want me to move to Chicago? I will. I was a high school teacher before so I can find work anywhere," she murmured, a mix of hope and fear in her voice. Fear that he'd reject her? No way in hell. This female was it for him.

"I'm not the enforcer anymore. You can move there if you want, but I'll move here." He'd told The Council to start looking for his replacement immediately. Whether they found one soon or not wasn't going to be his problem. He'd put in his time with them and they owed him. Something they knew, which explained why they'd agreed almost immediately when he'd told them they needed to change their laws. In truth, he hadn't expected them to be so acquiescent but stranger things had happened. Now it was just a matter of getting the rest of the packs on board with the new laws.

He could sense her nervousness, but she didn't say anything. She just shifted on his lap and over his erection. Having her sit on him with so little clothing was worse than torture.

"I'm scared," she whispered.

"Of me?" His gut clenched at the thought.

"No! Of the future, of us, of everything."

"Shit, sweetheart. I'm scared too, but we're meant to be together." More than anything, he was afraid of losing her.

"How can you be so sure?"

He shrugged. There was no answer. He simply knew how he felt about her and that wasn't going to change.

"You'd really move here?"

"If this is where you want to live. I'll move anywhere you want." He had a few homes dotted around the country but he'd wait to tell her that another time. She'd seemed freaked out when he'd bought her all those clothes. He didn't want to admit how much money he had just yet.

She paused as she digested his words. Then she spoke. "You want to help me grab the rest of my stuff? I'll head back to the beach house with you and we can talk some more if you want."

He nodded because he didn't trust his voice as he stood with her. She walked ahead of him and he wanted to howl in frustration. She wore one of those Brazilian-type bikinis that didn't cover the bottom half of her ass. He wanted to reach out and run his palms over that tight skin but restrained himself.

She'd only said she wanted to come back to the house with him. He couldn't jump her bones just yet. Convincing her to take up permanent residence in his bed was likely going to take some time.

Paz felt as if her insides were shaking as she led Adam inside. She couldn't believe he loved her. She loved him too but was scared to say the words. After the past couple days without him, she'd been miserable. Even though she'd been hurt and angry as hell, she'd still missed him. That had been the most maddening part of all. She thought he hadn't wanted her and had been avoiding her. She'd run from him, but she hadn't been hiding. She'd just assumed he knew where she was staying. And she'd thought he hadn't wanted her anymore.

His heated gaze on her as they walked toward her room was scorching. Without even seeing him, she knew what he was focusing on. She'd taken most of her belongings to the guesthouse and hadn't picked up anything in the last two days. And she definitely didn't need his help bringing her meager belongings over to his place. That wasn't why she'd asked him to her room at all.

Thankfully they had the house all to themselves. Her sister was still gone and would be for a few more days.

As they entered her room, she turned to face him.

His gaze raked over her body from head to foot with a heat she'd come to love seeing in his eyes. "What stuff do you want to bring with you?" The question came out scratchy and uneven.

She reached behind her back and pulled the ties of her bikini top loose. His eyes widened as she let it fall to the ground. Understanding quickly dawned in his eyes and was quickly followed by full-blown lust.

Her nipples tightened into hard points under his scrutiny. He started to move toward her but she held up a hand. "Wait," she whispered.

She shoved her bathing suit bottom over her hips and let gravity do its job. After it pooled at her feet, she covered the distance between them and wrapped her arms around his neck. She didn't want any more barriers or secrets between them. "I want to bond with you." It was the only way she could show him she loved him. While she'd been busy cursing his name, he'd been making more progress with The Council than anyone else had in hundreds of years. And he'd done it all for her. That knowledge simultaneously touched and terrified her. She couldn't believe he cared for her as much as she cared for him.

His hands settled on her hips and he tugged her flush against him. She could feel his cock pressing through his pants. But there was a question in his emerald eyes. "Are you sure?"

"I want this more than anything." And she also wanted something else. He'd tasted her—all of her—and she wanted to return the favor.

Glancing down, she freed the button to his pants, then slowly pulled the zipper down. She sucked in a deep breath as his cock sprang free. Her stomach muscles clenched as she stared at him. Something possessive stirred inside her. He was thick and perfect and all hers.

She ran her tongue over her lips but glanced up when he groaned. "What?"

"Are you trying to torture me?" he gasped out.

Grinning, she dropped to her knees. "Maybe I am."

He shoved at his pants and quickly stepped out of them. As she fisted his cock, she was aware that he'd stripped out of his shirt, but she didn't take her eyes off his hard length.

Holding him firm, she bent forward and licked the underside of his thick length, all the way to the crown. She took her time circling the head before stroking her tongue back down his length, then up again. His legs jerked once and she inwardly smiled.

"Oh yeah." His voice was tight and she knew he was barely holding onto his control.

She sucked his head into her mouth then took him as far as she could go. Until this moment she'd never understood why so many women loved this act. She'd never felt more powerful than she did right then. Even though she was on her knees, she held all the power. And it was an incredible turn on. Heat pooled between her legs as she tasted him.

As his fingers threaded through her hair, she moaned against him and kept sucking. Up and down, she took him deep. He pulsed in her hand and under her mouth, so she knew he was close.

With a low moan, he pulled away from her. She frowned and kept her hand snug at the base of his cock. "What's wrong?"

"I want to come in you."

His deep voice and words sent ribbons of desire curling through her. She wanted the same thing, especially after being separated from him for two days. Her wolf had been going crazy as much as she had.

Before she could stand, he hooked his hands under her arms and lifted her to her feet. Slanting his mouth over hers, he probed with little restraint. His tongue danced with hers in an erotic mating that made her crazy.

The heat coming off him was dangerous and hot. She was ready to feel his cock slide into her and felt she might combust on the spot if he didn't do something about it. What she'd learned about him was that he had a lot of patience, whereas she had very little. Her hands slid around his waist and she latched onto his backside. The firm muscles beneath her clenched. As she loosened her grip and slid her hands up his back, he covered one of her breasts with his hand.

She couldn't believe how much she'd missed touching him and having him touch her. They'd only been intimate a couple times but she felt such a strong connection to him and she'd ached without him. It had been the worst kind of torture. She'd been shown the most exquisite pleasure only to have it taken away from her.

Lifting one of her legs, she wrapped it around his back and ground against him. Her pussy was soaking wet and she needed to be filled. Needed that release. And she could only get it from him. She'd tried masturbating over the past couple days but her actions had been fruitless and frustrating.

He continued strumming her nipple in a perfect rhythm. Each time he tweaked her, it sent a jolt of heat straight between her legs. His cock rested against her lower abdomen and she was too short to impale herself on him the way she wanted.

Breathing hard, he lifted his head back. "You're sure you want to bond?"

"Yes." *Oh yes*. Very much so.

So much so, it scared her. She'd always felt a little out of place in the world, even in her own pack. With Adam, she belonged. In their own way they were both outsiders. Now she knew someone would always have her back. He'd already gone to great lengths to prove that.

He gripped her hips and turned her so that she was facing the foot of the bed. Without bothering to move the cover, she crawled onto the plush comforter and stayed on all fours. The cool material underneath did nothing to quench the heat burning through her. Her inner walls clenched with anticipation of her mate, of bonding with the male who had completely stolen her heart.

The bed dipped when he moved behind her but instead of plunging deep into her as she knew he wanted to, he kissed her backside. The soft, feathering action surprised her so much, she jumped.

"What are you doing?" she whispered.

"You looked so fucking sexy in that suit, this was all I could think about," he growled against her skin. Continuing his assault, he licked her, raked his teeth over her and continued the hot trail up to her back. She shuddered with pleasure under his gentle exploration and had to order herself to remain patient. It was hard to, however, when all she wanted was to feel Adam inside her.

Just seeing Paz in such a submissive position had Adam close to coming without much stimulation. But there was no way he was going to fuck up their bonding. All supernatural beings were superstitious, but werewolves were doubly so when it came to the mating ritual. If he screwed this up, he'd never forgive himself.

She was his and they both deserved to be happy. Holding onto her hips, he hovered behind her. He paused, giving her another chance to back out, but she just scooted back farther, pushing that hot ass of hers against him.

As he slid his cock into her, he didn't bother hiding his moan. She was so tight and wet. The woman was practically dripping. All for him. For the past two days all he'd done was think about her — and this moment.

He hadn't realized she'd want to bond so soon. While he'd known his feelings for her were real, he'd thought he'd have to work up to this. Use what little charm he had to convince her to be his forever. Something nagged at the back of his head that this was all a dream and he'd wake up with his fist around his cock instead of her tight sheath. But it wasn't. Paz was real and she was all his.

His chest squeezed painfully as he thrust into her again. She was putting so much trust in him, it touched him more than he wanted to admit. Prejudices among wolves ran deep and he'd shown his ass the first chance he'd got. The fact that she believed his intentions and his apology said more about her feelings for him than she could probably ever voice aloud.

Keeping one hand flat against her back, he used his other to reach around and stroke her clit. He'd learned that she loved the extra stimulation. When he rubbed over the swollen bud, she jerked and let out a tiny little mewling sound that made him positively crazy. It was music to his ears. He loved how responsive she was to his caresses.

He continued teasing her and each time he did, her inner walls contracted around him like a vise. Increasing his thrusts and his tweaks, he found a rhythm that had her panting and saying his name like a mantra.

When he lightly pinched her clit between his fingers and tugged, she let out a strangled cry and surged into orgasm. This was it. What he'd been waiting for.

As she rode through the waves of her climax, he leaned over her quivering body. Wrapping one hand underneath her, he supported her and dug his canines into her shoulder. Just enough to break the skin and to mark her for life. *She was his.* Now everyone would know.

Something foreign and moist burned the back of his eyes as it hit him they would have forever together. His life hadn't started until this moment, he was sure of it. She was exactly what he'd been waiting for. There was so much they didn't know about one another, but they had all the time they wanted.

Pushing back up, he thrust once more and her pussy clenched around him tighter than before. With a shout, he let go and let her drag a toe-numbing climax from him. He emptied himself completely inside her until his knees were numb and his hips were blindly jerking against her. His cock just didn't want to stop.

Somehow he managed to steady himself and pull out of her. When he did, she fell against the bed and rolled over to face him. A slight sheen of moisture dotted her forehead and her entire face glowed. Naked and stretched out, she looked like a goddess. A wide smile broke across her face. "In case you don't already realize it, I love you too."

Panting, he collapsed next to her. The tight vise around his chest snapped free, but he didn't trust his voice so he sidled up closer to her and gathered her into his arms, right where she belonged. She lay against him and splayed her hand against his chest. There was no other feeling in the world like having her next to him.

For the first time in his life, he felt like he was home.

EPILOGUE

Six Months Later

Paz glanced up from smoothing icing onto the last cupcake as Adam walked through the kitchen door. Her heart skipped a beat when she saw him in his beat-up jeans and button down plaid work shirt. It didn't matter what he wore, the mere sight of him raised her temperature a hundred degrees.

"Hey, sweetheart. You look beautiful." He unsnapped his work belt from his waist and dropped it onto the kitchen table.

"You look pretty good yourself."

When he headed toward her with a lecherous grin, she held up the spatula and waved it at him. "Uh uh. Take that crap upstairs. And please shower and change. We have to leave in twenty minutes." She felt a little bad that she wasn't giving him his normal greeting, but they had no time to waste.

His eyebrows rose at her commanding tone. "Feeling feisty today?"

"That's right. I do *not* want to be late to this."

"Where are we going again?" Completely ignoring her, he strode toward the refrigerator and popped open a beer.

She playfully swatted his butt, but when he reached for her, she took a step out of his reach. After a full day in his workshop, he was covered in dust and wood shavings and she was not changing her dress again. "You know exactly where. It's Alexandra's birthday."

With a grin on his face, he leaned against the counter. "Give me a kiss."

She eyed him warily. "Promise not to get me dirty."

"I swear." His grin was wicked, but she knew he wouldn't break his word.

She leaned into him and as their tongues clashed, she almost threw caution to the wind and wrapped her arms around his neck and legs around his waist. *Almost.* If they didn't make it on time with the cupcakes and half the decorations, her sister would give her hell. Somehow she pulled back, though her nipples were already hard from their brief kiss. "Please get ready, I promised Marisol we'd help set up."

"Fine, fine. They have too many parties. It wouldn't hurt to miss one." He grumbled as he grabbed his tool belt, but she knew he didn't mind. Not truly.

Since retiring as the enforcer for The Council, Adam had moved to Miami and started a business building custom furniture. Her mate was certainly skilled enough with his hands. He didn't need the money — as she'd found out not long after they'd bonded — so he was doing what made him happy and just starting to turn a profit. She had no doubt he'd be incredibly successful in a few years. As it was, he was already turning work away. Now that things had settled down, she was doing exactly what she loved too, teaching high school history. And thanks to the Lazos pack they'd found a new family.

"Sweetheart, Ethan just called. I told him we'd pick him up." Adam's voice carried down the stairs.

"That's fine. Please hurry up!" Ethan was slowly adjusting to his new life as a werewolf. He'd gone into business with Adam and so far things were working out. The young wolf had his own car but he depended on Adam a lot to get around. He was still reeling from the drastic changes his life had undergone and Paz understood that he'd come to depend on her mate for guidance. It had surprised her how well he and her mate got along but they were both outsiders so maybe it was only natural.

Of course he represented a new breed of wolf. One turned by science as opposed to nature, but The Council had accepted him. And slowly but surely, the rest of the packs were coming around to accepting mixed-bloods into their lives. As it turned out, there were members on The Council hiding their true mixed-blood identity, and next month a meeting had been set up between them and the queen of the faeries to discuss a peace treaty. It was long overdue but better late than never in her book.

While Paz was more than satisfied at the progress her people were making, she was simply happy she'd found a wolf to spend the rest of her life with. And she didn't plan on ever letting Adam go.

DANGEROUS CRAVING

She has nowhere else to go...

A century ago, the only man Nissa ever loved turned his back on her when she needed him. Now that her life is in danger from one of her own kind, he may be her only hope for survival. As a full-blooded faerie and next in line to be queen, Nissa figures the last place anyone would think to look for her is with a pack of werewolves.

So she turns to the one man who broke her heart...

Werewolf Thomas Lazos knows he screwed up by letting Nissa go and he's suffered the consequences for too long. Now that she's finally back on the same continent, he shows her what she's been missing all these years. The sex between them is as scorching as ever and the seductive faerie is still the only woman who makes him lose control in and out of the bedroom.

But who will protect her from him?

When he learns that someone wants her dead, Thomas will do whatever it takes to keep Nissa safe and finally claim what is rightfully his — her heart. But with an unknown enemy stalking her, it might be too late for a second chance.

CHAPTER ONE

"**P**hone's for you, boss." Stephanie, Thomas' head bartender slid the phone across the polished oak bar.

He looked up from doing the week's schedule and grabbed the portable. Probably one of the cocktail girls calling out sick. Again. His family's pack had been dealing with so much crap the past few months from crazed Immortals to rogue werewolves he'd been unusually absent at work. Some of the new hires thought they could take advantage. That was all going to stop tonight. "Yeah?" he barked.

"Hey, Thomas."

It was Paz. Immediately his demeanor softened. "Hey. Why are you calling the bar? Is everything okay?"

"I'm fine but your cell kept going to voicemail."

Piece of shit phone. For some reason he rarely got service inside his club. "What's up?"

"Ah, well...tomorrow's Alexandra's birthday party."

"Yeah, I know. She already called and told me I better bring her a good present. Sounded like she expected another bottle of Dom." His cousin Alex was turning twenty-two and last year he'd gotten her an expensive bottle of champagne. He shouldn't indulge her again but it was hard not to. She was by far one of the youngest in the pack. His Uncle Cosmo had mated late in life and they had a much younger generation of wolves. Barely over two decades old, Alex was the oldest of her three siblings and one of his favorite cousins. Not that he'd admit it to her face. She'd use it to her full advantage. More than she already did.

Paz cleared her throat nervously. "So, Adam and I will be there of course."

He frowned, wondering why she was acting so weird. "I kinda figured."

"I have this friend from work who I was thinking of inviting. She

296 | SAVANNAH STUART

teaches English and she's sweet and really gorgeous. Tall, blonde—"

He massaged his temple. "Damn it, Paz. I don't need you to set me up with anyone." Did he seem so desperate his friend felt the need to find him a pity date?

"It's been a century. You can't pine over someone that long."

Yeah, he really could. "Why did I ever tell you about *her*?" he muttered.

"Because I'm awesome—and a good listener."

That much was true. But he'd mainly told her because Paz was half fae. He'd been hoping Paz knew something about the gorgeous full-blooded faerie who'd stolen his heart. No one in his family knew that he'd fallen for a faerie over a century ago. And not just anyone, but a princess. Of course he'd fucked things up but good with her. God, he couldn't even think her name. It hurt too bad. An ache lapped across his chest like a slow building fire. He did not need to deal with this right now.

"I appreciate your concern but I'm fine and I don't need help finding a date." As owner of one of the hottest clubs in Miami he had his choice of gorgeous women. Not that he actually dated.

"I've already invited her, so—"

"Damn it." He gritted his teeth. If he didn't care for Paz so much he'd be pissed.

"I didn't tell her she was there to meet you. Just that my in-laws were having a party and it would be fun. She might not even come."

Thomas bit back a sharp retort, knowing he'd upset her. Paz was his sister-in-law's sister and after a year in captivity at the hands of a madman, she was strong, but still more sensitive than most. And the little she-wolf held a soft spot in his heart. He didn't have any sisters but if he did he'd want one exactly like her. "It's fine. Just…no more attempted set-ups, okay?"

She blew out a long sigh. "All right."

He could hear Adam, her mate, in the background so Thomas changed the subject. "Tell Adam that I'm ready to start construction on that Tiki bar on the top floor. He can start next week."

"I know you're trying to change the subject but I'll tell him. See ya tomorrow night."

He placed the phone on the bar. "Steph, I'm heading to my office. Unless the place is on fire, no interruptions."

The slim brunette absently nodded before returning to the inventory. Resisting the juvenile urge to slam his door, he shut himself in his office and collapsed onto his plush leather chair. After working on the accounts for over two hours he turned his computer off. He'd already caught himself inputting wrong numbers twice. His distraction could cost him too much money.

What he needed now was a drink. Lately all his thoughts had been consumed by *her*. His dreams too. And they were vivid. Not typical, fuzzy thoughts but real 3D quality dreams. Her long blonde hair fanned around her face as he rode her. Then it was streaming down her back as he took her from behind. Her eyes were like shards of emeralds, vivid and striking.

Every time he shut his eyes at night, there she was. And it was always the same thing. She was crying and asking him for help. He ached to reach out to her, to comfort her. To just hold her one more time. Even thinking about holding her made his cock flare to life. In his dreams he knew it was pointless but he responded that he'd help her any way he could if she'd just let him.

Hell, he owed her that much.

But in the morning he'd wake up and be alone. It was just wishful thinking. There was no way she'd come to him for help anyway. Not unless she was desperate. Even then, he just couldn't see that happening.

He headed to the VIP section on the second floor. Loud music thumped through the speakers, jarring him straight to his bones. With his extrasensory abilities, the music seemed overly obnoxious tonight.

Bruno, one of his security guys, held back the gold curtain as he reached the top stair. "Hey, boss. Didn't know you were still here."

Unsurprised by the statement, he nodded and glanced around. At ten it was still fairly early — for Miami — but the place was packed. "What's the status report for the night?"

"A few players are here tonight and they brought a ton of groupies so we're at capacity. Until it clears out a little, we're not letting anyone else in."

"Good." Players was a reference to the local basketball team. Any time a group of them partied at his place, they were sure to stay busy. He had four fully stocked bars located strategically around the two-story club and half a dozen cocktail waitresses milling around the place but he wanted to expand. It was one of the reasons he was adding another bar on the top floor. That and he wanted to add a more relaxed atmosphere so there was something for everyone.

"Oh, your brother's here. Just arrived a few minutes ago." He nodded behind him.

Frowning, Thomas looked around Bruno, then grinned. His brother

298 | SAVANNAH STUART

Nick sat at one of the high-top cocktail tables with his human mate, Carly, and a woman Thomas didn't recognize. Nick didn't normally frequent clubs and by the semi-scowl on his face, it was obvious he wasn't having the best time. Maybe it was because of all the men checking his woman out. "Thanks. I know I've been absent lately but I'll be here all night. Spread the word."

Bruno nodded. "Sounds good, boss."

Nick's expression changed when he saw him. His pale eyes lit up and he grabbed Thomas' shoulder as if he was a lifeline. "Hey, I hoped you'd be here tonight. This is Carly's best friend Stacie. She's visiting from Chicago."

After making polite small talk Nick practically dragged him toward the bar. "I need another drink. I don't know how you work here."

"I can work anywhere." Thomas motioned to the bartender and when she was close enough to hear, he ordered two beers for him and his brother and another round for the women. Then he told her to give him the final tab, much to Nick's annoyance.

"All this noise would drive me crazy." Nick's eyes narrowed when he spotted two male-model types walk up to Carly and her friend. They wore designer suits and drank martinis.

Next to him Nick's hand tightened around his beer bottle. One of his tattoos rippled dangerously under the flexing motion.

Thomas placed a light hand on his brother's arm when he sensed the subtle shift in him. As a mated male, Nick's human side might know the men talking to Carly were harmless and stood no chance, but his wolf side didn't care. And as an alpha in nature, his most possessive urges would be clawing to assert his dominance to the two strangers. "I know those guys, brother. Don't worry. They're just making their rounds, seeing who's single."

"That's easy for you to say, you're not mated." As soon as he'd uttered the words his pale eyes widened. "Shit, man. I didn't mean it like that."

Thomas' chest constricted but he just shrugged as if it didn't bother him. He was happy his two brothers had found their mates but it was a stark reminder he was alone. That he'd had a chance a century ago but screwed it up. "So why are you here tonight?"

"Carly wanted to show her friend all the hot spots in Miami and I got dragged along."

Thomas bit back a smile. "Her friend know what we are?"

Nick shook his head sharply. "Hell, no. Although she did mention seeing a couple big dogs running down the beach this morning."

"Nice." Their pack used their private strip of beach in Key Biscayne to run free whenever they needed so it wasn't odd to see dogs or even wolves running at any time of day or night. They picked up their beers and the mixed drinks for the women and headed back.

His brother stalked toward the table and before Thomas had reached it, the two men had scattered.

"So you own this club, huh?" Stacie asked.

"Yeah, I..." He trailed off as a woman caught his eye.

Not just any woman. His eyes widened and he actually had to blink. A flash of hot then cold curled through his body like a violent electric shock. It was *her*.

Nissa.

Her long, blonde hair was piled on her head in some sort of twist thing. It should have looked messy, but it was exquisite. Just like her. The shimmery gold dress—if she could even call that scrap of material a dress—fell against her willowy frame like it was a second skin. Among a sea of tanned, bronzed people, her ivory skin seemed to glow.

Around her, men and some women turned to stare. Part of it was because of her ethereal beauty but another reason was because of her natural appeal. Just like vampires, that same sensual magnetic pull emanated from all fae. It was just more prominent in her because she was royalty.

When her emerald-green eyes locked on his he forgot to breathe. Nearly a century had passed but she was just as he remembered. Some days he wondered if he'd created an illusion in his mind. But this was no figment of his imagination.

This was flesh, blood and pure sin in a dress. And she held the key to his heart. He might try to claim it was only a physical desire, but he wanted all of her. Mind, body, soul.

A hollowness settled in his chest as he remembered the last words they'd shouted at each other. The anger he'd felt when he thought she'd betrayed him. And then the inevitable suffering when he realized he'd been wrong. So fucking *wrong*.

"See you guys later," he muttered, not caring how rude he sounded.

He hurried toward the exit of the VIP room. When he pushed past the curtain, she stood at the bottom stair, one hand haughtily placed on her hip as she stared up at him expectantly. He loved that look, loved everything about this female.

He didn't remember moving but suddenly he was standing in front of her. "Nissa." After so long, her name felt foreign on his lips but her scent was familiar. She was like a sweet summer day. Fresh and intoxicating.

Addictive.

For a moment she looked almost nervous. Then her composed mask slipped back into place. "It's been a long time, Thomas." Her soft, slightly Irish accent rolled over him with an intimate warmth he missed. Despite having lived practically everywhere in Europe, she held on to a faint Celtic accent and it still drove him wild.

Nissa fought all her instincts to turn and flee. She'd forgotten how tall and intimidating Thomas was. And how quickly her brain short circuited in his presence. Around him she had to be strong, though. If he knew how much she still cared for him...she couldn't bear the shame. When he didn't respond, she cleared her throat. "Aren't you going to say hello or buy me a drink?"

His dark eyes narrowed. Wordlessly, he reached out and grasped her wrist. Not hard, but he put enough pressure on her that she couldn't pull away—and the hold was very, *very* possessive. Before she realized what he intended he turned and dragged her with him.

Despite the fact that they were surrounded by so many people, everything else around her funneled out as they continued behind one of the bars, through a swinging door, up a set of stairs and finally into a quiet office. If it had been anyone else she would have shaken him off and told him to get his hand off her. But she liked the feel of him touching her, much to her dismay. And she'd come here for a reason.

The office was definitely Thomas' by the look of it. The furniture was old, big and with lots of polished dark wood. Very masculine. Very him.

"Please have a seat." He motioned toward one of the plush leather chairs in front of his desk.

Nervously, she sat on the edge and crossed her legs. To keep her hands busy she traced her fingers over the intricate stitching of the chair. Maybe she shouldn't have gone with such a short dress but it had been a long time since they'd seen each other and she'd wanted to get his attention. It rode up against her legs revealing a lot of skin and reminded her how he'd kissed and licked every inch of her once. When his dark gaze raked over her legs she knew he was remembering the same thing. Yep, maybe not the best idea.

"Would you like a drink?" he asked and motioned to a small bar in the corner of the room.

She nodded. "Wine would be nice." Anything to take off the edge would work for her at this point.

After he poured two glasses he handed her one then sat in the chair next to her instead of across from her. With his legs stretched out in front of him, he looked almost casual. But she knew better. He was tense. Every muscle in that hard body was primed for action. Unlike her kind, shifters were born hunters, predators. Hundreds of years ago the fae had been forced to take on that roll when they'd become hunted but that was neither here nor there.

"Is it true your family has a half fae living with them?"

His dark eyebrows raised a fraction. "Yes."

"And...she is mated to the enforcer...ah, former enforcer, correct?"

He nodded.

Okay, he wasn't going to make this easy for her. "Is it also true The Council has changed their laws regarding the fae?" She'd heard that six months ago a half-werewolf, half fae had mated with the enforcer and as a result The Council had lifted their ban on mixed breed matings. Before that it would have been certain death if a shifter had chosen to mate with anyone of faerie blood. The change in law was fairly revolutionary for werewolves and it was why she was here.

"Why do you care?"

She'd taken a big risk coming to see him. No matter what had passed between them, she knew he wouldn't hurt her. At least not physically. And this was the last place anyone would think to look for her. The thought of her hiding among a bunch of shifters was actually laughable. "I need protection."

Something predatory and dangerous flashed in his dark eyes. He set his glass down on the desk and leaned forward. "From who?" he growled, murder in his dark gaze.

"My family."

CHAPTER TWO

Thomas pushed down the rage scorching through his veins. The wildfire of his anger was close to unleashing. He could actually feel his canines starting to lengthen. He, who was one hundred and seventy five years old, alpha in nature, and next in line to be Alpha of his pack, had learned to control himself well over a century ago, felt as if he were spinning out of control. Against his better judgment he scooted his chair closer and grasped Nissa's delicate hand just to convince himself she was real. Oh God, touching her was too surreal. He fought a shudder, not wanting her to see his reaction. "Why does someone want to hurt you?"

For a moment she started to pull away but to his relief she relaxed her hand. "I'm not exactly sure. As I'm sure you know, my mother...ah, the queen is supposed to meet with your Council next month to establish a truce between our people."

He nodded and tightened his hold, rubbing his thumb over the pulse point of her wrist. It thumped wildly against his skin. "I don't know all the details but my Alpha — my father — told me about the meeting. He'll be attending."

"My mother is sick and well, she doesn't have much time left. I'm next in line so I'll likely be the one to sign the peace treaty." Her voice was sad, dejected and clawed at his insides.

"I'm sorry about your mother." He'd never met her family but he remembered how close she'd been to them.

Brushing away his concern, she continued. "There are those who don't want this treaty signed. About a month ago someone tried to poison me and a few days ago...a masked man broke into my house and tried to kill me. He had an ancient iron dagger so I know he wasn't a typical intruder. I tried to neutralize him with a burst of energy but someone must have cast a protection spell around him. I managed to get away but just barely."

She shuddered lightly and he ached to reach out and pull her close. Comfort her.

The fae feared iron as much as werewolves feared silver. Thankfully they were just as fast, though not physically as strong as shifters. His stomach twisted painfully at the thought of someone trying to harm her. He wanted nothing more than to hunt her attacker down and rip him apart with his claws and teeth. The savage thought riled his wolf up. "And you think someone in your family is after you?"

"I didn't know where else to go," she whispered. A blonde tendril fell loose against her face.

Instinct kicked in and he reached out to brush it back. His hand froze as he grazed her soft cheek. She was just as he remembered. Everything about her made him insane, from her scent to her smile.

When her mouth parted slightly he knew what he was about to do was stupid, but was powerless to stop himself. Leaning forward, he inhaled her scent. Would she taste as sweet as he remembered?

Her emerald eyes flared with hot desire but she pulled back out of his reach. "I didn't... I can't get involved with you. Not like that. I'm to be married soon."

Her words were like a sharp, silver blade straight to his chest. His throat seized as he jerked back. "Married?"

Glancing away, she nodded but not before he missed the flash of pain flit across her face.

"Then why didn't you go to *him* for help?" he growled, hating the possessive note in his voice. He had no claim to her; had lost that right because of his own stupidity.

"It's complicated," she muttered.

"Do you love him?" *Why the hell did he ask that?*

Her eyes narrowed at him. "None of your business."

The hell it wasn't. "That's not an answer."

"No, it's not. The last man I fell in love with threw me out of his life and accused me of using my influence to make him fall in love with me. I can assure you that *love* is overrated bullshit."

And Thomas had done just that. Hearing her spell out exactly how he'd mistreated her made him want to jump into a dark hole. "Shit, Nissa. Don't say that. Don't ever say that, please." He scrubbed a hand over his face, unable to meet her piercing eyes because he knew he'd hate himself for what he saw there.

"Coming here was a mistake." She abruptly stood but he reached out and grabbed her arm, unwilling to let her go.

Not again. He'd fucked up once, but she was on the same continent as him for the first time in a century. She'd come to him for protection and he was going to give it to her. Whether she wanted it or not. He was not letting her out of his sight. Or out of his life. He didn't care if she was supposed to marry someone else. It wasn't going to happen. Not as long as he was breathing. He might not deserve a second chance but he had to try. "You didn't make a mistake. My pack will protect you. You have my word."

She nodded stiffly. "Thank you."

After he stood, he motioned toward the door. "I'd like you to meet one of my brothers, then we can head to my Alpha's home. He'll need to approve that you're going to be under his pack's protection and he'll want to meet you in person." Not that Thomas cared what his father said or thought in this instance. The only thing he cared about was keeping Nissa safe.

When the color drained from her face he wrapped his arm around her shoulder and pulled her close. She tensed but he didn't let go. He couldn't. "My father will protect you because I ask him to. Meeting him is just a formality, I swear." If for some reason his father said no, Thomas would still protect her with his life. No matter what.

She relaxed next to him. Not by much, but it was a start. "I have a few bags at my hotel. Can we—"

"As soon as we leave here we'll pick them up."

Even though he didn't want to let her go, when she stepped out of his embrace, he did. There would be time enough later to convince her that they still had a chance. Time and distance hadn't diminished his feelings for her. If anything, seeing her again after so many years reminded him of how much time they had to make up for. Being virtually immortal and going so long without his female, the woman he knew was his mate, was hell on earth.

———————⚫❘⚫———————

Nissa grasped the stem of her wine glass tightly. After meeting Thomas' father some of her earlier apprehension had dissipated, but she was still scared out of her mind. She'd left her home without telling anyone, fearful of who wanted her dead. Her sister had been acting odd lately and even though they were close, the hunger for power did strange things to people. It made her sick to think of her own flesh and blood betraying her but she knew it was possible. She'd seen it happen before. Far too many times.

The ironic thing was she didn't even want to be queen. She hated to think that her sister Kassia had been behind the attempts on her life but she couldn't think of another way someone had gotten into her home. Her security was damn near impenetrable and the intruder had known her security code and somehow gotten around the biometric scanner. Nothing added up.

"So who's this...man you're engaged to?" Thomas asked as he strode into the kitchen.

He'd gone to put her bags in his guest room and left her sitting at the marble-top island in his kitchen.

She thought she'd have more time to gather her thoughts but it didn't matter. All he had to do was walk into the room and she forgot to breathe. "Why do you care?" she snapped. Her haughtiness was her only defense. Let him think she was a bitch. It would be easier to keep her distance from him. After so many years she should be over him and she hated that she wasn't.

His dark eyes raked over her from head to toe as he pulled up a seat much too close for comfort. "I think that should be obvious."

It wasn't obvious. Not at all. But she didn't say that. "Technically I've never met him." Saying it aloud was worse than she'd imagined. Maybe she should have kept her mouth shut. She cursed her fair skin as she felt her cheeks warm up.

"You've never met him?" The slow way he asked the question made her feel even more embarrassed.

"He lives in Paris and his family is of the right bloodline according to my mother." She could hear her mother's voice ringing in her ears as she told Nissa who she'd be marrying next year. Told. Not asked. As usual. *You're getting too old and when I die I want to know you will continue* our *line.* Even thinking of her mother's words made her cringe.

"So you're not technically engaged?"

"I'm to be married to him." She understood what he was asking but her people rarely did engagements. At least not the royalty. Anyone else could marry or mate with whomever they wanted. And after next month, that included shifters. The world was changing and she was thankful the laws were about to be rewritten. It was time to throw out those archaic rules and regulations. If only her mother would rewrite some of the standards for the royal line.

"Where are you living now?" The abrupt change of subject surprised her.

"Dublin. I've been there for a few years now."

Something about his expression told her he'd known exactly where she lived before he'd asked. "Back in Ireland? Why not London?"

"Because that's where my mother and sister live. Which, I have a feeling you already knew." The truth was, she'd been born on the beautiful Emerald Isle almost two hundred years ago and had always felt safe living there. Well, until recently.

Thomas took a deep breath and his big, annoyingly muscular chest expanded when he did. She hated that she noticed. She hated that she'd seen it before. And she really hated that she still fantasized about it. Even if they didn't have a past, they could never be together anyway. She had her role to play for her people and it didn't involve him.

"Nissa, I don't even know how to say this without sounding like an ass but I'm going to try. I'm sorry for what I said to you a century ago and I'm sorry for turning you away when you came to see me that day. If I could take it back, I would."

Her throat clenched at his words but she steeled herself against her building emotions. She'd wanted to hear this in person for so long, but it was too little too late. She lifted her shoulders slightly because she didn't trust her voice.

He continued. "I came after you later when I realized how wrong I'd been. I...shit, I think I'm screwing this up, but I'm sorry. I know it's just words but it's all I have right now. If there was some way I could make it up to you—"

"It was a long time ago and we were so young. I eventually got over you." The lie rolled off her tongue so smoothly she even believed herself. Good, it meant he would too. "I received the letters you sent me apologizing and it's part of the reason I'm here. I knew you'd help me. So rest easy, it's all water under the bridge, okay?" She'd never gotten over him but actually saying that to his face was too shameful for words. A century was too long to pine over someone.

"It's not okay," he growled.

She scowled at him. "What do you want me to say? I'm still angry at you? Well it's not going to happen. We were young and naïve. It wouldn't have lasted so—"

He moved so fast she didn't have time to react. His mouth covered hers in a harsh, dominating kiss. She didn't want to give into this. To him.

She wanted to push him away. Grabbing at his chest, she fully intended to shove him back but instead she clutched on to his shirt and held tight. As if he was her lifeline.

Her legs opened wider as he positioned himself between her spread thighs. With her barely-there panties and only his pants as a barrier, she could feel his hardness pressing against her.

It would be so easy to get rid of the clothing between them. So easy to let him push deep inside her. To open herself completely to him. But if they crossed that line it would be that much harder when she walked away.

Instead of pushing back, her fingers splayed against his hard, muscular chest. *Push him away!* Her inner voice was very noisy but not loud enough. She wanted to curse her weakness but as his tongue stroked against hers it was hard to care.

The teasing reminded her of how gentle and sweet he'd once been with her. It was in opposition to the tight hold he had on the back of her head. One of his hands gripped her so intensely she knew he wasn't letting her go anytime soon. She hated herself for enjoying the feel of him so much, for wanting him so much.

His scent was so familiar it made her ache. A long time ago there had been no barriers between them and everything had been so easy, fresh and exciting.

But she wasn't that innocent girl anymore.

She wrenched her head back despite his hold. "Thomas, this is—" She stopped as he ripped her panties free with his other hand. She'd been vaguely aware of his hand inching up her thigh but the tearing sound seemed to reverberate against the walls.

He quickly shoved the material to the side as the skimpy strap against her hip broke free completely. Then he completely cupped her mound.

The feel of his hand against her sensitive flesh made all her good intentions vanish. A moan tore from her throat as his callused fingers began rubbing against her folds.

"I've wanted to do this for so long." His voice was a ragged whisper against her neck.

The words and the feel of him speaking against her skin sent a sensuous shiver curling through her entire body. She wanted to tell him she'd fantasized about this too—often—but held back the words.

It didn't matter. He continued anyway. "I've dreamed about having you stretched out beneath me with my face buried between your legs, or you wrapped around me like this so many times."

She swallowed hard at his words, wishing she didn't enjoy them so much. As he lightly scraped his teeth against the sensitive spot beneath her ear, the spot where he could mark her if he chose, she arched her back. At one time she would have given anything to be marked by him, to be his.

308 | SAVANNAH STUART

When she moved against him, he pushed a finger inside her. He understood exactly what she wanted without her having to ask. One of his thick, blunt fingers pressed deep inside her, filling her, and making her want things she had no right wanting.

He didn't give her time to get used to the intrusion. Thomas pushed another one into her wet sheath with skilled precision. The stroke was smooth and fast. He held his two fingers still, letting her body adjust.

Holding his fingers in place, he began a trail of kisses down her neck. Not bothering to push her dress to the side, he kissed her over the material until his mouth covered one of her nipples.

She hadn't worn a bra so there wasn't much clothing between them. He ran his tongue around the covered bud until it was rock hard and pebbled against her dress.

Then he did the same to her other breast, his wicked tongue driving her to the brink of her control. Clutching his shoulders, she tried to hold on to it but knew she was losing that battle.

While he teased and tweaked her nipples, he began moving his fingers inside her. Slowly at first. The action was smooth and her inner walls clenched around him with each stroke.

Part of her wished it was his cock inside her, but in her heart she was glad it was just his fingers. What they were doing was stupid, something he had to know.

"Stop thinking and relax," he murmured against one of her breasts.

Nissa hadn't realized he'd been able to sense her distress, but he was right. At this moment all she wanted was release. To feel something other than the weight of all her people's responsibility on her shoulders. No one was around to judge her.

Forcing herself to do exactly as he said, she shoved everything else out of her brain. Her fingers flattened against his shoulders and she allowed herself the joy of touching him anywhere she wanted. As he continued pushing deep inside her, she traced along the muscles and striations in his shoulders and arms. Savoring the feel of him, she closed her eyes and focused solely on the sensory pleasure.

When his thumb tweaked over her clit, she jerked. Her inner walls started contracting wildly, her body so close to the edge.

Moving away from her breasts, he lifted up so that their faces were barely an inch apart.

"Let go." The command in his voice sent a thrill through her. He'd always been like that, so dominating and demanding.

So she did just that. She let go. Covering the tiny distance between them, she met his mouth with her own as the climax ripped through her. Her kisses were jerky and wild as pleasure pounded through her in wave after wave.

Like a waterfall, her orgasm broke free with a sudden urgency. Her inner walls clenched around his fingers as she wrapped her legs tighter around his waist.

As she came down from her high, the only other sound in the room was their erratic breathing. Even though he hadn't come, he was still as affected as she was. The knowledge humbled her.

Slowly, he withdrew his fingers and she immediately missed his touch. When he slid his fingers into his mouth, tasting her, her cheeks warmed at the erotic act.

"Just like I remember." His murmured voice was as dark and sensual as the man himself.

She couldn't even begin to find her voice and thankfully she didn't need to. Holding on to her hips, Thomas pulled her farther past the edge of the counter and tighter into his embrace. He wrapped his arms around her waist and buried his face against her neck. The action was submissive and totally out of character for this male.

"I've missed you, Nissa." The quiet desperation in his voice threatened to crack the wall she'd built around her heart nearly a century ago. Why did he have to make this so hard?

Her vocal chords refused to work. She felt the same way but she couldn't return the sentiment. Not aloud anyway. If she started thinking about how much he meant to her, it would be that much harder when she had to leave him.

And leave him she would.

She had a duty to her people and once this whole assassin mess was figured out she'd have to return to her life. And he had no place in it. No matter what kind of treaty she signed with The Council, her people would never accept a werewolf as her mate. It wasn't as if he was asking anyway. He wanted her physically but he'd kicked her out of his life once. No matter that she said she'd forgiven him, the truth was, he'd turned his back on her when she'd been willing to leave everything behind for him.

Her family, her friends, her title.

Everything.

She actually had forgiven him. She just hadn't forgotten the pain. And she didn't know if she ever would.

"Share my bed tonight." His intoxicating voice sent a tremble curling through her. His rock-hard erection pressing into her abdomen left little to the imagination what he wanted. After what they'd just shared she wanted to please him as much as he'd pleased her.

However, she stiffened in his embrace, forcing herself to be strong—even as guilt ate away at her. "I can't, Thomas."

All the muscles in his body pulled tight as he pulled back to stare at her with those dark, penetrating eyes. "Can't or won't?"

"I won't." Why did her voice have to shake so bad?

When he didn't respond she had the irrational urge to fill the silence, something she rarely did. It showed weakness. "There's too much going on in my life right now. I just need to regroup, get in touch with those I know are loyal and figure out who is trying to kill me. This..." She motioned with her hand between them. "Is too complicated."

"Let me help you." Why did he have to sound so sincere?

"You are helping me by giving me a place to stay. For the first time in months I can sleep feeling safe." She might not get one minute of sleep under his roof but at least she knew no one would harm her with him around. The male was a force of nature and his pack was one of the deadliest.

"You'd be safer in my bed," he growled softly, his frustration clear.

Maybe physically but not emotionally. She resisted the urge to sigh. "When you kicked me out of your life—"

He cursed but didn't back away from her. If anything, his grip around her tightened. "If you'd let me make it up to you—"

"No. I'm not asking for that. I'm simply saying that when you...when we parted ways, I realized it was for the best. We're too different and things would never have worked. I don't know about you but I...I don't know if I could live through another breakup from you." It had nearly broken her the first time. So much so that she hadn't been able to even take another lover; had never wanted to. Which was freaking pathetic. Even admitting this much was stripping a huge chunk of pride from her, but if it got him to back off it'd be worth it.

Regret flared in his eyes but then that damn mask slid into place as he stepped back, his gaze shuttered. "Come on. I'll show you to the guest room."

CHAPTER THREE

Nissa swiped mascara across her eyelashes one last time before grabbing her clutch from the bathroom counter. Thomas had been gone practically all day but the house certainly hadn't been empty. His brothers and cousins had been coming by, never leaving her alone for one moment. For that she was grateful, even if she'd missed Thomas.

She'd wanted protection and that's what she'd gotten. Unfortunately she hadn't been able to contact her mother despite numerous calls. Her sister kept answering the house phone and even her mother's mobile phone. Since she didn't know if Kassia was behind the attack on her life, she didn't want to give away her whereabouts. If she could just talk to her mother everything would work itself out. She was sure of it.

As she exited the room she was struck by how quiet the house was. Unlike Thomas, she didn't have extrasensory abilities so she couldn't scent anyone. Her flat sandals were quiet against the bamboo flooring.

When she reached the kitchen and found it also empty, her heart rate quickened until she spotted Thomas and Stephan through one of the windows on the lanai. They sat on two loungers drinking beer and looking completely relaxed.

She wished she could loosen up around him but was finding it impossible—especially after the way he'd brought her to orgasm last night. More than anything she wanted to get Thomas out of her system once and for all. A century was too long to fantasize about someone, that being an understatement. He shouldn't have lived up to her expectations, but if anything he was better than her memories.

He laughed at something his brother said and her chest tightened. She'd been able to make him laugh once upon a time. He'd been all smiles around her. Back when he'd thought she was just human. Then he'd discovered her true identity and a switch had flipped. She'd seen him angry for the first time. His eyes had practically glowed with rage as he'd kicked her out of his life. Despite the even temperature, she fought off a shiver. That was such a dark time in her life and she hated thinking about it.

As if he knew she was watching him, he turned toward her. Averting her gaze, she smoothed down her sea-green halter-style dress. He'd told her they were going to a birthday party but she wasn't sure if it was dressy or not. His response when she'd asked had been to tell her she'd look good in anything. Such a male answer.

She jumped at the sound of the sliding glass door opening and met Thomas' gaze. In one swoop he assessed her from head to toe. His dark eyes were *very* approving when he reached her face again. Looked like she'd worn the right thing after all. Not that she cared what he thought. Or at least she kept trying to convince herself she didn't.

"You look beautiful." He spoke low, for her ears only.

She swallowed back her nerves. "Thank you."

An awkward silence started to stretch between them when his brother slid the door shut with a bang.

"I hope you're not shy, Nissa, because you're meeting the whole clan tonight," Stephan said with an easy grin.

She wasn't exactly shy but meeting a houseful of werewolves was intimidating. But as part of the royal family, she knew how to fake it. Plastering a smile on her face she nodded. "I'm ready to go if you guys are."

Sidestepping Thomas, Stephan threw his arm around her in a brotherly gesture as they headed toward the door leading to the garage. "My mate and sister-in-law are so excited to meet you. You already know that Paz is half fae but she's never met others like herself. She and Marisol spent all afternoon cooking."

Nissa didn't know if she should be more surprised by how nice Thomas' family had been so far. It sounded as if some of them actually *wanted* to meet her. If she'd brought Thomas home to meet her family he'd have been met with cold stares or snide remarks. Or worse, considering someone wanted her dead.

Thomas cleared his throat loudly as Stephan held open the passenger side door to Thomas' BMW coupe. Thomas glared at his brother.

Stephan just grinned and stepped back. "See ya at the party, Nissa," he said to her but kept his gaze on his brother, some unspoken conversation going on between the two males.

"Uh, yeah, see you," she muttered as he shut the door, unsure why Thomas was annoyed with his brother. Stephan had been nothing but friendly.

DANGEROUS CRAVING | 313

When Thomas slid into the driver's side, she squirmed against the leather seats. Alone with the frustratingly sexy male again. At least the drive wouldn't take long.

"I'm sorry if my brother made you feel uncomfortable." His words were practically a growl.

"He didn't. Why are you frustrated with him?"

"I don't like him touching you." His knuckles turned white as he gripped the steering wheel.

She frowned at his words. "He's very happily mated. Even I can see that."

"I don't care." He didn't look at her but his jaw clenched tightly, frustration clear in every line of his body.

His answer didn't invite much conversation so she crossed her legs and smoothed down her dress as he pulled out of the garage. Part of her wanted to ask what he'd done all day but it seemed a bit too familiar. Like they were a couple or something.

She truly wanted to know about his day but at the same time, she didn't want to get even more invested in him or his life. It would just cause her heartache later. Well, more heartache. For years she'd been shoving memories of him into a tiny compartment in her mind and she needed to keep doing that if she planned to survive.

As they pulled down a long, private driveway, her heart beat a staccato rhythm. His family owned a private stretch of beach in Key Biscayne and though she'd met his Alpha the night before, panic started to set in. Luxury cars, midgrade cars, an old muscle car, trucks — new and old — and a few hybrids lined the driveway. She'd known it was a party but the reality of her situation crashed over her. She was going to be in a house full of werewolves.

Werewolves.

She trusted Thomas, and his Alpha had been kind but what if —

"Stop!" Thomas' voice thundered in the enclosed space.

She jerked in her seat causing her purse to slide to the floorboards. "What?"

"I don't know what you're afraid of but the terror rolling off you is actually hurting me." There was no anger in his words, just sadness.

Oh, hell. Nissa bit her bottom lip as she looked into his dark eyes. She'd forgotten he could sense her emotions if she didn't keep them in check. "Sorry. I just started thinking and..." She shrugged as she trailed off.

Surprising her, he reached out and grasped one of her hands. "My

314 | SAVANNAH STUART

family would *never* hurt you. And if someone tried, I'd kill them."

She swallowed hard at his words, hating what the truth of them did to her. She'd forgotten how protective he could be. Since she didn't trust her voice, she squeezed his hand and gave him a small smile before plucking her purse from the floor. As she started to open her door, he'd already gotten out and was helping her out. Another thing she'd forgotten. How fast shifters were.

Thomas kept his hand firmly around her waist as they headed toward the front door. She tried to subtly step away but his grip only increased. Oh yeah, he was in protective, possessive mode and it was hard not to like it.

"Don't think you can run away from me," he murmured so low she wasn't sure if she'd heard him right.

Before she could contemplate it, the front door swung open and a dark-haired girl who couldn't be more than sixteen jumped at Thomas, giving Nissa the opportunity to put some distance between them.

The girl wrapped her arms around his waist in a tight hug. "Thomas! I'm so glad you're here."

He chuckled as he hugged her back, then gently set her away. "I take it you missed me."

"You missed the last party and you haven't been around lately." She pouted in the way only a young teenage girl could.

His lips pulled into a small smile as he shook his head. "Some of us actually have to work. Athena, I'd like you to meet Nissa. She's my guest."

The girl smiled shyly and held out a hand. "Hi, it's nice to meet you."

Nissa took her hand and some of her nervousness dissolved. "It's nice to meet you too."

Thomas covered the small distance between them and once again his hand was at the small of her back. "I'm going to introduce her to everyone, okay?"

Athena nodded and ran back inside. Thomas' hand moved from the small of her back to her waist once again. He held her in such a proprietary manner as he made the rounds, introducing her to everyone, and it surprised her. He'd said he'd protect her but he seemed almost proud to be standing with her. If anything she thought he'd keep her at arm's length because of what she was.

After meeting a dozen shifters, they stopped in the Mediterranean-style kitchen and she finally caught her breath. Under the hanging copper pots, there was a smorgasbord of exotic-looking food on the center island.

DANGEROUS CRAVING | 315

Through the sliding glass door she spotted a small bar outside. His brothers and most of the males were out there. She tensed for a moment when she realized he planned to take her out there.

He paused by the bar chairs lining the center island. "Are you thirsty?"

She nodded. She wasn't but she wanted to keep her hands busy and maybe get a little distance from him.

"I'll be back in a sec." Shocking her, he dropped a quick kiss on her cheek in plain view of *everyone.*

As he disappeared outside she turned away from the window so she wouldn't stare at him like some lovesick idiot. Her skin tingled where his lips had been and the deepest part of her heart wished he'd kissed her mouth. Which was just plain foolish. She knew they had no future together and after that mistake last night it seemed stupid to pretend otherwise.

"Nissa?"

She swiveled in her seat to find a petite, dark-haired woman sliding onto one of the high backed chairs next to her. "Yes."

"I'm Caro." She slid a glass of white wine across the marble top. "You can probably use this."

She pushed out a grateful breath and took the long-stemmed glass. Was she that obvious? "Thank you. Are you one of Thomas' cousins?"

She shook her head. "No. I'm his aunt, though I'm not that much older than him."

Nissa nodded and took a sip of her drink. That meant the woman was close to two hundred even though she looked as if she were in her early thirties. Werewolves and other shifters aged at the same pace as the fae. It was one of the few things they had in common.

The dark-haired woman's eyes narrowed a fraction as she assessed her. "I've never seen my nephew so smitten over someone before."

Nissa cleared her throat. She knew he'd told his family who she was and why she was in Miami, but he hadn't told everyone about their past. Or she didn't think he had. "We're just friends."

The female snorted softly. "Ah, *right.*"

Nissa would rather talk about anything other than Thomas so she tried to change the subject. "Is that your mate over there?" She tilted her head in the direction of the back patio where most of the males were. A dark-haired man with electric-blue eyes hadn't taken his eyes off Caro since she'd sat down. He watched her like, well, a predatory wolf watched his mate.

Caro glanced over her shoulder and when she turned to face Nissa her expression was dark.

Uh oh. "I'm sorry. Is mate the wrong word? I'm still not sure of all the correct—"

She shook her head and placed a gentle hand on hers. "I'm sorry, it's not that. No, he's not my mate. He's a very persistent... Never mind. I'm actually unmated."

"Oh." She racked her brain trying to think of a decent response, but was saved when two petite, slim she-wolves grabbed a couple more bar stools and pulled them up close, creating a small circle. "Hi..."

"I'm Paz." The smallest one spoke first.

"And I'm Marisol. We're sisters," the other dark-haired one said next.

"We're so happy to meet you. I can't believe how tall and gorgeous you are. You're the first full-blooded faerie I've met before. Actually, any of us have met. I thought maybe you'd be short like me. Are all full-blooded fae like you?" Paz asked.

Marisol nudged her sister and shot her a sharp look. "Let the woman breathe, *hermana*."

Paz's cheeks tinged pink. "I'm sorry. My social skills are crap. If I ask you anything inappropriate feel free to ignore me. You won't hurt my feelings, I promise."

Feeling immensely relieved—and amused—Nissa smiled at the sisters. "It's okay. Ask anything you want. And to answer your first question, the Gentry—the royal line—we're all fairly tall I suppose." In reality she was one of the smallest of her family.

Paz shot another question at her and for the first time in ages, Nissa let her guard down. She'd expected a cold reception from these werewolves but so far everyone was incredibly nice. So much so, it scared her a little. All these wolves were so welcoming and Nissa couldn't help but wonder why her kind had been at odds with them for centuries. She knew what her mother had told her about the Great War but this pack didn't seem like evil, conniving monsters.

Leaning back in her chair, she answered another question and found herself smiling at the sisterly banter between Paz and Marisol.

CHAPTER FOUR

"I really like your family—uh, pack," Nissa said as they headed back to Thomas' house. Now that they were alone again she felt the need to fill the silence.

"I think they were quite taken with you too." His voice had a sensuous quality she didn't think she was prepared to handle.

"I was surprised by how nice everyone was." She wasn't sure why she told him.

Thomas shot her a quick glance and a frown marred his sharp features. "Why?"

She shrugged. "Why wouldn't I be?" When she realized he probably thought she meant it as an insult she shook her head. "I meant that as a compliment, Thomas. I've never spent any time around your kind...well, except you of course."

At her words, he relaxed a little but not much. His fingers gripped the steering wheel a bit too tight and the muscles in his arms were pulled taut. She itched to reach out and stroke his arm. Just to feel all that power underneath her fingertips. She'd missed him so much.

Not only was he a skillful lover but he'd taken a piece of her heart when he'd kicked her out of his life. Maybe more than a piece. More like a huge chunk.

"I'm sorry my mother wasn't there. She's looking forward to meeting you though." The words were sincere, but still surprising.

Nissa frowned. Somehow she doubted his mother was *dying* to meet her. Her own mother would likely have a stroke if she found out she'd slept with a shifter. The Gentry didn't even like to intermingle with the common fae, preferring instead to marry those of similar social standing. Shifters, humans—they were all off limits. Vampires were accepted, but it was still a rare thing.

"You doubt me?" he growled softly.

She turned to him. "I didn't say anything."

"I can still sense it. When I say my family wants to meet you, I'm not lying."

"Well, my family doesn't have any interest in getting to know you, Thomas. They don't know I'm here and if they did, it would kill them. My mother especially. Treaty or not I don't think they'll ever truly accept the mixing of our kinds." The words were harsh but he needed to understand that just because times were changing, her family never would. She desperately needed to keep him at arm's length. Maybe if he realized that their two worlds would never mesh, he'd back off.

"What about you? Do you care what your family thinks?"

No. "Of course I do."

"Even if they want to kill you?" His voice was soft, concerned.

She shrugged, but his words were another reminder of the real reason she was in Miami. "I tried calling my mother again tonight." She'd sneaked away to one of the bathrooms and called barely an hour ago.

"And?"

"My sister answered again."

"You're sure she's the one trying to kill you? You always said how close you two were. Have things changed that much?"

Stark sadness filled her chest, spilling into her lungs, making it difficult to breathe. Her sister had been acting odd lately but actually trying to have her killed? It just seemed too diabolical. But the proof said otherwise. And it burned a harsh hole inside her. Her family might have their issues but trying to kill her? She pressed a hand to her stomach to quell her nausea. "I didn't think so, but I truly don't know. I can't take the risk of trusting her until I know more. If I could just talk to my mother…"

He sighed heavily as he put his car into park. "You can stay with me as long as you need, Nissa." Thomas reached out and grasped her hand. When she tried to pull away he threaded his fingers through hers. Instinct told her to yank her hand back, to make him let go, but her heart told her something entirely different. Instead, she let him comfort her and she savored the simple act of holding his hand. Since it would probably be the last time it ever happened, she tightened her grip.

"Nissa." Her name on his lips was an unsteady growl.

The car was still running but the engine was barely audible. Sitting in his driveway, she felt as if they were the only two people on the planet. As if someone wasn't trying to kill her. As if he wasn't a shifter and she wasn't fae. As if they *somehow* actually had a shot at making a relationship work.

DANGEROUS CRAVING | 319

"We should probably go inside," she whispered, though she wasn't sure why. If she spoke louder it would sound as if she meant the words. And she didn't. She didn't want to go inside and she didn't want to let go of his hand. Didn't want to let go of him.

With his free hand he reached out and cupped her jaw. The grip was positively possessive. His hand tightened as it slid back a few inches until he held the back of her head.

Her mouth parted slightly as she stared into his dark eyes. It was all she could do to breathe as their gazes clashed. Suddenly the interior of the car was too small, too stuffy.

The pad of his thumb stroked her cheek. "Stay in my room tonight, Nissa."

Yes. The word was on the tip of her tongue. She wanted to be in his bed right then. Wanted to feel his mouth and hands covering her entire body. Wanted to experience the type of raw, primal pleasure only he could give her. As she started to answer, the sound of his cell phone ringing cut through the air, breaking the spell.

Sliding out of his embrace, she gently removed her hand from his hold as well. She clasped her hands tightly together in her lap to cover her slight shaking. A rush of air entered her lungs as she escaped his hold. She could breathe again. Letting him touch her was bad news. When he did, she couldn't think straight. Didn't want to think, really. Just wanted to feel. That was too dangerous.

Thomas cursed under his breath then yanked his phone out of his pants pocket. "What?" he snarled. "Can't you take care of this yourself... Damn it... You're right, just give me some time. I'll be down there soon." As soon as he ended the call he looked at her. Regret burned in his eyes. "I'm going to take you to Stephan's house. I need to go to the club and—"

"I'll go with you." The words were out before she could stop herself, but she didn't want to be separated from him. Apparently she really was a masochist.

"You sure?"

"I'm probably not dressed appropriately but—"

"You look gorgeous, Nissa. You could be wearing..." He shook his head and kicked the car into reverse. "You'll be the most beautiful woman there tonight, trust me." Thomas said the words with such sincerity, something long buried inside her fluttered.

Thomas gripped the steering wheel tightly as he headed down Ocean

Drive. Nissa had been ready to say yes. He'd seen the decision in her eyes. Until that damn phone had rang. Then it was like she'd been wrenched out of a trance.

Now he wasn't sure she'd agree to share his bed tonight. The night actually hadn't been half bad. Not as bad as he'd expected anyway. The entire pack had been welcoming and Paz hadn't brought her human friend she'd wanted to set him up with. Nissa had seemed like she'd had a good time, which was important. If he wanted to convince her to make a life with him, she had to feel like she belonged.

The second he pulled up to the club, one of the valet drivers opened his door and another opened Nissa's. Thomas didn't miss the way the young kid stared at her. He seemed almost mesmerized as he looked her over from head to toe. When his gaze reached her face again he gave her a goofy grin.

Thomas' inner beast growled but he refrained from pummeling the kid. Hell, he couldn't blame him really. Hooking his arm around her shoulder, Thomas steered Nissa through the front door. He savored the feel of her against him. Even for a shifter he was tall, but so was she and he liked the way her entire body molded to him. It was too bad they had their clothes on.

A familiar song blasted through the air. The downstairs area of his club was always louder. Men and women danced and moved in rhythm with the hip-hop beat. Next to him, Nissa relaxed. The action was subtle and if he hadn't been holding her so close he might not have noticed.

The music soothed her.

He'd forgotten how much she liked to dance. Okay, maybe not forgotten exactly. He'd forced the image of her dancing from his mind because it always got him hot and hard. Before they'd met, her family had lived everywhere, including Egypt and Turkey. She'd learned the sensual art of belly dancing at a very young age. Years ago she'd performed many private dances for him, something he'd never been able to forget.

His cock pressed painfully against his pants. Damn it, he didn't need to be meeting with his staff with a raging hard-on.

"Hey, boss." Bruno ducked out from under one of the bars as they approached.

"Where are they?" Thomas asked. Bruno had called to let him know his best bartender and his best cocktail waitress had been ready to exchange blows. Whatever the problem was, this was something he needed to handle himself.

"Your office. I've got someone covering for both of them."

"Thanks. This is Nissa. Don't let her out of your sight." It was not a subtle order.

Bruno's eyes widened slightly as he nodded. "Of course."

Without giving her a chance to protest, Thomas pulled her close and captured her mouth with a dominance he knew would throw her off kilter—which was exactly what he wanted. She tasted sweet, probably from the wine she'd been drinking earlier. When he pulled back, her green eyes practically glowed. She ran her tongue along her bottom lip in a seductive manner that had his cock begging for release. So he turned away before he did something stupid like throw her over his shoulder and find the nearest secluded spot.

As he made his way to his office, he pushed down his inner wolf. Barely. Everything inside him told him to claim Nissa. Take what he wanted before she left again. His human side would never do that but the fierce battle waging inside made him uneasy. He took a deep breath when he reached his office door. Once the throbbing of his canines pushing against his gums subsided, he opened it.

"She's stealing my customers!" Ally jumped up from her seat.

Stephanie rolled her eyes at the other woman and shook her head. "She's crazy."

Sighing, Thomas shut the door behind him. This was going to take a while.

Winding her way to one of the dance floors, Nissa let her hips sway with the music. She couldn't remember the last time she'd gone dancing. Or done anything fun, really. Lately she'd been so consumed with Gentry business and trying to figure out who wanted to hurt her she'd been afraid to let her guard down.

But now she was with Thomas. In beautiful, sunny Miami. No one knew she was here. Sure, she and Thomas had already crossed an invisible line. One she knew she couldn't come back from. In the end she'd get hurt again but that didn't mean she couldn't enjoy herself. Just for a little while.

The rhythmic thump streaming in from the speakers was hypnotic. Exhilarating. Using her gifts, she projected a tiny bubble of space around her to keep others at a safe distance. Technically she was just spreading her wings, but humans couldn't see them unless she allowed them to.

Closing her eyes, she let herself be swept away with the sounds. None

322 | SAVANNAH STUART

of the music was familiar but it flowed through her like a rich wine, making her loose limbed and relaxed.

One song bled into another. She wasn't sure how much time passed but when a harsh sounding rap song blared through the speakers she slowed her movements. As she began to make her way off the dance floor she spotted Thomas.

He stood on the stairs that led to the VIP room. As he tracked her movements, his eyes were hungry. For her. She didn't know how long he'd been standing there but it was obvious he liked what he saw. The gleam in his gaze was potent, needy. Like he'd bared his soul to her so she could see every little thing he wanted to do to her.

Years ago she'd given him many private dances. Something she'd never done for anyone else. Had never wanted to. Now she knew why. It was something special they'd shared together and even though she'd been so hurt by him, he'd always held a special place in her heart. Even if it killed her, she wanted to experience everything Thomas had to offer again.

Pulling her wings in, she strode across the floor. She wove through the masses of people, determined to reach him as quick as possible.

Turning sideways, she tried to avoid a couple grinding on each other. When she swiveled, she spotted the blade first. Her gaze snapped up to find a man staring at her intently. The small dagger was gripped tightly in his shaking hands. She blinked as she saw the look in his eyes. They were glassy, unfocused and it was obvious he'd been influenced by one of her kind.

Shit!

He was on a mission. No doubt to hurt her.

An alarming tingle raced through her, telling her the blade was iron. She tried to take a step back but bumped into someone.

Without taking her eyes off the man, she moved to her right and tried to find another escape.

"Hey!" A drunk girl slurred something else at her but Nissa ignored it. The crowd had gotten too thick for her to bring her wings up to protect herself.

Sure she could zap this guy with energy but they were in a room full of people and this was Thomas' club. She couldn't bring that kind of scrutiny down on him. If someone had a cell phone and recorded what she did, it could be bad for all supernatural beings.

Quickly she glanced back toward the stairs. She needed to let Thomas know she was in danger. He wasn't there.

DANGEROUS CRAVING | 323

Fighting back the bubble of panic pushing up inside her, she shoved her way through a small group of people.

Glancing over her shoulder, she spotted the man still following. He looked even worse, as if he were drugged. Which in a way, he had been. His mind had been messed with.

She knew the influence on him wouldn't last forever but it could last long enough for him to hurt her or anyone who got in his way.

Nissa needed to get him away from these humans. If she had to, she'd protect herself with her powers, but she didn't think it would get that far. Mindless of the annoyed cries, she continued shoving her way through the crowd. Once she broke free she glanced around for Thomas again but he was nowhere to be seen.

Shaking her head, she hurried toward the bathrooms. They were down a long hallway. As she made her way she looked over her shoulder. Sure enough, the dark-haired human was still following. His movements were stilted and jerky but he was definitely tracking her.

And he wouldn't stop until the influence wore off. Depending upon how powerful the spell was, it could be a few hours. Possibly longer.

As she reached the hallway she frowned at the cluster of people standing around. There was no choice but to use her influence. She cleared her throat. "Go get a drink right now and don't come back to use this restroom for the rest of the night." Her voice was loud and clear. Command laced her words. Most of the fae had to make eye contact in order to exert their persuasion but since she was a member of the Gentry, she was more powerful. Her skills more tuned.

A few women turned to look at her as she spoke and did as she ordered. As they hurried away from the restroom, the dark-haired, wild-eyed man rushed past them.

"You have to die," he growled.

"Stop!" She put all the authority she possessed into the word. She didn't want to hurt this human but she wouldn't let him stab her.

He faltered and his grip on the blade slightly loosened. "You have to die?" Now his words sounded more like a question.

Sharp relief surged through Nissa. The spell was wearing off. All she had to do was convince him to put the weapon down. "You don't want to do this. You don't want to be here. Why not put the weapon down and — "

She fell back a step as a blur rushed through the hallway and slammed the man against the wall.

Thomas.

One of his hands was wrapped around the stranger's neck, and his other hand pinned the guy's weapon-toting hand against the wall with crushing force. Nissa could see Thomas' canines protruding from his mouth. "Did he hurt you?" The question was guttural, animalistic.

Hurrying toward them, she grabbed Thomas' arm. "Let him go. He didn't hurt me."

He didn't loosen his grip. "I saw him. The weapon. Tried to get to you. You moved through the crowd...too quickly." His breathing was labored and uneven.

She tightened her hold on him. Then she heard the sound of a blade hitting the floor. "He's under the influence. Someone did this to him. Let him go."

As if coming out of a dream, the man in Thomas' grip started to struggle as his eyes widened. He began clawing at Thomas' hand and arm, his movements pathetic and ineffectual. Nissa knew if Thomas had wanted to kill the human, he'd already be dead. It was a testament to how much control he was actually showing.

She brushed a gentle hand down Thomas' forearm. They needed to let this man go. Getting any information from him would be impossible. Whoever had influenced him would have wiped his memory. "Let him go. He's harmless now."

After a moment, Thomas' fingers loosened. The man slid down the wall and crumbled into a heap on the floor. Choking and coughing, he crawled away. "You're crazy, man," he muttered.

"Get. Out. And *never* come back here." Thomas bit the words out with barely concealed rage and Nissa noticed his canines still hadn't retracted.

Pushing to his feet, the other man stumbled away faster than she'd imagined possible.

She picked up the weapon by the handle and gave it to Thomas who quickly tucked it into his belt. Despite her better judgment, she smoothed her hands over his chest. When she did he looked at her. Really looked.

His dark eyes had started to turn a golden yellow.

She inhaled sharply. He was so close to shifting. This could be dangerous to everyone. Including him.

CHAPTER FIVE

Running her hands up his chest, Nissa encircled her fingers around the back of Thomas' neck. "Breathe, Thomas. Do it for me," she whispered, desperate for him to listen.

Then she leaned forward and pressed her lips to his. With his sharp canines it was difficult to avoid the points but as she molded against him, she could feel the tension subside from him. Like the tide being pulled back out to sea, his animalistic side quickly abated.

Well, most of it.

As their lips meshed and his tongue invaded her mouth, his kisses became more dominating. He grabbed her hips and pulled her tighter. "What were you thinking?" he murmured against her mouth.

She pulled back slightly to answer. "I needed to get him away from the humans."

"You could have been hurt." Now his words were a growl.

Her lips pursed. No, she couldn't have. He should know that but his animal side had taken over. It hadn't cared that she'd been capable enough to take care of herself. It had seen her in trouble and had wanted to kill.

The fact that he'd shown so much restraint spoke volumes about his abilities. She'd known he was next in line to be Alpha and now she knew why. Some shifters couldn't control their instincts when it came to their females, but he definitely could.

She faltered at the thought. She wasn't *his* female. So why did it feel so right to be crushed to him now? Chemistry, that was all it was.

Her nipples tingled as they rubbed against him. There was too much clothing in the way though. She wanted to feel his chest against hers, craved that skin to skin contact.

"My office, now," he murmured against her jaw as he nipped his way across her skin.

326 | SAVANNAH STUART

She didn't even think to protest. "Okay."

As they made their way through the club she felt as if she were floating. After they got to his office she thought maybe he'd offer her a drink or give some pretense of foreplay but she should have known better. He came at her fast, a sleek, sexy predator.

She stepped back until she ran into the edge of his desk, but Thomas didn't stop his advance. He caged her in with his size and strength.

Clutching the bottom of her dress, he pulled it over her head with quick efficiency. She hadn't worn a bra so the cool air rushed over her. But she barely had time to think about it before he lowered his head over one of her breasts. He certainly wasn't wasting any time.

The sudden contact jolted her straight to her core. He murmured something against her skin but she couldn't understand what. Didn't really care at this point. As he pulled one of her nipples between his teeth and tugged lightly, heat rushed between her legs.

She wanted to clench them together to ease some of that ache but Thomas positioned himself between her open thighs. She felt his hard length as he rubbed his cock against her with jerky thrusts.

It wouldn't take much for him to push inside her. Despite the loud voice in her head telling her how foolish it was, she desperately wanted him.

All of him.

Reaching between them, she tried to tug at his belt but he stilled her with one of his large hands.

Then he pulled his head back from her breast. There was something in his eyes but she wasn't sure what it was. Pain, maybe. But that didn't make sense. Did he want to stop? An ache welled up inside her at the thought.

She started to ask him but the pressure on her hands increased. He held on to her wrists.

"You're mine, Nissa." The words were guttural, strained.

She knew it. Deep inside her core the truth was there. While it might not change their future, she'd always be his. It was as if he'd claimed her so many years ago and she'd never been able to get out from under his spell.

"I know." Those two words made his dark eyes flash hungrily. Triumphantly.

Keeping her wrists captive, he slipped an arm around her waist and laid her on the desk. The smooth wood instantly cooled her back. Holding her wrists above her head, he began nibbling along her jaw toward her ear.

"If I was a more patient man, I'd wait until we got back to my place and tie you to my bed. Think of all the things I could do to you." In the past Thomas rarely talked when they were intimate, but his words lit her entire body on fire.

The thought of being at his mercy was wildly erotic. Years ago he'd been so dominating when they'd made love and each time it had been just as hot. She hadn't thought she'd like it but sometimes when he just took over it drove her wild.

He sucked her earlobe between her teeth and tugged. "Don't move your hands." His let go of her wrists but she did as he said, a slave to his command.

Wordlessly, he held on to her hips and shifted her position so that she was stretched out along the length of his desk. She heard something thud against the carpeted floor but he didn't seem to care what had fallen and she definitely didn't.

He continued kissing his way down her chest and abdomen, until he reached the sensitive section of skin right above her mound. He flicked his tongue against her skin, teasing her just underneath her panties.

She instinctively arched her back. She wanted him to kiss and lick her the way she'd been fantasizing about for years. Chuckling against her, he grasped the thin straps and tugged them down her legs.

Blindly, Thomas tossed the flimsy scrap of material Nissa considered underwear across the room. He didn't know why she even bothered.

Inhaling her sweet scent, he bit back a groan. Jasmine and honeysuckle. It was so distinctive he could pick her out in a crowd of thousands. God, he could have lost her tonight. Rage still thrummed through him and the darkest part of him wished he hadn't let that human go. It didn't matter to him that the male had been under the influence, all his wolf knew was that someone had wanted to hurt Nissa. Hurt what was his.

He leaned forward until he was inches from her pink folds. They glistened lightly with her wetness. He'd barely stimulated her and she was ready for him. Even if he couldn't scent her, he could see it clearly.

When she sat up and threaded her fingers through his hair, he glanced up and shook his head. "Lie back."

She paused for a moment then did as he said. Right now he didn't want to push her too far too fast, but he did plan to tie her up eventually. He hadn't been joking about that.

The thought of seeing her bound to his bed made his cock ache. It felt like a heavy club pulsing between his legs. But this wasn't about him. Not right now. Not tonight. This was entirely about her.

If he had to use sex and pleasure to bind her to him, he'd do it. He couldn't let her walk away again.

Instead of stroking her pussy directly, he ran his tongue along the crease by her inner thigh. He'd always loved teasing her, making her crazy with wanting him.

She groaned in frustration, but he continued a path with his tongue and teeth, moving higher over her mound but completely avoiding her clit and slick folds.

Her skin was silky smooth and the small bit of blonde hair covering her mound was just as fine and soft as he remembered.

"Do something," she finally moaned. She rolled her hips again, trying to force him to move faster.

He smiled against her. He'd always loved her impatience.

Moving lower, he slowly dragged his tongue up the length of her folds, making sure he put more pressure on her clit. She tasted sweet and the sounds she made were even sweeter.

As he circled the small bundle of nerves, she tunneled her fingers through his hair. He'd been fantasizing about this for too long and couldn't bear to tear his mouth away from her.

More than anything he wanted to pound into her. To slide his cock into her tight sheath over and over until they were both sated. But he couldn't. He knew he didn't deserve her. After the way he'd turned on her, abandoned her, accused her of lying to him all those years ago, it was amazing she'd come to him at all. Now he had to prove he was worthy of her. That he could give her everything she deserved.

Still teasing her with his tongue, he slid a finger into her. She was so tight, making his hips jerk. His cock had a mind of its own and he didn't blame it. He hadn't been with anyone since her; his wolf hadn't let him even consider it. Now he truly understood why. There was no one for him but Nissa.

Slowly, he pulled his finger out then pushed it back in. Each time he did, she rolled her hips until they found a perfect rhythm.

She came so fast she took him off guard. Her inner walls clenched tightly as her hips began to move faster and faster. Her breathing was as erratic as her thrusts, her movements sensuous and erotic.

"Thomas." His name was a bare whisper on her lips.

Hearing it tore a growl from him. His name should be the only one she ever said. And he planned to make that happen. She belonged with him.

Taking her clit between his teeth, he gently tugged. The action pushed her right over the edge.

Now it wasn't a whisper. It was more like a scream. "Thomas!" Her orgasm rushed through her and he could feel every quiver and tremble of her inner walls as she found her release.

Her fingers tightened on his head for a moment before she fell back against the desk, limp and satisfied.

The sight of her stretched out and naked on his desk was making it difficult for him to keep his original goal in mind. This was about her, not him. As her chest rose and fell and her aroused pink nipples taunted him, he was hard pressed to remember that.

With the taste of her pleasure on his lips, he moved until he was an inch from her face. Her green eyes were wide and her pupils dilated.

A soft smile touched her lips. "Thank you."

He couldn't answer. His throat was too thick. When she reached between them and started grappling with his belt, he did something he hadn't thought possible. He stopped her. He might want her but he didn't deserve to sink himself inside her. To feel her tighten around him. No, he deserved the torment of a fucking hard-on that wouldn't go away.

Those perfect lips of hers parted as a frown marred her face. "What are you doing?"

He pressed a soft kiss to her lips. "We need to get back to my place. Whoever sent that guy is still out there." He wasn't worried about that but it worked as an excuse. If someone had tried to enter his office he'd have scented them coming long before they made it to the door.

"But—"

He covered her mouth again. Stroking his tongue over hers, he invaded her mouth until she was panting and breathless. Though he hated to, he finally he lifted his head and quickly disentangled himself. If he didn't now, he knew he never would. After he picked up her discarded dress, he fished his phone out of his pocket and called one of the valet guys to bring his car to the side alley. He wasn't going to risk taking Nissa through a crowded club after what had just happened.

As he finished his call he turned to find a dressed Nissa sitting on the edge of his desk with a confused expression on her face. The look in her eyes told him she didn't believe his excuse one bit. At least she wasn't pushing him for more. If she did he knew he'd toss his restraint and self-induced torture aside and take her right on the floor.

CHAPTER SIX

Nissa set her iced tea on the table that separated her from Thomas' sister-in-law, Carly. Her husband Nick was out patrolling the house and grounds while his redheaded wife kept her company. The woman was sweet and surprisingly at ease around so many supernatural beings. Thanks to Thomas, Nissa knew that she'd only been turned less than a year ago through the mating process. "I'm sorry your friend had to leave."

Carly smiled and waved a dismissive hand in the air. "She'll be back next month. I think I've almost convinced her to move here."

Nissa's eyes widened. "And she doesn't mind that you're all...werewolves?"

"Ah, she doesn't know...*yet*. I plan to tell her...one day." Carly chewed on her bottom lip for a moment. "Eventually I'll have to or she'll realize I'm aging a lot slower. I don't know how she'll take it. Some days *I* still don't believe it. If it hadn't been for Nick I don't know that I'd have handled the transition so well."

Having a supportive mate made all the difference in the world. Something she'd never get to experience. Nissa shoved the abrupt thought away. Dwelling on something that could never be was a waste of time. And if she allowed herself to think about it, the hole in her heart she'd patched up long ago would rip right back open. Before she could respond Nick appeared from around the side of the house.

The tall, multi-tattooed shifter nodded politely at her but when his gaze landed on his mate, his entire face softened. "Hey, sweetie."

Carly's cheeks flushed as their gazes clashed and Nissa had to look away. Seeing two people so in love was another reminder of what she'd never have. It didn't matter who she ended up mated to. That person wouldn't be Thomas. Maybe she'd eventually learn to care for her intended husband but it wouldn't matter. Swallowing back a lump, she stood. "If you guys don't mind I think I'm going to take a quick nap."

Carly eyed her curiously. "Are you sure? I was about to make lunch."

Not trusting her voice, she nodded and strode inside. All morning Thomas' family had been stopping by to keep an eye on her and some just to meet her. Though Thomas hadn't told her what it was about, he'd had to take care of some business with his father. He'd certainly made sure she was looked after though. Something that didn't surprise her. Especially not after the way he'd taken such gentle care with her last night.

As she hurried up the stairs, she found it easier to breathe. After the hot interlude in Thomas' office last night he'd been quiet and hadn't pressured her to share his bedroom again. The disappointment she'd experienced was sharp.

Even though she knew the memories would torture her later she wanted to feel him inside her just one more time. When she passed by his room, she paused. His door was cracked open and his sandalwood scent twined around her, drawing her inside. She might not have his extrasensory abilities but his whole house smelled like him. It was subtle and it drove her crazy. Even when he wasn't around, it felt like he was.

Nissa glanced behind her to make sure no one was there then nudged the door open farther with her foot. Pushing back the tiny twinge of guilt, she stepped into his room. Since the two large windows facing the ocean had the blinds pulled up she didn't bother with the lights.

Instantly her gaze trained on the king-sized bed. She couldn't stop the way her legs clenched together at the sight. The thought of letting him take her on that huge thing sent a quick rush of heat to her core.

Shaking her head, she took a step back, ready to leave, when the painting above his bed caught her eye.

She froze. *How did he have this? How had he known?* Tears pricked her eyes. Turning away she started to wipe them from her cheeks but jerked to a halt.

Thomas stood in the doorway, watching her intently.

She flushed under his scrutiny. "I-I'm sorry. I was curious what your room looked like."

He frowned and covered the small distance between them. With callused thumbs, he brushed away her tears. "Why are you crying? Did someone upset you?" The second question held a surprising amount of underlying anger.

She shook her head and half-smiled. "I was surprised by the painting, that's all. I can't believe you have it. No one, not even my mother knows I paint." Annoyed with herself, she swiped the rest of her tears away. "I can't believe I started crying. I'm just being stupid."

Thomas' brow knitted together. "*You* painted that?"

Her tears dried as his question registered. "You didn't know?"

He shook his head and his gaze trailed past hers to stare at it. For a moment, his eyes glazed over. "I bought it because it reminded me of you. Of us." His words were barely audible.

The scene was a simple one. A villa right on the sparkling Med with a black wolf playing in the sand. Maybe playing was a stretch, but the animal lounged on the beach, soaking up the bright sun. Using oils — her favorite medium — she'd painted it with *him* in mind. It had taken forever to get the mixed blues and greens of the Mediterranean Sea correct. Known for its deep hues, she'd struggled with so many drafts but it had been worth it in the end. In her mind it had been the last time they'd been happy together and she'd put all her effort and soul into capturing that moment on canvas.

To her horror, more tears pricked her eyes. This time it wasn't just a few stray ones. Giant drops rolled down her cheeks with abandon. Though she ordered herself to get it together, it was a fruitless endeavor. She tensed and quickly headed for the door. Letting him see her cry this way was the last thing she wanted. He was still looking at that damn painting anyway. She should have burned it. Seeing it only brought her more sorrow. After she'd sold it she'd never thought to see it again. It was amazing he owned it now.

"Nissa." His hand on her upper arm stopped her.

Keeping her gaze low, she refused to make eye contact. "What?"

He gripped her chin between strong fingers and lifted her head. Not hard, but with enough pressure to make her look at him. The expression in his dark eyes was so concerned it sent a tiny crack through the ice surrounding her heart.

Slowly Thomas leaned forward and brushed his lips over one cheek, then the other. As he kissed away her tears she had to fight back more of them. Why did he have to be so sweet, so gentle? She'd known she'd find protection with him but time should have buried or at least dimmed their attraction. If anything, it was as if things were even more incendiary between them.

He started to step back but something primal inside her didn't want that to happen. Reaching out, she placed a hand on his chest. When he just stared at her she traced her fingers down the hard length of his body, feeling all those taut, lean lines until she reached the hem of his polo shirt. She started to grasp it with the intention of pulling it off him but he tried to stop her.

She frowned. "So you can touch me but I can't touch you?"

"I didn't say that." His voice was strained.

"You didn't have to." She still held on to the bottom of his shirt. When he didn't let go, her frown deepened. "My first night here you wanted me in your bed. Has that changed?"

He swallowed hard but didn't respond. That just annoyed her. He'd been all about this but now that she was offering he apparently wanted to back out. She swiveled away from him but instead of leaving, she shut the door and turned back to confront him.

His eyebrows rose slightly. Without giving him time to question her, she grasped the edge of her dress and lifted it over her head. The halter-style summer dress dropped to the floor with a whisper of sound. Since she'd arrived in Miami she hadn't worn a bra much. To torture him or herself, she wasn't sure.

Slowly, she reached up and cupped her naked breasts. His breath hitched and his gaze narrowed on her hands cradling herself.

As he stared, he looked mesmerized. And the huge bulge in his slacks made her smile. She liked that she affected him so obviously and so quickly.

"What are you doing?" he rasped out.

"If you have to ask..." Simultaneously, she rubbed her thumbs over her hardening nipples.

He tore his gaze away from her movements and focused on her face. "What..."

"I want you inside me." The invitation couldn't get any more blatant than that.

The movement was slight, but he shook his head. His neck muscles were corded tightly, the strain on his face evident. "I don't deserve you."

She wanted to reach out and wipe all that agony off his face, to tell him that wasn't true, but she knew words wouldn't matter now. So she slid her hands down her sides, over her waist, and moved to her hips. In a smooth movement, she pushed her thong down until it pooled around her ankles then kicked it away. If he wouldn't take charge of this, she would. "Take off your clothes."

He shuddered slightly, no doubt at the command in her voice. She ached so badly for him, she didn't care about much else other than feeling his hard length push deep into her. She desperately wanted to give back to him as much as he'd given her since she'd arrived. When he didn't make a move, she wielded a tiny amount of energy and zapped his shirt. It quickly disintegrated.

"Shit." Thomas ran a hand down his washboard stomach and her mouth watered at the sight. The male was absolute perfection and for now at least, he was all hers. "I forgot you could do that," he muttered.

Instead of responding, she headed for his bed. "If you don't hurry, I'm going to start without you."

As she tried to move past him, he grabbed her by the waist and pulled her tight against him. Without pause she clutched his shoulders and lifted up, wrapping her legs around him. The feel of all that raw power and muscle between her legs made her moan. A man didn't have a right to be so toned.

His hands slid down her back until he cupped her behind. Clutching her tightly, he dug his fingers into her cheeks.

Thomas fought to breathe with Nissa's breasts pressed up against his bare chest. He'd tasted and licked them the past couple days but to feel them was heaven. A small part of him wanted to stop this. She deserved a hell of a lot more than him but he was selfish. Once she'd stripped off her dress and bared herself completely to him, he'd known he was lost.

Her desire for him was still as potent as before. The fact that she'd taken this step without any pressure from him meant they had a chance together.

He wanted to make her forget anyone else existed but him. If there was a chance he could bind her to him, he had to take it.

Right now all he wanted was to slide into her and the bed was too far away. As he covered her mouth with his, he took the few steps until they collided with the wall.

Keeping her up with the weight of his body, he quickly unhooked his belt and shoved at his pants. He felt a little foolish with his boots still on, but before his pants had even fallen all the way down, Nissa lifted up and impaled herself on him. He groaned at the feel of her closing around him. All his senses went into overload at the feel of her surrounding him. It had been so damn long he could hardly believe this was happening, that she was in his arms.

She let out a sharp hiss as he thrust inside her. Her sheath was wet but still tight. So fucking tight.

The way her inner walls stretched and molded around him told him it had been a long time since she'd been with anyone. He shouldn't care but the most primitive part of him roared in satisfaction.

Nissa was *his*.

"Oh my...I'd forgotten how good you feel." She took a ragged breath as she lifted herself up and tried to adjust to him.

As he stared into her startling green eyes, he held her hips and kept her still against the wall. Then he pulled out until just the head of his cock was in her. He paused before sliding fully back inside.

The movement was slow and measured. She felt like heaven, like coming home. It was the only way to describe how he felt when he was inside her. It was why he'd never been able to be with someone else after her; she was his home.

Her mouth parted slightly as he moved into her again. His chest tightened as he watched the pleasure play across her face. He could watch her all day and not get tired.

Nissa's hands splayed across his chest before her fingers traced over every inch of him. She looked like a kid on Christmas morning and he was her present. She'd always been like this when they made love. It touched him that at least this much of her attraction hadn't changed, that the connection between them was still real.

Cupping one of her breasts with his hand, he captured her nipple between his teeth while still slowly thrusting. Her heat and tight embrace made it damn near impossible not to come but he held back. He traced a wet path around her areola, loving the feel of it hardening under his tongue.

She arched her back, pushing her breast farther into his mouth. With each lick he could actually feel her inner walls tighten around him. Every part of her body was receptive and attuned to his. Something he'd missed, but never forgotten.

It didn't take much to stimulate Nissa. He'd already put that satisfied smile on her face twice but it wasn't enough. If he could, he'd keep her in that state forever.

They'd never leave the bedroom if he had his way.

When she let out a loud moan, his balls pulled up even tighter. Her legs tightened around him and it was all he could do not to come right then.

Thrusting into her hard, he held himself there, filling her completely. She tried to move against him but he stilled her with his free hand. He wanted to feel her contracting around him.

Her breathing was becoming shakier so he knew it wouldn't be much longer until he felt her explode around him. Having her come around his fingers was nothing compared to the experience of her on his cock.

When he switched breasts, she dug her fingers into his shoulders. "I'm so close."

He smiled against her soft skin. Lightly, he sucked on her pebbled nipple. She jolted and tried to grind against him.

Using his weight, he pressed her harder against the wall and lifted his head so that their faces were inches apart.

336 | SAVANNAH STUART

"Who's inside you?"

Her green eyes were bright with need. "You."

"Say my name." His voice was rough and uneven. He didn't know why it was important, but it was. Every part of him needed to hear; both wolf and human.

"Thomas." She said it like a prayer. Soft and reverent.

His throat tightened. Unable to say anything else, he reached between their bodies and rubbed his thumb over her clit.

The bud was already swollen, just begging for his touch. When he began softly massaging it, her eyes glazed over and her pussy began wildly contracting around him. With each contraction, she moaned, each one louder than the last.

Her fingers, which had already been digging into him, tightened even more. He savored it, knowing he was the one giving her the pleasure.

Finally he started moving. She was tight but so wet. And it was all for him. As he began rocking into her, she abruptly arched her back. With her eyes closed, her head fell back and sent her blonde hair cascading around her shoulders.

As the climax tore through her, she pinned her gaze to his, watching him as she came. There was something so intimate, so real about the moment, he wanted it to go on forever. But he knew it couldn't.

As her orgasm subsided, she draped her arms around his neck and nuzzled him sweetly. With her teeth, she nibbled and scraped across his skin, the playful kisses making him crazy.

The subtle action made his already taut balls pull up even tighter. But he couldn't come in her. With things so uncertain between them and after the way he'd treated her, he didn't feel like he deserved it. He didn't know that he ever would. He should just fucking suffer.

When he started to pull out she straightened and her grip around him tightened. "What are you doing?"

With his jaw clenched, he didn't say anything. His entire body trembled with the need to let go. To claim her. To mark her while he came in her. But he couldn't. He desperately tried to tame his inner wolf, to make his animal side understand that couldn't happen.

It was no use. Nissa seemed to understand. Somehow, she'd always seen right through him. Her legs constricted even harder around him. Holding on to his shoulders she began grinding against him.

With her pussy tightening around his cock and the feel of her breasts rubbing against his chest, it was too much.

All the good intentions in the world were nothing compared to Nissa naked and willing in his arms. He didn't bother biting back the curse that tore from him. Giving into his need, he met her stroke for stroke. They fell into a raw rhythm that had him coming long and hard.

Hot jets of his come shot into her, filling her and soothing his most primal side. He was the one inside her, no one else. Nissa was his, always had been. If he could just convince her of that. Everyone else could go to hell as long as she accepted him. Even after his climax had subsided, his hips still blindly thrust against her. He hadn't realized how desperately he'd wanted that. Needed that.

Groaning, he buried his face against her neck. "I haven't been with anyone since you," he murmured, laying himself bare in the best way he knew how.

CHAPTER SEVEN

Nissa stilled against him, stopping all movement in that preternatural way only the supernaturals could. "What?" she whispered at his confession.

He raised his head. "I just wanted you to know." She deserved to know that there had been no one for him since her, that she had meant everything to him. Even if he had fucked up.

She stared at him for a long time, her green eyes glittering with too many emotions to sift through. For a moment, he thought she'd respond directly, but instead she looked away, her gaze almost troubled. So he just held her. He didn't need a response anyway.

After what felt like an eternity, Nissa untangled her legs. Unsteadily, she leaned on him and kept her arms wrapped around his neck. The skin to skin contact soothed him.

"Do you realize that's the first time you've ever come inside me?" she asked quietly.

"I know." When they'd first gotten together she'd been fertile. He'd believed her to be human and had been working up a way to reveal his true nature to her before he asked her to mate with him. There was no way he could have admitted he'd known she was basically in heat, so he'd used the excuse that he was being careful. In reality it hadn't been an excuse at all.

Back then times had been different and if she'd gotten pregnant before she'd been married she'd have been ostracized by her village. Of course she hadn't been a simple human living in a tiny seaside village like he'd assumed. She'd run away from her royal fae family. And she'd come to tell him just that the day he'd discovered her true identity.

But he'd turned on her.

A shudder rolled through him at the memories of their fight. It had been brutal. Even thinking about it now made him nauseous. He'd have erased those memories if he could have. Instead he was determined to show her how much he loved her. Shaking the thoughts away, he stepped back and pulled off his shoes.

She laughed lightly under her breath. "We made quite a picture."

Despite the intense emotions running through him, he grinned at her as he finished stripping off his pants.

She revealed a perfect row of white teeth as she returned his smile. She opened her mouth to say something else when she stepped back unsteadily.

Alarm jumped inside him, worry for his mate punching through him. "Are you okay?"

When she nodded and smiled again, the light didn't quite reach her eyes. "I'm fine. If you'll excuse me a second." She nodded toward his bathroom before hurrying past him.

Instinct told him to go after her but if she wanted privacy he'd give it to her. It was the least he could do.

Nissa shut the heavy bathroom door and sagged against it. But only for a moment. She wasn't sure if Thomas would follow her. A brief but searing pain had shot across her right shoulder moments after they'd finished making love.

Walking to the full length mirror, she brushed her long hair back and turned to the side to get a better view of her shoulder.

A crushing weight settled against her chest and she fought to breathe as she stared at the intricate Celtic symbol that had formed on her skin. Though lighter in coloring than a tattoo, it was still visible.

She didn't know if she wanted to curse or cry. This was her own fault. She'd felt Thomas pulling out of her and she'd desperately wanted to feel everything he had to offer. Just once she'd wanted to experience him releasing inside her. Now she wanted to kick herself as reality crashed over her head.

Mates.

They were honest to God, *true* mates. Bondmates to be exact. *How was that even possible?* She was fae and he was a shifter. It didn't make sense. She knew his kind mated differently than hers. The male took the female from behind and marked her with his teeth as they climaxed. That bonded them for life and usually linked them telepathically. Even though most shifter mates recognized one another before bonding, there was always a choice. With her kind, however, bondmates were rare and often times had no idea they were fated for a certain mate.

Reaching up, she ran her fingers over the symbol. It was raised enough that she could feel every line and groove. *The bonding symbol.*

The very thought was ludicrous but she'd seen it before on other mated fae so she knew exactly what it was.

A flash of cold snaked through her. Would he have one too? He hadn't reacted at all so maybe he didn't. The males of her kind developed an identical symbol but it usually appeared after the official bonding ceremony.

Something she'd never thought she'd have to worry about with Thomas. "Shit," she muttered. *Shit, shit, shit.*

Thomas had turned his back on her once because she hadn't been honest about what she was. What if he thought she'd lied about this too in some attempt to trap him? Straightening, she turned away from her reflection. She wouldn't tell him. That was the simplest answer. Even if he loved her—and after his admission about not being with anyone else, she was certain he had to. She still couldn't wrap her mind around the fact that he'd been celibate, just as she had. But she hadn't wanted anyone else.

Even so, they'd never have a future together. She was destined to be queen and her people would never accept a shifter as her mate. If they did mate, he'd become a target. Maybe not at first but someone would eventually come after him.

And he probably wouldn't be willing to leave his family anyway. Even if he was, she couldn't tear him away from his pack. He was destined to be Alpha of his pack and whether he admitted it or not, he couldn't live without his loving family surrounding him. No, she'd just keep this to herself. If he hadn't been marked with the bonding symbol then he'd never have to know. Now she'd never be able to mate with anyone else but maybe that wasn't such a bad thing after all.

CHAPTER EIGHT

Nissa slipped on her light cardigan as she descended the stairs. Thomas was in the shower, giving her a little time to decompress and come to terms with...holy crap, she was mated to a shifter.

She didn't know if she'd ever come to terms with *that*.

As she entered the kitchen one of the women she'd met the night before was pressed up against the center island by a very lustful-looking shifter. The woman's name was Caro but she didn't know the male's name.

Her head snapped up as Nissa faltered in the entryway.

"I'm sorry. I... Uh, I'll come back." She started to backtrack when the dark-haired she-wolf pushed against the male's chest.

"No, please come in. I was just leaving anyway. Please tell Thomas I stopped by." She ducked out from under the male who had his arms caged around her.

Nissa bit her bottom lip as she looked at the tall shifter standing almost bereft in the middle of the room. "I'm sorry. I didn't mean to interrupt."

He shook his head and sighed. "Don't worry about it. We're just friends anyway," he muttered. "I'm Ethan by the way. I don't think we met last night."

Smiling, she crossed the distance and took his extended hand. She remembered him as the male staring at Caro. "Nissa."

"Nice to meet you. At least now I don't feel like the only freak outsider."

Her eyes widened at his words.

Almost immediately he held up his hands apologetically. "Shit. I didn't mean you were a freak or anything. I just meant it's nice to have another outsider." He scrubbed a hand over his face.

She couldn't help the smile that spread across her face. "It's fine, trust me. You must be the human who was...turned?"

He nodded, but his expression was still wary. "Yeah. Maybe don't tell Thomas I called you a freak?"

A burst of laughter escaped. "Stop worrying. I won't say anything though I doubt it would matter."

Ethan's eyebrows raised in disbelief. "I'm starting to learn that mated males don't always think straight around their females."

Her throat seized at that word. "We're not mates."

"Right." The shifter snorted, clearly not believing her. He headed for the stainless steel refrigerator. "Want a drink?"

"Sure, a bottled water would be great."

He grabbed one for himself then slid another one across to her. "So what's the deal between shifters and the fae? I know there's a big treaty that's going to be signed in a couple weeks but I don't get what's so big about it. We're all supernatural right?"

Stark sadness filled her at his questions. There was no simple answer. "You were a soldier before you were turned, right?"

Frowning, he nodded. "Yeah."

"The 'deal' between us is probably the same deal between most humans across the planet. Hundreds of years ago there was a misunderstanding or a skirmish between a few shifters and the fae. One thing led to another and an all-out war started. To this day I don't know who officially started the Great War. I honestly don't think anyone does. There's more to it than that but if you want our history in a nutshell, that's the very condensed version." Which was why she'd hidden her true identity when she'd met Thomas. She had a gift for masking herself that most didn't. Immediately she'd known what he was but instead of fear, she'd been fascinated by the handsome shifter.

He hadn't been scary or terrifying or without conscience like she'd been taught from the time she was able to walk. He'd been sweet and considerate and he'd made her ache every time he looked at her.

The first time they'd made love had been seared into her mind forever. He'd been so careful, so gentle, he'd completely wiped out her previously conceived notions of shifters. A monster wouldn't treat someone the way he'd treated her. At the time he'd thought she was simply human of course, but it was too late for her heart. She'd fallen for him. She'd been taught that shifters just took what they wanted and didn't care who they hurt. It had all been lies.

Ethan's eyebrows drew together. "That blows."

Nissa smiled at his vernacular. "Yes, it does."

He started to say more when his gaze trailed past her. "Thomas.

DANGEROUS CRAVING | 343

I'm sorry to stop by unannounced but I really need to talk to you."

Nissa clutched her bottle of water tightly and turned to face Thomas. "I'll leave you two alone then. It was nice meeting you, Ethan," she murmured to the other wolf.

As she hurried past him, Thomas stopped her with a light touch on her arm. Before she realized what he intended, he leaned down and brushed his lips over hers. Not a searing, dominating move, but more of a gentle caress. Light and sweet though still somehow incredibly sensual.

It sent a shock wave through her entire system. Her nipples tingled against the soft material of her cotton dress. She knew both men could probably smell her desire so she hurried from the room. As she strode away she instinctively pulled her sweater tighter around herself. She wasn't cold but it was the only bit of protection she had right now. Thomas was sharp and if he saw the mark on her body he'd ask about it. Of course, that was if he didn't figure out for himself what it was.

Once she was alone in the guest room, she pulled out her burner cell phone. She stared hard at it before trying to call her mother one more time.

Her sister answered again on the first ring. "Hello?"

Nissa started to hang up, but stopped. She couldn't run forever. "Why are you answering mom's phone?"

"Nissa! Where are you? We've been worried sick! Your place has been trashed and you haven't been answering your phone. Where are you calling from? I don't recognize this number." Kassia sounded genuinely worried as she spouted off questions, but Nissa steeled herself against any emotions.

She ignored all her sister's questions. "*Why* are you answering her phone?"

"Because someone tried to kill her! Most of the Gentry have barricaded themselves in their homes and we've tripled security here."

Nissa's heart thumped wildly against her chest. The fear in Kassia's voice was real. "Is she okay?"

"She's...resting for now. I'm scared, Nissa." Her voice cracked on the last word.

The tone of her sister's voice set alarm bells off in her head. Kassia rarely worried about anything. Or at least she didn't show it. "What happened?"

"One of the new chefs tried to kill her. He put slivers of pure iron in her food. With her already being so weakened it's amazing she survived at all."

Nissa gripped the phone tighter. "Who did this?"

"We think it's Venetia. She's gone missing and the man who poisoned mother had been influenced. The spell was very powerful and I can't imagine who else would be able to wield that kind of energy."

"Venetia," Nissa growled. Why hadn't she thought of her before? Her cousin was a power-hungry dissenter. She'd been causing trouble within the Gentry for the past decade. But she'd never been to her house so Nissa hadn't suspected her of being part of the break-in. If she was determined enough, though, anything was possible.

"A few members of the Gentry have come forward and admitted that Venetia has been trying to start a coup. She wants the throne and she doesn't want the treaty to go through."

Nissa sat on the edge of the bed. "And you don't know where she is?"

"No. Are you sure you're safe?"

Nissa laid back and covered her face with her arm. "Yes. I'm safe," she muttered. As safe as she could be. If anyone could protect her, it was Thomas. She wouldn't have come to see him otherwise. After the attempted attack last night she felt more uneasy than before, but she didn't want to worry her sister. The one thing she did know was that at least Kassia hadn't been behind it. Even if she'd influenced someone into trying to kill her, the spell wouldn't have lasted for the length of time it would take someone to fly from London to Miami. And Kassia was still in London. "Can I talk to mom?"

"Let me check... She's awake. Hold on."

Nissa finally relaxed when she heard her mother's voice. After her mother confirmed everything her sister had said, relief slid through her in potent waves. Despite their differences and her mother's almost Draconian view of their laws, she was still her mom. She wasn't sure what was going on with her cousin but she knew she had to get home.

And soon.

The strain in her sister's voice had been apparent, even though she'd tried to hide it. Their mother had been sick for a while and if she'd been poisoned, it was a miracle she was still hanging on.

No matter what else was going on, she had to get to her mother.

Thomas stared out at the ocean as if it could somehow give him the answers he wanted. He'd spent the morning with his father and had laid out his intentions to offer to mate with Nissa. Even if she was too good for him, he was too much of a selfish bastard to let her go.

He couldn't let her walk away from him. Especially not after what they'd shared last night. There could never be anyone else for him, something he'd realized long ago. Having her in his life again only drove the point home. Even if he had to give up his position in the pack and move across the ocean, he'd do it.

Hell, he figured it was the only way for them to stay together. Of course, that was if she accepted him. Which was why his father had decided to hold off on naming his replacement. As next in line to be Alpha, he'd have to step down and Nick would likely take his place. Something he knew his brother would hate. But that was the way pack law was sometimes.

The sound of the sliding glass door opening caused him to turn, though he knew who it was before he looked. He could sense or scent her anywhere.

Nissa stepped out onto the lanai wearing another one of those silky summer dresses that swayed around her hot body with each step she took. Unfortunately she also wore a sweater, which covered too much skin. Hell, anything covered too much. He wanted her naked and underneath him.

"Hey." She took a tentative step toward him so he moved over on his lounge chair and patted the seat.

"Sit with me."

The elongated chaise lounge was made for one person but he didn't want any space between them. As she started to sit on the edge, he grasped her hand and pulled her into his lap. Right where she belonged.

Instead of tensing, like he expected, she stretched out on him and settled between his open legs. Turned on her side, she laid her head on his shoulder and began tracing small circles on his chest. Something he remembered her doing when she was nervous.

His cock was rock-hard but there wasn't much he could do about that. If he was honest, he didn't care all that much. It was simply enjoyable to hold her like this. After so many years of missing her, having her in his arms was a small pleasure he'd missed more than he'd admit to anyone.

"What's on your mind?" he murmured against the top of her head and tightened his embrace around her.

She sighed and the sound was so heavy, a band tightened around his chest. "I finally spoke to my sister and mother."

He straightened at her words but didn't lessen his hold. "What did they say?"

"To make a long story short, my cousin Venetia is likely the one behind the attacks. They think she influenced a human to poison my mother and she's probably the one who sent someone after me. The spell cast on the human in my home was strong. Whoever did it has to be a member of the Gentry. My money is on her."

He frowned as he digested her words. "Is your mother okay?"

"I-I don't know. That's what I want to talk to you about. I'll be leaving soon. With my mom sick and Venetia probably stalking me in Miami, I need to get away from here. I'll be going tomorrow morning if I can get a flight."

Full-blown panic set in. It wormed its way directly into his bloodstream and coursed through his system with lava-like intensity. Even if she was leaving to get back to her ailing mother, he felt fucking pathetic. His muscles tightened and he had to fight to breathe at the thought of her gone. "I'm going with you."

She stiffened in his arms and stopped tracing designs on his chest. "Thomas—"

"I'm going, Nissa, so save any argument."

She pushed up to look at him and her blonde hair spilled across his chest. "Don't do this."

He could barely control the anxiety roaring through him. His wolf was just as pissed, clawing and swiping at his insides. "Do what? Admit that I love you and want to protect you? That I fucked up once and all I can do is promise not to repeat the past? Why won't you let me in your life, Nissa?"

"That's not it!" She shoved up fully now, her eyes blazing. "You're next in line to be Alpha of your pack and I'm next in line to be queen. On what planet could this ever work?"

He started to answer but she continued with her rapid fire argument. "It wouldn't. Even if you decided to give up your life here, you'd *hate* living with me. Treaty or not, my people would *never* accept you. You'd have no friends, no family nearby, and you'd constantly be looking over your shoulder. And when you weren't, I would be. I'd tear myself up with worry that one day, one of my own people would try to kill you. I'm sorry but I love you too much to put you through that."

The band that had been around his chest for so long snapped. "You love me?" He squeezed the question out.

She pushed out an exasperated sigh. "Did you hear anything I just said?"

"Only the important stuff." If he was with her he didn't give a shit about anything else. Let someone try to come after him. He could handle himself. He'd spent a century without her and it hadn't dulled his love and need for her. Living without her again was a hell of a lot worse than worrying some asshole might try to kill him. "At least let me come back with you to London. You shouldn't be traveling by yourself. Especially not right now." If he managed to convince her to let him travel to London with her to see her mother, he'd just never leave. Simple as that. He reached out and fingered a lock of her thick, blonde hair. When he did, he trailed a finger down her cheek.

She closed her eyes at his touch and swallowed hard. "Thomas." The word was barely a whisper.

He'd won. He could feel it straight to his core. She'd let him go with her. Not that it mattered at this point. He'd just follow her either way. Pride be damned.

As he started to lean forward, ready to capture her lips, a loud explosion from the direction of the beach jerked him back.

CHAPTER NINE

Nissa whipped around at the sound and started to get up but he grabbed her and rolled her under him on the chair. "Stay here."

He didn't bother to see if she'd obey him. Jumping up, he strode toward the beach with tensed muscles, his wolf right at the surface. Flames licked into the sky behind a sand dune but it was obvious someone had torched a few of his Adirondack chairs. If someone had done it to scare him, they'd only succeeded in pissing him off *and* announcing their presence. Yes, this would likely be the fae female after Nissa. Any sane shifter would have crept up on them using more stealth.

Breathing deeply, he scented the air. In addition to the smoldering fire, he scented something or someone foreign. Piney, earthy, with a slight mix of patchouli.

He quickly scanned the area. He didn't see any of his pack nearby but that didn't mean shit. If one of the younger members was out jogging or just playing they could become an unintended target.

Slowly, he took a step back only to run into Nissa.

She sidled up directly next to him, which only infuriated him more. "She's here," Nissa whispered.

His logical side knew she was capable of taking care of herself but his most primal side didn't care. It just wanted her safe. "How do you know?"

"It's got to be her," Nissa murmured as she clutched his arm. "We should go inside."

He ignored her. Running and hiding wasn't in his nature. "Does she smell like patchouli?"

"Yeah, why?"

"She's here then." Stepping in front of Nissa, he began moving back toward the sliding glass door. Their feet were silent against the stone patio but they were in plain view of anyone. He needed to get Nissa to safety

DANGEROUS CRAVING | 349

then he was going to take care of this problem. "Go inside and call my brothers using my cell."

"But—"

A burst of light flew past them. It crashed through the glass door, sending an explosion of shards flying everywhere. Without pause he grabbed Nissa and practically tackled her. He used his body as a shield and his arms to soften the impact as they slammed against the concrete. They rolled behind one of the stone columns on his porch, blocking them from view.

On instinct, he changed. His inner wolf took over in an instant, ripping his clothes to shreds. With the breaking and shifting of his bones, inescapable pain swelled through him. His muscles and tendons strained under the pressure. Just as quickly, it subsided as his body realigned.

In his animal state, everything was intensified. The salty ocean was potent but more than that, the danger nearby invaded his senses with perfect clarity. His wolf now associated that patchouli scent with the unknown threat and he knew exactly where it was coming from.

Growling low in his throat, he pawed the stone ground as he looked at Nissa. To his undying relief, she nodded and stayed crouched low.

If she followed him he couldn't focus on what he had to do. Whoever this bitch was, she was going to pay for putting his mate in danger. He and Nissa might not be technically bonded but she was his. Someone was going to suffer for this attack. Not to mention a faerie attacking them on a werewolf's turf so close to the treaty signing was insane. This was the kind of shit that could start another war. That all ended here and now.

With lightning speed he darted behind the next column. Just like vampires, his kind had impressive speed and agility. Since he was a born alpha, he was faster than most.

Peering from around the column, he saw a flash of movement behind one of the lounge chairs lining his Olympic-sized pool. At that moment, he wished it was a little darker. As it was, he didn't have many angles of approach.

Their would-be attacker could obviously harness energy as a weapon but she wasn't very good at controlling it. If she had been, she'd have hit them earlier.

"You stupid whore! I can't believe you're here with a shifter!" The loud voice was definitely female.

Thomas looked toward the other column where Nissa was still crouched behind. In his shifted form he could see her wings clearly. She had them pulled in tight against her back. By the tense lines of her body it looked like she might be contemplating doing something stupid.

This non-communication thing sucked. He howled loudly and her gaze snapped in his direction.

"It's Venetia," she whispered.

He knew what she was doing. Her cousin wouldn't be able to hear Nissa and any human wouldn't be able to at the distance they stood, but Thomas' extrasensory abilities were even stronger as a wolf.

"You're both trapped but if you give my whore cousin up, I'll let you live, lycan!"

If he'd been in his human form, he'd have laughed. Drawing on his strength, he darted to the next column. The patio wrapped around the pool in a giant L shape. All he had to do was get to the other side.

Then he'd be able to attack her. Sure he might get zapped, but he was strong enough to withstand more than a few blows.

"Have you lost your mind, Venetia? Trying to kill me and my mother?" Nissa's voice was loud and strong.

Good, keep the bitch talking. Thomas lunged toward the other column. Only two more to go.

Then he'd have the crazy faerie in his sights.

"Your mother is too weak to lead and you're just as pathetic. If I'd known you liked to slum it with these animals, I'd have killed you decades ago."

"Even if you kill me, Kassia is next in line, not you."

"She's easily disposable. Your entire family has gotten weak these past few years. You're hurting the Gentry... God, how can you stand the stench of these animals? After what they did to our people?"

Thomas guessed someone she loved had been killed during the Great War. Undeniable pain laced her voice. Even though she was obviously unhinged, Thomas could sympathize with anyone who'd lost family during that time. Hell, if the enforcer could mate with a half fae after faeries had killed his parents, everyone else should be able to get over their own bullshit. The war had ended centuries ago and no one from this generation had started it.

"That was a long time ago," Nissa called out.

Thomas made it to the next column. He was fast and sometimes indiscernible to the human eye when he moved, but another supernatural being should be able to see him. Not to mention the column didn't exactly hide all of him in his wolf form and he was a giant black animal. Hard to miss if someone was looking. But so far she hadn't tried to fire at him again.

Even if she did, her fire wasn't laced with silver. He'd burn but he'd heal. As he inhaled again, he realized she was a lot closer than he realized. Peering around the column, he froze for a moment.

She wasn't hiding behind anything anymore. Standing boldly out in the open, all her attention was solely focused on the column Nissa stood behind. The faerie was tall like Nissa. Maybe a little taller, probably six feet one.

Her long blonde hair was pulled back into two tight braids and she wore a pair of cargo pants and a tight tank top. She looked like a fierce Amazon warrior. In her left hand a flaming red ball of fire hovered. Her entire body was tense, ready to spring.

Thomas crouched back on his haunches. Using all his lower body strength, he darted out from behind the column and lunged.

Gasping, she turned and threw the ball of fire at him. Flames singed the back of his coat as he sailed through the air but it didn't stop him.

She dodged out of the way as he landed on a solid wood lounge chair. It cracked under the impact but he used it as a springboard.

His front paws slammed square in the middle of her chest, knocking her on her back. A scream tore from her throat and she raised her hand to strike him but he snapped down on her wrist. He tasted blood and felt tiny bones break beneath his grasp.

She screamed again, this time louder and more shrill. When she did, he raised back, ready to tear her head off.

As he went in for the kill, an incredibly powerful gust of wind knocked him off her. He rolled to the side, ready to strike again but stopped when he saw Nissa.

She was the one who'd pushed him off.

With her hands held out in front of her, a bright green flame — the same color as her eyes — burned in both her hands. It was like fire but somehow different. Like pure energy.

Venetia scooted back against the concrete. "No, please don't — "

But Nissa didn't listen. Her eyes were glassy as she concentrated on Venetia. Before her cousin finished her plea, the powerful stream of energy burst from Nissa's hands.

Thomas stared in shock as Venetia turned to stone. She held up her arms as if to protect herself but it was too late. Her body transformed rapidly, posed with an expression of utter anguish.

He snapped his attention to Nissa only to see her collapse into a rumpled heap. Without pause he shifted back to his human form. His muscles and bones strained under the pressure until he found himself on all fours trying to catch his breath. Shoving his discomfort aside, he hurried to Nissa's side.

Her eyes were closed and her skin unnaturally pale. Lifting her into his arms, he held her tight against him and checked for a pulse. At least her heartbeat was strong. It was a miracle because she looked like death.

"Nissa. Please wake up." He shook her lightly as he hurried inside, desperate for her to open her eyes. Mindful of the glass shards, he didn't stop until he'd stretched her out on the center island. Seeing her this way was like déjà vu. Barely half a year ago his friend Paz had been injured and laid out just like this.

But she'd survived.

And Nissa would too. "Nissa, God, please wake up." He cupped her head and held one of her hands.

When she lightly squeezed, some of his panic subsided. But not much. *Wake up, wake up, wake up.* He chanted the words over and over in his head.

Her eyes flew open suddenly, the sight stealing his breath. "What the hell was that?" The words came out harsher and louder than he intended. He cringed but a ghost of a smile played across her face.

"I didn't have time to warn you. I'm fine, I promise. Just really tired. I'll need to rest for a few hours." She sounded strained as she spoke.

Scooping her up, he headed for the stairs. "What was that?"

"I can only turn other fae to stone. It won't kill her but she'll be stuck like that until I change her back. I'm going to let my mother judge her."

He'd known she was gifted but he'd had no clue what the extent of her powers were. "Why did you collapse? And are sure you're okay?" He wanted to call his aunt Caro to check on Nissa.

There she went with that smile again. Soft and loving, as if she hadn't just turned someone to stone then passed out looking like she had a date with death. "It takes a lot of energy to wield that kind of power. I've only done it once before and I was knocked out for a day. It's not something I can do on a whim."

His throat seized at the thought. If she'd been unconscious for a day he'd have gone absolutely mad. "Then why did you wake up now?"

She frowned for a moment and he saw the moment the answer registered with her. But she shook her head. "I-I don't know."

She was lying. He didn't know why, but he could read it clearly on her face, could scent it rolling off her. "Nissa..." He trailed off when her eyes drifted shut again.

Sighing, he laid her on his bed then slid in next to her and pulled her back tight against his chest. He needed to call his Alpha and clean up the aftermath of Venetia's destruction, but right now all he cared about was holding her close.

CHAPTER TEN

Nissa stirred as she felt the soft brush of something — lips — tease against her neck. With her eyes closed, she smiled. Thomas' spicy, masculine scent was unmistakable. "What are you doing?" she murmured.

"If you have to ask, I must be doing it wrong." His voice was directly next to her ear. He was so close she felt his hot breath caress her skin like a soft breeze. When his teeth tugged her earlobe gently, she didn't bother to bite back a moan. The nip of his teeth made her inner walls clench with need. She desperately wanted to feel him inside her, thrusting and taking.

The bed dipped and Thomas' hard body stretched out next to hers. When his muscular chest rubbed against her bare arm and the side of her breast, it registered she was naked. She opened her eyes and looked down. "When did you undress me?"

"While you were sleeping." That deep voice should be illegal it was so hypnotic.

She stretched her arms above her head and turned slightly to face him. Lying on his side, one elbow was bent as he propped up and looked down at her.

"Pervert," she said, trying not to smile.

"I never claimed to be otherwise." Pulling the duvet back farther, he placed his big hand on her bare stomach in a proprietary manner. "How do you feel?"

Testing her motor functions, she wiggled her toes and rolled her ankles for a moment. "Fine. Still a little tired though. How long have I been out?" Drapes covered the windows, keeping the room plunged in a muted dimness. She could see it was still light outside, but it was impossible to tell how late it was.

"A few hours." He trailed one of his fingers over her abdomen and teased her belly button.

354 | SAVANNAH STUART

Under his touch, her muscles clenched.

When he ran his finger over the sensitive area above her mound, she tensed even more. She didn't want his finger or much foreplay, she just wanted to feel him inside her.

Spreading her legs in invitation, she started to push the cover completely off when abruptly he stilled.

His hand tightened against her stomach but then he quickly withdrew it. Sighing, he said, "I'm sorry, I know you need to rest."

She might be tired but she was also incredibly turned on. When he started to get up, she reached out for his arm. "Stay with me for a little while?"

With a clenched jaw, he nodded.

She didn't know why he was holding back, but she didn't plan to let him. Turning away from him, she smiled against the pillow as he pulled her tight against his body. She loved the feel of him holding her, didn't know if she'd ever get tired of that strong embrace. And she hated that soon she wouldn't get to experience it anymore.

With her marked shoulder against the bed and her hair draped across it, the Celtic marking was hidden. And she didn't think he'd be looking for it anyway. Not when she could practically smell the lust coming off him.

His muscular chest pressed against her back and the feel of his erection was unmistakable. Even if he wanted to, he couldn't deny how much he desired her right now. He only wore a pair of boxers, but he'd taken the privilege of completely undressing her, panties and all.

And she planned to take full advantage of that by teasing him. Wiggling her bottom over his covered erection, her smile grew even wider when he groaned under his breath.

"You okay?" she asked quietly while trying not to laugh.

"Fine." It sounded as if his jaw were wired shut.

One of his hands was thrown across her middle so she placed her own over his. Threading her fingers through his, she slowly slid his hand lower until he cupped her mound. Oh yeah, that was the perfect spot.

"Nissa, I'm trying to let you sleep. You've been through a lot." His voice sounded strained even as his middle finger slowly began to rub over her clit.

In response she pushed back against him and didn't bother to keep her movements subtle. She rubbed her butt over his covered erection slowly and seductively. "Take your boxers off."

After a moment, he withdrew his hand. Behind her she could feel him rustling around and knew he was doing as she'd said. While her body mourned the loss of his touch, she smiled in triumph when he pressed up against her and this time all she felt was his hard cock.

She tried to move against him but he placed a dominating hand on her hip. "Don't move, Nissa."

Though her body strained to writhe against him, she did as he said. She was already wet but the underlying note of command in his voice sent another rush of heat between her legs.

She was slick and wet and willing. "Please touch me."

Since she couldn't see him she couldn't be sure, but she thought she felt him smile against her hair.

The firm hand on her hip slid up to her breast and cupped it. But he didn't make an attempt to do anything else. "I *am* touching you," he murmured.

She growled in frustration. "You know what I mean."

"Hmm." He didn't say anything else, just held her like that.

Gritting her teeth, she decided not to give in. Instead she slightly lifted her leg and placed it on top of his. When she did, she opened herself up to him. The head of his cock inadvertently breached her opening.

Barely.

What she wouldn't give to have him push fully inside her.

Thomas chuckled against the top of Nissa's head. "Always so impatient."

Without warning, he thrust into her. She gasped at the intrusion but he didn't give her time to get used to it. He drove into her again and again. She was slick and tight and he knew it would take all his restraint not to come right away. After almost losing her, he still felt unhinged, the need to mark her overwhelming.

The sensation of her clenching around him raced through his entire body, making it difficult for him to think about anything else but her tight sheath.

He actually had to clamp down on the need to come, on the need to score her flesh with his canines, marking her for everyone to know she was his. His balls pulled up so tight it bordered on painful.

Nissa panted and moaned as he thrust in and out of her. Her inner walls clenched tighter and tighter, letting him know how close she was.

Maybe he was being selfish. He knew how tired she was, but he wanted to prolong this. Hell, he needed it. She was alive and in his arms. He stopped moving and kept himself buried inside her, all the way to the hilt.

If he could, he'd stay like this for hours, deep in the pure essence of her. Even after the time they'd spent together he kept thinking that somehow this was a really messed up dream. That Mother Nature was just screwing with him and he was going to wake up and she'd be gone again.

"You're such a tease," Nissa groaned testily.

No, this wasn't a dream. In his dreams Nissa never had an attitude. Which made real life that much better. He loved it when she got feisty with him.

Reaching over her, he began teasing her clit again. She sighed contentedly when he did. "Touch your breasts," he whispered into her ear. He needed more hands to touch her everywhere.

He felt her shudder at his words.

While he tweaked and slowly rubbed his finger over her sensitive bundle of nerves, she cupped one of her breasts.

Thankfully he had excellent vision in the darkness. Despite the dim room he watched as she gently held the perfectly rounded globe. As she started rubbing her thumb over her hardened nipple, he nuzzled her neck. Seeing her like this brought out his most animalistic side.

When he raked his teeth over her sensitive skin, her inner walls tightened around him. The small action made his inner wolf roar. What he wouldn't give to be able to mark her right now.

To sink his teeth into her just enough to claim her. To bond them.

But he couldn't do that. Even if his inner animal wanted to, his human side could never take that choice from her. Things were still too fresh between them. He wanted to take things slower, prove he'd always be there for her.

Then he'd mark her and bind them forever. Everyone would know she belonged to him. And vice versa.

Suddenly her back straightened and she jerked against him. Her climax came fast and hard and was totally unexpected.

Her inner walls clamped around his erection, squeezing him relentlessly. Increasing his rhythm, he rubbed her clit faster. As he did, she shouted out his name. Reaching out, she clawed against the sheet as he slammed into her, over and over.

The sound of his name on her lips had always made him crazy. Now was no different.

"Yes, yes." She repeated it as her orgasm rippled through her.

Without giving her time to react he pulled out and flipped her on her back. She opened her mouth but to say what, he'd never know. Slanting his mouth over hers, he pushed into her once again.

DANGEROUS CRAVING | 357

Immediately her legs wrapped around his waist as she met him stroke for stroke.

He increased his rhythm, pumping and pushing until finally he exploded inside her.

As he released into her, he pulled his head back and let out the groan clawing at his throat. Filling her this way gave him a primal satisfaction that almost scared him. Waiting for her was the best damn thing he'd ever done. There was no one else in the world for him but Nissa.

He continued driving into her like a male possessed until she'd finally wrung everything from him. Breathing hard, he collapsed onto his elbows above her.

Smiling, she reached up and gently cupped his face. The expression in her eyes was filled with satisfaction and happiness, exactly the way she used to stare at him after they'd made love.

His throat clenched, knowing that he'd put that look on her face.

Leaning down, he kissed her again but this time it wasn't hungry or needy. He feathered light kisses all over her face. Her forehead, cheeks, then finally her mouth.

As his tongue danced with hers, his cock started to harden again and her inner walls once again tightened around him.

Chuckling, she pulled back a fraction. "I think I might be too tired," she whispered almost drowsily.

Gently, he withdrew from her and pulled the covers tight around her. But he didn't leave her. He just gathered her in his arms and waited for her to fall asleep.

Nissa opened her eyes and stretched her arms above her head. The room was empty and when she rolled over and saw the time, she winced.

It was almost seven. Good Lord, she'd slept most of the day away.

After showering and changing into jeans and a T-shirt, she went in search of Thomas.

In the kitchen she found Caro and a young girl bent over a textbook and open spiral notebook at the center island. She thought she'd met the girl at the party, but couldn't remember her name. There had been so many pack members there. Nissa hovered in the doorway as she watched the two of them, unsure if she should interrupt.

Caro looked up first and smiled. "Hey, I was wondering if you'd sleep the whole day through. Thomas told us about what happened."

The giant stone statue outside had probably invited a lot of questions so she didn't blame him. Nissa took a few steps inside. "Hi. Uh, where's Thomas?"

The older woman's smile didn't falter. "Meeting with his father and brothers. Pack business. He left not too long ago so he'll probably be a few hours."

"Do you mind if I grab something to eat?"

Caro laughed at her question. "Of course not. Athena wanted to do her homework over here and I just wanted to see my nephew. Trust me, you have more business being here than we do. Take whatever you want."

Nissa wasn't sure how to respond so she ignored it and hurried toward the fridge. After losing so much energy earlier she was beyond famished. As she stared at the contents of Thomas' fridge, she couldn't help but overhear Caro and the young girl's conversation. They were talking about perfectly mundane family stuff but it made her ache.

While she loved her mother and sister, they'd never been a particularly warm family. Not even close. After she'd run away — and subsequently met Thomas — her mother had kept a much tighter rein on her. She'd been convinced Nissa needed more discipline in her life.

Sighing, she pulled out a couple containers and peered inside. When all she found was different meat products, she frowned.

"Uncle Thomas probably doesn't have anything you'd like but we can order take-out if you want," the young she-wolf said as she slid her book away from her.

"Athena," Caro murmured, "leave her alone."

"It's fine. I'm sure I'll be able to find something." She smiled reassuringly at the young girl who only blushed and returned to her book.

Nissa slid the containers back into the fridge and ignored the emptiness filling her. The sensation had nothing to do with hunger, either.

It was sadness. Plain and simple.

Thomas' family was hanging out at his house for no other reason than they wanted to spend time with him. No one in her family ever simply stopped by. And she didn't either. Her family always called first and there was usually a purpose to the visit. Never just to say hi.

It made the differences between their families suddenly and blindingly clear. What had she been thinking? She'd known from the start this could never work.

Swallowing back the lump in her throat, she mumbled an excuse and hurried back to her room. Since she hadn't technically unpacked, it didn't take long to gather her things.

No matter what Thomas said, she couldn't stay here and she couldn't drag him back to Europe with her. His family meant too much to him.

It was so obvious. No matter what he said she couldn't tear him away from his pack. They were the only family he'd ever known and the thought of bringing him to meet and live with her distant family was almost laughable.

If it wasn't so heartbreaking.

She had to get out of here before Thomas came back. No way would she be able to go through with this in front of him. He'd just talk her out of it and she would cave because she loved him too much. Fighting back tears, she fished out her cell phone and called a taxi company. Leaving this way would piss Thomas off but in the end he'd thank her. Maybe not now, but eventually he'd get over this and realize how right she was.

Love and attraction weren't enough sometimes. Not when the real world was glaring so bright in her face. Besides, real love shouldn't result in making her mate sad or endanger his life.

Cutting ties now would be so much easier than dealing with years and years of resentment. In the end, she knew that was what would happen.

When the taxi company told her they could pick her up in twenty minutes, she allowed herself a small moment of relief. By the time she got to the airport and left, Thomas would just be getting home. She'd be able to send someone to pick up Venetia later so that wasn't even an issue.

Hating herself for leaving this way, she quickly wrote him a note, then fled the house like a thief in the night. She knew it was totally the coward's way out but the thought of facing him and having "the" conversation with him was too much. At least this way she wouldn't have to take the memory of another argument with her. Or the agony in his expression before she walked away.

Not that the knowledge was much of a consolation. Her heart was shredded to ribbons at the thought of never seeing Thomas again.

CHAPTER ELEVEN

Two Weeks Later

Nissa smoothed her hands down her black pants as she exited the elevator to the fourth floor of the designated building for the treaty meeting. They'd picked New York City as their destination and chosen neutral ground in the form of a perfectly bland office building. Located in the middle of Manhattan, it was owned by humans none of them knew. Despite the cool temperature in the hallway, her palms were clammy.

Today was the day.

With her mother dead, she was the interim queen and would soon be meeting with The Council. Technically only two out of the eight Council members would be at the meeting, but they'd been permitted to bring Alphas from four of the strongest packs. That meant Thomas' father would be at the meeting. Hence her ridiculously damp palms. She was so ashamed at the way she'd left Thomas, then ignored all his attempts to contact her.

"You okay?" her sister whispered as she gave her hand a small squeeze.

Swallowing hard, she flicked a quick glance in Kassia's direction but she was mindful of the six other Gentry members walking with them. She couldn't appear weak in front of them or she'd have to deal with the fallout later. Even if she hated all this political crap it was unfortunately her life now. "Of course."

But she wasn't. Nausea swirled inside her mercilessly. She'd skipped breakfast in lieu of three cups of steaming hot, black coffee. Now the bitter liquid swirled around in her stomach like acid.

After the way she'd sneaked out of Thomas' house in the middle of the night weeks ago, the thought of seeing anything or anyone related to him made her shiver. Her traitorous nipples hardened at the thought of his callus-roughened hands or sensuous mouth teasing them.

He'd been so insistent that everything between them would work out and he'd make a place in her life but she knew better. Instead of arguing or dragging things out, she'd simply left. Yes, she was the worst kind of coward but she'd needed to get to her dying mother and she hadn't had the energy to go up against a dominating man like Thomas.

And no matter what he said, she couldn't allow him to suffer throughout the rest of their life together. She loved him too much and she knew he'd eventually resent her for taking him away from his pack. His resentment would be worse than anything.

She steeled herself as one of her men opened the heavy oak door to the conference room. Entering before her sister, she nearly stumbled in her heels but thankfully caught herself.

Thomas sat at the table with five other shifters. And they were all hulking. No wonder her people had lost the war all those centuries ago. All these men were giant predators.

Her throat tightened as his dark eyes narrowed on her. Oh yeah, he was pissed. Beyond angry. And she didn't blame him.

Forcing herself to breathe, she looked at the two Council members she'd held a video conference with the week before and smiled at them. "Gentlemen, it's nice to finally meet you in person."

Both Adama and Brenner nodded politely at her as they stood. "Nissa," Brenner said first. Then he motioned toward the other males. "This is Calder, Haki, Isandro, and you've already met Thomas. We heard about what happened with your cousin and since the Lazos pack gave you protection, we granted the request that Thomas come in place of his father even though he is not yet an Alpha. We hope this is acceptable?"

She nodded stiffly. "Of course. My people are very grateful for the protection afforded me by the Lazos pack. They were incredibly generous and we are in their debt." Nissa couldn't believe her voice didn't shake. Her insides felt like jelly yet somehow she managed to sound completely unaffected. Or maybe that was just wishful thinking on her part.

At her words the two Council members visibly relaxed. One of them motioned toward the seats across from them at the long, rectangular table. "If you're ready to start, we are."

Gratefully she took a seat and barely refrained from collapsing onto it. Her sister and four of her men sat, but two stood back guarding the door.

Brenner lifted a briefcase from the floor and spread a handful of papers on the table.

Even though she was doing her best to avoid looking at Thomas she could feel his heat-seeking gaze searing into her. Her underarms dampened and beads of sweat popped up across her forehead and down her spine. Inwardly cursing him for being here and throwing her off her game, she slipped off her slim-fitting, two-button jacket.

As she turned to drape it across the back of her chair, her sister gasped. Nissa's back went ramrod straight as she swiveled back to face the shifters.

Under the table, Kassia grasped her leg in a death grip. "You have the bondmate mark? When did this happen?" she whispered.

Gritting her teeth, she slightly shook her head. The shifters could all hear her no matter how quiet Kassia tried to be. "Not now," she said through gritted teeth. She'd been wearing sweaters and jackets the past couple weeks. *How could she have been so stupid?* She wanted to put her jacket back on, but couldn't without looking obvious or crazy.

But her sister didn't listen. "I didn't know you'd *bonded* with anyone. Holy shit, Nissa. *Who?*" Her voice was so low Nissa could barely hear her, but she knew the others across the table could. Even if they politely pretended to ignore them, they'd just heard every single word.

Thomas loudly and obnoxiously cleared his throat. "Permission to speak, Council?"

The two older wolves looked at each other, then him curiously, before nodding.

"I thought the queen was to be married soon. I'm just curious where her mate is. If we're all signing this treaty shouldn't *he* be here?" The others might have missed it but the slight cut of sarcasm wasn't lost on her. Neither was the angry — betrayed — glare he sent her way.

"Nissa will not be taking a mate anytime in the near future. She's called off her impending nuptials," one of her councilors answered for her.

"Then why does she bear the bonding mark on her shoulder?" His question silenced the entire room.

She could feel everyone's eyes on her but she kept her gaze trained on Thomas. "How is that important to this meeting?" To her horror, her voice shook.

He paused for a moment, as if weighing his words. "If you're mated we should know his politics and views on shifters. We have a right to know who he is."

Brenner, Adama and the three other Alphas nodded and murmured their agreement.

DANGEROUS CRAVING | 363

Traitorous tears pricked her eyes. She couldn't answer him in front of everyone. How could he do this to her now? Embarrass her like this? She would not cry in front of all these people. Her mother would have never showed such emotion. Or any emotion at all. Neither would her sister. More proof she was just an imposter and had no business as queen. Feeling sick, she abruptly stood. "If you'll excuse me for a moment, I need to confer with my sister."

Let them all think what they wanted. She needed to get the hell away from him so she could think straight. Or simply breathe. As she strode down the hallway she felt Kassia fast on her heels.

She turned to speak to her, but came face to face with Thomas instead.

"Where the hell are you going?" he growled.

Without looking at him, she tried to yank away, but he just pulled her tighter against him until she was flush against the length of his body and there was nowhere for her to run. Not that she really wanted to. Being next to him felt like coming home.

"Hey." Kassia shouted from down the hall as she raced toward them. "Get your paws off her."

Nissa held up her free hand. "It's fine."

"Damn right it's fine," Thomas muttered. He glanced around, then dragged her toward another door. They'd rented the entire floor but she didn't like being manhandled.

"Get your hands off me." She tried to pull away but he only released her once he'd dragged her into another bare room with the same style conference table as the one they'd been in. He locked the door with an ominous click.

"You're mated?" His words were a low, feral growl.

He didn't realize it was him. She didn't know if she should be relieved or not. "What do you know about my kind's mating rituals?"

"I heard what your sister whispered to you. You've become fucking *mated* in the past two weeks? How could you do this to me? *To us*? How could you let someone else fucking touch you?" His voice rose with each word and he advanced on her fast.

Retreating, she kept going until the backs of her legs hit the table. He just kept coming until he caged her in. "Who is he?"

She couldn't hold his dark gaze. Looking at his chest, she bit her bottom lip. He was already pissed and she knew he'd freak when she admitted the truth.

"Who. Is. He." His angry words sent a chill through her. She'd never heard this particular tone from him before and it actually frightened her.

"Why?" Anything to delay the inevitable.

She was vaguely aware of her sister banging on the door but she tuned out Kassia.

"Because I'm going to kill him." He breathed out the threat so low she wasn't sure she'd heard him right.

"You don't mean that."

His jaw was clenched tight and he still didn't back up to give her space. "Why'd you bond with someone else, Nissa?" Raw pain laced his words and she realized he truly had no clue about the fae's mating process.

"The fae don't have a choice who our bondmates are. Mates, yes, if we so choose. But we can technically leave—or divorce—our mates. With bondmates, there's no choice." She turned slightly to the side and pushed her hair out of the way to reveal the small Celtic knotting symbol on her shoulder. "This happens once we bond with our destined mate. I didn't have a choice."

He glared at her shoulder. "You chose to fuck him though, didn't you?"

She almost jerked back at his words, but more than anger, she could actually feel his physical pain. Reaching out, she placed a light hand on his chest. Despite the tension in the air, she felt the overwhelming need to soothe him. He tensed but surprisingly didn't pull away. She racked her brain, trying to find the right words. There weren't any so she just blurted it out. "This is from you, Thomas. I got this after we made love."

"You haven't been with anyone else?"

She shook her head.

A ragged sigh tore from him and he cursed under his breath. For a moment he just stared at her. "Why didn't we..." He trailed off as if answering his own question. "We didn't bond before because I never came inside you."

Still afraid her voice would shake, she simply nodded at his words.

Relief filled his expression. "Did you know we'd bond?"

Her eyes widened. "Of course not."

"But you left Miami *knowing* we were bonded." It wasn't a question.

"Yes." Even if she wanted to, she couldn't deny the obvious.

Her sister continued banging on the door, throwing out curses, but they both ignored her.

"Why'd you leave without even a fucking goodbye then? And that letter was pathetic." The words came out raspy and angry.

Shame filled her because he was right. She should have stayed and stood her ground, but deep down she hadn't been sure she could actually leave him. The most selfish part of her wanted to bring him home with her but it wouldn't have been fair to him. "Because I don't want you to give up your life and family for me. You'd eventually resent living with me and constantly looking over your shoulder."

"Don't you have any faith in this treaty?"

"Of course I do. But being mated to the queen—before or after the treaty—would make you a constant target."

"So *you're* a constant target?"

"Sort of. I mean, not always, but if Venetia's attack on me is any example, do you really want that kind of life?"

"I want the choice, Nissa. And I choose you."

Her throat tightened. "What about your pack? I see how close you are to them." And they were absolutely wonderful. She hated the idea of taking him away from all of that love.

"You'll be my family. I'm a big boy, Nissa, and I know what being away from them will mean. I still choose *you*."

Unbidden tears rolled down her cheeks. Even though she tried, she couldn't control them. Why did he have to say the perfect thing?

"Ah, shit." He reached up and cupped her face, using his thumbs to brush away the wetness. When his lips pressed softly against her cheeks, she shut her eyes tight and tried to pull away. To block him out. It was an impossible task.

"Why do you have to say all the right things, Thomas?" she muttered.

He ignored her attempts and wrapped his arms around her waist. When he did, she gave in and laid her head against his chest. She savored his strength and warmth. "I was never with anyone during our separation—not the first one and not this recent one." He'd confessed his celibacy to her and deserved to know she'd been unable to be with anyone else either.

"It wouldn't have mattered if you had." But she could still hear the relief in his voice, could feel it in the way he shuddered. His chin rested on top of her head as he stroked her hair and down her back. "Were you ever going to tell me we'd bonded?"

She was silent, not wanting to admit the truth.

He sighed against her. "It's okay, I'd have found out anyway. The world is only so big and I'd have found you wherever you went. I'm not letting you—*us*—go that easily, sweetheart, so get used to having me in your life."

She smiled against his chest, but didn't respond. She loved this male.

"How have you been since your mother's death?" he continued.

Awful. She shrugged instead of telling him the truth. "I haven't had much time to mourn. There's been too much to do." Political, mind-numbing stuff she had no interest in. But duty required it.

As if he read her mind, he said, "Do you even *want* to be queen?"

Pulling back slightly, she looked at him and shook her head. "No." Not even a little bit. Being queen had never been her dream. She was an artist and that's all she'd ever wanted to be. Even that aspect of herself she'd hidden from most of her people.

"Then why don't you step down?" His gravelly voice wrapped around her, sending delicious shivers rolling through her.

"I don't have a choice."

"You *always* have a choice." His heated statement made her head snap back.

"You don't—"

"Understand? I'm stepping down as next in line to be Alpha of my pack, Nissa. I do understand. Don't force yourself into a life you don't want. I'll be happy anywhere I'm with you, but will you be happy as queen?"

No. Actually, it was a big, fat no. She hadn't even been able to judge her cousin. That had been handled by her mother. The last order she'd given had been for the statue of Venetia to be destroyed. Nissa knew her mother had wanted her to give the order but sentencing someone to death—no matter how evil—wasn't something she wanted to live with. It wasn't who she was.

Nissa had hated every single day of the last two weeks and not just because she'd been separated from Thomas or because she'd been mourning her mother. Where her sister took to politics like a fish to water, she felt wildly out of place in all the meetings and dealing with the Gentry and their petty demands. She missed her quiet townhome in Dublin, she missed painting, she missed her peaceful Sunday mornings, and more than anything she missed Thomas.

"You make it sound so easy," she whispered.

"It is easy." He lowered his voice to a dark whisper at the same time he bent his head.

His lips covered hers in a hungry fervor. As their tongues danced and intertwined, another loud bang sounded on the door.

"Nissa? Are you okay?" It was Kassia.

"Go away!" Thomas shouted.

"I'm fine!" she said at the same time.

DANGEROUS CRAVING | 367

It was the wrong time and totally inappropriate but she didn't care. She'd never thought of herself as animalistic but at that moment she embraced her most primal side.

She desperately needed to feel Thomas inside her. Needed to feel his hot, naked skin against hers.

And she wanted him to mark her, to take her the way she'd fantasized about for decades.

Arching her back against him, she scooted back on the table and spread her legs wider before wrapping them around him.

Thomas' breathing was erratic as he looked down at her. "Why didn't the bonding mark appear on my shoulder?"

"I have no idea," she said truthfully. It could be because he was a shifter or it could be because they hadn't undergone the fae's traditional bonding ceremony. Or more likely, it could be because he hadn't marked her. There was no science to this and it was a mystery that a full-blooded fae had bonded with a full-blooded werewolf in the first place.

"Will it eventually?"

"Does it matter?" she whispered.

"I want it." His voice was just as low as hers.

The admission surprised and touched her. She'd expected him to be averse to the marking. Before she could respond, he kissed her again. This time it was deeper and there was nothing tender about it. This kiss was a soul-searching, primitive one that took her breath away.

Clutching his shoulders, she used him to balance as she tightened her legs around him even harder.

His hands slid under her silky sleeveless top and gently held her breasts. He pulled the cups of her bra down and lightly rubbed her nipples in a teasing, erotic manner.

Feeling like an animal in heat, she arched and writhed harder against him. Her inner walls clenched and heat built low in her belly with the need for him to fill her. She wanted his cock to slide deep into her. Was dying to feel that thickness already.

When she felt her shoulder tingle and almost burn, she knew this time they'd complete the bonding process.

Thomas jerked his head back abruptly, leaving her dazed.

"What?" Her gaze narrowed on him.

"I can feel my canines extending."

"What's the problem?"

"I'm ready to mount and mark you," he muttered, sounding disgusted with himself.

368 | SAVANNAH STUART

She blinked once. "Don't you want..." she trailed off, not understanding.

"I want to mark you so much I ache, but I'm not going to take you on a conference table with a dozen people waiting next door."

"I don't care."

"I do."

Before she could respond the door swung open and Kassia stormed in. Two guards stood behind her, their eyes wide. Her sister faltered as she stared at Nissa and Thomas. Whatever her sister thought about them, it was obvious their embrace was mutual.

Nissa's hands still dug into his shoulders and Thomas' hands were shoved high up her top.

"Shit," Kassia muttered. Instead of leaving, she turned back to the slack-jawed guards. "We'll just be a moment." Then she shut it and leaned against it. Her green eyes were almost a mirror of Nissa's, just a little darker. Right now they were wide with shock. "I take it you and Thomas are more than just 'friends'?"

Nissa nodded and fought the heat creeping across her cheeks. She'd lied to her sister about why she'd gone to Miami for his protection. "Yes."

Her blonde eyebrows arched. "So is this who you bonded with?"

"Yes."

Kassia shook her head, sending her long blonde hair swishing around her shoulders. "Holy shit. I didn't even think that was possible."

"Well it is," Thomas growled.

Kassia held up her hands in a gesture of mock surrender. "I don't care who or what you are as long as you treat my sister right. If that ever changes, I'll kill you myself."

At the deadly edge in her sister's voice, Nissa glared. Kassia was definitely the stronger of the two, at least physically. Her sister had trained with the fae warriors from a young age. Since she was royalty she'd never been inducted into the private sect. And Nissa didn't like anyone threatening her mate, no matter how harmless. "Stop it, Kas."

Ignoring her, Kassia sauntered over to the table and leaned against it. "Think you two could untangle for a few minutes so we can talk?"

Thomas actually looked uncomfortable for a moment as he glanced down at their bodies. Withdrawing his hands, he smoothed Nissa's top down but didn't move far out of her embrace. She tried to subtly adjust her bra but finally gave up the pretense and pushed the cups back into place—and ignored her sister's muted snicker. Thomas threw an arm around her shoulder as they turned to face Kassia.

"Everyone's getting a little restless in the other room. Is this treaty still going to happen?" Kassia looked back and forth between the two of them with raised eyebrows.

Nissa nodded as she melded tighter against Thomas. "Yes, but—"

"You don't want to be queen?" Kassia finished.

Her shoulders relaxed. "Not even a little bit."

"I know. I've known for a while."

"Why didn't you ever say anything?"

Her shoulders lifted slightly. "I'm the youngest. It's not my place."

"So...*you* want to be queen?" Please say yes. Nissa had never considered the possibility, would have never wanted to put all that responsibility on her sister.

Kassia nodded tightly. "Yes. So many changes need to be made right now and I don't want to miss an opportunity to bring true peace between our kinds. I think I could implement..." she trailed off, suddenly looking unsure of herself. "I don't mean to speak out of place."

Shrugging off Thomas' embrace, Nissa stepped forward and grasped her sister's hands. "You're not. I've always admired how well you stand up to the Gentry and immerse yourself in our politics. Sometimes I feel guilty because all of it doesn't mean more to me. I just had no idea you wanted this role."

"Well you'll be taking a big step toward bringing our races together by bonding with him." She nodded slightly back toward Thomas. "A member of the royalty bonding with an Alpha is the perfect alliance to solidify this treaty."

A ghost of a smile touched Nissa's lips. "Always the diplomat."

Kassia smiled and blushed. "I can't help it."

"What do you think the councilors will say?"

"I think they already have a pretty good idea what was going on in here between you two and truthfully, I think the only thing anyone cares about is having this treaty signed *today*."

"Do you want to sign it?" Nissa asked.

Kassia jerked back slightly. "I have no right."

Nissa slid off the ornate platinum ring her mother had given her. The huge marquis-cut emerald stone in the middle of it twinkled brightly under the fluorescent lights of the room. There would be an official induction ceremony later—probably as soon as Kassia returned to London—but all she truly needed was the ring. It signified her role as leader and truthfully, she didn't need the ring anyway. Nissa, the Gentry and Nissa's own councilors usually looked to Kassia for important matters. Just like their mother, she had a gift for diplomacy and could make those impossible decisions without questioning herself later. She was a lot harsher, more Draconian in her views of the world than Nissa, but most of the fae were. Placing the ring in her sister's palm, she closed Kassia's fingers over it. "You do now."

CHAPTER TWELVE

Thomas wiped sweaty palms on his pants as he ascended the stairs. He was almost two hundred years old and he'd made love to this woman countless times. When he closed his eyes at night, her naked body was what he dreamed about. She'd been all he dreamed about for as long as he could remember. There was simply no one else for him.

But this time was definitely going to be different. Shifters were very superstitious and if the bonding didn't go right, it could set the tone for their whole relationship.

On a logical level he knew it was complete bullshit, but his inner wolf was terrified he'd fuck this up and Nissa would leave again.

It didn't matter that she'd practically moved in with him. After the treaty signing she'd opted to return with him instead of going home. She'd promised her sister she'd return to London for the official induction ceremony and then she wanted to head to Dublin to spend a couple weeks packing up her stuff—and he planned to be right by her side the entire time. Partially to ensure her safety, but mainly because he loved her and couldn't stand to be apart from her. Never again.

Until then, she was living under his—their—roof. Somehow he'd forced himself to keep his hands off her since they'd gotten back from New York. It had only been a few hours but it felt like an eternity.

Part of him still feared this was a dream. Until he marked her, he feared that feeling wouldn't go away.

When he pushed the door to his bedroom open, he froze at the sight before him.

Nissa sat up on her knees in the middle of his bed wearing nothing but a seductive smile.

His heart actually stuttered as he drank in the sight of her. With her silky blonde hair spilling over her breasts she looked like Aphrodite come to life. Only more beautiful. Those perfect pink nipples were rock-hard and begging for him to touch and kiss.

As his gaze tracked down the flat planes of her abdomen to the soft patch of blonde hair covering her pussy, he could feel his canines throb. His abdomen muscles pulled taut and his arms tightened as he clenched his fists to keep steady. The instinctive need to mark her was overwhelming, but he would do this right.

Her long, lean arms rested gracefully against her sides. When she twisted her hands nervously in front of her he realized he'd been staring too long.

Quickly he averted his eyes to meet hers. "You're so fucking beautiful." Immediately he cringed. He'd wanted to be smoother, more charming and he wasn't off to a great start.

When her lips pulled up into a smile some of his apprehension faded. "You don't look so bad yourself."

For the past few hours he'd been dealing with unavoidable pack business but all he'd been thinking about was getting back to Nissa. He hadn't expected her to be waiting for him like this. He'd known tonight was "the night", but damn.

This was the best way to come home. "How long have you been waiting like this?"

"You'd like me to say hours, wouldn't you?" Her nose crinkled as she laughed lightly. "I heard you downstairs so…" She placed her hands on her hips and her green eyes brightened as she looked him over. "You're wearing too many clothes." The sudden, sensual drop in her voice made him ache.

Without wasting time he stripped off his shirt, shoved his jeans down and stepped out of them. He wasn't wearing any boxers. With Nissa living here now, it seemed pointless.

As he strode toward her, her gaze zeroed in on his rigid cock. When she licked her lips, he groaned. The sight of her running her tongue over her pink lips brought back too many memories of her licking and sucking his cock.

But that wasn't going to happen tonight. At least not at first.

Tonight he had to claim her. He refused to wait any longer.

Once he'd had his fill of her a few hours from now, maybe he'd be able to think straight again. Right now his inner wolf was howling in demand that he mark his mate. "On your back."

She looked surprised at his abrupt demand but she quickly complied. Soon he'd have her on her stomach and he'd be driving into her but for now he needed to taste her.

DANGEROUS CRAVING | 373

Spread out on his dark sheets, her golden hair was a sharp contrast. Since it was night, the drapes were wide open and the moonlight streaming in was their only source of illumination.

It bathed the bed and her in a soft bluish glow. Thanks to his extrasensory abilities the effect made her eyes that much brighter and intense.

He could drown in that gaze if he let himself. Right now he didn't actually care if he drowned in Nissa's arms. All he wanted was to wrap himself up in her and never let go.

As she lay before him, her thighs fell open invitingly. Lifting one of her legs, he pressed a kiss to her inner ankle. When he did, she shuddered lightly and an unexpected tremble rolled through his own body. It was as if he could actually feel her pleasure curling through him.

Moving a couple inches higher, he scraped his teeth over her calf then followed with his tongue. Blowing on the moist area earned him a moan at the same time a potent burst of lust rolled off her. He remembered exactly what turned her on. Since the bottom of her feet had always been sensitive, he lightly massaged her instep with his hand as he continued tracking kisses along her leg.

Her desire was stronger than anything he'd ever scented. Unlike his kind she never masked her need and he loved that. All her emotions and hungers were right on the surface.

Her fingers tightly clutched the sheet underneath her as he trailed higher. As soon as he reached her inner thigh he was nearly bowled over by her sweet scent. Clenching his jaw tightly, he paused and tried to rein his inner wolf back in.

He wanted her panting and pliant and so fucking needful for him all she could think about was that final release. He couldn't just pound into her like he wanted and it took all his control to stop at her thigh then start on her other leg.

When he kissed her other ankle, she arched her back and moaned lightly. "Why do you have to keep teasing me?"

He paused and tried to find his voice. "After I'm inside you I'll be staying there for a long time. This is all the foreplay you're getting tonight, Nissa." Even to his own ears his voice was raspy and uneven.

A mischievous smile played across her face as he ran his tongue along the inside of her other leg, up toward where he planned to bury his tongue then cock for hours.

His hips jerked at the thought. It was taking all his strength not to flip

374 | SAVANNAH STUART

her over and start pounding into her from behind. Sometimes his wolf and human side played havoc in his head and now was one of them.

As he moved higher, her hands splayed across her stomach then gently cupped her breasts. His throat tightened as he watched her. Slowly, seductively, she began strumming her nipples with her thumbs.

When she pushed the soft mounds together and began caressing herself more insistently, he didn't hold back anymore.

Burying his face between her legs, he stroked his tongue along her pussy lips. Tasting her sweet essence, he licked and laved relentlessly. A low growl tore out of him. As he delved deeper into her core she moved against his face and moaned her excitement.

For a moment her legs squeezed around his head but when he started to pull back they loosened almost instantly.

He knew she was getting worked up and forcing herself to relax. In a hundred years, some things still hadn't changed especially her sensitivity and reactions.

Tall, lean and so hot she made him ache, the woman was like a box of explosives.

Utterly combustible.

Slowing his strokes to drag out her pleasure, he shifted position until his tongue zeroed in on her clit. All it took was one flick of his tongue and she jolted against him. Smiling, he added pressure and began sweeping over it in a rhythmic dance.

Her fingers tunneled into his hair and held his head tight. As she dug in, her breathing became more shallow and unsteady.

The sweetness of her arousal was stronger. And her hips were writhing faster and faster against him.

She was close.

He could feel it. And he didn't want her coming until he was buried deep inside her.

Abruptly he pulled his head back.

"Wha—"

She didn't get to finish. Roughly he grabbed her hips and flipped her over. Immediately, and before he had a chance to do anything, she wordlessly stretched her arms up on the bed and pushed her ass back toward him. Part of her hair spilled down like a silky curtain. It highlighted the long lines of her back, the sleek bands of muscle outlining her spine.

The action was so submissive it made his inner wolf absolutely crazy.

DANGEROUS CRAVING | 375

Seeing her splayed out like this was his darkest fantasy come true. Taking her this way and finally being able to mark her made something deep inside him howl with satisfaction.

Shuddering, he ran his palm along the curve of her spine, continuing down until he cupped one of her firm cheeks.

She tensed under him but only for a moment. He slid both his hands back up her sides and waist until he reached under her and cupped her breasts. This was his female.

Leaning forward, he pressed lingering kisses along her back as he fondled and massaged her hardened nipples. She moaned at his teasing and began rubbing her ass against his cock.

He moaned in turn but didn't give in yet. He wanted her worked up and ready to come when he finally pushed into her.

As she continued squirming, he continued his stroking. Trailing one hand between her breasts and down her stomach, he didn't stop until he cupped her mound.

Using his middle finger he lightly rubbed over her clit. Her moans turned to incomprehensible mumblings and he knew she was ready.

Without giving her warning, he fisted her hips roughly in a dominant grip and plunged into her.

She gasped and her sheath tightened around him with no mercy. As he pulled out then slammed into her again, he felt his right shoulder start to burn.

The bonding symbol.

He knew he shouldn't care whether it appeared on him or not but his basest side desperately wanted it. *Needed it.* Satisfaction roared through him as the burn spread, heightening his gratification. He wanted her mark as much as he wanted to mark her pale, soft skin.

Her inner walls clenched tighter around him. The sudden fluttering was his sign she was ready to come. Grasping her hips tighter, he knew he was going to leave bruises. Some logical part of his brain told him to ease off but he couldn't hold back. Not now.

"Come for me, Nissa." Command saturated his voice and he knew it would push her over the edge.

It always did.

Feisty as she was, she loved to be dominated. Nissa's back arched as she clutched the sheets underneath her. He could feel her slickness and climax as she found her release.

His own orgasm was a loud drumroll in his head. "If you want to back out say it." Somehow he managed to growl the words. His inner wolf shouted at him to shut the hell up but he needed to make sure she wanted his marking.

"Want...this," she panted as he continued to pummel into her in a barely controlled frenzy.

God, yes. He'd been waiting over a century to hear those words.

His canines lengthened fully. Bending slightly, he reached under her and palmed her stomach. After he lifted her to meet him, he scraped his teeth against the side of her neck.

Hard enough to break the skin and mark her forever. When he punctured her sensitive neck she let out a low yelp but arched again and he could feel her inner walls contract even harder.

That was all it took for his own control to snap. The orgasm ripped from him violently and he didn't bother trying to rein in his shout. Shuddering, he emptied himself as she continued milking and taking everything from him.

After what felt like an eternity he finally forced his hips to still and gentled his grip. He'd been blindly thrusting into her even after he'd climaxed. His cock didn't want to leave her warm embrace.

Nissa's head was bent forward against the bed, laying in between her outstretched arms. While he could watch her in that submissive position forever, he needed to take care of her.

As he pulled out of her, he reached under her and gently rolled her onto her back. She smiled at him as he stretched out next to her. Before she could say anything, he leaned forward and nuzzled her neck where the tiny markings were. "Did I hurt you?"

"Hmm, a very good hurt," she murmured as she threw a leg and arm across him.

Wordlessly she reached over his shoulder and gently circled his new bonding mark. The subtle action sent an unexpected punch of pleasure through his entire system.

His cock started to throb again and he just gritted his teeth. It would be a little while before she was ready for more. As he pulled her close and stroked a gentle hand down her back, another thought occurred to him. If he had the same bonding mark as her it stood to reason she'd likely acquire some of his gifts.

Both his brothers could communicate telepathically with their mates but he wasn't sure if he and Nissa could since she was full-blooded fae. Since her eyes were closed he decided to go for it.

Are you hungry or thirsty? he projected with his mind.

"I don't know how you can even think about food," she muttered.

DANGEROUS CRAVING | 377

It soothed him to know they were true mates in every sense of the word. He didn't laugh out loud but she must have heard his laughter in her head because she opened her eyes and regarded him curiously. "What's so funny?"

Looks like you're not going to be able to keep secrets from me anymore.

Her eyes widened for a fraction of a second but just as quickly she grinned. *That works both ways, buddy.*

His heart stuttered at her contented smile. She was like a miracle to him. After all the time they'd been separated he didn't want to keep anything from her ever again and he was relieved she felt the same. All that mattered was that they'd finally found their way back to each other's arms again. He knew they'd likely face prejudices and danger again because of their union but as long as they were together, they could handle anything. "I love you, Nissa."

Her smile was blinding. "I love you too. Always."

DESIRE UNLEASHED

She triggers all his possessive instincts...

Turned into a shifter against his will, Ethan Connell would have died if the Lazos pack hadn't given him shelter. While he's grateful to all of them, there's one she-wolf he can't get out of his head. Sweet, sensuous Caro, who not only saved his life but sets his body on fire and triggers every possessive instinct he has. But she's made it clear she just wants friendship from him.

At first he scoffs at the idea and after months of biding his time, he makes his move. Instead of rejection, she meets him with a passion every bit as intense as his own. But Caro was burned in the past and won't admit she wants more than just a physical relationship. Ethan has no doubt that he's playing for keeps — if she'll only let him.

CHAPTER ONE

E than tugged on his T-shirt as he trudged across the patio. The run along the Lazos' strip of private beach was always exhilarating but after six months he still hadn't gotten used to the fact that he could turn into a wolf. Some days it was just too surreal.

Little more than a year ago he'd simply been a human. An ex-soldier working for various security companies across the globe. Until a crazy doctor had injected him full of some sort of organic serum that turned him into a wolf. Or werewolf to be precise. He'd been a mess after he'd escaped and if it hadn't been for the Lazos pack, the local shifters who made their home in Miami, he'd be dead. Or worse, locked up somewhere in a government lab while scientists did experiments on him for the rest of his natural life.

He opened the sliding glass door to the house where he lived with Paz and Adam, also new members of the pack.

Paz looked up from where she was dicing tomatoes. The petite woman smiled warmly as she always did. "Hey, how was the run?"

"Good." He racked his brain as he tried to think of something normal to say. He always felt awkward around her. Okay, that wasn't fair. He felt awkward around *everyone*. His new pack had all been born with the ability to shift to animal form. He was a freak of nature who'd been turned by a mad doctor. He wasn't one of them and he wasn't sure he'd ever fit in. "Uh, you need help with anything?"

She shook her head and smiled softly. "No, but Caro will be here any minute if she's not already. She's bringing over decorations for tomorrow's party. Will you help her carry everything in?"

At the mention of Caro, his throat went dry so he simply nodded. As he stepped outside the two-story palatial house, he spotted Caro driving up the stone driveway. Though he could only see her silhouette through the windshield, he could picture her anyway. Could see her if he simply closed his eyes. The petite, dark-haired she-wolf had starred in all of his fantasies over the past six months. Her shoulder-length hair was always pulled back in a ponytail or some sort of twist. Just once he'd like to pull it free and watch it fall around her face as she rode him. Before being turned into a shifter, sex had always been a pretty regular part of his life. He'd never had a serious relationship, had never wanted to. Since being turned he hadn't been with anyone—he hadn't wanted to. The only female he craved was Caro.

His heart pounded erratically and when she climbed out of the vehicle, full-blown lust surged through him. Almost as if she could read what he was thinking, she slammed the door shut and muttered something under her breath. Hell, maybe she *could* read his emotions. According to his mentor Adam, all shifters had learned to cover their emotions since they were pups, but Ethan was still learning to hide his. Hell, around Caro he didn't want to mask his desire. He'd been trying to get her alone for six months and he wasn't going to fuck up his chance to ask her out. "Hey, Caro."

The dark-haired doctor ducked his gaze as she pulled the trunk of her car open. "Hey, Ethan."

He hurried over and took the wide box she'd lifted from her hands, forcing her to look at him.

Her espresso-colored eyes widened slightly. "Uh, thanks."

He scrambled to find the right words. "Listen, Caro. I never got to thank you properly for all you did." When he'd first been found by the Lazos pack he hadn't been able to control his shifts and it had been killing him. Even though Caro was a pediatrician, she'd used all her medical training to help keep him alive. In short, he owed his life to her.

Her cheeks tinged pink. "You've already said thank you enough. I'm just glad I could help."

"I'd like to take you out to dinner. Saturday if you're free."

Her eyes darkened for a moment but she simply shook her head. "Thank you for the offer, but it's just not going to happen."

Sharp disappointment forked through him. He might not be as advanced at controlling himself but he could sense she was attracted to him too. "Why not?"

"I think you're interested in more than thanking me?" Her voice was soft and intoxicating.

He could listen to her all day. He nodded at her question. Hell yeah he was interested in doing more than thanking her.

"It would be too complicated, okay? You're young—"

"I'm almost thirty," he ground out.

"And I'm almost two hundred. You have a lot to learn about yourself and until you do, the last thing you need is to worry about dating. Besides, I don't want anything casual anyway."

"Neither do I." The words came out more forceful than he'd intended, but as soon as they were out of his mouth he realized he meant them. The woman had consumed his thoughts for months. He didn't understand his wild attraction to her, but it was anything but casual.

Her smile was almost patronizing, but he guessed she was trying to let him down easy. She was just nice like that. "You say that now, but trust me, in a few years you'll figure out what you want and you'll settle down with a she-wolf your own age."

"I'm not some teenager going through puberty," he snapped, angry at her words. They looked the same age anyway so he wasn't sure what her deal was.

Her expression immediately softened and it made him feel even shittier. She was just so damn sweet. "I know that. You're a *very* attractive wolf and I'd be blind not to see that, but... All I can offer you right now is friendship." She almost seemed wistful as she said it but quickly continued. "If you're okay with that, then good. If not, let me know now because we can't hang out otherwise."

Friendship. *Awesome.* "Friends?"

She nodded once and he wanted to tell her hell no, that wasn't enough. But he wasn't stupid. Or maybe he was.

"Okay, friends," he managed to squeeze out.

"Good, friends then." She grabbed another smaller box from the trunk then turned on her heel and strode toward the house.

His eyes narrowed on the soft sway of her ass. Where so many of the women in the Lazos pack were lean, Caro was a little softer. Curvier. And he wanted to feel all of her curves. Stroke, lick, kiss them. His attraction had nothing to do with gratitude and everything to do with a burning, searing need deep inside him. He could barely understand it let alone explain it. When he was with her, his wolf just wanted to mark her, to claim her so everyone knew she was his. It was such a primal feeling he wasn't sure it was normal.

When his cock started to harden he cursed under his breath. He knew she could sense his lust and he desperately wished he could cover its intensity. One way or another he was going to convince Caro to give him a chance.

Ethan strolled through Lucas and Alisha's house, trying to act casually

384 | SAVANNAH STUART

even though he felt anything but that. He'd gotten caught up in a conversation with Adam and when he'd turned back to find Caro, she'd been gone. He just wanted a few minutes alone with her. He opened the last door in one of the downstairs hallways and froze when he saw Lucas sitting behind his oversized desk.

"Sorry, Alpha." He started to backtrack when his Alpha stopped him.

"It's fine. Come in and you don't have to constantly call me Alpha. Lucas is fine." The dark-haired wolf was over two-hundred years old but he didn't look much older than his three sons.

Ethan did as he said because, well, he was the boss and somewhere in his most primal being, his inner wolf feared and respected Lucas. Not because he'd hurt him without cause but because he was a tough wolf. A warrior. Ethan also knew that his Alpha would protect him and the rest of the pack at the risk of death. "Ah, sorry Lucas."

The older wolf smiled as Ethan pulled up a seat. "And you can stop saying sorry to everything."

"S...okay." *Would he ever get used to this werewolf thing?* He relaxed a little as he sank down against the leather seat.

"Why aren't you at the party?"

"I am...was. I'm just looking for someone."

"Caro?" Slight amusement laced Lucas' voice.

He nodded, wondering if she'd complained about him. Maybe he'd pushed her too far yesterday. She'd said they would be friends and he'd agreed. He tried to contain his lust but she always seemed to sense it so maybe she'd changed her mind.

Lucas leaned back in his chair. His dark eyes seemed to penetrate right through him. Instinctively, Ethan averted his gaze. On one level he knew it was because the other shifter was an Alpha, but his human side was annoyed because he wasn't used to anyone having control over him. Sure, when he'd been in the Corps he'd taken orders but that was different. If he'd chosen he could have disobeyed any order. Sitting here with Lucas, he felt almost mentally compelled to avert his gaze.

"You are very conflicted right now." It wasn't a question.

He looked back at his Alpha. "I'm still getting used to...everything." That was an understatement. Since he was so new, he needed to shift four or five times a week and each time brought a new kind of pain.

"Adam has been a good mentor though?"

"Yes." Adam was the best friend he could ever ask for. He was like a father, brother and friend all at once. Something Ethan had never had. Explaining all that in words was impossible so he didn't try.

"Go on back to the party, Ethan. I know you didn't come here looking for me. And take some advice from me. Caro has been single a long time and it's by choice, not for lack of suitors."

Ethan nodded and headed toward the door. He paused with his hand on the handle as the meaning of his Alpha's words sank in. "Did someone hurt Caro?"

Lucas paused for so long Ethan wondered if he'd answer. It wasn't like the Alpha owed him anything, but finally he spoke. "Not physically."

His canines tingled at that, a new sort of rage pumping through him at the thought. "Who?" The word came out as a soft growl.

Lucas blinked in surprise, probably from Ethan's tone. But he hadn't been able to help the reaction. The thought of someone hurting Caro had his wolf swiping out in anger.

"That's not for me to tell," Lucas said quietly, authority in his voice.

Ethan nodded once before he shut the door behind him. How could anyone hurt that sweet she-wolf? As he stalked back down the hallway, he ran into Adam.

The blond wolf frowned at him, but didn't comment on his dark mood. "Paz and I are about to head home. You ready?"

"Nah. I'm gonna go for a run but would you leave some clothes on the patio?" Ethan didn't relish the idea of walking through the house naked. Paz and Adam had taken him in and while nudity seemed to be no big deal to shifters, he didn't like strutting around in the buff if there was a chance Paz might see him. Not that he worried she'd particularly *care*, he just knew how territorial Adam was where it concerned her. Adam had explained that sometimes their inner wolves didn't listen to their human side when it came to reasoning. Especially if a mate was involved. So, he kept covered up at all times.

Adam looked at him thoughtfully. "All right. If you need to talk later, I'll be awake."

God, was he that obvious? Ethan nodded and continued toward the kitchen. When he got there he saw Marisol chatting with a handful of females. Still no Caro. He ducked out the side door and avoided looking at anyone as he made his way to the beach. For the most part the party was still in full swing. Hell, he didn't even know whose birthday it was. One of the younger females, he thought. There were too many pack members to keep track.

He took off his shoes and stripped off his shirt. As he started to unbutton his jeans he spotted a lone figure sitting in the sand close to the shoreline. *Caro.*

Not bothering to stay quiet, he strode across the sand, the need to be next to her all-consuming. His toes sunk into the soft grains until the ground hardened and leveled out.

"I just want to be alone, Ethan." Her voice was barely audible over the sound of the crashing waves.

Ignoring her, he sat next to her. She glanced at him and he didn't miss the way her espresso eyes quickly flicked over his bare chest. For a brief moment, desire flared in them, but just as quickly she looked away.

He was careful to give her space even though he wanted nothing more than to reach out and touch her. Hold her. "What's wrong?"

"It doesn't matter," she muttered.

"It does to me."

She sighed heavily. "Ethan, you can't keep—"

"I don't know what you think I'm doing right now. You're part of my pack and I just wanted to see what was wrong. I thought we were friends." Hurt more than anything slammed through him. It seemed he couldn't do anything right lately. He started to push up from the sand. He might want the she-wolf but he wasn't a masochist for her rejection.

Her delicate hand shot out and grasped his lower arm. "You're right, I'm sorry."

Surprised by the gesture, he lowered himself next to her and savored the feel of her fingers holding on to him. "So what's going on?"

"It's nothing important. I just needed some space, that's all. I love these parties but with so many of our pack getting mated lately it's a reminder of..." She shook her head. "Sometimes space is nice, that's all," she trailed off, repeating herself.

Ethan couldn't believe she'd opened up to him even this much. He knew he needed to tread carefully. The last thing he wanted to do was push her away. He scooted a few inches closer and inhaled her sweet scent. Taking a chance he wrapped his arm around her shoulders and pulled her to him. He could do this friends thing.

Maybe. She stiffened for a brief moment but laid her head on his shoulder. When she let out a tired sigh his entire body ached to comfort her in other ways. Yeah, being friends would likely kill him but he could deal with it. For now.

CHAPTER TWO

Six Months Later

Ethan shut the door to his truck, but paused to get his lust under control. It was Friday, which meant his weekly ritual of popcorn and a movie at Caro's house. It also meant he had to control his dominant, sexual urges for the next couple hours.

This "friends" thing they had going on was getting old but even so, he loved the time they spent together. He knew she wanted him physically, but she refused to let them out of this annoying holding pattern. In reality she was the best friend he'd ever had and he didn't want to screw that up, especially since he was the newest member of the Lazos pack. Yeah, he considered Adam his best friend too, but that relationship was different since he was more of a mentor and father figure to Ethan.

With Caro, Ethan felt completely free to be himself. But he couldn't just sit back and pretend his feelings had gone away. If anything they'd gotten stronger.

He wanted her so bad he ached for the need to sink himself deep into her and stay that way for hours. Just once would never be enough. On a primal level he didn't quite understand, he wanted her more than he'd ever wanted anything or anyone. It was starting to make his wolf edgy.

After hurrying up the stone walk, he knocked on her door. When she didn't answer, he tried again.

Nothing.

Her car was in the driveway and he knew she wouldn't forget about tonight. Frowning, he tried the door but it was locked. So he headed around the side of the house. As he trekked across the yard, he noticed the thick, green grass needed to be cut. He made a note to take care of it tomorrow.

388 | SAVANNAH STUART

When he rounded the back of the house he scented her and paused. She was nearby. He just couldn't see her.

The Olympic-sized pool glistened under the setting sun and the palm trees slightly waved against the breeze blowing up from the Atlantic. He started to cross her backyard but froze when he spotted her walking up from the beach.

Completely naked.

Curvy and gorgeous, the petite she-wolf made his cock ache by simply looking at her. Beads of water rolled down her sleek body, tracking from her neck to between her breasts all the way down to the juncture between her legs.

Exactly where he'd like to bury his face, then his cock. The dark tuft of hair covering her mound was perfectly trimmed. His erection jerked as he stared at her and he found it impossible to control his lust.

He knew she wasn't aware of him or she wouldn't be so free with herself. Most of the pack was unabashed about their nudity—himself included—but around him Caro was different. Shy even. Thankfully the wind was blowing toward him or she'd have known he was there.

She'd probably gone for a run in wolf form then decided to take a dip in the ocean. She ran her hands back through her wet hair and squeezed it, wringing the salt water from it.

As she did, she glanced in his direction. Her dark eyes widened and she immediately covered her breasts. Not that it mattered. He'd seen the perky mounds and those hard, light brown nipples already. That image wouldn't be leaving his mind any time soon.

"Do you mind?" she practically shouted, her cheeks tinged bright red.

Grinning, he shook his head and strode toward her. "No, I don't mind."

"Damn it, Ethan. Turn around. *Now*," she said through gritted teeth.

Shaking his head, he turned toward the back of her house. In the big windows that took up a lot of space he saw her in the reflection anyway. Grinning to himself, he watched as she grabbed a towel from one of the wooden lounge chairs and wrapped it around her body.

"I'm decent now." When he faced her again, her cheeks were still red. "What are you doing here so early? I thought I'd have time to get in a run before..." She trailed off and nervously cleared her throat. And that's when he noticed it.

Lust.

It emanated off her in subtle waves. Like a fresh spring rain it rolled over him, bathing him in its purity.

DESIRE UNLEASHED | 389

He shrugged as if seeing her naked were an everyday occurrence, despite how his cock was wedged against his suddenly too-tight zipper. His inner wolf howled and clawed at his insides. The primitive part of him wanted to draw her towel away and visually feast on everything she'd just covered up. "It's no big deal, Caro. You've seen me naked before too." It had been in a medical capacity but still, she'd seen all of him.

"Well that's different," she muttered and broke his gaze. "Come on. I need to get changed and you need to wipe that smirk off your face."

But he didn't. He couldn't.

Seeing her off kilter like this brought out all his animal urges. Maybe tonight was the night when she finally admitted they were meant to be more than just friends. He'd been holding back, but if she was off-balance he could push just a little harder than normal. "You want me to start the popcorn while you get changed?"

"Yeah." She mumbled something else as she opened the French doors leading to her living room. Then she hurried across the room and disappeared down one of the hallways.

Ethan blew out a breath and headed for the kitchen. Yep. Tonight was it. He'd make sure of it.

Caro hated that her face was still bright red when she made it to the privacy of her bathroom. After a long day she'd needed a run in her wolf form but she hadn't expected Ethan to show up early.

Around him she was always off kilter. Still, she couldn't seem to stay away from the young wolf. Sure, he was thirty in human years but he'd only recently been turned into a shifter and she didn't want to get tangled up with someone who could just as easily change their mind about her once they'd slept together.

She'd been through that with another shifter before and didn't want to go through that kind of pain again. With Ethan, however, she was really tempted to throw all her rules out the window. The past six months she'd gotten used to the ritual of hanging out with him on Friday nights and seeing him whenever she wanted. She was afraid to get too comfortable because she knew he'd likely meet someone soon and that would be the end of things between them. He was simply grateful she'd saved his life. That was all. She couldn't take advantage of his gratitude because in the end, they'd both get hurt. He'd meet his mate and she'd be alone. Again.

Shaking her head at herself, she jumped in the shower and washed the salt water out of her hair. After cleaning off and changing into jeans and a T-shirt, she found Ethan in the living room lounging on the couch.

It was hard to quell the jump of desire inside her when she spotted him. His long, muscular legs were stretched out casually and his broad shoulders and muscular arms pulled impossibly tight against the shirt he wore. He worked as a carpenter with his mentor Adam and all those long hours he put in showed. What she wouldn't give to let him wrap those arms around her just once.

When he saw her, he set his beer down and stood. The predatory gaze he raked over her body made her shiver. She couldn't be sure but it felt like he was imagining her naked again. "I didn't make the popcorn because I wasn't sure how long you'd be."

"Okay, we can make it now. I need a glass of wine anyway." Maybe several. Glancing away from him and his heated stare, she hurried toward the kitchen. For some reason she was sure he was staring at her butt as she walked. She hated that she liked the thought of that. A lot.

We are just friends, she reminded herself.

As she poured herself a glass of wine, acting like his friend was the last thing on her mind. She spared a glance at him as he grabbed a bag of popcorn from one of her cabinets. He looked so comfortable in her kitchen. So right. Like he belonged.

Knowing she shouldn't stare, she did anyway. His hands had always fascinated her. So strong, rugged and callused. Even though he was a big, muscular guy, his fingers were long and lean. The fantasy of what it would feel like for him to push them inside her, to stroke and tease her to orgasm — She jerked her gaze up when she realized he was looking at her strangely.

His blue eyes darkened as he assessed her face. As if he could read her mind. Her inner most thoughts.

Shit. She'd been so caught up in her fantasies she hadn't been controlling her desire so he could probably scent it on her. She could scent it and even untrained as he was, she had no doubt it was knocking him over right now.

"How was your day?" She tried to make the question casual, hoping he'd ignore her scent, but he didn't bite.

"Fine. But I think it's about to get more interesting." He moved away from the counter and microwave and lithely moved across the tiled floor toward her.

She could barely hear his movements but she couldn't tear her gaze from him. The man moved like a lethal jungle animal. Like he was stalking something.

DESIRE UNLEASHED | 391

Her.

She was his prey.

And she found she didn't mind all that much. Or at all really. Her panties dampened so much it was embarrassing. All he had to do was train those blue eyes on her and she felt lost. "Interesting?" she squeaked out.

"You want me." He said it so boldly her first instinct was to deny it.

But she didn't bother. He'd know she was lying. Even as she tried, she couldn't hide the lust she desperately wanted to cover. "So?"

"So...what are we going to do about it?"

"You're my friend, Ethan."

"Fuck being friends. I've never wanted *just* that from you. You *know* that," he growled.

"It's all I can offer," she whispered. She might fantasize about him but panic started to thrum through her. This would end badly. She just knew it. Once he found his mate—and she doubted she was it—he'd be gone. Probably sooner. It would shred her to have to go through something like that again. This time it would be a hell of a lot worse. Ethan was sweet, gentle and even though he was young, he was mature for his years.

She cared for Ethan way more than she had for her ex-lover. Maybe even more than cared.

CHAPTER THREE

"Bullshit." Ethan closed the distance between them until he stood inches from Caro. She was petite so he had to look down at her.

He didn't want her to feel like he was towering over her intentionally but he liked the thought of dominating her in the bedroom. He couldn't count how many times he'd fantasized about it. Before he'd turned, before he'd met her, he'd never thought much about it, but he craved her submitting to him now. Not with bondage or shit like that. He just needed her to admit that she was his and he was hers. He wondered if it was a shifter thing but was too hesitant to ask anyone.

Reaching out, he grasped her hips and pulled her tight against him. His cock pressed firmly against her belly. "You feel what you do to me? Anytime I'm near you, *this* happens."

Her dark eyes flashed once as she nodded. His normally talkative, sweet Caro seemed speechless. She placed her hands on his chest as if she were going to push him back. But she didn't. She just held perfectly still, as if she couldn't make up her mind what she wanted to do.

He decided to make the decision for her. She either rejected him or she didn't.

He crushed his mouth over hers, catching her moan. For a moment her delicate hands pushed at him and he knew she was battling herself. Some demons were wreaking havoc inside her and if he knew what they were he'd try to ease them. Show her that he was different than whatever asshole who'd hurt her in the past. But he wouldn't force her so he teasingly stroked his tongue against hers, waiting for her to move forward or pull back. After what felt like an eternity, her hands slid up and grasped his shoulders.

He couldn't bite back a groan. "Damn, Caro," he murmured against her mouth, nipping her bottom lip between his teeth. The way she started to melt into him was making him crazy.

Her fingers dug into him so tight that if he'd been only human, she'd have definitely left bruises. She was nervous. He could feel the tension humming through her entire body and in the way she gripped him as if her life depended on it.

His heart squeezed. What was she so afraid of? Definitely not him. He needed to soothe whatever fears she had but what the fuck did he know about that? He'd joined the military when he was eighteen, then after that he'd done contract work overseas. He didn't know shit about real relationships or dating. Sex, yes. Relationships, no.

Caro deserved better than him, but right now he didn't care. He was a selfish bastard and she was finally giving him a chance. He might not know the right things to say but he'd figure it out.

All he knew was that they weren't stopping at kissing tonight. He planned to make love to her half a dozen times before the night was through. When she woke up tomorrow morning, she'd feel him on her. In her. Her skin would be permeated with his scent. Hopefully she'd realize that they belonged together.

Cradling her closer, he ran his hands through her thick hair and cupped the back of her head in a dominating but gentle grip. He wanted her to know he wasn't going anywhere. Whatever she was afraid of, they could work out. Because she had all the control over him. He wondered if she even realized it.

The longer he held her, the hotter his body grew and the stronger the scent of her desire grew. The sweet scent curled around him, making him dizzy with need.

Right now he needed to touch and mark her. Releasing her head, he slid his hands to the bottom of her T-shirt and began tugging it up. She froze and stopped kissing him.

"What are you doing?"

She sounded nervous and he desperately wanted to soothe her. If she wasn't ready he'd stop but he knew she was. They'd been building up to this for a year even if she didn't want to admit it. They'd just been dancing around their attraction. Well, she had. She just had to get past whatever issue was holding her back. "I've already seen you naked once today. I want to savor it this time."

Her cheeks flushed that delectable shade of crimson and when she hesitated, he leaned forward and raked his teeth over her neck before nibbling on one of her earlobes. "You're fucking perfect, Caro. Let me see you." He inwardly cringed at his language but as he spoke, she relaxed.

"If you undress me, I get to see you too," she finally murmured.

It was obvious she was still nervous but the fewer clothes they both had on, the better. Without pause, he stripped off his shirt.

Something totally primitive stirred inside him as she stared at his bare chest. Thanks to his time in the Marine Corps, he had his fair share of scars but she didn't seem to care. Her gaze tracked over him with undisguised lust. She'd shot quick peeks at him before and he'd gotten a hint she liked what she saw, but this was different. Her dark eyes tracked over him in a way that made him shudder knowing she wanted him as much as he wanted her.

Before he could take off her top, she leaned forward and kissed his chest. Lightly, she traced her tongue over one of his nipples then tweaked it with her teeth.

He trembled at the feel of her mouth on him and though he wanted her to keep going, he wanted her bare to him even more. Seeing her naked earlier had been a tease of what he'd been missing out on. The need to see and lick those light brown nipples made him ache all over.

As she kissed him, he grasped the hem of her shirt and tugged upward. She made a brief protesting sound at having to pull back, but the sound died as he removed her shirt, then bra.

Tossing them on the floor, he reached for her again. Her eyes were heated as she stared at him. Whatever had been holding her back before, she was ready to take the next step. This time he didn't bother with the pretense of being gentle.

He reached around her and clutched onto her gorgeous ass. Then he hoisted her up so that she had to wrap her legs around him. Even with clothes on, he could feel her heat. All he could think about was burying himself inside her sweet pussy. The faster they got to her bed, the better.

As she teased his tongue with her own, he headed for her bedroom. He'd never actually been in there — even if he had fantasized about it — but he knew how to find it.

He just followed her sweet scent. The farther he moved down the hallway, the stronger it got.

When she arched her back, rubbing her breasts against him and practically purring in delight, he tripped and lost his balance. It happened so fast but he managed to throw out a hand and take most of the brunt of the fall.

Instead of jerking her out of the moment, Caro simply laughed lightly under her breath as they tumbled to the ground. Then she grappled for the button of his jeans. She didn't seem to care that they were on the carpeted hallway outside her bedroom.

He definitely didn't. If he was honest, he was so afraid she'd change her mind that he didn't bother trying to make it the rest of the way to her bed. Desperate? Hell yeah. The need to taste her, to be in her, was driving him and his wolf like nothing he'd ever felt before. Before he could let her finish undressing him, he needed to taste her.

Had been dreaming about this for too long.

Grasping her hands, he stilled them. "Not yet," he murmured.

Her dark eyes shimmered with lust as she stared at him. But she withdrew her hands and watched while he slid her pants off instead.

The scent of her desire hit him full force, wrapping around him like a warm embrace. *Do this right*, he ordered himself when all he wanted to do was strip off her panties and thrust into her, foreplay be damned.

Her breathing became more erratic as he grasped the thin straps and slid them down her smooth legs.

"Just like I imagined," he managed to rasp out. And she was. She made a sound as if to dismiss his words but when his gaze locked on hers she swallowed hard. "You're perfect, Caro."

Her cheeks reddened in that delicious way he loved but she didn't say anything. He was glad because he didn't want words now. Just wanted to taste and touch. When he'd fantasized about her pussy he'd wondered if she had hair and was pleased that she did. He didn't like women bare and she had a perfect little thatch of dark hair covering her mound. Even though he'd seen her in the backyard earlier, this was up close and personal and better than he'd imagined.

With one finger, he slowly parted her pink folds. Her lips were wet and inviting and practically begging for his tongue. Running a finger along the slit, he bit back a moan when she shuddered.

"Ethan," she murmured, a mix of emotions in that one word. *His name.*

The sound of his name on her lips while she was naked and underneath him was enough to drive him over the edge. Almost.

His finger wouldn't be enough though. Though he wanted to kiss a trail up her legs, tease her a little, he couldn't right now. He was barely hanging onto his control as it was.

Leaning down, he teased his tongue over her already swollen clit. She jerked at his kiss but ran her fingers through his hair and held on.

Feeling her clutch onto him as he began to stroke between her folds made his cock ache with an almost painful need for release. He fought it back, determined to give her pleasure. Show her they were meant for each other — and how much she meant to him.

Caro couldn't believe she and Ethan were doing this in the middle of her hallway but for the first time in years she decided to let go of her inhibition. She'd been hiding behind her broken heart for too long.

She didn't want to think about that though. For the last year Ethan had started to show her all that she'd been missing. She was still terrified that this was a mistake, but with his face between her legs, it was hard to think about anything but the way he was making her feel.

When Ethan plunged his tongue inside her slick folds, she arched her back, urging him deeper. She needed this so desperately and she truly trusted Ethan.

As he stroked her, she didn't hide her desire. She wanted him to know exactly how much he affected her. "I want more." The breathless words slipped out before she could stop herself.

She loved the feel of his tongue but it wasn't enough. He looked up at her with those striking blue eyes and wordlessly slid a finger inside her.

Her body contracted around him and her head fell back. Before she could respond, he slid a second in and began slowly moving in and out. Her lips parted but she couldn't think of anything coherent to say. Maybe words were overrated anyway. All she wanted was more of this.

More of Ethan.

He pushed deep inside her, over and over, in a slow rhythm that had her heart beating out of control and her inner walls clenching tightly around him. Suddenly he pushed deep, holding his fingers still as he rubbed his thumb over her clit. Her inner walls clenched around his fingers as she drew him into her. Everything about her body felt so sensitized.

Her nipples tingled and itched and all she wanted to do was stroke herself, but she held back. She might trust him with her body but this was a huge step. They'd gone from having a friendly date to *this*. Letting herself go completely was a little scary.

As if he read her mind, he partially lifted his head and stopped his beautiful torture. "Touch yourself," he murmured against her mound.

When she tensed he must have sensed it because he fully drew his head back and stared at her. "Now."

The subtle command in his deep voice sent shivers rocketing through her. He'd never talked to her that way. But she liked it. Maybe too much.

Lifting her hands, she tentatively cupped both her breasts. He continued staring, those blue eyes like lasers burning her. Liking his attention, she lightly pinched one of her nipples between her thumb and forefinger. The grasping action made her clit ache even more. When she did, he began moving his fingers inside her again.

It was like the erotic sensation in her nipples was connected to what he was doing. With each stroke of his fingers inside her, her nipples tingled and tightened even more.

Laying her head back on the floor, she closed her eyes and began strumming her thumbs over both hard buds.

Ethan growled against her before he sucked her clit into his mouth with an abrupt, sensual tug. The action took her by surprise but only pushed her closer to orgasm.

"Ethan," she moaned out.

He growled again, the sound wildly erotic.

Her inner walls continued to tighten around him with each stroke until finally it was too much. She didn't know why she was trying to hold on to any sort of control, but she was tired of denying herself what she wanted. Tired of denying herself Ethan in her bed.

When he lightly raked his teeth over her clit, stimulating that sensitive bundle of nerves in the best way possible, she pushed over the edge and found that elusive bliss she'd needed for too long. The exquisite pleasure raced through her at lightning speed, making her entire body tremble.

Her legs tightened around his head but he didn't seem to mind as he continued tweaking her clit. He didn't stop until he'd wrung every bit of pleasure from her. Her climax came in wave after wave until finally she fell limp against the floor, breathing hard but still needing more.

She needed to feel all of Ethan inside her. That had only taken the edge off.

Something primitive inside her had wanted him since the moment she'd seen him stretched out and injured on that examination table — though she'd never tell anyone that. Now was her chance. She wanted him to claim her. Take control.

Ethan moved up Caro's body, savoring the feeling of her underneath him as he covered her. Her dark eyes were slightly dilated as she came down from her high, but he wasn't done with her. Not yet.

Feeling those tight walls clasp around his fingers wasn't enough. Not even close.

"That was amazing," she murmured, trailing her fingers up his bare chest.

He loved the feel of her touching him. Skin to skin contact was important for shifters, something he'd learned, but he craved her touch more than anything he'd imagined.

"We're not done." The words came out like a growl, much harsher than he'd intended. But he was barely hanging on. He kept his gaze pinned to hers as he shoved his jeans off.

Her fingers dug into his shoulders as he settled fully between her legs. His cock nudged her slick entrance, his balls pulled up tight. She still stared at him with heavy lidded eyes. She opened her mouth to say something else but he didn't give her the chance to finish.

A year ago he'd have had to worry about putting on a condom but since they were both shifters, it didn't matter. Thanks to their DNA they couldn't give or get any diseases.

When he pushed the head of his cock against her opening, she reached down and grabbed his ass. Clutching hard, she dug into his skin and lifted her hips against his. As he thrust into her, he thought he'd die from the pleasure.

She was so fucking tight it pushed him right to the edge. He'd known she would be after feeling her with his fingers, but this was heaven.

Though every part of him demanded he thrust into her until he was sated, the way his animal side demanded, he stayed deep inside her, savoring the feel of her tight sheath milking him. Even slick and wet as she was, the woman felt like a silk glove around his cock. She pulsed around him as if they were two puzzle pieces, perfectly fit together.

He cupped her cheek, barely holding onto his control. "Caro..." He had no idea what he'd planned to say, just that this meant everything to him. *She* meant everything to him.

"Fuck me, Ethan," she whispered as she stared at him with that soulful dark gaze.

Three words he'd never thought to hear from her and they made his cock throb in agony. A primal growl tore from his throat as he pulled back and slammed into her.

Her mouth parted invitingly as she let out a gasp of pleasure and he was lost. Crushing his mouth over hers, he let go, thrusting into her, over and over.

She clawed at his back, meeting him stroke for stroke. The sounds she made would forever be etched into his mind. Unable to stop his harsh rhythm, the driving need to claim her, he needed her to come again one more time.

Reaching between their bodies, he tweaked her clit, strumming it with more pressure than he'd used before. He knew it would still be over-sensitized.

She made a brief protesting sound, as if it was too much, but just as quickly let her head fall back. He watched as she arched up into him, her dark hair pillowing around her face as she closed her eyes and found another release.

That was all it took for him to let go. The climax that had been building inside him burst free in a tidal wave of pleasure.

It felt like he came forever, her tight walls clenching around him until his hips were just blindly thrusting against hers. Finally he ordered himself to stop. Breathing erratically, he stared down at the female who'd stolen his heart a year ago. The sharpest sense of rightness slid through his veins.

When her eyes opened to meet his gaze, he found he liked the satisfied half-smile pulling at the corners of her full lips. Yeah, he was going to keep that smile there for a long time.

Moving off her even though he hated to pull out of her, he reached underneath Caro and lifted her of the ground. He cuddled her close, savoring the feel of all that bare skin against his. Wordlessly he headed into the bedroom and placed her in the middle of the bed. Reaching out, he cupped her cheek and softly stroked her.

They weren't even close to being done for the night.

CHAPTER FOUR

Caro opened her eyes and inhaled deeply. The scent of French roast coffee and bacon teased her nose. Her heart did a little flip-flop at the realization that Ethan was cooking breakfast for her. Not that she should be surprised. The male was always so thoughtful.

Stretching her arms above her head, she smiled at the soreness she felt all throughout her body. Especially between her legs.

They'd made love too many times to count last night. The man had been a tireless machine—and she had no complaints. The delectable stiffness she experienced was totally worth it.

Even though she wanted to lay there for another few minutes she forced herself to get up. After putting on a robe, she headed for the kitchen.

She found Ethan standing at the stove with his back to her. Shirtless. Letting her gaze rake over the sharp lines and striations of his very muscular back, she smiled. Not an ounce of fat on the man.

He glanced over his shoulder and smiled when he spotted her. "Morning."

"Morning." She wrapped her arms around her chest as she took a few steps into the kitchen, hating that she suddenly felt shy around Ethan of all people.

Too many old insecurities threatened to overwhelm her as she looked at him. What happened if he found someone else? His true mate? She'd lose not only a lover, but a friend. Her best friend if she was honest. Other than the members of her pack she hadn't let too many people get close to her in the last century. Since they had to move to a new city every couple decades it was hard forming lasting relationships.

"What's wrong?" He frowned and stepped away from the stove.

Not wanting to discuss it, she pasted on a bright smile and shook her head. "Nothing. Something smells really good."

His frown lessened but it didn't disappear. "There's coffee on if you want."

"Great." She averted her gaze and made a beeline for the coffeepot. As she started to grab a mug from one of the cabinets, she felt Ethan's hands settle on her hips before she even scented him. He was getting a lot better at masking himself, she realized. He might be young, but he was definite alpha material. The way he'd dominated and ordered her around in the bedroom made that clear enough.

From behind, he lightly nuzzled her neck, sending a shiver rolling down her spine. "After breakfast I have to help Adam for a couple hours but I can come over and we can hang out for a while before the party tonight." His words were low and sensual and there was no doubt in her mind what he wanted to do while they "hung out".

She wanted that too but what happened afterward? Would they go to the party together? They'd just had sex, it wasn't like they were a couple now. But they were part of the same pack so even if she wanted to it's not like she could avoid him. And there were always so many parties or get-togethers. The pack didn't need a reason to party.

"Uh, okay." Why did she have to sound so unsure? She wanted to shake herself and snap out of the insecurities plaguing her but couldn't. Fear of abandonment bloomed inside her now that they'd taken such a big step in their relationship. It seemed so fast even if she knew that they'd been building up to this. She might not have wanted to admit it, but subconsciously she knew they'd been working toward something more than friendship. But what if they'd just screwed everything up?

His hands still loosely gripped her but he raised his head slightly, pulling away. "If you have plans then I can just pick you up tonight." Now he sounded unsure, making her feel like crap.

"I...have a lot of errands and other stuff to do today so why don't I just meet you there?" God, she sounded so lame even to herself. She should just let him pick her up, but then she would just over-analyze everything to death.

He let his hands drop. "Sure." She could hear the distance in his voice but she couldn't find the words to make things right. Everything she thought of saying sounded silly and insecure and she didn't want him to see that part of her.

Behind her she could feel him waiting for her to say something more but she just pretended nothing was wrong and started spooning sugar into her coffee.

***

Ethan slammed the door to his truck before stalking up the drive

402 | SAVANNAH STUART

toward Adam and Paz's house—well, his house too. Sometimes it was hard to remember that. Hell, sometimes it was difficult to remember he finally had a place to call home. He'd grown up in the foster system and had never had anyone. The Marine Corps had been his family after he turned eighteen. Now he felt as if he finally had another one. One he could count on forever. As he walked, the front door opened and Adam strode out carrying Ethan's tool belt.

"You ready?" his mentor and friend asked.

"Yeah," he muttered. Adam—former enforcer for The Council—didn't miss shit. Whenever Ethan was in a mood or worried about something his friend called him on it.

Half-smiling, he handed Ethan the tool belt. "So...stayed at Caro's last night? Bout damn time."

Feeling awkward, he shrugged his shoulders. While he and Caro might have spent a lot of time together in the past months he'd never stayed over. He might have fantasized about it but he always ended up right back here at the end of the night. "I don't want to talk about it."

Adam pressed his key fob, unlocking his truck. "I can smell her on you."

Ethan gritted his teeth and ignored him as he slid onto the passenger seat. Caro had been perfectly polite at breakfast but completely distant. As if last night hadn't happened. He wanted to punch something. Or maybe go for a long run. He couldn't understand what was going on with her. Maybe she'd changed her mind about them. He knew she was insecure about their age differences—or at least that's the bullshit she'd tried to feed him months ago—but after last night it was pretty damn obvious how compatible they were together.

Adam started his truck and steered out of the driveway. They were headed to their pack member Thomas' nightclub to do some custom work on one of the new bars. Ethan settled against the seat, hoping the conversation was over when Adam continued. "Whatever bullshit going on with you two, you'll work it out."

Ethan grunted. Easy for him to say. He was happily mated.

"Just talk to her," Adam pressed.

"Since when did you get so fucking talkative?" He hated the defensive tone of his voice and he really hated that he was taking his aggression out on his friend but he couldn't stop himself.

Adam just chuckled. "I'm getting daily sex from my hot mate. Take my advice and just *talk* to your woman. If Paz and I can get past our differences, so can you and Caro."

DESIRE UNLEASHED | 403

Ethan didn't respond but glanced out the window instead. As he stared at the palm trees passing by he knew Adam was right even if he didn't want to admit it. Paz was half fae, half-werewolf. Because of some Great War between faeries and werewolves that happened a hell of a long time ago and way before Ethan's time, the blood running through her veins made her and Adam natural enemies. They'd sure as hell worked past their differences.

Ethan knew he just needed to talk to Caro and they'd figure things out, but he didn't know how to get her to open up. How to break through that polite wall she'd erected between them. Whatever had spooked her this morning was fixable. It had to be. The thought of life without her wasn't something he was willing to consider.

Nick sat on the other side of his Alpha's desk, across from his father while he waited to see whatever it was that had been so important to take him away from his mate and the party—

His dad turned his laptop around so Nick could see the image on screen.

A grin tugged at Nick's mouth. A Ducati Monster with definite custom work. It was one of Nick's favorite bikes. Naked, with an exposed engine and trellis frame, all that raw power was on display like it should be. "Very nice. Mom's finally letting you get one?"

Lucas stiffened slightly. "Your mother doesn't...know about this yet."

Nick snickered, which only earned him a glare from his dad. Lucas might be Alpha, but Nick's mom had him wrapped around her finger. "It's a quality bike, especially with that custom work. And that was a good year."

"It's a local sale. I want you to come with me to look at it."

Nick nodded. "Anytime this week works."

"Good. So... how do you think Shea is doing?" Lucas turned his laptop back around and closed it.

Nick figured this was the real reason his father had called him away from the party, not because of the bike. They could have talked about that anywhere and his dad could have just shown him the image on his phone. It surprised him that his father was asking at all. "She's living with you guys."

"But she's spending a lot of time with Carly. I think she's doing well, but I want your opinion."

This was the reason his father was such a good Alpha. He checked on every single one of his pack members no matter what. "Good as far as I can tell. She's not skittish anymore and she really seems to enjoy knitting with Carly. Carly said it's some type of therapy." Whatever it was, Shea sucked at knitting. But if she enjoyed it and it helped her heal after her year of captivity, it was a good thing.

Lucas' mouth twitched. "Yeah, she gave me a blanket or something. I'm not really sure what it is."

Nick didn't bother to hold back his laughter. "You're not alone. I know she's planning to make something for Caro too." He'd overheard Shea tell Carly it was a sweater but it had looked more like a blanket with random holes in it.

"I just want to get her settled with a mate, someone who will take care of her. Alexandra too," he tacked on.

Nick just snorted. "If my mate could hear you, she'd call you sexist."

"You disagree?"

"No. Wolves should have a mate to take care of them." Carly certainly took care of him as much as he took care of her. They were a team.

"I think we might have another mating sooner than I'd imagined." His father looked exceptionally pleased by that and Nick knew why.

Everyone loved aunt Caro and wanted her to be happy. "Yeah, I smelled Caro all over Ethan when I passed him in the kitchen."

"He's a good male. It still hard to digest that he became one of us by being injected with something."

It disturbed Nick as well. This was one of the reasons they kept what they were from humans. Any number of governments would love to get their hands on shifters to find out what made them different, stronger. "He loves Caro."

Nodding, his father stood. "I know. And she's too stubborn to admit it, but I know she loves him, or at least cares for him more that she'll admit. They make a good match."

Nick knew his father had worried about Caro for decades, wanting her to settle down. He'd never pushed her because she was his sister-in-law, but this was a good thing for the pack. One of their most giving pack members was finally taking a mate. Or she would be if she got over her insecurities. Another reason to celebrate. "Let's get back to the party before my mate kills me."

Lucas clasped Nick's shoulder as he rounded the desk. "That sounds like a good idea. And happy anniversary. I have no words for how pleased your mother and I are that you and your brothers have finally found the happiness we have."

Feeling his throat tighten, Nick just nodded. He'd given up hope of finding a mate decades ago. Then within a year he and his two brothers had all found their other halves.

The wait had definitely been worth it. Now he couldn't and didn't want to imagine a day without his Carly.

CHAPTER FIVE

Caro strode through Nick and Carly's house, mingling with her cousins, nieces and nephews. Her nephew Nick was celebrating his one-year anniversary with his human mate and everyone in the pack had shown up.

She knew Ethan was there because she could scent him even if she couldn't see him. In the huge crowd, that spicy, earthy scent was unmistakable. It made her ache to run her fingers all over him again.

As she made her way through the kitchen she smiled at Alisha, her younger sister, but didn't stop to talk. She didn't miss the way her sister looked at her curiously but she ignored it. Obviously her sibling could scent Ethan on her. Or maybe Alisha had already scented Caro on Ethan. Didn't matter, she had no plans on hiding her relationship with him.

Caro wanted to talk to Ethan. After the stupid way she'd acted that morning he deserved an explanation, but she didn't know how to fix it. When she reached the sliding glass door, she froze in the entrance.

Ethan wasn't doing anything wrong, just talking to Shea, the very pretty new she-wolf of their pack. She'd been rescued from the same doctor who'd injected Ethan and in her former life she'd been a runway model. Yeah, she wasn't just pretty, she was gorgeous and tall and thin. The opposite of Caro. Self-consciously she wiped her hands down her dress and cursed her curves as she did.

Ethan must have said something funny because Shea laughed and lightly stroked his lower arm. Glancing away and taking a step back, Caro retreated back into the kitchen.

Her throat tightened and it didn't matter that she knew she was being beyond stupid, she couldn't help it. She cared about Ethan more than she'd admit to anyone. The thought of him with another female tore her to shreds inside. Hurrying through the house, she ducked down one of the hallways and found an empty bathroom attached to one of the guestrooms. Out of the way from the normal foot traffic where she'd have a chance to breathe.

Shutting the door behind her, she set her purse down and splashed cold water on her face. As she started to pat her face dry, the door swung open.

In the mirror she watched Ethan step into the smaller room with a look she couldn't quite put her finger on. Had he followed her? Her heart did a somersault against her ribs. "Hey, Ethan."

His blue eyes narrowed on her. "Why'd you run away back there?"

She shook her head, as if she didn't know what he was talking about. "I needed to use the bathroom."

He took a step closer so that he pressed against her back. The feel of his erection on her lower back was unmistakable. "Bullshit," he whispered.

Her eyes grew heavy for a moment as he rubbed himself against her. She was still sore from last night but God help her, she wanted more of him. A lot more. Swallowing hard, she didn't respond.

"I don't want anyone else but you, Caro." The statement came out as a possessive growl. "Shea and I are just friends if you need me to spell it out for you."

"I know." She hated the embarrassing flush she felt creep up her neck. "I'm sorry I...got a little nervous this morning." That was an understatement. She'd been scared and had acted like a coward by pushing him away.

He snorted. "You can't put me back into your friend category after last night. I won't let you. If you're worried about us or me, fine. We'll talk about it. But I'm not playing games and I'm not letting you go."

His words sent shivers of pleasure skittering over her entire body. Didn't he know how to say exactly the right thing? She needed to tell him about her past so he understood why she'd been acting so stupid. After taking a deep breath, she forced the words out. "About a century ago...I fell in love—"

He growled softly, possessively and the sound made her smile. It also made it easier for her to continue. "We'd been together a long time. Had grown up together, in fact. I was never in a rush to officially get mated because I assumed...well, long story short, he left me when he found his true mate. We loved each other—or I thought we did—but the biological pull they felt for each other...well, I couldn't compete with it." Her throat tightened as she remembered the day her lover had told her that he'd be mating with someone else—directly after they'd made love. It had been humiliating and heartbreaking. She didn't tell Ethan that part. It was too embarrassing.

"Any man who left you is a damn fool." His hands slid down her hips to the hem of her dress. They were creeping into fall weather but it was Florida so the temperature was still in the seventies. She'd worn the short summer dress tonight for him, even if she hadn't admitted it to herself.

As he slid the light blue dress up and over her hips, his eyes darkened to molten hot. He wasn't a big talker and normally that would have bothered her but after what she'd just told him, she didn't want words of sympathy or anything else. She just wanted to feel how good they were together. Staring at his reflection and seeing how turned on he was made her nipples instantly harden. Whatever happened later, at least she had this time with him.

His gaze tracked down to her chest and he smiled seductively. Without a bra, her reaction was visible. Not that he couldn't scent her desire anyway.

He *had* to. Both their cravings filled the air with a potency that made her entire body hum.

She'd worn a thong so cool air rushed over the slick heat between her thighs. He hadn't said a word but she could read in his eyes what he planned to do. Maybe she should feel a little bad that they'd left the party to have sex in the bathroom, but right now she didn't care.

Propriety could be damned. Especially when she had a man like Ethan who wanted her. Even if it wasn't forever, it was enough for now. At least that was what she was telling herself.

While keeping one hand bunched on the bottom of her dress — and keeping her butt exposed for him to softly grind against — he reached up with his other hand and pulled the tie on the halter free. The top of her dress slackened and fell, revealing both her aching breasts.

She couldn't stop her erratic breathing as he stared at her. His eyes practically glowed in the dim light of the bathroom as they tracked over her chest. Like he wanted to devour her.

"I'm going to fuck you right now, sweetheart." His voice was rough and scarcely controlled.

It mirrored the way she felt. Even though they were barely moving, she felt as if she could crawl out of her skin. She braced her hands on the countertop as he reached up and cupped both her breasts, knowing it would drive him crazy.

The hem of her dress fell back down but she still felt exposed to him, especially with the slight way he kept rubbing his pelvis against her backside.

His hands were callused but gentle as they held her. "These are mine to touch."

DESIRE UNLEASHED | 409

His words sent off fireworks in her body, making the ache between her legs even hotter. She sucked in a deep breath as he began tweaking her already aroused nipples. The feel of his hands on her like this sent another rush of heat to her core. This male made her want to lose all control.

When she didn't respond, he stilled. "Say it, Caro." Ethan needed to hear the words come from her. After the day he'd spent twisted up and worried about what was going on with them, he wanted everything she had to give tonight. To pull her out of her comfort zone and get her to open up.

"They're yours." Her voice was shaky but definitely aroused.

He felt almost drugged as he palmed her sensitive breasts. Touching her and watching their bodies in the mirror like this was erotic and better than any of his fantasies. He wanted to strip her completely but he didn't want to pull away long enough to do it. Feeling her up against him like this was exactly what he craved. Her heat, her body, just...Caro.

When her eyes grew heavy and started to close, he lightly squeezed her breasts. Her dark eyes instantly snapped open.

"Watch us," he commanded.

She nodded and the hungry shimmer in her eyes was unmistakable. She wanted this as much as him.

They were far enough away from the party that no one should hear them but they were in a house full of wolves with extrasensory abilities so he knew they'd have to be fairly quiet. Not that he cared if anyone heard — he wanted the entire world to know she was his. But he didn't want to embarrass her. He hated pulling away from her, but his cock ached and was demanding to push inside Caro's tight pussy.

Lowering his hands away from her, he quickly unfastened his jeans and let them fall halfway down his legs. He rarely bothered with boxers and now that he and Caro were involved, he doubted he'd ever bother again.

His cock sprang free and he grasped the edge of her thong. With shaking hands he shoved it down her legs.

She let out a small little gasp as he palmed and rubbed her ass. Everything about her was perfect and taking her from behind had quickly become one of his favorite positions. Last night they'd made love countless times and each time he'd had to resist the urge to actually mark her.

Right now was no different.

His canines ached to extend and sink into the soft flesh of her neck. The sudden need was more overwhelming now than it had been last night. Somehow he pushed it back. If he marked her without her consent she'd never forgive him. Hell, he'd never forgive himself.

The whole mating thing was still a mystery to him but he knew what he felt for her was different than anything he'd experienced before. He knew it was real and that it wouldn't change. After what she'd told him about her past he wondered if it would matter to her. He knew he needed to talk to his Alpha about this, to confirm what the mating pull felt like.

When she pushed her butt back against him, he groaned. Grabbing his cock in one hand, he guided himself to her entrance and thrust inside her.

Her tight sheath wrapped around him like hot silk. He could feel her rippling and tightening around him. Moaning, she tried to push back on him. His inner wolf told him to take her hard and fast but right now he wanted to enjoy being inside her.

They'd only been apart a few hours but all the uncertainty he'd experienced had been foreign and he needed to convince himself she was real. That *this* was real. That she wasn't walking away from him or putting up walls between them. Never again.

"Do something." Caro clutched onto the counter and tried to move against Ethan but he held her firm.

If anything, his eyes danced with humor. She didn't know what was so funny and she didn't care. Her body burned for release and she'd kill him if he didn't give it to her.

When she tried to move back against him again, he sighed and seductively nipped her neck. "You have no patience," he murmured, chuckling lightly.

As he nibbled against her neck she had a sudden vision of him biting her, marking her for life. A quiver of longing ran through her. She'd thought she wanted that with her ex, but the hunger she felt for Ethan eclipsed any feelings she'd ever had for anyone. He was all she could seem to think about, day and night. It was his face she saw when she touched herself.

Wanting to make sure he was as worked up as she was, Caro reached between her legs and began stroking her clit while he watched.

All humor fled his face and his eyes turned to dark storm clouds. He grabbed her hips in a tight, dominating hold that made her entire body light on fire. She loved it when he took control. Right now she didn't want gentle, but hard and fast. She'd been aching for him all day and only he could ease it.

As he began moving inside her, she increased rubbing her clit. The added stimulation and the feel of him completely filling her made her knees weak.

The harder he pounded into her, the tighter she clenched around him. The higher she felt herself rising. Erotic ecstasy poured through her veins as they watched each other in the mirror.

She couldn't take her eyes off him. His arm muscles clenched furiously and his neck corded tightly as he moved. Harder and faster.

A flash of color sparked in front of her eyes for a brief moment as her climax hit fast and out of control. Clutching the counter with both hands, she used it for support as her orgasm bloomed, spreading to all her nerve endings in wave after wave of pleasure.

Behind her Ethan let out a loud cry as he came inside her. His thrusts were harsh and untamed. She could feel his heat inside her as he found his own release and the most primal part of her loved it.

Gently, he pulled out and turned her to face him. Cupping her face, he said, "Don't ever doubt my need for you. What we have…this isn't going away for me." The soft spoken words made her throat tight with emotion but she didn't respond.

Thankfully he didn't seem to expect her to. After he grabbed a washcloth from beneath the cabinet, he wet it with warm water and surprised her by gently swiping between her legs.

Holding her dress up, she leaned against the counter and kept her legs spread while she watched him clean her up. His consideration touched her on the deepest level. She couldn't remember the last time a man had taken care of her. Not like this anyway.

Watching his big hands move with such gentleness brought up a foreign swelling in her chest. She could definitely get used to this. And she wanted to trust him, but that old fear whispering in the back of her head warned her that things *would* eventually end between them.

When Ethan looked up at her with nothing but warmth in his gaze, he covered her mouth in a soft, tender kiss that took her breath away, silencing the noisy bitch in her head.

CHAPTER SIX

Caro didn't bother knocking when she reached her sister's house. The majority of the pack lived on the same strip of private beach in Key Biscayne and it was uncommon for anyone to lock their doors. Alisha had woken her up with a text stating she had an emergency so Caro had hurried over. It had only taken her minutes to get here.

Knowing Alisha, it could be something along the lines of 'clothing emergency', but she doubted her sister had woken her up early on a Sunday morning for something like that—and she hadn't answered her phone when Caro called to check.

A little chime dinged as she opened the front door, letting whoever was inside know that a door had been opened somewhere in the house.

"In the kitchen," Alisha called out.

Caro hurried through the foyer and down a hallway to the kitchen—where she found her sister sitting at the granite-topped island drinking a cup of coffee and looking completely fine. Her long, dark hair was down, fanning around her face in perfect waves.

Her sister smiled warmly at her. "Did I disturb your sleep this morning?"

Caro narrowed her eyes. "Is there even an emergency?"

Alisha's smile just widened. "Depends how you define emergency." She nodded at the nearly full coffeepot. "Grab a cup because you're not going anywhere until I hear all the dirty details about you and Ethan."

Caro stood still for a moment, staring at her sister. "Tell me that's not why you pulled me out of bed early this morning."

"Then I'd be lying."

"You suck... Do you have muffins or croissants?" she asked as she headed for the coffeepot. The aroma of the rich roast teased her, erasing most of her annoyance. Her sister knew the way to her heart.

"Hungry? Did you get a good workout last night?" Alisha continued with an interested gleam in her eyes.

"Oh my God, you're such a pervert!"

"You're the one who had sex in a bathroom last night at a party full of our pack mates."

Horrified, Caro swiveled to look at her older sister, mug still in hand. "Does everyone know?"

Alisha just snickered. "I wasn't even sure you had until right this instant."

Caro inwardly cursed herself and turned back to the pot. She wasn't having this conversation without caffeine. "Where's your husband?"

"Running along the beach. But I don't want to talk about him. Tell me what's going on with you and Ethan. Are you finally going to settle down and mate with that boy?"

"He's not a boy." The words were out before she could think about censoring herself. She knew she sounded a little defensive, and she'd used that same argument against Ethan himself; that he was too young. But he was definitely a man at thirty. She'd just wanted to put barriers between them.

Alisha just laughed as Caro snagged creamer from the refrigerator. "Oh, I bet he's not."

"Better not let your mate hear you say that."

"Don't even try to change the subject. Come on. You two have been dancing around this for a year. I want details and I shouldn't have to hear them second hand from pack gossip."

Sighing, Caro leaned against the counter and took a sip of her coffee. She'd find food later. "I really care for him. It's a little terrifying."

"He's nothing like your ex-douche. Ethan might be younger, but he's not selfish and he cares for you so much."

"Did you just say ex-douche?"

"It's something I heard Carly say."

"I think the phrase is douchey ex." Because Caro had heard Carly say the same thing. The human female had an amusing and colorful vernacular.

"I like my way better. And don't get off topic." Alisha shook her head slightly. "Or I won't tell you where Shea hid her homemade chocolate chip cookies."

Caro hoped that Shea baked better than she knitted, but didn't say it out loud in case the other female was in the house. Shifters had exceptional hearing and she didn't want to hurt her feelings. "They're good?"

"Melt in your mouth."

"Fine... I don't know what you want me to say though. We're having an enjoyable time together." She knew that wouldn't be enough to pacify her sister, but it was too scary to put into words how amazing things were with Ethan.

Her sister cut her a sharp glance. "That's lame, even for you."

"Hey!"

"You know what I mean. You haven't given me sex details in a long time. I deserve them."

"Why, getting bored with your mate?" she asked as Lucas opened the sliding glass door. His wet hair was slicked back and he'd wrapped a towel around his waist, probably because he'd known his mate planned to call Caro over here. And she did *not* need to see her brother-in-law/Alpha naked, so she was grateful for his courtesy.

"Maybe a little," Alisha said without turning around, though she'd definitely heard and scented him given her mischievous smile.

"Then maybe I'll have to get creative later," Lucas murmured, striding right for his mate. He bent down and nuzzled her neck from behind.

The sight used to make Caro ache. Not all the time, but so many happy mates was difficult to see, especially when her nephews recently started mating, one after the other. She'd been so happy for them but also a little sad for herself. Now she felt nothing but absolute joy. And yes, it did scare her because everything about Ethan was perfect. Maybe a little too perfect. She kept waiting for the other shoe to drop.

"Why didn't you bring Ethan over this morning?" Lucas asked, raising his head.

"Because my devious sister told me she had an emergency."

Lucas' lips twitched but he didn't respond. Just kissed Alisha on the head and left the room.

"I will tell you one sexy thing he's doing right this instant—mowing my lawn and trimming my hedges."

Alisha shook her head. "That has so many dirty—"

"I mean that in the literal sense. He's kind of perfect. It's weird."

"Why? You deserve it. And your ex was a douche no matter how you look at it."

Caro certainly wasn't going to defend the guy, but she didn't want to talk about him. Not when she was talking and thinking about Ethan. Her ex didn't deserve the space in her head. "Ethan's really...he's really dominating in the bedroom." It had surprised her too.

Alisha sat up straighter. "Oh, really?"

"Yeah, he... he's very vocal about what he wants and he loves taking control."

"Good, that's what you need. Not some lazy pup."

Caro might have argued a couple weeks ago, but the truth was, both her wolf and human side enjoyed it when Ethan took control. She'd never thought she'd like that in the bedroom but wow, there was definitely something to it. "He's really special, Alisha." She would only fully admit it to her sister. Her big sister who knew her better than anyone.

Alisha's expression softened. "I know. Just don't be afraid to let him in. If you're afraid, your wolf might not be open to admitting that he's your mate."

Caro frowned and took a sip of her coffee to hide it. She didn't want to be afraid anymore. She just wasn't sure how to let go of all her old insecurities. And she wasn't sure if he was her mate. Her heart told her one thing, but she'd gotten so burned in the past that it was scary to be open to getting hurt again.

———————◆◆———————

Caro thanked the server as he pulled out the chair for her at the outdoor patio table. This morning had been long so she was glad that Ethan was able to sneak away for a lunch break. He was working on the interior of Thomas' club with Adam only a few blocks away from the restaurant they were meeting at.

"Caro Angel?"

She turned at the sound of a vaguely familiar male voice. When she saw Edward Bergman, a man she'd collaborated with five years ago at a medical conference, she smiled and pushed up from her seat. In his fifties, Edward had a distinguished look to him. Instead of the suits she'd seen him in before he was dressed casually in a cashmere sweater and slacks. Before she'd moved away from her chair, he'd managed to maneuver through two of the mosaic-topped tables. Umbrellas fluttered in the cool breeze as he reached her, a smile on his face.

"It's been a while." She opened her arms for a brief hug. "What are you doing in Miami?"

"Vacation this time." He nodded to a woman who she assumed was his wife, sitting with another couple. Caro gave a short wave. "You're so lucky you live here," he continued.

"I am," she said, smiling. Of all the places her pack had lived over the years, Miami was a favorite. "How long are you in town?"

"Two weeks. My wife and I are down here with friends renting a timeshare. If you're free we'll have to meet up. Or you can at least recommend a few places to eat."

"I can do both," she said laughing. "My number's still the same. And if you like Greek food, I know the perfect place." Her pack owned a string of restaurants around the city.

"Sounds good. We're about to pay so I'll text or call you later."

"I'll look forward to it." She turned and moved back to her table, surprised to find Ethan mere feet away, striding toward her.

As if on cue, butterflies launched in her stomach. Just being near him and she felt off her game and out of control. Which wasn't necessarily a bad thing. She loved the way he made her feel and hoped he felt the same. She smiled as he reached her. "Hey—"

His hand fisted around her hip in a tight, possessive grip as his mouth brushed over hers, warm and sensual. The kiss was a bare meeting of mouths but she could feel a pulse of raw energy rolling off him. When he pulled back it felt as if an eternity had passed, when in reality she knew it had been only seconds.

He pulled out her seat for her and when she sat, he leaned down and gently nipped her earlobe with his teeth, before sitting next to her. The action was so primal it made her toes curl and she struggled to find her voice.

"Who's that male you're going to call later?" he asked, a thread of something in his voice she wasn't sure how to define. Jealousy?

"Who?"

Ethan's blue eyes seemed somehow darker as he watched her. "The male you hugged." That was definite jealousy.

Caro's eyes widened and she tried to stop the laugh that escaped but it just popped out. "Ethan, please tell me you're not jealous of a happily married man who's a couple decades older than you."

To her surprise, Ethan's cheeks flushed red. "I don't know what's wrong with me. I saw you hug that guy and my wolf went crazy," he muttered, rubbing the back of his neck. "I had a serious violent urge to knock his teeth in—and yes, I know that's insane."

When he did, the muscles in his forearms flexed, drawing away all her attention. She cleared her throat, forcing herself to focus. "Nothing's wrong with you. It's just the way we're built. It's a wolf thing," she said, whispering the last part.

"Yeah?"

She nodded. Technically his reaction wasn't exactly typical. It was a behavior that mated shifters portrayed. But he hadn't been born a wolf so maybe things were different for him. It had taken him a while to get his shifts under control. But now wasn't the place to talk about it. "So, how was—"

Her cell phone rang in her purse and she gave him an apologetic smile. "I hate to do this, but it could be the office."

"No worries," he said, smiling at their approaching server.

"Green tea," she whispered to Ethan so he could order for her as she answered her call. She didn't recognize the number, but there were a few new nurses who were in training at work so she'd told everyone they could call her with any emergencies. "Hello?"

"Caro, it's good to hear your voice."

Everything around her funneled out for a long moment as she heard her ex's voice coming over the line. She hadn't talked to him in years. *Decades.*

What. The. Hell.

None of those feelings she'd always associated with him flared up at the sound of his voice. No sadness, no longing...nothing. Well, except annoyance. And she had absolutely no desire to talk to the bastard. "I'm busy right now." She hung up, feeling incredibly proud of herself.

The old Caro might have talked to him out of social decency but she didn't owe him anything. And she wasn't going to waste one second of her time, especially not when it would take away from her time with Ethan.

"Everything okay?" he asked as she slid her phone back into her purse. Even if work called she wouldn't be answering, she decided. They could survive without her for one hour.

"Yeah, just work." She inwardly winced at the lie but now wasn't the time to get into anything with Ethan. Especially not when he was already feeling edgy. She slid her hand across the table and linked her fingers through his.

When he immediately tightened his fingers around hers, any residual annoyance at the interruption dissipated. She was done living in the past and letting it dictate her future. Not when she had a male like Ethan in her life.

CHAPTER SEVEN

"What's going on with you?" Adam nudged Ethan with his elbow, drawing his attention back to the grill on Adam's back patio.

"What?" He took a swig from his beer and forced himself to focus on his friend and not the woman he wanted to mate more than he wanted his next breath. He could see Caro through the wall of windows in Adam's kitchen laughing at something her sister said.

He loved it when she let her guard down and seeing or hearing her laugh soothed all his edges out.

Adam turned back to the grill and flipped a burger. "You've been edgy the past few days at work. What's up?"

Ethan glanced around the patio area. A few of the pups were in the pool swimming and laughing and his Alpha and the Lazos brothers were on the other side of the huge pool deep in conversation about something. He wondered if this was something he should talk about with his Alpha or what. But Adam was still the only one he felt truly comfortable opening up to. At least about something like this.

"I think something's wrong with me," he murmured, hoping everyone else was so preoccupied they wouldn't hear him. Everyone at the barbeque this afternoon was a shifter but he'd learned that almost all shifters were pretty polite about not eavesdropping.

Adam stilled his metal spatula under one of the burgers and turned all his focus on Ethan. "How so?"

"Every time Caro and I have sex I want to mark her. My canines are actually hurting now when we're naked. It's like they have a mind of their own." And he felt like a rabid fucking animal for it. The urge to flip her over and bite her as he sank into her, to claim her so that everyone knew she was his, was getting worse.

"Oh." Adam turned back to the grill, all the tenseness in his shoulders loosening. "That's normal when you're with your mate. Once you actually

DESIRE UNLEASHED | 419

mark her the urge will go away. For the most part. You'll still mark her sometimes and she'll probably do the same to you, but no worries. Nothing's wrong with you."

Ethan still wasn't sure though. "I-I wanted to beat the shit out of a human male she was talking to the other day. The guy was no threat and I knew there was no attraction between either of them, but my wolf got fucking pissed. I can't explain it." And he felt crazy trying to.

But Adam just nodded. "All normal." He flicked a glance at the big windows, then looked back at Ethan. "Look, I don't know Caro well but she's been pretty reserved the last year with you. Now it's like you guys have always been together. If her wolf side is accepting you, your wolf can tell and he's ready to get down to the business of claiming. Until you actually mark her, those feelings won't go away. So don't stress it. Just mark your female and be done with it." He said it with such authority.

It wasn't as simple as that. Or Ethan didn't think it was. Caro had made comments before about how when you met your true mate you'd know. Well he was pretty damn sure he knew. But she hadn't let on anything so maybe he was wrong.

Only, he'd bet his life he wasn't. Caro was *his*. He knew it on the most basic level. Now he wondered if maybe he was the only one with those intense feelings.

----------••----------

Caro silenced her cell phone and shoved it in her pocket. Seriously, take a freaking hint.

"What's that look?" Alisha's gaze narrowed on her.

Caro plucked Alisha's mimosa from her hand and took a sip, knowing it would drive her sister crazy — and that it would divert her sister's attention. She so didn't feel like talking about the fact that her ex had been calling once or twice a day for the last few days. It was weird and annoying. They had nothing to say to each other and as far as she knew, the male was mated. And even if he wasn't, she didn't care.

"Get your own drink."

"Pretty sure I just did." Grinning, she stepped back and made her way to the fruit tower that someone had brought. She popped a grape into her mouth. Today wasn't an actual party, just a normal pack get together at Adam and Paz's place. Ethan's home too, though he was pretty much living with Caro now. He stayed over every night and she hated the thought of him leaving her bed. "Do you think I should ask Ethan to move in with me?" she blurted to Alisha—then cringed when every single female in the kitchen stopped talking to stare at her.

"Yes!" Four different women shouted at once while the others nodded their agreement.

"Cosmo says to put that poor wolf out of his misery," Melina added, piling fruit and cheesecake onto a dessert plate. "Mate with the pup."

"He's not a pup," she grumbled even as a smile tugged at her lips. "He's freaking thirty." The past few days Ethan had been acting a little strange, edgier than normal. Part of her hoped it was the mating call but gah, she was too afraid to ask. She didn't want to screw up what they had, not when this was the happiest she could ever remember being.

As if he knew she was thinking about him, the sliding glass door opened and Ethan stuck his head in. "Caro, I need to show you something."

"I bet you do," Alisha murmured, giggling into her tulip-shaped glass like an adolescent instead of the Alpha's mate.

Ethan clearly heard though because his cheeks flushed red as he looked at all the women with something that looked a lot like terror before he ducked back out.

"You guys are mean." Caro set her glass down.

Melina waved a manicured finger at her. "We're not the mean ones. Put him out of his misery."

Not responding to that, she left the kitchen. Ethan took her hand, linking his fingers through hers practically the moment she stepped outside. Despite the cooler fall weather creeping in she'd worn a summer dress tonight. "What did you want to show me?"

"I'll show you on the beach." His voice was pure sin.

"Is this what I think it is?" she whispered, realizing her sister's assumption was right.

He lifted his broad shoulders as a wicked grin lit up his face. Yep, he wanted to have sex on the beach. And she was all for it. The old Caro would have been careful and too concerned about what others might think, but right now all she wanted to do was get naked with the male she loved.

Loved.

The thought nearly brought her up short, but it was true. She had completely fallen for this male in every way that mattered. Now she just had to figure out a way to tell him.

CHAPTER EIGHT

One Week Later

Caro set her hair dryer on her marble countertop and paused. Was that a knock on her front door? It was still too early for Ethan to be here. He'd had to work late on a new job today, but she'd given him a key anyway. Technically she hadn't asked him to move in yet, but he had a key and had already started moving his stuff into her closet. Well, their closet. She wanted to share everything with the sweet, sexy male.

As she ran a brush through her hair, she heard a definite, loud banging. Frowning, she hurried toward the front door. When she neared it, she froze. The scent of the male outside was unmistakable.

Francisco. Her ex.

Years ago she would have done anything to see his handsome face one more time. Now she felt...annoyance. What the hell could he possibly be doing here? She'd ignored his incessant calls and he'd finally stopped bothering her four days ago. Frowning, she pulled the tie on her silky robe tighter around herself.

"Caro? Are you home?" Same, deep voice.

Yep. Definitely him. She should probably just ignore him, but after his calls and now this, maybe she should see what he wanted and get it over with. Sighing, she opened the door and couldn't even plaster on a fake smile. "Hello?" It came out like a question because she couldn't help it.

"Caro. You look beautiful." He smiled warmly and made a move to embrace her but she crossed her arms over her chest and leaned back. Yeah, that so wasn't happening. She didn't want anyone's hands on her except for Ethan.

Her ex looked exactly the same. Maybe a few years older but he'd aged very well. Same olive complexion and lean, dark Italian good looks. And he wore a tie and suit. Armani if she had to guess. So obnoxious and so very Francisco. She wanted to know why he was on her front porch. "What are you doing here? Have you contacted my Alpha to let him know you're in town?" Pack law dictated that any outsider encroaching on another territory—even if they were just passing through—had to notify the residing Alpha of their presence.

He shrugged, as if it were no big deal. To him it wouldn't be. "I wanted to see you first. You're his sister-in-law. I figured it would be okay."

She gritted her teeth, annoyed at his arrogant attitude. "So what are you doing here?"

He shrugged again in that nonchalant way of his that she used to love. As if nothing in the world mattered. God, she'd been so young and naïve then. "I was passing through and thought I'd look you up." Evasive answer. Likely a lie, if she scented right.

"We haven't seen each other in decades and you just wanted to look me up?" She arched an eyebrow.

"Well I've been calling." There was a silent question in his eyes, wondering why she hadn't returned any of his calls. When she didn't respond, he continued. "Aren't you going to invite me inside for a drink?" He pasted on a smile she supposed was meant to be charming but just came off as fake. After being with a man like Ethan it was hard to believe she'd ever wanted someone like Francisco.

"Fine. You can come in for a quick one but I'm calling my Alpha first." While she didn't want to share a drink with him, she also didn't want to chance her Alpha finding out he was hanging around Miami. Lucas was diplomatic but he also hated Francisco with a passion and she didn't want any unnecessary drama.

"You look really great, Caro. You're practically glowing," he said as she shut the door behind them.

Instead of responding, she turned on her heel and led him to the kitchen. After calling Lucas and letting him know there was a visiting wolf in town—much to his very loud annoyance—she grabbed a beer from the fridge for Francisco.

He picked up the bottle and eyed it with slight disdain. "You don't have anything foreign?"

"That's what I've got. Take it or leave it." She didn't care that she sounded rude. It was just like him to barge in and then be picky about his choice of drink. And that was Ethan's beer. For some reason it annoyed her Francisco seemed to think it was beneath him.

"You're not happy to see me." He frowned slightly, as if hurt, and she felt a twinge of guilt. Maybe she was being too harsh.

"It's not that. I don't understand why you're here." Plus she had plans with Ethan soon. Plans that did *not* involve someone else.

"I... Maria..." His voice trailed off and for a moment she felt like a total bitch. If his mate had died she'd never forgive herself for being so cold to him.

"Is everything okay?"

He shook his head and gave her a mournful look. "Can we go outside and talk? I need some fresh air."

"Uh, sure." She nodded at the sliding glass door that led to the lanai. As he strode toward it, she grabbed a beer for herself. She might not like him but if he needed a friend, she could be decent.

Outside she sat on one of the chairs next to him at the patio table. "What's going on?"

"Maria left me."

Caro jerked back slightly at his statement. *That*, she hadn't been expecting. Mated wolves didn't just leave each other on a whim. The biological bonds were practically unbreakable, especially if the couple was in love. Leaving was virtually unheard of. "Left you?"

He nodded and took a big swig of his beer.

She frowned at him. "What happened?"

"I don't want to talk about it. I just wanted to see a friendly face." He leaned forward and made a move to cup her cheek.

Her eyes widened in shock as it clicked why he was there. Did he think he'd get some sympathy sex from her? Good God, he'd lost his freaking mind. She started to pull away when a loud, unexpected growl ripped through the air and Francisco went flying across the open patio. Caro's eyes widened as she realized Ethan had tackled him. She hadn't even heard him enter the house.

Still wearing his tool belt, Ethan stood over Francisco in his dirty jeans and T-shirt, a dark expression on his handsome face. "What the fuck do you think you're doing?" His voice was a low, deadly growl.

Francisco had never been a fighter but he pushed up and snarled back. "Who the hell are you?"

Ethan took a menacing step forward. "Answer the fucking question."

Francisco looked past Ethan to Caro for help but she just stared at him. She wanted an answer too.

Finally he faced Ethan again. "I'm just visiting an old friend."

"Looked like you had different intentions."

Francisco shrugged. "We were once more than friends and—"

Lightning fast, Ethan's hand wrapped around the other wolf's neck and lifted him off the ground. "I got a call from my Alpha that you were here after he got word from *your* Alpha. You can't even stay faithful to your own mate and you want to come sniffing around *mine*? Just because your whole pack is pissed at you doesn't mean you get sniff around here."

Caro gasped. "You cheated on Maria?" No wonder she'd left him.

"Not only that, he got her sister pregnant," Ethan ground out without taking his eyes or hand off Francisco.

Caro felt sick to her stomach. She'd never actually met the other she-wolf, but no one should have to deal with something like that. "What's the matter with you, Francisco?"

He coughed and struggled until Ethan finally put him down. "I don't care about her sister. I just wanted to continue my line. We've tried but Maria can't get pregnant and—"

"Get out." She shook her head. She didn't care what his excuse was and she didn't care about him. Looking at him now made nausea rise inside her. He was a pathetic excuse for a male and if he wanted sympathy from her, he was looking in the wrong place.

"But, Caro—"

Ethan grabbed him by the collar and dragged him toward the door as he sputtered. Caro didn't try to stop him. As he shoved the other wolf inside, she collapsed on one of the lounge chairs and stretched her legs out. What a crazy day. It was a little surreal that her ex had shown up but she felt surprisingly fine about it. And it wasn't even that surprising really. If his entire pack was truly pissed at him then he probably thought he could come see her and get sympathy, if not sex. He'd always needed someone to baby him. At one time she'd liked taking care of him but that was a lifetime ago and she'd been such a different person then.

When Ethan walked back through the sliding glass door, she frowned at his dark expression. "Did he give you any trouble?"

Instead of responding, he unhooked his tool belt and let it fall as he stalked toward her. She started to push up to a sitting position, but he moved fast and covered her body with his much bigger one. She spread her legs wider to accommodate him as he settled between her thighs.

His breathing was harsh and erratic. "Did he hurt you?"

She frowned and shook her head. "No. He's harmless. Stupid, but harmless." And she didn't want to talk about him. Not even a little bit. Rolling her hips, she smiled as Ethan's eyes darkened.

"Is he the one who's been calling you?"

Feeling guilty, even though she had nothing to feel bad about, she nodded. "I didn't say anything because he's not worth it. I ignored him and thought he got the hint."

"Obviously not." Caressing her face, he growled softly. "I don't like anyone touching what's mine."

Her pussy dampened at his words. She hadn't bothered putting on panties while getting ready because she'd known he'd be home soon. If she'd been wearing anything, it would be soaked. "Yours, huh?" she whispered. He'd been calling her that since they'd crossed the line from friendship to lovers and she loved it.

His hand covered her mound and he pushed a finger inside her. The unexpected intrusion made her inner walls tighten. When he pushed another one inside her she raked her teeth over his neck. He was salty, earthy, and all male. All hers.

As he began dragging his fingers in and out, something he'd said earlier registered in her mind. *You can't even stay faithful to your own mate and you want to come sniffing around mine.* He'd basically called her his mate when he'd been yelling at her ex. She quickly drew back, wondering if he'd meant it.

His blue eyes glittered with need. "You finally realize what I said before, huh?"

She didn't want to jump to conclusions but her heart started beating just a little faster. Did he mean he wanted to claim her? Ever since that night in her nephew's bathroom she'd known Ethan was it for her. She'd felt the mating call in a way she'd only dreamed about. It registered inside her soul deep but he hadn't mentioned anything so she'd held her tongue. Because if she was wrong, it would shred her. "What *did* you say?"

The intense expression he wore made her heart pound. "You are mine. I intend to mark you tonight, Caro. I don't want to wait any more." His eyes seemed to glow against the fading daylight.

He'd been waiting? "Are you sure?" The question was a strangled whisper. Unexpected tears pricked her eyes.

"I've been sure since you decided to put me in your little *friend* category. I didn't understand it was the mating desire at first, but it's more than that to me. I...I love you, woman. If you want to wait, fine, but—"

She didn't let him finish. She sure as hell didn't want to wait. Her mouth met his in a hungry dance. His tongue stroked hers the way it had countless times in the past couple weeks. The absolute rightness she felt with him was overwhelming.

Like they were meant to be together. Something she'd never felt with anyone before. Whatever she'd felt for Francisco all those years ago, it hadn't even been close to this. Ethan was everything to her. Thoughtful, giving, and so sexy she ached just looking at him.

The front of her robe slackened then fell open as Ethan moved with deft hands. The cool Atlantic breeze flowed over her even though she was covered by his body.

He began a trail of kisses along her jaw until he stopped to nibble on her ear. "Mine," he murmured.

Shivers rolled over her as he began softly rubbing her breasts, teasing her nipples with exactly the right pressure he knew she liked.

"Is your pool heated?" he murmured against her neck.

Since it was close to fall she'd turned on the heat to combat the sometimes breezy wind. She hadn't used the pool much in the past couple weeks but now she was thankful she'd kept the heater on. "Oh yeah."

He quickly pushed off her and began stripping off his shirt, boots, and finally his jeans. She'd already shrugged out of her robe but the shudder she experienced had nothing to do with the slight wind and everything to do with the rock-hard, perfect male in front of her.

The past couple weeks with him had helped her shed her insecurities in so many ways. When Ethan looked at her with such raw hunger, it was hard to doubt herself. Now that she knew he felt the same way she did, she experienced the sharpest sense of freedom.

As she sauntered toward the shallow end, she watched as he tracked her movements. He looked every bit the predator as his gaze followed her.

The warm water rushed over her feet, calves and thighs but she didn't go any deeper than that. Not until Ethan joined her.

When she scooped water up with her hands and let the warmth spill down her breasts it was as if he jerked out of a trance. His movements were purposeful as he slipped into the pool and glided toward her.

Ethan had been biding his time, waiting to tell Caro he wanted to officially mate. He hadn't planned to ask her today, but after seeing that asshole try to touch her something had snapped inside him. As soon as he'd gotten the call from his Alpha—who'd likely known what his reaction would be—he'd rushed over. Her ex was lucky he was still walking.

Ethan didn't care about that now, though. All he wanted was to claim Caro as his. He didn't know why he'd been waiting. They fit together.

When he wasn't with her, he was thinking about her. And when he was with her, he'd never been more content in his entire damn life. Even though she hadn't said it, he knew she loved him too. He'd felt it in the way she'd kissed him after he'd admitted his feelings. She wouldn't be bonding with him otherwise.

Before he reached her, she'd lifted her hands out for him in a welcoming gesture that made him ache for her even more. She made him feel as if he was coming home for the first time in his life. Her delicate fingers slid up his chest and around his neck as their bodies joined.

She kissed his neck and shoulders as she lifted up and wrapped her legs around him. Just the feel of her lips on his body was enough to make him combust. Her sweet, unique spring rain scent surrounded him, making his wolf scrape against the surface, demanding he take her now.

Holding her hips, he moved them through the water until they were near the wall of the pool. They'd done things hard and fast then soft and slow but right now his inner beast needed the mating.

Needed to mark her.

Sliding his hands up from her hips, he lightly cupped her breasts and bent to nuzzle her neck. His heart felt like it was going to explode. "I need to be inside you, sweetheart."

She drew back from kissing his neck and softly smiled. Wordlessly, she let her legs drop and turned toward the wall. Over her shoulder, she looked at him so trustingly, he felt honored she'd chosen him to be her mate.

Palming one of her hips, he grabbed his cock with his other hand and guided it to her entrance. He didn't bother to test her slickness since he'd felt it on the lounge chair. She was soaked and it was all for him.

It seemed it didn't matter how many times he had her, he was always hungry for more. Seeing her like this, bent forward, surrendering to him, hands braced on the ledge, it pleased the most primitive part of him in a way he'd never imagined.

He needed to mark her but he needed her to come first. His primal side might be telling him to take her hard but the man in him wanted her to feel as much pleasure as he did. Since he'd been a part of their world, he'd come to learn that shifters were a superstitious bunch. This mating had to go right. There was simply no other choice.

When she pushed back against him and moaned, his throat tightened. Yeah, it was going to be hard to keep his control now.

"Hold onto the edge," he whispered against her neck. His chest rubbed against her smooth back and even that got him hot.

While she held on, he began thrusting. Slow, steady strokes. Reaching around her, he palmed her breasts and tweaked her nipples.

The moment he started teasing her, he felt the reaction in her tight pussy. She clenched even harder around him. With each push inside her, he felt himself spinning out of control.

Her inner walls gripped around him with no mercy. The faster he moved, the more she rippled around him until she was panting in the same erratic rhythm he was.

His heart thumped rapidly and his cock felt like a steel club between his legs. When she let out a loud groan, those ripples intensified until her climax crashed over her. It was almost as if he could feel her pleasure as she cried out his name. The way she said it was like a prayer and as she moaned, he finally let go of his control.

His canines extended the way they'd ached to for months when around her. His inner wolf had known they were linked even before he'd realized it. There was no one but Caro.

Brushing her hair to the side, he bent to her neck and let his canines sink into her soft flesh. The instant he broke the skin, he came. His orgasm ripped through him like a freight train, the intensity like nothing he'd ever experienced as he emptied himself inside her.

Pleasure shot to all his nerve endings and his abdomen bunched tight as he let out a loud growl. He didn't care if all of Miami heard them. She was so slick and tight, absolute perfection.

Caro was his.

And he was hers.

He withdrew his mouth from her and even though he hated to pull out of her, he forced himself to. But he didn't keep his hands off her sweet body. Turning her around, he drew her close and buried his head against her neck while she nuzzled his chest.

He wasn't sure how much time had passed while they held each other but he finally broke the silence. "Did I hurt you?"

He could feel her smile against his chest. She shook her head. "Not even close." Then she pulled her head back and looked at him. Her dark eyes glittered with desire and satisfaction. Keeping her gaze on him, she reached up and gingerly touched where he'd bitten her.

Can you hear me? Her voice sounded clear in his head.

Smiling, he nodded. *Now you're going to know every wicked thing I want to do to your body.*

"Good." She grinned mischievously and wrapped her legs around his waist. "I love you so much, Ethan. I can't believe I ever thought we could just be friends."

"Me neither," he murmured before capturing her mouth with his. But he was glad that they were friends too. With Caro he had a lover and a best friend and he was never letting her go.

Thank you for reading Shifter Bonds! I really hope you enjoyed it. Please consider leaving a review at one of the major retailers. It's a great way to help other readers discover new books. If you don't want to miss any future releases, please feel free to join my newsletter. Note that this newsletter is for both my author names, Savannah Stuart and Katie Reus. The signup is available on either of my websites:

www.katiereus.com

www.savannahstuartauthor.com

KATIE REUS COMPLETE BOOKLIST

RED STONE SECURITY SERIES
No One to Trust
Danger Next Door
Fatal Deception
Miami, Mistletoe & Murder
His to Protect
Breaking Her Rules
Protecting His Witness
Sinful Seduction
Under His Protection
Deadly Fallout
Sworn to Protect
Secret Obsession
Love Thy Enemy
Dangerous Protector

THE SERAFINA: SIN CITY SERIES
First Surrender
Sensual Surrender
Sweetest Surrender
Dangerous Surrender

DEADLY OPS SERIES
Targeted
Bound to Danger
Chasing Danger (novella)
Shattered Duty
Edge of Danger
A Covert Affair

Non-series Romantic Suspense
Running From the Past
Dangerous Secrets
Killer Secrets
Deadly Obsession
Danger in Paradise
His Secret Past
Retribution
Merry Christmas, Baby

Paranormal Romance
Destined Mate
Protector's Mate
A Jaguar's Kiss
Tempting the Jaguar
Enemy Mine
Heart of the Jaguar

Moon Shifter Series
Alpha Instinct
Lover's Instinct (novella)
Primal Possession
Mating Instinct
His Untamed Desire (novella)
Avenger's Heat
Hunter Reborn
Protective Instinct (novella)

Darkness Series
Darkness Awakened
Taste of Darkness
Beyond the Darkness
Hunted by Darkness
Into the Darkness

SAVANNAH STUART COMPLETE BOOKLIST

MIAMI SCORCHER SERIES
Unleashed Temptation
Worth the Risk
Power Unleashed
Dangerous Craving
Desire Unleashed

CRESCENT MOON SERIES
Taming the Alpha
Claiming His Mate
Tempting His Mate
Saving His Mate
To Catch His Mate

FUTURISTIC ROMANCE
Heated Mating
Claiming Her Warriors
Claimed by the Warrior

CONTEMPORARY ROMANCE
Adrianna's Cowboy
Dangerous Deception
Everything to Lose
Tempting Alibi
Tempting Target
Tempting Trouble

ABOUT THE AUTHOR

Savannah Stuart is the pseudonym of *New York Times* and *USA Today* bestselling author Katie Reus. Under this name she writes slightly hotter romance than her mainstream books. Her stories still have a touch of intrigue, suspense, or the paranormal and the one thing she always includes is a happy ending. She lives in the South with her very own real life hero. In addition to writing (and reading of course!) she loves traveling with her husband. For more information about Savannah please visit her website at: www.savannahstuartauthor.com. If you would like to be notified of future releases, please join her Katie Reus newsletter, found at www.katiereus.com

Made in the
USA
Monee, IL